Midnight SUN

MIDNIGHT SUN

elwood reid

DOUBLEDAY New York London Toronto Sydney Auckland

PUBLISHED BY DOUBLEDAY
a division of Random House, Inc.
1540 Broadway, New York, New York 10036

DOUBLEDAY and the portrayal of an anchor with a dolphin are
trademarks of Doubleday, a division of Random House, Inc.

Book design by Bonni Leon-Berman

Library of Congress Cataloging-in-Publication Data
Reid, Elwood
Midnight sun / by Elwood Reid—1st ed.
p. cm.
1. Wilderness survival—Fiction. 2. Adventure and adventurers—Fiction.
3. Wilderness areas—Alaska—Fiction. 4. Alaska—Fiction. I. Title.
PS3568.E47637 M53 2000
813'.54—dc21   00-022719

ISBN 0-385-49736-9
Copyright © 2000 by Elwood Reid

For Nina and Sophia Alaska

Midnight
SUN

There is always some one thing which the ignorant man knows, and that thing is the only thing worth knowing; it fills the ignorant man's universe.

—Joseph Conrad, *Outcast of the Islands*

BEFORE

The best I can say was that I went to Alaska to build houses on an army base with my buddy Burke. We'd been chasing the buck together for two years, jobbing up and down the coast, never staying in any one place too long. All that mattered was the work, the coin and those brief moments just after punch-out when I walked back to my truck, bone tired and feeling like a king for having laid it down yet another day.

I was in love with Alaska—the trees and mountains; the rivers without end full of dying salmon and the grizzly bears ready to pounce on them. Everybody was searching for something—whacked-out Vietnam vets waiting for war, Christians praying for the rapture, hippies looking for paradise, strippers rolling dirty bills in their garters, backpackers trekking for that last untouched place. All this put to the soundtrack of sled dogs howling for winter from the back of pickup trucks.

And then there were the wolves—wolves that circled in packs where the roads ended and the maps became blank spaces.

This was the interior, not the sea-struck coast with its mild winters, but the vast middle where winters came early and hard—seventy below and dark by noon. Fairbanks, the Golden Heart of Alaska, former boomtown, now a flat, unremarkable grid of Native American gift shops, pipeyards, bars tricked out to look like log cabins, pull-tab parlors and dusty liquor stores.

The summers were long shadow-filled things. People wandered around, hungover from too much sun and not enough sleep. By

June the Alcan was clogged with convoys of fat tourists in over-priced RVs chasing the last of the midnight sun, stuffing them-selves at salmon bakes in between trips to Denali, Circle Hot Springs and dramatic reenactments of Robert Service poems at the Malamute Saloon. Locals dragged dead salmon through the bar and told bear stories to the RV crowd hoping to mooch drinks, while the midnight sun lasted. It was one big show until winter came.

I don't know what Burke wanted or what he thought was at the end of it all. He was a tall, thick-chested man with blunt hands and deep work-haunted eyes; a journeyman who could walk beam dead drunk and drive nails with one swat. His face was scuffed and worn from bar fights and outdoor labor. When he spoke he made fists with his hands and jabbed his chin, daring someone to take a swing. There was nothing soft or false about him, just the dogged pursuit of the physical. He lifted weights, skied, hiked, fished and taught himself obscure things by poring through old books on knots, blacksmithing, beekeeping and metallurgy—anything he thought the common man might have forgotten. He was impossi-ble to know, but I caught glimpses—small snatches of what made him tick, usually after too many beers or shots of bourbon. But then I was too far gone to put the pieces together and I'd wake the next morning knowing I'd forgotten something.

•

Burke always held the fact that I'd had a little college over me. I quit one morning after taking stock of the giggling, backpacked horde and realizing that I was hip-deep in a shallow pond. I felt like a fraud. Maybe it was some midwestern inferiority complex or perhaps it was the suburbs—but I felt soft and useless. I was smart, but not that smart. Women found me easily resistible. My hands were pale and unscarred and except for being tall everything about me screamed average.

I'd been in exactly one fight my entire life and lost—got my face rearranged by some frat boy. For some reason this began to eat at me. I reasoned that in ten years I'd be married, worried about money and what school to send my kids to or what color Volvo I should buy. Did I want leather seats? Cell phone? It was like looking slow death in the face and saying, "Okay, I'd like a piece of that." The alternative was to sit and do nothing or worse, belly up to the treadmill and get taken.

One benefit of my underwhelming mediocrity was that I had options.

I could fight back. Or I could fail miserably at something and live in the shadow of that failure the rest of my life.

What I needed most was a temporary fix, a reprieve from the ruin and doom I saw coming if I stayed my pleasant course of college. So I tried karate and couldn't get past the bowing and black belt crap. Boxing was no better. Got my nose broken by some old Croatian guy who said I punched like a fag. Several guys I knew had nutted out and joined the marines. But that was too obvious. I wanted to be blindsided and led down some dark extraordinary alley, where I might carve out a life.

So I took a job hauling lumber and running errands for the foreman on a housing development, figuring that at the very least the job would toughen me up if not force me to find something better. My old man pissed and moaned about how I wasn't realizing my potential, wasting my life and selling myself short. But the pay was good and it wasn't school. I got up every morning and knew my job. Hit a nail and you'll know what I mean. There was an art to it and there were times when just setting nails into wood seemed a deep and important thing to do. I liked coming home smelling of pine boards, my palms stained with nail grease and tired in a way that seemed real.

Five years later I was a carpenter with a belt full of tools and a late-model Ford F-150. The soft college kid my old man wanted was buried under calluses and thick slabs of job muscle. I hit the road and headed west through Great Falls, Portland and Seattle, working jobs until they were done. I learned to walk away and leave everything behind—the long hours, the accidents and near accidents, foremen getting in my face, the nail-shooting contests— and move on to the next job where empty foundations waited like graves to be filled and built upon and then abandoned for families or factories. Either way it didn't matter because I was letting it roll. Jobs. Friends. Life.

It was honest work. Clock in, clock out and don't think about it in between. And I liked it. I figured that as long as I didn't let the job break me, I could stave off the creeping softness that attacked men and forced them indoors to wait out the end of their dreams.

Most jobs were populated by zombies and God squadders who did what they were told and were easy to let go when the work ran out. The Christians chalked up the hard-luck nature of the job to the will of God while the zombies, drunks and ex-cons received the frequent layoffs and freak accidents as proof that it was a cold and cruel world out there. I didn't believe in much of anything; God, country, dead Elvis and I'd read enough books to know that if you stared hard enough at anything it would turn into crap. Nothing lasts forever. Everybody dies—cue the tiny violins.

Then I met Burke and went to Alaska. I found a small apartment on the outskirts of town—a place I could pick up and leave at a moment's notice. No attachments, nothing to keep me except the paycheck.

Burke rented a geodesic dome from an old hippie named Day-Glo Bob who grew hydroponic dope and said he'd fucked Janis Joplin when she was good, before she went lesbian and started ignoring her hair. Day-Glo spent most of his time listening to short-wave radio, drinking homemade beer and worrying about the Feds busting up his little paradise.

Our first job was a small subdivision called Bear View, which promised "Spectacular" views and "Amazing" wildlife. What the prospective buyer got though was cheap materials, nonunion hackwork, a couple of scraggly moose and a view of a small valley that had been clearcut. Corners were cut wherever they could get away with it; floors sloped, walls leaned off level. The units were stacked shit—the kinda work you crept away from at the end of the day with that sick feeling in your belly. But there was money and Burke and I were chasing it.

At night I saw moose grazing in front yards, heard wolves and sled dogs howling and listened to men tell bear stories. It put a blaze on things, made the work we were doing seem dangerous and important. We weren't just building houses. We were building houses in Alaska—the last frontier. But after ten hours of beating a nail gun and humping 2x4s the mountains seemed as far away as Ohio; tall snow-covered ghosts taunting me into daydreams until the boss reminded me to pick up the pace. Winter was coming—men would be laid off. Alaska would be left to the Alaskans.

After work we drank, shot pool and blew our hard-earned money on strippers and pull tabs. Burke never backed down from a challenge even if it meant matching shots of rotgut with terminal rummies or arm wrestling pipe fitters in for a little R&R from Nome or Barrow; Puppy Chow to Burke. What he was after was the messy life-and-death stuff because the years on the job had dulled his pulse.

As for me, I wanted to work a little longer and then get out, maybe go back to school or see about a real job, one where I could grow old but not soft. I wanted to come away from Alaska with a pocketful of money and plot a course to some sort of life I could see living. In two years I would be thirty. I had friends who lived in three-hundred-thousand-dollar homes, drove BMWs and Porsches, took vacations in Vail and Barcelona. They were growing richer by the moment. They had families who counted on them. On the other hand I had nobody to answer to, no ties, no obligations, and there was nothing a little muscle or hammer couldn't take care of. What I was searching for wasn't on any map, it was inside—a soft and dark place I'd discover when there was nowhere left to go. But then one morning I got a glimpse of that soft dark place.

It was early and the beams were wet with dew. I had the beer sweats. The whitehats were on the ground barking at us to brace the trusses and Burke was giving it right back to them. I was at the edge watching a forklift crank over a Dumpster when the deck began to shudder under my feet, slow at first and then faster. I looked up to see the trusses coming down like dominoes, slapping toward me, braces flying as they picked up speed.

I froze.

Then I saw Burke racing through the jungle of half-built walls and braces, hatchet held over his head, face burning like a star as the trusses snapped at his heels. And there I was letting it run down my leg. He shoved me over the edge where we seemed to hang forever in the empty blue sky.

Then we crashed hard with two dull thuds on the ground, followed by wood cascading off the deck. Burke was up before I could figure out what had happened, tugging at my tool belt asking if I was okay.

Work came to a halt as the whitehats swarmed and started asking questions, getting up close and personal, sniffing for booze or dope on our breath.

Burke backed the foremen away with his hatchet. "I wanna know who set the trusses," he demanded.

Some fat-ass whitehat in pressed jeans checked his watch. All the rubbernecking was making him nervous, his company brain silently toting up lost work time.

"Leave it to us," he said.

One of the sheetrockers started coughing "asshole" loudly.

"We could have been killed," Burke said.

"Take a minute if you have to," the foreman said. "Then get back to work, let's all get back to work."

Two other bossmen stepped up tapping clipboards with gold pens. One of the laborers everybody called Dog Dick groaned, stuck his arms out like some sort of zombie and said, "Time to make the donuts."

The sheetrocker kept coughing, "Asshole."

"Get back to work!" the whitehats shouted in unison.

That was all Burke needed. He swung at the tallest bossman in the bunch and they came at us, white men in white hats with lots to prove. I threw a few punches—halfhearted jabs because there was no fight in my heart, just the thought that I should have been up on that deck, smashed to bits, jabbed full of wood and nails: dead or maimed at twenty-eight.

Before I knew it we'd fought our way to the parking lot. Dog

Dick was right behind us, his eye opened up like a smashed frog. I could tell it wasn't the first time he'd been booted from a job and it wouldn't be the last.

"At the tone the time will be beer-thirty, and I'm buyin'," Dog Dick said. "You guys comin'?"

He grabbed a used tissue that had been fluttering around the parking lot and stuck it to his wrecked eye where it just kind of hung there getting redder.

Burke shook him off. "We just snatched one away from the job," he said.

"What about me?" Dog Dick asked, pointing at his eye.

"You'll live," Burke said. "Go on, we'll catch up to you."

Dog Dick shrugged, climbed into his Hornet and took off, music blaring through a shattered window, tailpipe dragging.

After he was gone I looked at Burke. "You wanna go?"

"With the way that boy's luck is running some of it's bound to hop off and stick to us."

I laughed.

"Let's go drop off some résumés," Burke said, holding up his callused hands. "Before we end up like Dog Dick."

So we hit the road with our tools and went looking, knowing that unemployment had a way of growing on you.

By lunch we'd found work on the army base, a government job. Government jobs were referred to as the Good, the Bad and the Ugly. The good—tall wages and plenty of OT. The bad—periodic piss tests to make sure you weren't doping it on Uncle Sam's time. The Ugly—not much pussy to stare at on an army base. So we split a bottle of vinegar and pickled our kidneys. The next morning we pissed in a cup, filled out W-2s and went to work building three-family condos.

•

On the weekends we drove north on the private haul roads owned by oil companies and the government: the places not on any map. We fished for salmon and grayling until our arms ached. Walked mountains with no names searching for hidden lakes, venturing

down logging roads that didn't end so much as go wild. We used
shitty, second-rate gear because the trip was the thing, it was the
only thing and all those outfitted jag-offs with their slick gear were
missing the point. They were trip yuppies, not above calling their
wives or girlfriends on cell phones from the middle of nowhere.
They navigated with GPS units and buried their trash in messy fire
pits while we on the other hand used compasses and never left a
mark on the land.

Once we came upon a herd of caribou that stretched across the
whole valley, their caramel-colored backs blotting out the hillside.
Burke laughed and ran at them, spooking the herd farther into the
valley until their hooves drowned out his shouts.

He came back panting and sweating.

"Hey, Dances with Caribou," I said, "you wanna set camp?"

"You shoulda tried it."

"Chasin' after a herd of caribou?"

He nodded.

"I prefer not to," I said in a flat, dead voice.

Burke started to say something then stopped, his eyes narrowing, not wanting me to know he'd gotten the joke.

"You savin' yourself?"

"It's just that chasing after caribou somehow don't seem all that
much fun."

"You're wrong, Jack," he said. "It felt like the ground was coming up and for a minute I lost myself. I mean I had no goddamned
idea who I was or what the hell I was doing."

"You were chasing caribou and screaming like an idiot."

"You don't get it, do you," he said.

"Get what?"

"Fuck it," he said.

"No, get what?" I asked.

He grinned. "I don't know what. I just did *it*—you either get
that sort of thing or you don't."

I stared at him and said flatly, "Chasing caribou?"

He started laughing. "Just shut the fuck up before I start chasing *you*."

I laughed and looked out over the valley. The dust the caribou had kicked up hung in the air glowing in the sunlight like some low fire. I could still hear the distant thrum of their hooves and started to say something to Burke, but he was already spreading the tent on the ground.

On Monday we were back at work, staring at the mountains again. The walls went up, trusses boomed in and slowly we worked our way through the one hundred and thirty-five units. Each day, a little closer to working ourselves out of a job. Leaving seemed inevitable. There would be another job and then one after that. It was life on the punch card.

During a break Burke explained how he'd chased enough work.

"I been ratting away money," he said.

"What for?"

"Homesteading."

"Forty acres and a mule type shit?"

"They're opening up some parcels down by McCarthy next spring."

"And?"

"And I'm gonna live off the fat of the land. Five acres and a cabin. Kill my own food, chop wood, fish, run a trapline. Take life on its own terms. And best of all, no bossman holding a paycheck over my head."

"You're forgetting a few things," I said.

He turned. "Yeah?"

"No women, not to mention the bears and bitter cold. The months of darkness. That doesn't sound all that fun."

He shook his head and then put a finger against my chest.

"Depends how you look at it."

"It looks cold," I said. "Or maybe this is like chasing caribou."

He didn't smile. "Yeah, well, it's a shitload better than stoopin' to the job with all that romantic working-class crap swirling around your head," he snarled.

He jabbed me again until I grabbed his finger and twisted.

"What's this got to do with me? You're the one who wants to do the Jeremiah Johnson thing, not me."

He doubled over, wrenched his finger free and drew his framing hatchet, laughing. "I should just bash your head open right now, you stupid bastard."

I picked up a nail gun, its compressor cord hissing, and pulled back the guide. "Bring it on," I said.

"What's a matter," he said. "Scared you'll end up like your father?"

I thought of my old man then, trudging through life. Twenty years at the same job, working his way up until he had an office, a secretary named Donna and the occasional corporate golf outing. He was a man going to work on Saturdays, taking phone calls that pulled him away from the dinner table and sent him to the den with a glass of scotch.

But he'd been to Vietnam, shot and killed men. He was sort of a hero, though he never talked about it. Mom was in on it, hiding his medals in her underwear drawer, distracting me with questions about school whenever I came home and asked about the war.

Once, when I was sixteen he took me fishing and told me he'd saved three men and killed six others and no amount of thinking could balance the sheet in his favor. He said he could still see the eyes of the dead men, the way their hands shook white against the muddy ground.

"I was this close," he said. "Some of their teeth had been shot out."

I looked into the water at his line, hoping no fish would bite and interrupt him.

"They smelled like jungle and blood and all I wanted was to take my bullets out of them and go home. When it got dark and we were waiting for a Medevac a tiger came into the clearing and dragged one of the bodies into the woods. The guys wanted to shoot it, but I wouldn't let them. I knew the tiger had to live. It was the only thing that made any sense in that war."

We didn't catch any fish. My father just stopped talking as if he was embarrassed or thinking about the tiger. And that was my big father/son moment.

I thought about that tiger though. It came to me in dreams lit up with gun flash and flare, slipping in and out of the jungle, purring, trying to tell me something.

•

Burke laughed and then swung the blade side of the framing hatchet down on the air hose line, severing it. The hose slapped and hissed between us. "I'm right about your old man then?"

I shook my head. "He did what he had to do, nothing more, nothing less."

A whitehat named Anderson was making his way toward us across the muddy lot, jaw clenched tightly, clipboard under his arm.

"Fucking the dog again?" he shouted at us.

Burke saw him too and made for the cut line through a cloud of sawdust.

"I got it, Anderson," he said, reaching down and snapping the cut hose off at the joint. In the basement, the compressor caught its breath and stopped laboring.

We put on a show. Burke bent a few shiners and I revved a Skil-saw until Anderson stomped past us but not before he'd marked something on his clipboard.

"I shouldn't have saved your ass," Burke said, after. "Maybe those trusses would've beat some sense into you. Take a look around and tell me how many fifty-year-old carpenters you see?"

I looked at the men bent over their work, hammering and sliding walls into place. Sun beat down on the deck. Heat rippled off in waves. And there was the ever-present thunder of generators and forklifts. "Well, there's Harry Lime on the garage crew and Pete with the siders."

"Okay," he said. "Two, maybe three guys. Next time you're talkin' retirement with Lime look at his hands and tell me how many fingers he's got left. Or Pete, the motherfucker can't even straighten his back he's been hunched so long."

"That's not the point," I said.

"You think the people who move in after we're gone are gonna think about how we sweated and lost fingers to give them a house? Fuck no, man, this ain't no monument to your labor, it's a tar baby and nobody gives a shit what we do as long as we keep doing it."

"Now you're the jobsite philosopher?"

He stepped out to the edge of the deck.

"Before you flap your wings out of Alaska I'm gonna find us one last big-time adventure."

He shook his head and cracked a smile before he disappeared down the ledge and left me staring out through a glassless window at the sun on the mountain.

During the off-hours I followed him up rivers for hours, looking for the wild untouched spots, thinking that at any moment Burke would turn around and release me from his promise. And that would be okay with me, because he was right—there weren't a lot of fifty-year-old carpenters around.

By the end of July the first pink slips began to flutter onto the jobsite. The drunks and half-breeds were the first to go, sent packing with complimentary thermoses and promise of work next season. There was a lot of talk about who would be laid off next. The basement rats were sweating it out. Burke was already looking for something to take him into October while I'd made plans to work the winter at a truss factory in Texas. The pay would be good and I could return in the spring with coin and spend a little time finding the right job. I kept quiet about this fact, because most of the blather about cake jobs turned out to be bullshit as did most of the talk about leaving and coming back. The carpenters I knew spent off-seasons on unemployment, getting fat, staring at beer bottles and satellite television, going back to work in the spring only after they'd drunk up all their money.

A couple of the guys had already quit, run off with pretty Eskimo women to Anchorage or taken jobs as maintenance men in Seattle. Each day there were a few less pickup trucks in the muddy lot. Sometimes I had a whole building to myself, the floor littered with crushed Marlboro packs and empty soda cans, evidence that other men had leaned, tired and sore, against this very same wall, talking about their dreams—how they hated work but loved the money and how lunch was too short, the whitehats were jobbing them, stealing minutes, days of their lives, so fuck 'em, fuck 'em all. By then I was too tired to care that other guys had been unfairly pink-slipped because somewhere there was one with my name on it. And I would move on, leaving the ghost of my labor behind, maybe some blood on a dusty plywood sub-floor.

Then Bryce, one of the bad-luck boys, killed himself in a basement. Bryce had put into the job late, worked like a demon and then started fucking up, hurting himself and others. Guys got superstitious and refused to walk beam with him or stand nearby when a forklift set a bunk of lumber on the deck, fearing that Bryce's bad-luck pull would get them killed. They talked behind his back, called him an accident on two legs, Job with a hammer and a step dick. So the whitehats stuck him on basement detail where he picked up scraps and braced joist. It was retard work and nobody gave him any respect. He became a troll with tools who ate by himself. He grew pale and fat. Sometimes you could hear him under the plywood floors, talking to himself, crying, pouring his life out to the dank basement. At punch-out time when the crew would gather around the tool crib Bryce would lurch out of one of the basements shrinking from the light like one of those blind cave frogs.

Then one morning he just snapped. He pressed a nail gun to his skull and pulled the trigger—three times. He didn't die fast or beautiful, but slow and alone with the whine of Skilsaws and the whump of nail guns above.

One of the laborers found him when he went down to take a piss and tripped on the body. Work stopped long enough for the state troopers to question the remaining crew and lecture the whitehats about job safety. His body was hauled out of the basement and into the sun where it was loaded into an ambulance and driven off the jobsite.

At quitting time Burke grabbed Bryce's time card and punched it out and then hung it above the clock. Guys waiting to punch out stared up at the card. Some even fingered that last clock-out, their fingers tracing the ink like Braille.

The next day Bryce's girlfriend showed up and collapsed by the tool crib, crying. She was a chubby woman with limp brown hair and wide-set eyes that Bryce had met a month before at the Boatel Bar during Mexican night, which meant free chips and salsa with your shot of tequila. The bartender had on a sombrero and was pointing cap guns at the drunks, pretending to shoot them. Somebody had strung red-pepper lights on Eddie the dead elk's rack to go along with the faded lei left over from Hawaiian night.

Bryce had been limping around, sozzled to the gills, yammering about how the company had it in for him. Then he saw her. She was dressed in a flowered smock, large fake gold cross hanging on her ample breasts, ass squeezed into grimy Dacron slacks as she handed out Bibles to the Eskimos huddled around the large-screen television watching *Gilligan's Island* reruns. They were whistling at Ginger and cheering whenever Gilligan took a coconut to the head or pissed off Skipper. By closing time Bryce had lured her away and was buying her pull tabs and white wine spritzers, telling her he believed in God, family and country. Within weeks they were another of Fairbanks's doomed seasonal romances, barhopping, holding hands and making empty promises.

Three nails later and one of the whitehats was handing her Bryce's last paycheck and tool belt. She wasn't wearing the cross anymore and she looked sad and out of place standing in the muddy road next to the stacks of lumber waiting to be built into houses for military families.

After work we went to the bar, sloshed Bryce's name around and guzzled toasts in his honor. The girlfriend arrived drunk, eyes red with tears, and sat in a corner, staring at us, waiting for somebody to stagger over and bend her ear about Bryce. Finally Clarkson, one of the laborers, pumped some money into the jukebox and asked her to dance.

Clarence Carter was singing "Strokin'" on the jukebox and I was tossing darts with Burke, kicking his ass in cricket. The bartender set bottles out on the bar and men were lining up to pay their respects with a shot in Bryce's honor. On the dance floor, Clarkson had his hands all over the girlfriend's ass, dirty face pressed into her hair. They looked happy.

Something about seeing the two of them together filled me with desolation.

I wanted to throw darts at them, tell them to take it outside and leave Alaska before the snow came crashing down out of the mountains.

Burke pounded his beer and shook his head. "Fuck this funeral bullshit. I don't need to stick around for this. You comin', Jack?"

I nodded and followed him to his truck. It was still light outside. The sun hung just above the rim of mountains reflecting off the snow that soon would blanket everything in its deep white hush.

"We gotta meet someone."

I hesitated.

"Now?"

"Unless you want a spin with Bryce's old lady," he said. "Lemme know and I'll tie a board to your ass so you don't fall in."

"I'm not that drunk."

"Good then, get in."

I hopped in the truck and we drove out of Fairbanks until the roads turned to gravel. We crossed a couple of creeks, speeding down birch-lined roads hung with that crazy kind of light that made me think anything was possible in Alaska, even happiness.

I kept quiet and looked out the window hoping to see a moose or wild dog, something to remind me I was still in Alaska and that in a month I would be in treeless Texas, punching the clock and assembling trusses.

Burke laughed and punched the dash. His cheeks were red with liquor and he took his eyes off the road to look at me. "You bought the plane ticket yet?"

"No," I said.

"All right then, we're still in business."

We followed a twisted creek for a ways, down a washed-out

road. There were a few old cabins sprinkled among the trees.
Burke pulled out a flask and took several long hits before offering
it to me. I thought about work the next morning and shook my
head no, but he kept the flask out until I gave in.

"Live a little," he said as we bumped down a long deeply rutted
dirt path that was overgrown with brush. At the end of the path
was a small brown cabin tucked under a bank of jack pines. A
busted-out Bronco and an abandoned tractor sat in the tall grass
like skeletons, picked over by rain and snow, frozen with rust.

"Where are we?" I asked.

He parked the truck alongside the cabin, put the flask away and
got out of the truck without answering.

It was close to eleven o'clock and the sun was still in the trees. A
few ravens drifted lazily in invisible columns of air, the mountains
tall and distant behind them. And for a moment I could not imagine leaving a place like this. Burke was right to want to conquer its
vast unknowable places. But I also knew that it was just as easy to
lose yourself and surrender in some small cabin, surrounded by
dogs and garbage. Or worse: drink yourself blind, shoot your dog
and freeze to death. They'd find you after breakup, another
Johnny Doe Alaska done in by stubborn Arctic dreams.

A man appeared on the porch. He had long gray hair braided
loosely down the back of his neck and he moved slowly, bent
at the knees as if his back had been broken and only recently
healed. His face was red and wrinkled and I couldn't make out his
eyes.

Burke waved and the man waved back, motioning for us to
come up on the porch. As I got closer I could see that he wasn't
that old, just weathered in a particular way I'd seen a lot of men in
Alaska weathered, beaten down and hunched against some imagi-
nary assault.

I stumbled after Burke, caught up in his beery sense of adventure, feeling reckless and full of great things.

"Jack, meet Duke," Burke said.

Duke winced and stuck out a large hand for me to shake. His
grip was surprisingly strong, his hands thick and callused.

"You lookin' for a little adventure?" he asked.

"Drivin' drunk with Burke's enough," I said.

Burke held out his hands. "Hey, man, I'm steady as a rock."

Duke smiled and pushed open the door. "Come on in. Listenin' never hurt nobody."

Burke laughed and slapped Duke on the back as I followed them inside. The ceiling was high and crossed with hand-hewn beams which made me think that Duke had built the place himself back when he was young and land could be bought with the lint in your pocket. I'd heard plenty of stories of the pipeline days from barflies who claimed they used to light joints with hundred-dollar bills and for ten bucks and a six-pack you could get your ashes hauled by some Indian chick. There was a bear pelt mounted on the wall, its glass eyes dull and dust-covered. The pelt was surrounded by rows and rows of bookshelves filled with yellowed paperbacks, burnt-down candle ends, old leghold traps, shell casings, a cribbage board made out of whale bone, several small wood carvings and a half-empty bottle of scotch.

I figured Duke had his stories of the good old days and maybe Burke had brought me out there to hear him ramble on about how it was all gone now, the land fucked, all the good people dead or reformed, the boom busted.

Duke led us over to a round table and sat down heavily, slumping into the chair as if the bones in his shoulders had melted. I could see his eyes now, deep red-rimmed holes above the thick arch of his nose, which looked as if it had been broken a few times.

On the table before us was a map held open by two old paper ten-gauge shotgun shells. It was a detail of the land just above the North Star Borough where the Yukon splintered into the flats. Fairbanks was at the bottom, a square of gridlocked streets, the Tanana River slicing it in half.

Duke looked at it and sighed. "Thought you were comin' by earlier," he said.

"We stopped off at the Boatel," Burke said.

"Some guy at work greased himself with a nail gun," I said.

"It was a wake then?" Duke asked.

"Yeah," Burke said. "Now enough depressing shit, let's get to the good stuff."

Duke cleared his throat and focused on the map. "She's here," he said, pointing.

There was nothing under his finger, just green and a blue line of a river.

"Who?" I asked.

"My daughter."

I looked at them waiting for something more.

"Her name's Penny," he said. "I need someone to go get her for me."

"From where?" I asked, thinking that at any minute Duke would give it up, break out a bottle and we'd get drunk.

But he didn't.

"From him," he said, his voice rising above the tired croak.

"What's this about?" I asked, suddenly sober.

"Just listen to the man," Burke said. "He wants to hire us, for a little side job."

I looked at the map again.

"What sort of job?"

"Go get his daughter—hero kind of shit," he said, winking at Duke.

"I don't get it," I said. "Rescue her from what, there's nothing up there."

"Observant motherfucker," Burke said. "Hell, if she was in Anchorage Duke could go scoop her up himself."

"I'm sick," Duke said. "Tumors in the stomach and who knows where else. I've got a little time though and I don't wanna say she's all I got, but that would be the truth. It's time to get things in order, say what's gotta be said and get ready to die." He coughed into his hand. "She went willingly, at least at first. And now?" He raised his shoulders. "Now I don't know. I'm worried something bad is happening up there."

"Who is she with?" I asked.

"His name is Nunn," he said. "But I don't know what he's calling himself these days. Could be anything, could be she's not even there anymore." He stared at the map. "Hell, I thought she'd be back after the first snow. But she stayed and it's been a year since I've heard from her."

"What sort of place is it?"

"It's a commune or something like that. Maybe there was some reason for it a long time ago—I don't now." He folded his hands over the map. "I started hearing things," he said. "A friend of mine on the state troopers says they picked up a few backpackers stranded in the flats who said they'd been up there. They'd almost starved to death trying to get out."

"So you want us to find her?"

Duke stared at me. "Yes," he said.

"It's nothing," Burke said, slapping me on the shoulders. "We can do it in a weekend."

I studied the map. There were no roads leading into or out of the spot Duke had pointed to. It was just inside the Arctic Circle and although the days were still warm it would be winter soon and no place to be.

"For what?" I asked. "I mean why us?"

Duke glanced into the kitchen. "If you want money—"

Burke shook me by the shoulders. "You're missing the point, Jack."

"What about the job?"

He laughed. "You said yourself that we've about worked our way out of it. And then what? Where are you gonna go? What are you gonna do?"

"Texas," I said.

"You're not going to Texas. You were never going to Texas," he said. "First we do this thing."

"I have something lined up," I said.

"Lined up?"

"Yeah," I said. "Just like you were gonna go native and home-stead. I got something lined up."

He thought about this a moment, eyed Duke and then spoke slowly. "Yeah, but this is bigger than that, Jack."

I shrugged.

"If it's about the money," Duke started again.

Burke waved him off. "We'll get to that. Just say you'll think about it. We help Duke out, have a little fun, see some of the country. Besides, don't tell me you aren't at least a little curious about what's up there."

"I still don't understand what she's doing there," I said.

"That's a bit complicated," Duke said.

"Complicated how?" I asked.

He sighed and rubbed his eyes. "Because I introduced her to Nunn."

"The guy who . . ."

"Yes," he said, nodding. "A long time ago I did a few jobs for him after he'd first come into the country. This was after the pipeline money was drying up. The party was over for a lot of people and without the work things were getting a little rough. There was a shooting gallery over on Lacy Street. A couple of bouncers had been shot over drug money. There was even a rumor going around about a ring of pedophiles snatching Eskimo kids off the street in Anchorage and bringing them up here."

"We've heard the stories," Burke said impatiently.

Duke stared into the map. "Yeah, well, that's the way it was. So when Nunn came up here nobody noticed him. His full name was Gregory Blake Nunn, but nobody called him that. He blended right in with all of the other freaks, except for the fact that he had plans. The rest of us were just trying to get lost. In my case it was a bad marriage."

"What sort of plans?" I asked.

"He wanted to start a community, which wasn't out of the ordinary. Plenty of hippie types had already tried and failed because the land's too hard this far north. Problem was that Nunn wasn't really a hippie. He knew how to play the game though. He came from money—one of those trust fund guys, went to Harvard and was studying to be a doctor or something. Then one day he just left and started walking, hitching across the country, livin' off his parents, nothing too radical. Hated the government, but then so did everybody else. He read a lot, had some ideas about the way things ought to be. He had big parties on the solstice with these great big bonfires and bands, people skinny-dipping in the tailing pond. He watched and made sure nobody got hurt or too high. When it was over he would come over and just sort of sum up the whole evening for you, whispering in your ear. He was smart about people."

"Smart how?"

"He knew things, I guess," he said, shrugging. "Told you things about yourself that even you didn't know. It made some people uncomfortable. I guess that's where it started."

I looked at the map again, knowing that what Duke was telling me was important.

"Then he began collecting people," he said. "I used to see him in the bars talking them up, seeing which women bought him drinks when he asked them to. That was how he knew he wanted them, because they listened and would do things for him. I'll give him credit because a lot of folks come here and live like it's Los Angeles, but not Nunn. He was always trying to figure things out by quizzing old prospectors and hunting guides about the country, learning their tricks and how to live off the land. Sometimes he'd disappear into the woods and be gone for months, testing what he'd learned. And then just when we all thought he'd finally met up with a bear or crashed in some bush plane he'd show up again and talk somebody else into going with him."

Duke stopped to cough a couple of times. "He has a power over people. It's in the way he talks, you'll see. He has this voice and if I tell you it sounds important somehow, you wouldn't know what I mean."

"As long as it's not one of them Kool-Aid-sipping cults, we're still in," Burke said.

"You said you introduced them?" I asked.

"Penny was back from college, thinking about moving to Boston and getting a job. We had a good summer, almost no fights—went canoeing at night, took long walks and really got to know each other all over again. Then one day we were at Safeway grabbing a few groceries when I ran into him."

"You mean . . ."

"Nunn," he said. "He looked different. His hair was longer, but I recognized him right away and introduced Penny to him. He didn't say much, just stared right through me like I was doing something wrong mentioning the good old days. There was another guy with him, a skinny fellow about Penny's age, and he had a book tucked under his arm that she'd read so they started talking about it. I could see Nunn eyeballing her and I knew what he was thinking."

"That's it?" Burke asked.

"The next night Penny said she was going down to the Howling Dog Saloon to hear a band. She didn't come home until morning. She hadn't slept much. I asked her where she'd been and all she said was 'out.' I even remember her hair smelled like campfire and I knew she'd met someone because she didn't want to talk about Boston or anything else. It was like that for a while, sneaking around, coming back late. Two weeks later she was gone. At first I thought she'd decided to hitch back to Tucson or Boston, but I found a note that said she was going to 'the camp.' I knew right away it was Nunn, but I figured she was an adult, she could do what she wanted. She'd find out for herself it was no paradise and she'd be back. It wasn't the first time she'd done this sort of thing. She'd dropped out of college to follow some band around, drop acid and sell pot brownies in the parking lot. The only thing that brought her back then was her mother's death."

He swallowed hard, pecked his lips with his dry, papery tongue.

"Why don't you ask her to come back—write her a letter and have it dropped with the supplies?" I asked.

He shook his head. "There's been no answer."

Burke stood up. "I'm in. It's on you," he said, pointing at me. "We're gonna get the pink slip anyway."

"Yeah, but . . ."

"You can still go to Texas if we finish this before the first snow."

"Finish?" I asked.

"Get Duke's daughter," he said. "Hell, Jack, all we've gotta do is boat up this river, hike across here and we're there. Country club stuff. It's the best of it."

"What about getting her to come—sounds like all we're doing is kidnapping her back."

"No, man, it's just a bunch of old hippies, trying to live off the land, listening to this Nunn asshole talk about revolution. All we gotta do is offer her something better."

"Yeah and what's that?"

"Reality," he said. "A way out."

Duke looked at me and shook his head at Burke.

"What do you say, Jack?"

I thought a minute. Duke was dying right there, slipping away, wanting to see his daughter. I was drunk. Texas was flat. It would be hot, and the job, well it would just be a job, punch the clock, drink, sleep, wake up sore. I knew the routine.

I nodded.

"What does that mean?" Burke asked. "You in or not, Jack?"

"I'll give it two weeks," I said.

Burke beamed at Duke. "It's good as done, Duker."

"You sure?" Duke asked, looking at me.

"Somebody's gotta make sure they don't brainwash Burke here."

Duke winked, rose stiffly and walked toward the small eat-in kitchen and pulled a coffee tin off the shelf, brought it to the table. He popped the faded plastic top off and inside was a roll of bills rubber-banded together. "There's five thousand dollars here," he said, setting the roll in front of me. The money was dirty and smelled like smoke. "That oughtta at least cover the work you'll miss and then some."

I pushed the roll back at him. "You don't . . ."

He clamped a hand on my wrist. "I'm going into the hospital next week for more tests and I don't expect good news. It's just money—take it, use it for supplies, whatever you want, just get her for me."

"We'll take it," Burke said, plucking the wad away from me.

Duke nodded and then shuffled over to the bookshelf to a line of framed photos. He took one of them down and blew a scrim of dust off the glass before handing it to me.

"That's her," he said. "Five years ago, right after her mother died."

The girl in the photo was thin and smiling. Long brown hair fell over her smooth tan shoulders. I traced the curve of her collarbone and casually imagined fucking her because of the way her eyes glared back at the camera, confronting it with a deep seriousness. There was something in the curl of her mouth, a slight sneer or hesitation that said she wanted this to be the last picture of her youth.

"Go on and take it," he said. "I have others."

As I took the photo from him his hands shook slightly.

"This too," he said, handing me a plain white envelope. "It might help you convince her to come. It's a letter I wrote telling her about the cancer and some other things."

"Great," Burke said anxiously. He was staring at the bear pelt, sticking his fingers into the frozen mouth, tapping the teeth, the wad of bills clenched tightly in his other hand. "Are we set then?"

Duke pulled me aside. "Don't let yourself get wrapped up in what goes on up there—they want to be with him, even Penny," he whispered.

"What?"

But before he could answer Burke spun around. "Did you shoot this?" he asked, pointing at the bear pelt.

Duke nodded. "Took six shots and died at my feet. It was the last animal I ever shot."

"Got your blood moving?"

"You could say that," Duke said. "Took six shots, three to the skull, two in the shoulder and one right through here." He pointed at his heart. "The sonofabitch still almost got me."

Burke looked around the small cabin and examined one of the leghold traps.

"You ready?" he asked.

I walked to the door and shook hands with Duke, hoping he'd smile and tell me not to worry. But he didn't and I was left won-

dering about his cryptic warning and the people in the valley and
most of all, Nunn.

Outside the sun hung low in the west. Wild dogs or wolves
were howling somewhere off in the distance, their voices echoing
through the trees. I scanned Duke's trash-strewn yard. It was full
of grownup toys left to rust, projects half finished and I thought
that maybe this was how Burke would end up after he'd burned
himself out on his homesteading dreams and settled for a shack
close to town. Duke nodded at me silently as we stepped off the
porch and got in the truck.

Burke waited until we were on the road before he spoke. "A
week or two, we get the girl, have some laughs, see the country
and then you can shuffle off to Texas."

"What about work?" I asked.

He pulled Duke's money out of his pocket and waved it at me.
"Fuck work. This should about cover it. We're not sick with
money but it's enough for us to do this one last thing together."

"You sure we can find this place?"

"I guess we'll find out, won't we? Hell, that'll be half the fun."

He pulled into the driveway that led to my building, the headlights briefly illuminating a dead pine tree somebody had planted
in an old oil drum.

I popped the door and stepped out of the truck.

"Here's to . . ."

Burke's face darkened. "Don't go getting poetic on me,
college boy. It's just you and me goin' up a river looking for a little
something to get the blood moving and all that other good stuff."

He laughed. I shut the door and watched him back out of the
drive.

•

Inside my dark apartment I stared at the familiar heap of dirty
work clothes in the corner, the cracked plaster and my tool belt
slumped in a plastic milk crate by the door. It was near the end of
August and I had planned on being in Texas by Thanksgiving, just
about the time the bitter cold would settle over Fairbanks. But this

plan to rescue Duke's daughter had pulled me back from the plane and the job chasing.

I found the battered Rand McNally road atlas, popped it open to the map of Alaska and tried to remember where Duke's finger had pointed. There were rivers everywhere and patches of green ink next to the blank spaces. It was out there, past even the small roadless native villages.

I studied the map a long time until sleep came thick and heavy.

I did not dream.

When I woke I thought about just going to work and ignoring my promise to Burke and Duke, letting the routine roll over me. But that feeling soon passed as I scraped together my gear: fishing rods, nylon two-man tent, a pair of Gortex boots, knives, day pack and gun, a Winchester .338 Magnum that I'd bought from a pawnshop. The snap and click of gathering gear stirred something in me and for a minute I thought this was what I'd come here to do.

An hour later I drove over to Burke's house. Day-Glo Bob was blasting Janis's "Piece of My Heart" and walking around with a cigar-sized doobie, reading one of his trivia books and talking to himself.

His eyes widened like coals when he saw me coming around the corner. He did a little hippie head shake, knocking his hair out of his eyes.

"Jumpin' Jack Flash," he said, blowing the sweet dope smoke in my face.

We did the soul shake.

"Did you know Genghis Khan died fucking?" he asked, pointing at the trivia book. "Fascinating shit in here."

I noticed a Visine bottle on a rope around his neck and pointed.

"For puttin' on the man," he shouted. "If you've got a searching mind like I do, you gotta go undercover, look like the man, talk like the man—know what I mean, Jack?"

"Where is Burke the Man?" I said with my best hippie hiss.

"Everywhere and nowhere," he said. "But for you, he's out back, chief."

He led me into the backyard shouting with Janis.

Burke appeared, lugging an armload of gear, his face bright with our mission.

"You wanna go by the job?" he asked.

Bob stopped his screeching. "Working fools," he shouted. "You two need to be deprogrammed, unscrambled, rewired, before . . ." Suddenly he launched back into song, belting right along with her, tearing his heart out, pleading.

"Not no more," Burke said, but Day-Glo had already ambled away, shaking his head in disgust.

•

At the jobsite I told the girl in the office that we wanted our last paycheck. She stared at us a moment, scratching her stiff halo of ash-blond hair with glue-on nails she'd painted bright green with little silver streaks. Her sweater was covered in dog hair and food stains.

"You boys find yourself some greener pastures?" she asked.

"Just get the checks, honey," Burke said, winking and staring at her ample ass as she trudged into the back room.

While we waited in the stuffy double-wide that functioned as an office, Taft, one of the whitehats, entered the trailer. He was drinking coffee out of a thermos top, a newspaper folded under his arm. He had college written all over him; soft face, softer hands and perfectly white teeth. The plumbers called him the Shaft behind his back because he handed out pink slips like Christmas presents and hassled them about their time cards.

"What are you guys up to?" Taft asked.

"Not work," Burke said, puffing out his chest.

"Leavin' just like the rest of the wage chasers, before the pink slips get you, eh?"

"Something like that," I said.

Taft nodded and winked at us. I could see Burke's hands go into fists. He was not above pounding him right there in the trailer.

To his credit the Shaft stood his ground, smart-ass smile pasted on his lily-white face. But then the woman came around front with our paychecks, asking us to sign for them, and Burke let Taft slink out of the trailer without swinging on him.

In the truck on the way over to the outfitters Burke told me that Duke had loaned us his boat, a fourteen-footer with a Johnson outboard. "We're gonna fish our way up," he said. "And fish our way back."

"What about the girl?" I had her picture in my pocket and had looked at it enough times already that I had memorized the smile and the soft curve of her dark eyes. If it was possible to fall in love with a picture I was close to gone on her.

"If she's there, we'll get her," he said. "If not then we'll fish ourselves stupid."

"Maybe there's a reason she's up there."

"What's that mean?" he growled.

"It means we'll find what we're gonna find, see what we're gonna see," I said. "I don't trust anybody."

"You need to get laid or something," he said.

"I thought I needed an adventure."

"That too."

Burke pulled into the outfitter's parking lot. It was chock full of Alaskan limos: pickup trucks with empty beer cans rolling around in their beds and NRA window stickers.

We jumped out of the truck and headed for the wooden ramp that led to the double glass doors and emerged an hour later with MREs, topo maps, boxes of shells for both the rifle and the .45, groundsheets, life preservers, coils of good rope, flares and a case of mosquito repellent.

Afterward we ate lunch at a small diner south of town that served open-face roast beef sandwiches and homemade blueberry pie.

Burke laid out the trip.

We'd drive up this government road as far as we could and then put in the river. He figured it would take a day or two if the weather held and we spent a little time fishing the clear water sloughs. Duke had told him that the trail leading into the camp from the river would be marked and that there would be canoes, maybe even a makeshift dock. As for the hike to the lake he figured it couldn't be more than a day, but it would be rough, swampy going. Trails weren't easily cut in the bush. There would be black flies and mosquitoes as well as the ever-present threat of bears.

"I'll get us there, the rest is up to you," he said. "I'm gonna swing by Duke's tonight, grab the boat and pump him for more info about his daughter."

I tried to picture us out on the river, but the diner kept intruding: people eating and jabbering all around us, the waitresses snagging tips, busboys bussing—the whole show just clicking along around us.

"You ready?" Burke asked, dropping a twenty on the grease-stained check.

I nodded and followed him outside.

In the parking lot a skinny woman in satin hot pants was checking her lipstick in the side-view mirror. Her boyfriend, a tattooed biker, stood nearby sucking on a cigarette, making sure we weren't eyefucking her. Burke gave him a wink and the guy just stood there staring at his cigarette.

At my apartment we unloaded half of the gear while the chubby couple from 2B were arguing across the hood of a Jeep plastered with SAVE THE WHALE bumper stickers. The plates on the truck still read New Jersey, the Garden State. Their dog, a skinny collie who crapped all over the parking lot, was tied to the rear bumper, yapping.

"Happy, happy, happy," Burke shouted at them.

They ignored us and kept arguing.

Burke grinned and got in the truck just as the wife began sobbing into her hands. The husband circled, flapping his arms and shouting at her to stop. He glanced over at me and waved, his face tensing into a smile for a second before he turned his attention back to the wife.

I thought of the girl in the photo again and the letter in my pocket. When I closed my eyes her face appeared and then was gone.

•

There were a lot of odd people in the bush surrounding Fairbanks. Whole families living in dugout cabins, miners sitting on played-out gold claims, men and women who ran sled dogs and tended fish wheels in the summer. They were people trying to get away from something, testing themselves against the wilderness. I saw them occasionally at the diners and truck stops on the outskirts of town, greasy men with long beards and soot-stained coveralls. They sat alone, drank coffee and stared at people. Their hands were black and thick with calluses from splitting wood and tending to stoves. More than a few times Burke and I had run into spooky prospector types living in trailers along small creeks. Some of them guarded their claims with wolf dogs and guns, others took small fortunes out of the water each year, gambled and bought expensive machinery only to have the claim peter out and leave them with a lot of rusty bulldozers and gold fever. I wondered if Nunn was one of those restless types: a seeker, a man looking for himself in the middle of nowhere.

I called a few of the full-timers from the crew and asked them if they'd heard anything about Nunn. A roofer named Fred told me he'd met a woman who'd mentioned the name once. "Wanda June," he said. "She used to read palms and mooch drinks down at the Club Alaska."

I thanked him and hung up.

I'd been in the Club once, after five or six other bars, during my first week in the state and could remember virtually nothing about it except that I'd seen a pregnant woman passed out on the floor next to the jukebox, vomit hanging off her lips, and in the bathroom I'd met a man dressed like Santa Claus who tried to sell me acid. When I refused he lowered his beard and said, "Welcome to Alaska, Cheechako!" and placed a tab of acid in his eye.

Later I swung by the Club Alaska. It was a dark hole with rough unfinished floors, cheap beer mirrors on the wall, a long sticky bar running the length of the room and two useless pool tables propped up with cinder blocks. There were a few hard-core types fingering drinks at the bar, watching television and eating pickled eggs from napkins. There were no women.

The bartender nodded when I asked for a shot of bourbon with a beer back. He was a large man with rotten teeth, thick Coke-bottle glasses and dull blond hair.

He set the drinks in front of me. "Five dollars," he said, holding up his hand. One of the drunks watched me dig through my wallet, working up the nerve to cadge a drink. I knocked back the shot and took the beer down to the end of the bar and sat thinking of the trip. I had that same gut-level uneasiness that had accompanied every job hop with Burke. It was like stumbling around a dark room, groping for the light switch. What got me through was his confidence—the look on his face that he'd seen worse, a lot worse, and come through it okay.

I finished the beer and raised the empty bottle at the bartender, who shambled down the long bar, knocking dirty napkins onto the floor with his big hands and stacking tin ashtrays.

"'Nother?" he asked.

I nodded.

When he returned with the beer I asked him about Wanda June.

"She's been banned since breakup," he said. "Hope she's not a friend of yours. 'Cause if she is I don't wanna hear about it." He smiled, black gums and nasty bridgework. "Plenty of other bars for her to plague, don't know why she's attached to this one."

"Not a friend," I said.

"Well then that'll be two dollars," he said, pointing at the beer and frisbeeing the cap into a trash barrel.

I put three bills on the bar, pushed one to the drink rail. His eyes followed it. "She ever mention anything about a man named Nunn?"

"Wanda June?"

I nodded.

"She said a lot of stuff, man," he said. "That's why she's banned—pestering the customers, stealing toilet paper. General, all-around pain in my fucking ass. She's not the only one either."

I looked around at the Club's customers. It was a blighted dick farm of terminal liver beaters who woulda been lucky if someone so much as nodded in their general direction.

"So it's not the Sands," he said. "But I still got standards. Guys come here to drink and get away from their wives or lack of, the last thing they need is some hippie chick babbling voodoo shit at them."

I drank my beer and waited for him to stop his rant.

"You're not from here," he said.

I shook my head. "How about you?"

He leaned over the bar. "Cleveland," he said. "But that was twelve years ago and well this place it sort of gets in your blood and fucks everything else up. Try Ohio after you've seen Denali in July or watched the ice break on the Yukon. The rest of the world's boring." He laughed. More rotten teeth. "You wanted to know about Nunn, my friend?"

"Sure," I said.

"You gotta understand, there are lots of crazy people living up here. Half the shit you hear is just stories."

I looked at him. "Yeah?"

"Well, like that guy who strapped steaks to his wife's back and fed her to a bear."

"In Kodiak, right?"

"Well, it didn't happen that way," he said. "He shot her then put the steaks on her. But the story about finding a head in the grocery store Dumpster—that one's true."

"Where was the body?"

"Just the head. They haven't found the body yet." He leaned over the bar. "I got a friend who's a state trooper, tells me all kinds of shit, stuff they don't print in the papers, like all the rapes."

"What about Nunn?"

"I've heard his name," he said, pouring himself a glass of schnapps. "But have I met the man or shaken his hand? Fuck no. So until that happens the name's just another ghost story as far as I'm concerned."

"I still wanna hear it."

He looked around before pushing his glasses up and leaning heavily on the bar.

"Well, besides Wanda June I only heard his name once before," he said, sipping the schnapps. "It was right after breakup. Man came into the bar. He was drunk and he started telling me a story about how he and two other guys had been up one of the Yukon tributaries fishing. I've heard a million of these stories, tourists mostly, yakking about fishing or seeing a bear. But this guy was different. It was like he didn't want to tell the story, more like he had to, like he was trying to figure out what went wrong."

"What do you mean?"

"Well, three days into the trip one of his buddies falls down a ravine and breaks his leg bad. Fun's over—the man needs a doctor. But when they get to the boat there's a sow bear and two cubs playing with the rope, batting it around while mama bear sniffs around for food. All of their gear's in the boat, even the guns. The one with the broken leg is bleeding. They try scaring the bear off but she gets one of the guys pretty bad—chews his face up, punctures his lung. It gets dark, the wolves start howling—real up shit's creek without a paddle stuff, right? So just when they're thinking this is how they buy it, out of nowhere comes this canoe, drifting down the river. There's a woman in it and get this, she's singing. Before they can do anything she paddles over to the bears, claps the paddles together and boom! Off go the bears and she just floats past them without saying a word. They get back into the boat and get ready to go and abra-fuckin'-cadabra the woman shows up again only this time she's got two men with her. They reset the broken leg and then something bad happened."

"What?"

"I dunno, he wouldn't say. They had to hike through the woods all night and the next morning they're in some sort of camp or village."

"Indian village?"

"Fuck no, man—white people."

"What were they doing up there?"

"He thought they were running some kind of small-time mining operation because there were tailings everywhere and the people had jars of gold flakes and nuggets. But there was something else going on. Some other reason they were up there."

"You mean Nunn?"

"That's the name he gave me," he said. "This guy Nunn owned the land and the people were there because of him. If you ask me it sounds like a bunch of hippies trying their hand at paradise."

The bartender stopped to grab a drink for one of the rum hounds who was grumbling and jiggling the ice in his empty glass. No money changed hands. The man had half the drink down before the bartender could turn his back.

"That's it," he said. "All I ever heard about the man, just a name is all and that crazy story. The only reason the story stayed with me is because only one of them came back."

"What do you mean?"

"The one with the broken leg stayed at the camp."

"And the one that got mauled?"

"Like I said, something happened," he said. "Hell I don't know, maybe there was more but I didn't get to hear the rest 'cause it was last call."

"What?"

"Last call—end of party. No more stories." He paused. "Don't tell me you're thinkin' of going up there?"

I stared at my hands.

"A little piece of bartender advice," he said. "You go too far out and there's no coming back, believe me, I've seen plenty of it. Nice little hippie kid comes up here to work on the boats because he heard he can make big money. Only when he gets here and there's no job, not even one of those shitty cannery gigs gutting salmon in the freezer. So he starts hangin' with the freaks or maybe he thinks he's some kind of wilderness man. Either way he ends up going out there, into the bush, hoping to find himself—know what I mean?"

I smiled.

"All I know is sometimes they go out there and don't come back," he said, taking in the last of the schnapps, even the ice cubes. "Everybody figures they hopped a plane back home or something like that so nobody asks too many questions. But like I said I got friends on the force who tell me things, like how every month some parents come lookin' for their kid because they haven't heard from him."

"Thanks for the advice," I said.

He shrugged. "Just come back and have a beer sometime."

I shook my head, swilled the rest of the beer and let him go back to work, wondering if the woman the moose hunters had seen was Duke's daughter. Or maybe the bartender was right and the story had been just another bar story, something to fill dead air between rounds.

One of the rum hounds stumbled off his stool. "Wanna see something?" he asked.

He was a small man, his face a bright pimiento red, shoulders hunched, mouth pulled into a frozen scotch sneer.

"Out back," he said, curling a finger at me.

"I'm not going to buy you a beer," I said.

"Don't want a beer," he said, letting out a high trilling laugh. He inched closer. His skin had that long-term booze gloss, mapped with broken blood vessels, pockmarks and nicotine stains.

He kept moving toward the back door, shoelaces dragging behind in the beer scum and shattered peanut shells.

I shook my head and he laughed some more.

"If you don't look you'll always wonder," the man said. "What's worse than that, you'll dream about it."

"What's that?"

"Come on," he said. "A little look never hurt nobody."

A few of the others at the bar looked up. Some raised drinks, another ashed his cigarette on his pants. I looked to the bartender for help but he just shrugged. Figuring I had nothing to lose, I followed the man out the back door into a small fenced-in cement pad. A couple of broken pool tables sat at one end. The ground was littered with broken pieces of beer mirrors and brown beer glass. The moon hung low in the sky, just above the teeth of the fence. Cars rattled by on the road and some small animal scurried out from behind a clump of blown trash bags.

The man led me to the far corner where a large chest freezer sat under a blue tarp. An extension cord ran out the window to it.

He grinned.

"You ready?" he asked, picking up a flashlight that had been stashed next to the freezer.

I stepped closer and waited as he opened the lid of the freezer. No light came on. There was only the frost curling over the edge and then evaporating.

"Closer," he said, clicking on the flashlight.

I peered into the freezer and saw in the flashlight's dull beam a solid block of ice.

"Yeah?" I said. "So you got a block of ice."

He laughed. "You're not looking hard enough. What's wrong with you, boy?"

I moved closer. There was a dark blurry figure under the ice that looked vaguely human. Trapped air bubbles and a good three inches of freezer burn had distorted it. The face resembled a punched-in mask, plum-colored and clenched tight as if against the cold. A pair of hands were visible near the surface. But on closer inspection they appeared to be rubber and the fur rimming the man's dented head also looked fake.

"It's a frozen Eskimo," the man said. "Webster found him up in Prudhoe this spring and brought him back. We were going to put him behind the bar but Ronnie said the owner wouldn't go for it, fuckin' health department or some tribal council or something, so we had to settle for this. What do you think?"

I bent over the freezer until my nose was a few inches from the ice, trying to determine whether or not this was some sort of joke. Two cigarette butts lay just under the surface, frozen. The ice smelled faintly of beer and freezer burn.

"I think it's bullshit," I said.

The man stood there blinking a moment. "It doesn't matter what you think, you owe me five bucks."

I looked at him.

"Admission fee," he said. "Remember we had ourselves a deal."

"It's a fake," I said.

"Maybe, maybe not, it's still five bucks, pal—you took a look."

I turned and began walking toward the door. I heard the freezer slam shut and before I could get to the door he was standing in front of me, blocking the way.

"Five bucks," he repeated, poking me with the flashlight, hopped-up grin painted across his face. For a minute I thought about tossing a short jab to his already wrecked nose. I was a couple of inches taller and sober to his staggering drunk barker act and my fist could have caved his jaw in, taken a few teeth.

But I hesitated.

There was the flashlight. Suddenly my hands felt very heavy. My stomach fluttered as I tried to hold his bloodshot stare.

"Five's the discount rate, buddy," he said. "I'm going easy on you. Not everybody gets to see the bar mascot, especially you being a stranger and all."

He nudged me with the flashlight again until I gave up on the idea of punching and running. If it was a joke then his buddies were probably watching and would be waiting for me. This was Alaska, the northern knife and gun club where a bar fight wasn't even worth mentioning unless it involved some near fatal injury or creative use of available weapon.

So I gave him a couple of singles instead which he let flutter to the ground.

"That's all you get," I said, walking back into the bar, my hands trembling, neck tense, expecting the thump of flashlight at any moment or maybe a gun. But nothing happened. When I turned to have a look he was scraping the bills off the cement and swearing at me.

In the parking lot I examined my face in the mirror, forced a sneer, wanting whiskey and two or three beers to stop my guts from shaking.

UPSTREAM

The next morning Burke was pounding at my door. The .45 was strapped to his leg and a canvas coat hung loosely off his broad shoulders. His eyes were clear, gone was the usual hungover look. Burke stone-cold sober was a dangerous thing and I half expected him to pull out the gun and start shooting streetlights.

I was still thinking about the bar and how I should have scrambled the drunk's face.

"Daylight's burning," Burke roared.

I pointed at the pile of gear.

"I'm ready."

He grunted, grabbed some of the gear and headed for the truck. I picked up my fly rod, bedroll and backpack and followed him.

In the back Duke's boat sat tied and red-flagged. The boat did not inspire a lot of confidence. The bottom had been patched a few times with pop rivets and silicone. The sides were dented and the gunwales crooked. Two weather-beaten oars hung in the oarlocks. But the outboard motor looked good, clean and well taken care of as were the pull cord, spark plugs and fuel lines, which looked new.

"It'll get us there," Burke said, somehow sensing my doubts.

"Let's hope," I said.

After stacking my gear neatly next to his on the jump seat I crawled in, pushing laminated topo maps and food wrappers out of the way.

"Breakfast?" he said, pointing at coffee in a to-go cup and a box of powdered donuts.

I grabbed for the coffee as we sped out of the driveway, heading straight north.

He rolled the window down, letting the air whip his hair around. The radio was going full blast and I started getting into the spirit of things. But at the two-lane he suddenly doubled back, heading toward the army base and the jobsite.

"How about we give our last respects?" he shouted over the radio.

I nodded uneasily, hoping he was joking. But he kept driving until I could see the airstrip and rows of barracks set against the sunrise like tombstones. A massive drab-colored C-130 sat refueling near the B hangar and there were other planes just breaking over the rim of mountains like large aluminum ravens.

Burke pulled up to the guard shack, pointed at the sticker on his windshield and was waved through.

The early birds were rolling out the tools. Forklift operators jostled by, setting the day's wood supply on the second-story decks. We circled the muddy road, Burke blasting the horn and flipping off the whitehats who sat in their new trucks, drinking coffee, listening to the radio, waiting for the rest of the stiffs to show.

"Burnin' bridges, Jacko," he shouted. "Now this little mission's been o-fuckin'-ficially launched. Go on and get some."

I hesitated.

He forearmed me until I flipped off Gabe Peltz, a fat foreman who'd once put me on shiner detail for punching in ten minutes late. Peltz looked up from his coffee and glared as the truck spun around racing toward the gate.

Back out on the base road men in army fatigues marched in long rectangles, feet moving in unison, their faces blank circles attached to cookie cutter bodies. Burke saluted them and raced to the guard shack where the same somber-faced MP stood fingering his rifle, giving us the once-over. He nodded and the gate rose like a trap.

And like that we were sprung from the base. Anything could

happen, even the air felt different as it whipped in through the open windows, numbing my cheeks and forcing me to gulp it down.

We hit the two-lane blacktop and climbed out of the valley into the foothills, leaving Fairbanks, square and ugly in the rearview mirror. Mist hugged the edges of the road. The mountains were distant purple humps that seemed to grow larger the farther we got from Fairbanks until it was impossible to tell the valleys from the hills.

We followed the pipeline, a thick steel tube supported by concrete footings, out of town as it stitched its way above and below the earth.

The Tanana River ran along a ravine to our right, high and heavy from the recent rains, tree limbs floating just below its muddy surface. Pines stretched forever, an endless carpet of green broken only by the patchwork of clearcuts and the occasional cabin or house shoved into the landscape like a sliver.

There were a few truckers on the road pushing their rigs up the long slow inclines on their way north to Barrow or Prudhoe Bay. As we passed the truckers I caught sight of their gaunt faces through the windshield, eyes locked on the road scanning for moose or soft shoulders that could suck an entire truck over a cliff suddenly and without warning.

An hour out of Fairbanks the rock-and-roll station faded into a crazed preacher spouting Bible verse and ranting about the coming Apocalypse in a heavy Canadian yawp.

"Maybe we ought to turn back," I joked.

"Fuck that," Burke said, turning the radio off and grabbing his crotch. "As I walk through the valley of death my rod and staff comfort me. They maketh me lay with strange women."

"Praise the Lord."

He punched the radio off. "That shit has always freaked me out."

"Baby Jesus and your Lord Jesus Christ?"

"No, man, I'm serious, people that believe like that aren't fucking around."

"You mean the ones with the WWJD bumper stickers?"

He looked at me.

"What Would Jesus Do," I said.

"I'll tell you what he did. When I was little I used to mow lawns on the weekends. Most of them were mow-and-go jobs, but there was the Kellys' lawn—overgrown, bees' nests, sticker bushes, roots. It was hell."

"What's this gotta do with baby Jesus?"

"I'm gettin' to it," he said. "So one day after I finished the Kellys' lawn, Mrs. Kelly asked if I wanted lemonade or some shit like that. I said sure and followed her inside to the kitchen. I sucked back three glasses and just as I was about to go Mr. Kelly said he wanted to show me something in the den. So I sit down and they tell me they have a film they want me to watch. I still wasn't sure what the hell was going on, so I just sat there and waited while he messed with the projector."

"Was it one of those stupid Davey and Goliath films?" I asked. "You know the ones with that clay kid and his dog who were always fucking up and then being taught these Christian lessons."

He shook his head. "No, I wish, man. This was dead babies, shots of 'em in trash cans and Dumpsters and interviews with all these hysterical women who regretted having abortions. After some minister came on and talked about how special life was and how the killers had to be stopped."

"What did you do?"

"What could I do? I needed the cash 'cause I was saving up for my first car. The worst part was that Mr. Kelly gave me a Bible instead of the usual fifteen bucks."

"You ever go back?"

"Yeah, but it kinda messed me up with the girls because I kept seeing those dead babies every time I tried to get into some chick's pants. I remember beating off a lot that summer. I even did it once in their backyard."

We laughed as the truck dipped through the mountains into lush green valleys crazy with trees. Ravens sat in treetops watching us. Small ponds whipped by with abandoned mining equipment hunkered down around their gravel shores like animals poisoned with inactivity, seized by rust. Every once in a while we spotted a trailer tucked away off the road, papered with POSTED signs, the windows rocked out.

The blacktop gradually gave way to hardpack gravel. Then the guardrails disappeared and there were just snow poles dangling over the road fifteen feet high, markers for when the snow and winds came and the roads could only be opened with bulldozers. We saw fewer and fewer cars and then only trucks gearing down the sudden curvy declines, checking their brakes every thirty yards. Off in the distance the larger snow-covered peaks of the Brooks Range gradually came into view, sunlight shattering off their steep faces, not quite heaven but close. I could see Burke taking it all in, imagining himself out there, all alone, pitted against the winter and some contest of his own making.

I'd almost forgotten about Duke's daughter and Nunn. The more I took in the vast snarl of wilderness the more I began to see how somebody might want to lose themselves and start a camp. But I knew that under all that green was a tangled buggy mess chock full of a million ways to die.

"How about it?" he asked, pointing at the snarl of snow-covered peaks. "How far do you think they are?"

"Far," I said.

"When I first saw them I thought you could walk right up to them."

"The mountains?"

He nodded.

"I never thought about it," I said.

"Well I did, then I gave up thinking about them," he said. "Like climbing that mountain there—the one with the sheer face. Hell, gimme half a chance and I'd still do it."

"What's stopping you?"

"Same thing that's stopping you," he shot back.

I looked at him. "Nothing's stopping me. I'm happy to look at them without having to get to the top."

"When was the last time you got laid?"

"What's that gotta do with *you* wanting to climb mountains?"

"You tell me, Mr. I'm-Happy-to-Look," he said. "Rumor on the job was that you hooked up with Nannette of the North over at Cheap Charlie's. You weren't looking there."

"Nada," I said. "But I did bang some Greenpeace chick."

"No shit?"

"She came to the door wanting a donation to help stop drilling on the North Slope. I invited her in and . . ."

"And?"

". . . and she had hairy legs, but a nice set of tits. I stepped up for the environment."

"I thought we were talking about climbing mountains?"

But he let it drop as we drove into a deep valley. The silence broadened between us and the truck ate up road. We topped a long rise and several volunteer fire trucks and an ambulance passed us in the opposite direction. More cars followed—beat-up pickup trucks, a sputtering VW van and two strap wreckers. Burke looked at me, raised his eyebrows and hit the gas.

Fifteen minutes later we saw the skid marks. They were at least a hundred feet long and led up to a single-lane bridge spanning a narrow creek. A state trooper was setting flares on either side of the bridge, holding his brim hat as he stooped.

There were a few other cars parked and people staring over the embankment.

"Accident?" Burke said, pulling the truck to the berm. The thick smell of oil and gas hit me the minute I stepped out of the truck and I followed it to the lip of the bridge. Two men in Carhart coveralls nodded at us and pointed over the edge. A tractor trailer lay half buried in the opposing bank. There were blown bits of tire rubber scattered all over the ravine. The cab was a mangled mass of twisted sheet metal and the tank behind the rig had collapsed, spilling thick crude oil into the creek. Oil-covered fish struggled, dying in the water above the wreck.

"What about the driver?" Burke asked one of the men, a short guy with stained teeth and curly black hair who looked as if he'd just crawled out from under a car or some hole in the ground.

"They cut him out in pieces," the man said, pointing at a band of red on the crushed cab door. "Buckets of blood, looked like the animals had been at him too."

Burke whistled. "It get anybody else?"

The man shook his head. "Just him. The trooper thinks he fell asleep at the wheel, snapped awake and hit the brakes, but it was too late. Spilled a quarter load of crude and no way they're gonna get a HAZMAT team up here in time."

"When did it happen?" I asked.

The man shrugged. "This morning, maybe sometime last night."

I walked onto the bridge and stared at the motor which lay at the creek's edge like some carved stone. The oil slick stretched along the creek as far as I could see, poisoning the water as it worked itself like blood into the main river and then downstream, killing fish and birds as it flowed into the heart of Fairbanks.

"You ready?" Burke asked. He was standing behind me, staring at the trail of guts on the shiny steel door. "Better than a cup of coffee. Nothin' like a little smashed steel and death to get the blood flowing."

"Not a bad way to go," I said.

"When I go it's gonna be epic and alone," he said, swaggering back to the truck.

Before leaving I glanced at the accident one more time. Blood and oil glinted dully in the sun. I wondered if the driver had left a family or if he was one of those sad bottled-up Alaskan types who'd come here looking for something only to get lost in a zombie job. Now he was dead and after the land had managed to knit over the oil and crushed remains of the truck there would be nothing to mark this place except a poisoned creek and fish skeletons.

•

We drove for hours, blasting through the town of Circle where the Yukon River unfolded in front of us, a wide gray band weaving through the forest. I scanned for the trail leading down to the river.

The road was empty, the sky devoid of jet trails or birds. A wall of clouds hung to the west of the mountains, threatening the blue. Small creeks spun by and then disappeared as we descended into the broad pan of the Yukon River drainage where rivers tangled through brush-covered hills, pooling into dense backwater swamps.

When I finally spotted the trail it didn't look like much; just a muddy pull-off leading through the maze of trees. There were a few tire tracks, some faded soda cans embedded in the gravel and a piece of neon-pink marking tape fluttering from a branch.

"How would Duke know about this unless he's been here?" I asked.

"Got me," he said. "He did say there was a small beaver pond full of rainbow just before the river. You interested?"

I nodded, watching as a dark column of clouds blotted out the Brooks Range. Fairbanks, with its winter-proof architecture and buckled sidewalks, seemed to be in another state, a part of the past we'd left far behind.

We got out of the truck and surveyed the dim overgrown path. It looked just wide enough for a single vehicle and nothing more. A tractor trailer thrummed by heading toward Fairbanks in a cloud of gravel dust. It was good to hear the sound of an engine and I hoped the driver had seen the two of us contemplating the trail, stepping off the map.

•

"You could get lost and die," Burke said, pointing. "Good money says that no man's walked more than a hundred yards from this road."

"There's no reason to," I said.

"Fuck that," he said. "Watch."

With that he bolted off into the thick undergrowth. I could hear him crashing around and swearing and then after ten minutes, nothing. It was as if the woods had swallowed him. I went back to the truck, dug a sandwich out of the cooler and waited for him to finish making his point, figuring he'd give up a few hundred feet into the tangled bush and come back.

But the woods stayed quiet.

When he didn't show after twenty minutes I began walking down the narrow road. The trees blocked out every sound except for my footsteps. Stumps and roots coiled along the edge like frozen snakes. I could see only fifty feet or so up the road before the light became dark green and then black as if the forest was trying to close a hole that had been cut into its chest. A gray ground squirrel scampered across the trail, disappearing silently into the woods. Birds flashed in the branches above and with each step delicate spiderwebs broke across my face.

I heard several large thuds behind me and spun around half expecting to come face-to-face with a black bear or, worse, a grizzly. My pulse jumped into my throat, but stopped cold when I saw it was just Burke, covered with pine needles, his hair a tangled mass of small twigs. He was smiling and holding something small and white in his hands.

"Thought I was a bear, didn't you?" he asked, laughing.

"Find anything, Magellan?"

He nodded and held out the white object.

"Porcupine skull."

"Maybe it got lost and died."

"Wolves, probably."

"Anything else?"

"A whole lot of nothing," he said. "Now I know why no man's walked those woods, 'cause it's some miserable ass-going. I had to crawl, then I had to slither."

"Imagine what it's like in winter."

He grunted, tossed the skull at me. "We're just gettin' started," he said. "Wait 'til we're up that river a ways if you wanna see desolation."

I followed him back into the light of the roadside, locked out the hubs on the truck, and off we went down the path. Pine boughs scraped at the boat and brushed through our open windows. It was slow going. In several spots the road deteriorated

into a series of deep muddy troughs and more than once I had to
leap from the truck and drag fallen branches out of the way. We
couldn't see the sky, just the slender ghost of a road that seemed
to go on forever, twisting down into the river valley. Twice we
topped small rises in the path, hoping to spot the pond or the river
only to be confronted by more trees and potholes. The sight of
empty beer cans was the only thing that gave me hope, that others,
even recently, had slid and spun down this same track and lived to
tell about it.

Burke was clearly taken with the challenge, nursing the truck
through the rough patches, picking up speed when he could and
whooping things like "Off the fucking grid!"

I wanted to see the river and open sky. The whole time I was
thinking not about Duke's daughter or the bartender's story of
the missing moose hunters, but of Nunn—wanting to know what
sort of man we were driving at and what he'd built here in the
middle of nowhere.

•

After two hours the pond appeared on the right. It was a small
treelined pool of water with deadfall knitted along its weedy
banks. Trout rose, breaking the surface with their speckled noses,
flashing silver like hundreds of small electric charges.

Burke stopped the truck and we got out to examine the pond.
For the first time in hours I could see the slate gray of the sky
hanging above us.

There was a clearing to one side and the familiar blackened circle of a fire pit. More beer cans lay scattered in the weeds and the
remains of an old tent hung in the treetops like a stranded sail. A
large beaver dam ran along the north side of the pond and beyond
that I could hear the slow rumble of the river as the current moved
boulders under the water.

Burke pulled out his fly rod, tied on a mosquito pattern and
within minutes stood stroking out a long beautiful cast at the
pond's edge, his line arcing across the flat mirror of the pond to
deliver the fly gently on the water.

I geared up and moved to the far side of the clearing, false casting, hoping that some large fish would smash the fly the very second it hit the water.

I wasn't disappointed. Deep-bellied trout quickly rolled to our flies, dragging them under and then leaping with the sting of the hook. It was all too easy and I began to notice the clumsiness of it all. Even the rod felt heavy and deliberate in my hands. I glanced over at Burke to see the poetry go out of his cast as he dragged another fish to shore and dashed it dead against a rock.

Within fifteen minutes we had three fish between us. We put the rods away and gutted the trout, moving on instinct, having enacted this very same ritual dozens of times.

He built a small fire in the ring while I wandered into the woods and peeled three pine branches, sharpened them to points and impaled the fish on them.

"We'd be punching out just about now," Burke said, propping the trout across the fire.

I turned the fish and looked up at the bank of clouds that had moved in over the clearing. Burke saw them too and didn't say anything. Rain or no rain, we both knew there was no turning back now. We were hooked into the drive of the trip: the simple forward motion of getting there and grabbing her no matter what got in the way.

We ate quickly, washing the fish down with a couple of beers before pulling the truck down to the river.

The water was a menacing sheet-metal gray, swollen with recent rain. Large rocks and jumbled snags littered both sides of the river. The whole place looked as if it was in a state of constant flux, gravel banks undercut by the rushing water, trees clinging to life as their branches draped into the current. A low mist seemed to creep into the surrounding willow and alder like cigarette smoke.

Overhead bald eagles pitched, swooping into the muddy shallows along the bank, coming up with small grayling. I glimpsed a flash of brown on the opposite bank, perhaps a moose or the flank of a bear, but when I squinted the brown changed into a large stone. I was more shaken than if it had been a real bear because I knew they were out there, lurking in the chest-high ferns, feeding on wild blueberries and waiting for some stupid carpenter who ought to be in Texas to disturb them. The fear was good.

But there I was staring upriver waiting for Burke to break the moment with action.

He snuck up behind me. "There's no going back," he said.

I nodded, still staring at the bear-shaped rock. It was just about seven o'clock and true dark wouldn't come for several hours, so we unstrapped the boat and set it on the bank. I hauled the plastic fuel cans and secured them inside the boat while Burke mounted the outboard and snugged our gear with cords against the gunwales. We worked quickly and silently, the suck and drag of the river urging us on.

Next he backed the truck up the trail until it was partially obscured behind a tangle of uprooted pine trees.

"You ready, partner?" he asked, dousing himself with bug dope and then tossing me the can.

I sprayed until my lips were numb and my eyes burned. "Let's do it," I said, taking one last look at the truck, abandoned in the rutted turnaround.

He smiled, punched me on the shoulder and we shoved off. The current swept us downstream quickly, swirling us in circles before he got the engine to catch and could nose the boat upstream. I perched in the prow, scanning the water for rocks or submerged logs that would shred the prop.

We hugged the bank where the current sluggishly lapped against the shore. Clear water sloughs splintered off the main river, wending their way into nowhere through dark brush-clogged tunnels. Twice we came upon bull moose feeding in them, their antlers strung with rotten felt and weeds. Burke made a gun out of his hands and shot at them. They stood blinking stupidly at our intrusion.

The boat plugged away through the flat valley. Gradually the land on either side of the river began to steepen as we rode through a series of small foothills. There were trees strung from here to hell and not a whole lot else to look at except the water moving beneath the boat, dark and heavy with silt.

Every once in a while Burke would tap me on the shoulder and point out a steep rock cliff or a bald eagle, pacing our slow progress upstream.

We chugged around several bends and twice had to portage the boat across shallow gravel bars. I was sweating and my back ached, but it felt good just to be out there in all that landscape going after something, working for it.

The clouds held off, stacking themselves to the west as late evening sun slanted through the trees in bright shafts, turning the water into a blinding silver treadmill. For a moment everything seemed right and I could not imagine doing anything else. It was as if my whole life depended on this trip, that it would remake me somehow; teach me something I needed to learn. In return all I had to do was work the river, follow it upstream and let the hours unfold without a clock. For the moment work seemed a million miles away, as if my hands had never held a hammer or known the recoil of a nail gun.

I looked back and saw that Burke too was lost in the vastness of the place, his eyes tracing the banks trying to take it all in, thinking of the fish in the pools—fish who'd never felt the sting of the hook, caribou who'd never heard the crack of a rifle and farther back the bears in their dark places waiting for us to step wrong and come to them.

●

When the sun sank the rest of the way the spell was broken and the river seemed dangerous, indifferent to our presence.

"Put out?" Burke yelled over the roar of the outboard.

I made a casting motion with my arm. "Before it gets too dark," I said.

We rounded another bend and the river flattened out into a large stillborn pool. To our left was a long gravel bank with several wide sloughs jutting off the main river. We cut across the current, ran the boat into the shallows and beached it. Within minutes we had our rods out and were sizing up the river. I waded out past a flat pool to where the water gathered itself into deep riffles and fished the small boiling pockets of water behind boulders, dropping the fly into the tumble and foam, waiting for the flash of a fish while Burke worked the tailwaters with a large streamer. I knew he was after a fish to erase the easy foolish grabs of the pond rainbows.

Several casts later I missed a strike as the pre-dark gloom had settled over the river like a blanket, shutting out all sound except for the constant hum of the river. Then a small grayling rolled to my fly. I set the hook and it struggled briefly before panning over and letting me reel it to shore, where I popped the hook and let it swim back into the current.

"Put something smaller on," I yelled downstream to Burke.

He shook his head, stubbornly casting the oversize streamer into the river, stripping line in pursuit of his trophy.

After ten minutes he finally gave up on the main river and stalked off into the shadows toward the slough.

Stars began to glow in the darkening sky. I stopped fishing and for a moment I felt more alone than I'd ever felt.

The silence was broken by the crash of a large fish coming from Burke's direction.

"Got one?" I yelled out. I began running toward Burke, who was standing on the bank, rod bowed, wind whipping his hair like some primitive man. The water exploded as the fish shook and rolled. "It's a pike," he said. "A big ol' mean fucker."

He laughed and cranked down on his drag, pulling the fish to the bank, line singing with tension.

I got out my flashlight and played it across the surface of the water to where the fish was holding Burke's line steady. It broke water, its green-and-white-speckled back flashing, gill plates rattling as it tried to shake the large streamer from its mouth.

He fought the fish in, the water slipping and boiling as it zigzagged toward the gravel bank.

Just as I'd waded into the shallow mud to kick the pike ashore it broke free and the rod snapped back. Line whistled past my face. I looked out into the water, hoping to catch one last glimpse of the fish, but the water was calm and smooth.

"Ate right through the leader," Burke said, staring at the line.

"There's more where that one came from," I said, half tempted to tie on a wire leader and streamer myself.

"Fuck it," he said. "I don't wanna snap my rod for some bony-ass pike. Maybe I'll throw a few setlines and see if we can stir up any burbot."

"How far you figure we got today?"

He reeled in his line, scanning the river. There was no moon yet, just an early rush of stars low on the horizon struggling under the clouds like sparks thrown from a fire.

"Ten, fifteen miles," he said. "We're gonna have to push it. We're in for some weather."

"Maybe it'll hold off."

"Get you out on the river and you become the optimistic Eagle Scout," he said. "It's gonna rain and we're gonna get wet and then my guess is we're gonna get miserable."

"Then what?"

"Then the fun begins," he snapped, starting toward the boat. I took my rod, walked back to the main river and sat on a large stone, looking upstream. I watched Burke cradle a fire to life between two rocks near where we'd decided to pitch the tent, embers swirling past his face and then blinking out against the night.

When I got back to the boat he tossed me an MRE and a can of beer. Out on the river I could hear larger fish feeding noisily in the shallows, but neither of us felt like wading the cold water again. Mayflies and caddis dove into the small fire, burning themselves up on quick little missions to the glow.

"You know," Burke said, dropping the empty MRE bag into the fire, where it melted into a black fiery ball, "seems like I've gotta keep remindin' myself what we're after."

"You mean her?"

He nodded.

"How come Duke didn't just ask one of his state trooper buddies he was telling us about?" I asked.

"Maybe it was bullshit," he said. "Either way it don't matter. We took his money and his boat and here we are."

I took out her picture and set it on a stone between us. "Not bad," I said.

He picked up the photo, holding it carefully at the edges. "Too skinny, but yeah, I'd do her, how about you?"

"Yeah, but . . ."

"But what?"

"Why do you think she's really up here?"

He shrugged. "Probably just what Duke said, she followed some guy, then . . ."

"But up here?" I asked, pointing at the dark wood.

Burke sipped his beer and set the photo down. "You ever meet Vern?" he asked. "Drives that panel van with all the bumper stickers."

"Works with the God squadders, right?"

He nodded. "He's not a half-bad guy."

"What's Vern got to do with Duke's daughter?"

"He told me a story once about how he was hiking down in the Copper River Delta looking for a place to pitch a fish camp for the salmon run," Burke said. "This was before he got saved. Two days up the river he finds a dip in the canyon. There's a good back eddy where the salmon were bunched up nice and tight. He goes to work and catches a few, sets them on the bank, lands some more and when he turns around the fish are gone. At first he thinks it's a bear and that he's the next course, so he climbs a tree and waits. He starts hearing voices, smells smoke and something cooking, which is fucked because he's off the trail and hasn't seen a person in two days. So he climbs down, follows it and sees a couple of cabins and people sitting around naked under an old parachute strung from the trees. White guys mostly, Indian women sitting lotus in front of them. And there are his fish, roasting on spits. One of the women sees him and comes over to where he's standing. He starts to ask her what they're doing this far up the river, but she doesn't let him talk. She's naked like the rest of them and stoned out of her mind. The men are stoned too, playing with guns, grabbing the women. Vern said there were kids too, half-breeds watching him from the cabins. All of them naked. But he goes with it, figuring it's a whole lot better than trying to find someplace to pitch his tent. So they feed him his own fish, get him stoned and one of the women even takes him in the woods and fucks him. In the morning they tell him to get dressed and never come back or they'll kill him and throw him in the river."

He finished and reached for another beer.

"Did he say what they were doing up there?"

"Besides having a good time?" He laughed. "Growing dope, he thought. This was before the BLM got its shit together and started chasing the hippies off state land into homestead tracts."

"Hard to believe Vern getting stoned," I said.

"He was a pretty wild guy before he got God," he said. "So old Duker can call this place whatever he wants. It ain't the Masons or Boy Scouts, that's for sure."

"Maybe it's just some rinky-dink thing, a guy and two or three gals roughing it, reading *Walden* and thinking big thoughts."

He shook his head. "If it looks like a cult and smells like a cult . . ."

". . . but what if she don't wanna go? Or maybe one of us wants to stay?" I said.

"Why the fuck would we wanna stay? You been starin' at the picture too goddamn long."

"I meant you," I said. "Maybe this Nunn guy's onto something. Could be what you've been looking for. You get some like Vern, freeze to death in the winter, kill bears—you know, real manly shit."

He tipped his beer at me. "Or maybe they don't like us, skip the dope and naked women and just shoot us."

I tossed another branch into the fire. "How old do you think she is?" I said.

"Duke's daughter?"

I nodded.

"Twenty-five, twenty-eight," he said. "Duke's gotta be fifty or so. He's got Vietnam written all over him. Probably came here after some hippie spit on him figuring he'd better get hip to what was going on."

"Where did you meet him?"

"At a bar," he said. "Same place you meet everybody in Fairbanks."

"And?"

"And that's it. He told me his story. Asked if I'd been out in the bush much and I told him I'd poked around a bit."

"So then he just comes out and asks you to get his daughter over a couple of beers?"

"It wasn't like that," he said, knocking back a beer. "I mean it sounded like something we should do and I got to thinking about how soft the job was making me, figured maybe you had something you wanted to prove, so I listened to what he had to say."

"Prove myself?"

"You heard me," he said. "It's okay. I can keep a secret, I've got plenty myself."

"How long are you going to hold the fact that I wasn't born a carpenter over my head? I drive a nail same way you do, lay down the hours and what—there's some fundamental difference because I went to college a long time ago. Is that it?"

"Relax, Jackson, I'm not saying that . . ."

"What about you?" I blurted. "What went on that made you take the job?"

"Absolutely fucking nothing except the money and fine company," he said, tipping his beer at me.

"I forgot I was talking to Burke, Shane of the carpenters—the man with no past."

He shook his head.

"Okay then, tell me how I'm doing," I said.

"Tell you what?"

"Am I *proving* myself?"

He smiled but didn't answer and I sat there just staring at the fire. Finally I grabbed the photo, tucked it into my pocket and dragged the tent out to set camp.

The moon had risen low over the trees, casting a dull yellow light across the river valley. I worked by feel, snapping the fiber-glass ribs into the tent, steadying it with rocks when the sand and gravel wouldn't hold the stakes. I thought about how we were going to find the trail in all these miles of nothingness. It would be a test and when it was over we'd have the story of how we'd found Duke's daughter and brought her back to watch him die. I took out her picture and put the flashlight beam on it. There was that smile and those eyes, not empty like her father's but full of some new kind of hope, the kind that visits you only once or twice in your youth before the world begins to twist and compli-cate itself.

After I'd finished with the tent Burke baited a few large treble hooks with egg sacks and pickled chicken livers he'd stashed in the bottom of the cooler. He strung the hooks on a thick piece of waxed twine and tied it off to a long flat rock that would settle in the muck bottom.

"Be right back," he said, disappearing without a flashlight toward the slough.

Several minutes later I heard a splash.

He returned, popped another beer and took his boots off, set-ting them next to the fire to dry. Neither of us said a word and after a while I crawled into the tent and tried to forget Burke's crack about proving myself.

Hours later he woke me with a shove and flashed the .45 in my face. I came to quick and started to say something, but he put a hand up to quiet me. It took me a minute to remember that I was in a tent on the river, miles from anyplace.

Something was very wrong.

I reached out for the flashlight and felt something large bump into the nylon wall to my right, bowing the tent until I could hear the fiberglass poles splintering around the edges as something heavy and familiar with the night circled us.

I knew immediately that it was a bear and reached for my rifle and brought it up to my shoulder.

Then everything went silent.

Burke clicked the safety off the .45 and pulled the hammer

back. I began imagining the slow chomping death I'd read about in all those cheap-ass grocery store Bear Attack books, the ones they kept next to the Miracle Diet and Astrology ones.

"Bear?" I whispered.

He nodded. There was another bump against the tent wall and then a flurry of swats as if the bear was testing its discovery to see if it would fight back. We pressed against the opposite side, guns pointed.

When it finally stopped its assault there were two yard-long tears in the nylon.

My heart beat against my ribs so hard I could no longer hear the river or the bear, just blood clanging through my veins. Burke, however, seemed calm and deliberate as he waited for the bear to rush the tent again.

It grunted and coughed, taking a few more blasts at the tent, and then was quiet.

Ten minutes passed and then we heard the inevitable crash of the bear rummaging around inside the boat.

Burke unzipped the tent fly and in the moonlight we could see the bear's dark outline as it pawed through the cooler, gobbling up the contents. It appeared almost human, sitting back on its massive brown haunches, looking around the camp, chewing on the hard plastic MREs.

Burke cursed himself for not tying the food up in a tree like we'd done dozens of times on other camping trips where we knew there would be bears. Twice he took aim, locking his arms out, squinting down the barrel.

I waited for him to shoot the bear dead out of sheer rage, but he didn't, and after an hour of watching it sift through our gear for every last bit of food it ambled away into the dark and was gone.

There was nothing to do except crawl under my sleeping bag and try to close my eyes. The bear would come back for us or it wouldn't. I fell asleep with Burke sitting in the far corner, gun drawn, face pressed through the tent flap, waiting.

•

The next morning we surveyed the damage. The bear had totaled the cooler, chewed and drunk the last of our beers and ripped up our packs, leaving only a trail of empty MRE wrappers dotting the bank.

Burke walked the gravel bar, gun drawn, stalking around the large rocks, hoping to spot the bear, while I picked up trash, groggy-eyed.

"I hope Yogi's sick to his fuckin' stomach," I shouted.

"Well," Burke said, "we wanted an adventure and it looks like we just fucked ourselves into one."

"It ate everything, even the turkey a la king," I said, holding up several empty packets.

"That's one hungry-ass bear."

"What the hell are we gonna do?"

He rummaged through his fishing vest and brought out three foil-packed granola bars. "Eat these and then starve."

"That's it?"

He shook his head. "Unless you want this corned beef hash." He held up a mashed can of the stuff, slathered in bear drool.

"Think I'll take a pass," I said, packing the last of the trash into the wrecked cooler.

Burke chucked the can into the river.

"I hope we don't regret that," I said.

He shrugged. "We'll live." His face brightened. "Who knows? Maybe we got a few nice fat burbot," he said, heading toward the slough to pull the setlines while I broke the tent down and rolled and stuffed the bags.

He came back several minutes later holding a stringer of bare hooks.

"Not a goddamn thing," he said, stuffing the whole rig into a canvas sack. "We'll ride hungry."

"Why don't we try fishing a little?"

"With the bear around—go right ahead, be my guest. After that turkey a la king we'd taste like filet mignon." No sooner had he spoken when for some reason I found myself staring at a band of small cedars that had begun to shake violently as an enormous brown haunch rolled into view. It was the griz, not the biggest one I'd ever seen, but fat with muscle that hung from its neck and shoulders like sacks. In the morning light its fur seemed to be tipped with fire and its mouth hung open red and wet, a low rumble coming from somewhere inside. Its claws made hollow clacking sounds on the uneven river stones and I knew that if it wanted it could be on us in seconds.

Burke grabbed for his gun and I stood, slowly raising my arms to give myself a larger profile.

"It's circling," he said, stepping up with the pistol.

The bear was still fifty feet away, and if it charged, Burke would have two, maybe three shots at best. Not enough to stop it unless he got lucky with one of the bullets. I comforted myself with the statistic that most bears will retreat or at the worst offer a false charge, a sort of game of chicken to determine if you are prey or fellow predator. Prey runs, predators stand their ground. But this bear had already cleaned us out and it wouldn't take much for Burke to start shooting.

So I eased back to where the boat lay beached and began stashing gear, keeping one eye on the bear as it stomped back and forth in front of Burke. My arms moved, heavy with dread, wanting to be back in safe little Fairbanks and far, far away from this nowhere.

When I turned to look at the woods again, the bear had vanished. Something was lost. The woods were just woods—green nothingness, the horizon now drab as if the bear had put a shine on things and now that it was gone the world was an infinitely more boring place.

"Still wanna fish?" he asked, pistol locked in front of him.

"Maybe I can *prove* myself," I shot back.

He smiled grimly and helped me drag the boat to the water's edge. Within minutes it was in the water, rocking, ready to go. He holstered the gun, jumped into the boat and we were off.

The river sucked us broadside downstream again before Burke got the outboard to catch and we puttered back up the gravel bank, scanning the woods for the bear. Just as we'd pulled into the deeper water, it appeared, phantomlike, walking with rippling purpose toward the bank.

When the bear reached the end of the bank it froze and stood staring at us, its eyes dark and empty. They were the most vacant things I'd ever seen.

Burke laughed and steered the boat closer to shore, taunting the bear before it faded into the background as the motor pulled us upstream.

"We're probably the only people it's ever seen," Burke said, looking back.

I resumed my perch in the prow, calling out rocks as the sun disappeared behind a wall of heavy black clouds.

We rode, the water twisting and turning us until everything began to blend into a pleasant blur of rocks and trees and an eerie stillness fell across the surrounding vegetation. I scanned the thick brushy banks, hoping to catch a glimpse of something alive, a flicker of movement in the impenetrable green. But there was nothing. It was as if all the animals had disappeared or were hiding. The sky was gray and birdless and there was only the river.

Around noon it began to drizzle and we started looking for a good place to fish before the weather really turned. I pointed out a small island surrounded by a nice set of thigh-deep riffles. The surrounding banks were littered with driftwood, old salmon bones and dead aspen leaves that slipped under our wet boots.

After tying the boat off on a snag we geared up the rods in silence as a light wind kicked across the water, blowing the drizzle sideways.

I was hungry and sore. The simple motion of casting felt good, shaking the stiffness out of my arms and shoulders. I worked a seam while Burke waded into the heavy water casting a large Mickey Finn into the gray chop, stripping line, feeling for a strike. I kept an eye on the surrounding bank, wary of another bear after the encounter on the gravel bar. But part of me wanted that sharp heart-quickening feeling to return.

After an hour neither one of us had so much as gotten a rise and the drizzle had turned into a harsh whipping rain that made casting difficult and then finally impossible.

Burke turned and pointed at the boat and we broke down our rods, slipped our rain gear on and hunkered into the shallow aluminum shell as the motor churned upstream.

We split the remaining granola bar and stared ahead at the river. Burke locked onto the outboard, weaving us farther and farther up the river as the rain and wind intensified and the woods gave way to steep rock walls split occasionally by thin waterfalls that spilled into the river.

The outboard labored as it fought the thickening current. The river narrowed, growing deeper until I could not see the bottom.

The hull began to fill with rainwater as a hard cold settled into my bones. I glanced back at Burke, who stared right through me, his eyes locked on the high stone corridor. And so I gave in and drew inward, lured by the endless pitch and rock of the boat until the landscape fell away and I could have been anywhere, on any river, wet, cold and nowhere. The lost feeling was back and I welcomed it.

Two hours went by like that as we entered a new phase of the river. Thick fog hung over the water. The rain neither increased nor decreased its steady beat on the sides of the boat and the cold finally brought me back. I began to focus on my surroundings, peering over the gunwales into the water where the silt-gray current battered rocks, thinking how easy it would be to slip over the edge and die.

"I'm some new kind of cold and miserable," Burke croaked from the back of the boat. His hands were bright red, his face gaunt and poached with rain.

I nodded.

"Hungry too," I said.

He shrugged. The boat bucked against the current as the propeller chopped water. I wanted to find the trail or see a woman come down out of the mist on a canoe. I refigured the story so the woman in the canoe was now the girl in the picture and she was coming for us, wanting to take me to a place I'd never seen before, a place deep in-country, new and wild.

"We'll catch something tonight," he offered. "If not, well then hell, we don't deserve to eat."

I nodded and we rode until the rock walls gave way to forest on either side and the river fractured off into shadowy sloughs and temporary islands of deadfall and rock.

The girl in the canoe vanished from my thoughts and the

rest of the day passed in an unremarkable blur as we scooted past large spinning eddies that made sucking sounds. Burke dropped an empty water bottle into one of them and watched as it disappeared.

We cut upstream in silence, observing the twist and flow of the river, letting it take the hours away, while I scanned the shores, hoping some boat or makeshift dock would appear along the bank and we would be on to the next leg of the journey. But the country remained monotonously wild and by evening the river had flattened out again into a slow-moving sprawl. The rain stopped and the water began to darken with runoff, swelling into the low-lying floodplains, erasing land, lifting low branches like bridal veils and causing waves of mosquitoes, black flies and gnats to swarm out of the brush.

Around ten o'clock the sun mounted one last attempt, streaming through a break in the clouds and burning off the fog. The river continued to rise. Logs washed downstream and boulders loosened their grip in the stream bed, tumbling into submerged valleys.

Burke swung the boat across the current to the left-hand bank to avoid the rock-strewn shallow while I scanned the woods, trying to fix on anything besides the wall of spruce and snarled brush. Then I saw it—a flash of gray fifty yards beyond one of the sloughs in a narrow pocket of trees.

Burke caught on and nudged the boat closer to shore until the propeller began to churn noisily in the shallow water, roiling sand and silt in our wake.

"Maybe it's a diner," he said as a small cabin gradually came into view. It had been built on stilts and was nearly hidden by a thick cape of underbrush and bent trees.

"I'd kill for biscuits and gravy."

"Don't get your hopes up, Jack," he said, shutting the outboard down and motioning for me to drag the boat ashore. I jumped out, grabbed the gunwales and put my back into it until I felt the comforting thud of the boat hitting mud.

There were thousands of other cabins just like it scattered all over the bush, half of them built illegally on state land by moose hunters. The cabin meant food, perhaps a stash of dry rations left for when the owner returned to hunt.

Burke waded ashore and unholstered his gun with a poised calm as if every step contained both life and death. I pulled the rifle from its sling and walked behind him, up the bank until the cabin disappeared from sight again.

That's when I saw the footprints in the sand running along the bank before they dissolved at the edge of the slough. Burke inspected them briefly and then looked up at me, nodding toward the cabin silently. We approached the slough, found the least foreboding span to cross and waded its muck-lined bottom, our guns held high like soldiers treading rice paddies.

When we were close enough to make out the door, Burke shouted a warning that echoed through the trees. Nothing stirred. The area looked deserted, but we waited a minute before advancing on the overgrown cabin. There was an ax stuck in a log off to the side and what looked like the remains of an outhouse twenty yards behind the cabin. I stepped onto the narrow moss-covered porch and peered through a window. The glass was thick with dust and cobwebs and I couldn't see inside.

Then a gunshot split the air.

Bits of wood stung my cheek and I hit the ground. Two more shots exploded several feet from us, smashing through the rotten porch boards. I gripped the wood tightly, trying to make myself small as I studied the sweep of green for clues as to where the shots had come from.

There was nothing for a minute and then a bright blast from upstream. Whoever had fired at us was hunkered down in a thick patch of willow saplings.

"Come on," Burke said, jerking into action and sliding into a clump of ferns.

I was right behind him, coming alive in the moment, wanting to open fire on the willow grove.

"Split up," he hissed. "Get to the boat and make sure it's okay."

I nodded and slithered down a narrow scoop of mud and weeds

that emptied into the slough, moving blindly, the rifle out in front of me, arms and legs flailing.

With some effort I reached the slough, slipped in and began paddling slowly across its surface, certain that at any moment there would be a shot and I would be forced to go under or risk having my head blown off.

I could see Burke threading his way through the pines, gun flashing in front of him. Something moved out of the willows, but when I turned to look again it was gone.

Several minutes passed without any more shots and I dragged myself from the water and headed toward the boat, racing through the boulders and dead logs.

Fifteen feet from the boat I heard the click of a gun at the back of my neck and felt the air move. My hands clenched the rifle tightly as I turned to see the dull gleam of gunmetal hovering inches from my face.

There was a man on the other end. He was young and working thin as if some hardship had trimmed his large frame down to the essential ropes and pulleys. His hair was stuffed into a dirty knit cap and he was wearing coveralls that were spattered with mud and other stains.

I froze, hoping Burke was nearby and getting ready to save me.

"Why don't you just let go of the gun," he said. His voice was surprisingly calm. "Go on—let go of it."

I began to lift my fingers one by one.

"Drop it," he screamed.

I let the rifle drop with a loud clatter, hoping it would alert Burke.

I raised my hands and turned slowly to face him. He had several days' worth of stubble and his hands and arms were laced with small scratches and scars from bushwhacking.

"We just saw the cabin," I said. "We didn't mean . . ."

". . . that was your first mistake," he said.

"Please," I said. "We'll leave—"

I got more barrel to the head, his whole body shaking down through the gun. It would be nothing for him to love that trigger back a little and cough some lead into my brain.

"Now go on and tell your buddy to put down his gun before I blast your brains out on the rocks."

He kept pushing with the gun until I was down on all fours looking up at him.

"He won't do that," I said. "He'll shoot you first."

"Well, I guess that's too bad for you," he said. "Because I'm not going back. I'm getting the fuck out of this place even if I have to shoot the both of you to do it. I got people counting on me."

He stepped forward and flipped my rifle away with his boot.

"Go back where?" I asked, trying to buy time.

He let out a sandpapery laugh. "Very clever. Next you're gonna tell me you're on some sort of fishing trip. Is that it—you're just a couple of tourists out for trout?"

"No, I . . ."

His face shifted. "Just get your buddy out here. There's only one reason to be on this river."

"What's that?"

He shoved the gun at me again.

"Because, you're *lost* and *looking*. Fuck—I don't know and I don't care what you hope to find, I'm getting out. Now get your goddamned buddy out here front and center."

"Can't do that," I said.

He thought about this a moment, scanning the bank quickly for Burke.

"You got a boat, don't you?"

I nodded.

"Well then," he said, "crawl us out of this mess or you're gonna die."

"What?"

"I said, crawl, goddamn it!"

I started moving toward the boat before I remembered the picture of Duke's daughter. I stopped.

"Move!" he screamed.

I pulled the picture out and held it over my shoulder, praying he wouldn't shoot.

"Penny," he gasped. "Hey, man—what the fuck is this?"

"We came to get her," I said.

Nothing happened for several long minutes and I wondered if I should have kept my mouth shut about what we were up to.

His face softened. "I thought you were looking for me—to take me back," he said. "I was elected to get out . . . I had to get out and get help or else they'll starve."

". . . I don't understand . . ."

"He sent them after me and they were waiting at the dock with knives. I had to double back to the swamp. Then I got lost, really, really lost, and I thought that was it—that he'd finally got me . . ."

He jabbed me with the gun again.

"Is she still there?" I asked.

"Who?" he asked dreamily.

I shook the photograph at him as something caught my eye in the water—a roll of flesh in the gray river that rose and then disappeared.

"Yes," he said. "With the others. She chose sides and she's still there unless there's been another accident."

"What about Nunn?"

The gun dropped to his side. "But Nunn, you'll never . . ."

I was looking into his eyes when I heard the crack of the gun and saw them go dead, light draining out of his pupils. I flinched, waiting for the bullet to rip through me. But it didn't. When I turned back to look at the man his profile had been replaced by a fine pink mist that drifted over me, dampening my skin, cool and soft as larger drops rained down on the river stones, staining them.

I scrambled to my feet.

He was on the ground, half in the water. The rifle was at his feet, tethering him to the bank, preventing the river from taking him downstream.

Burke bobbed out of the water, pistol in front of him, his face a calm mask as he walked toward me. I went over to the man and watched his legs slither against the gravel. There was a hole in his chest and blood whorling out of it, clouding the water and then fading.

My shirt was covered with blood and a few pieces of what looked like lung. I picked the photograph up, wiped the blood from it and stuck it in my pocket.

"You all right?" he asked, keeping the gun on the man.

I nodded, trying to stop the words from catching in my throat as I studied the dying man's face bobbing just inches below the water like it wanted to come up once more for air and leave the body behind. Bubbles rose out of the mouth. His lips pulsed and his eyes seemed to come out of their sockets as he clawed at the water briefly and then was still. For a moment he looked like the frozen Eskimo I'd seen at the bar, real but not real.

"You killed him," I shouted.

He picked up the man's gun and heaved it into the current and turned. "What would you have done?" he asked flatly.

"He wasn't going to shoot. He just wanted to get out is all."

"Out of where?"

"The camp."

He looked at me hard.

"He thought Nunn had sent us out to get him," I said.

"Bullshit," he said. "He would have shot us both on the porch if he could have."

"They were warning shots."

Burke pointed the gun at the air and squeezed off a shot. "That's a fucking warning shot. From where I was standing it looked like he was fixing to do you."

The man gave one last shudder and his body went slack as the current began to flutter his arms out like wings. The water had washed some of the grime from his face. He looked younger, no older than thirty.

"You don't know that," I said.

"Fuck it," he said. "I came out of the woods and saw him with a gun on you. There was no other choice, Jack."

"I showed him the picture."

"What picture?"

I took it out of my pocket and flashed it. The blood had filled up small pin-sized holes around her face and eyes.

"So what?" he said. "All I saw was you on the ground . . ."

". . . it was still the wrong thing to do," I shouted.

He backed off and raised his hands, looking at me coldly.

"I told him why we'd come," I said.

"It don't matter now, does it?" he said, shaking water out of the .45. "It's done."

"What do you mean *done?*"

He got up in my face. "You can take it apart any way you want. He shot at us and got himself killed—that's some rough sledding, but we leave it right here, between the two of us."

"We have to report it," I said.

"Report what?"

"How it happened, how we shot him—how you shot him."

He walked away, tapping the pistol against his leg.

"That's not how it's going to work."

"What?"

"We're not reporting this."

"He shot at us first—"

"Listen to me, Jack—there's no way we're gonna involve the police in this. I mean we'd have to drag his body downstream."

"It's wrong, Burke—"

"—no, no, what's wrong is when they punch my name into a computer and they come up with a few things."

"What?"

He coughed, glancing down at the body again. "Maybe there's a reason I chase the job, Jack. And maybe there's a reason Alaska's pretty fucking good place for a guy like me to be."

"What are you saying?"

His gaze drifted from the body to the far riverbank where a raven sat on a large log pecking at something. "I'm saying we do this right and nobody has to know."

I studied him a minute. "Do what right?"

"This," he said, pointing at the body. I forced myself to look at it, floating calm and poised in the water, blood still leaking out of the holes.

"You mean hide the body?"

He nodded.

"Why?" I asked.

"I already told you."

"No, fuck that, tell me or I'm gonna take the boat and see the police."

He gave me the eye, jaw working overtime.

"I hurt a man in Arizona," he said. "Maybe I killed him, it doesn't really fuckin' matter now, does it?"

"Tell me," I demanded.

He sat down on a rock. "I was doing this thing—"

"Whaddya mean thing?"

"A deal," he said. "We'd scored a whole bunch of speed and were gonna sell it, because we wanted to make a little coin. But something went wrong."

"Yeah . . ."

"I didn't have much of a choice, not with the crowd I was running with. So I made my point and beat him, beat him real good, and then disappeared because I wasn't going to stick around and see if he croaked. I cut all my ties, parents, girlfriend—all of it and I never looked back—not once."

"Shit," I said. "How long ago?"

"Right before we met up," he said, wringing water from his shirt, "I figured that as long as I didn't stay in any one place too long that they wouldn't look too hard. You gotta understand that this guy had it coming. The sonofabitch crippled a friend of mine and took off with a lot of money so I gave him payback, plain and simple, that's all it was. He knew the rules. And then I walked and kept walking and here I am, a thirty-eight-year-old carpenter who can't go home, whatever that means."

"You don't know if he's dead?"

He shrugged. "Does it matter?"

I waited a minute, still trying to absorb what he'd just told me.

"You didn't have to shoot him," I said, pointing at the man in the water.

"Well, I shot him and if we report it I go to jail no matter if it was self-defense or not. You with me, Jack?"

I looked at the body again and then at Burke. He'd put the .45 away and was staring at me. "We're in this knee-deep and if you're not okay with that then we walk away right now and I disappear."

"Are you threatening me?"

"Take it any way you want," he grunted. "I'm telling you what we've got to do to make this thing work—what's it gonna be?"

I nodded.

"Good," he said, grabbing the man's boot and dragging him out of the water. He started going through the pockets, setting the contents on a palm-shaped stone: a rusty barlow knife, ball of string, fishhooks, some monofilament wound around a stick, several scraps of paper which were soaked and unreadable, a small sack of dried nuts and raisins. The last thing was a small jar filled with a thick sludge.

He held the jar up and shook it.

"Gold?" I asked, bending to take a closer look at the dull coppery sludge which moved along the glass like congealed blood.

"Sort of changes things," he said.

"How do you mean?"

"Tell me what he said again."

"He didn't want to go back," I said, watching him unscrew the jar. "Then I mentioned Nunn's name, he froze and you shot him."

Burke played some of the gold out on his palm, watching it glint for a minute.

"No sense reading anything more into it than that," he said, scraping the gold back into the jar. Then he pulled his gun and emptied four shots into the man's belly. Guts splashed all over the bank, gray, red and the white of spinal cord in the mess.

"What the hell are you doin'?" I shouted, ears ringing with the gunshot, gunsmoke burning my eyes.

"So he won't float," he said, tossing the spent shells into the water and reloading. "Now grab him."

I reached down and took hold of his arm. The skin was still warm. We turned the body over and kicked it out into the current, where it floated a moment, rolling faceup and then disappearing.

When we were sure he wasn't coming back up we took a minute to scrape the bank clean of blood and other bits.

"What if somebody finds him?"

"That silt sinks trees," he said. "In two days it'll be buried in the mud for the fish to work on. No one will ever find it and if they do there's no way they're gonna connect him to us unless you decide to start running your mouth." He paused to look around. "You still with me?"

I waited, tossing things around. I was soaked to the bone, hungry and spattered with blood and lung. They were all good reason to drift downriver to Fairbanks, get on a plane to Texas and try to forget everything.

"Okay," I said.

"Okay what?"

"I said I'm with you."

"All right then."

I hid my shaking hands as the river swallowed Burke's past for him. After a minute we walked back through the slough toward the cabin.

•

The inside of the cabin did little to erase my doubts about the man. It had been a long time since anybody had lived in it. What furniture there was lay in pieces as if some small storm had passed through the cabin, leaving only the walls intact. There was a plank set across two sawhorses for a table, some cheap wooden chairs that were rotted and unusable, several oil lanterns, which despite being a bit rusty contained oil and enough wick for further use, and a musty steamer truck with a squirrel's nest in it.

Burke walked over to the stove and opened it. Neatly chopped chunks of kindling sat atop a pile of crinkled newspaper and small pieces of bark, waiting to be lit.

"What more could you ask for?" he roared, poking around for matches while I scanned the dim surroundings for clues as to the cabin's owner.

There was little evidence to suggest he'd even stepped inside. A heavy coating of dust covered everything. A ratty-looking mattress sat in one corner, its stuffing chewed out by some animal. Empty tin cans and other bits of trash were huddled in the corners.

I heard the familiar hiss of a match being struck, followed by smoke as the fire pushed a quivering light into the cabin's darkest corner. That's when I saw the bloodstain on the far wall and hunkered down to inspect the timbers. Chunks of dried flesh were stuck to the rough bark in a wide halo of blood. Several long-dead beetles lay nestled against the wall like tiny abandoned cars.

Burke came over with one of the oil lamps, wooden match clenched between his teeth. He struck the match, lit the wick and put the glass globe back on its cradle.

"Take a look at this," I said, pointing at my discovery.

He crouched, took one look and nodded. "It's blood all right."

With his knife he poked at the logs until the blade hit something metal and he brushed away some of the dried pieces of meat to reveal a neat hole in the wood.

"Bullet?" I asked.

He nodded, then set the lantern on the floor and stepped back to survey the area. "What the hell happened here?"

I noticed a smashed chair near the stain.

"Coulda been a suicide," I said, imagining some sourdough crazy with cabin fever wanting to end it all before the ice broke on the river.

"How many suicides you know got the paste to bury themselves after they're done splattering their brains on the wall?"

"Good point."

I stared at the rough wood. It was scalloped with old blood and dried tissue and I wanted it all to somehow fit with what had just happened and lift the guilt I felt about going along with his plan to hide the body and keep going. But it didn't.

"Maybe it's what he didn't want us to see."

He shook his head. "There's no connection," he said. "What happened here happened a while ago, at least a season or two—could be longer."

"Maybe it was a dog or some other kind of animal."

He stopped and went through the debris with the knife again, holding up something for me to see. It was a piece of white bone with hair on one side.

"That's no dog," he said, letting the thing drop from his knife. It hit the floor with a dull chink.

"Let's have a look around," he said. "See if we can find any other surprises."

When we stood the whole room seemed to vibrate. The heat from the stove stirred wasps awake and they bounced drunkenly around the room, knocking against the window.

We stepped onto the porch and scanned the back side of the cabin for signs of a trail leading west into the forest. Except for a few small game trails the surrounding land was a damp impenetrable maze of muskeg. And what little clear ground there was looked untouched by a grave.

"Five gets you ten, whoever lost their head ended up in the river or one of these sloughs."

He nodded blackly and went back inside the cabin while I wondered about the bloodstain on the wall. Execution or suicide—it didn't matter. The law meant nothing this deep in-country and if what had happened in the cabin had gone undiscovered for as long as it looked, then we stood a pretty good chance of walking away from it all. What I couldn't escape was the sight of the corpse sinking and the plume of blood lacing across the water's surface.

•

After we'd dried and warmed ourselves next to the stove we waded back out to the boat. Burke rigged up the poles while I shuttled our sleeping bags to the cabin along with a few other supplies for the night.

The fishing was good. The grayling were feeding near the opposite bank, their backs flashing gray in the failing light, and the repetition of casting allowed my thoughts to drift back to where it was we were going and what we were after. For a while the trip fell back into its groove.

We caught three grayling and a rainbow and roasted them on sticks over the stove, letting the fat sizzle against the black iron vent plate. I could hardly wait for them to cook all the way through because the silence that had settled between us no longer felt comfortable.

When the skin bubbled and the eyes popped we pulled the fish and sat gnawing the warm white meat from the sticks until there was nothing left. It was good.

Afterward Burke hunkered down in front of the open stove, feeding wood into the glowing hole. "Don't get too comfortable," he said. "We're gonna go check on the boat one more time."

"Why?"

"Because maybe our buddy wasn't alone."

"He was alone."

"We're still gonna check."

I groaned and followed him out to check on the boat, making sure it was triple tied and well out of the way of the rising water. Coming back, I slid through the hip-deep slough, imagining all sorts of dark and slippery things hidden under the brackish water. Maybe even an old rotten body with its skull blown out.

I was shaking when I emerged from the water eager to get to the stove and roast the dank water from my clothes. Burke pulled a plastic flask of bourbon from his pack and we passed it between us silently until I was drunk enough to try sleep. I lay back on the sleeping bag listening to the wasps battering themselves against the window, trying to tack down the sense of dread blooming in my chest.

•

I woke the next morning stiff—all of the old injuries visiting me at once. The stove was going full blaze and I stood for a moment just hovering over the heat, thinking about having to find the trail and what would happen if we found her.

Burke came in from the porch looking as if he hadn't slept much and handed me two twelve-inch grayling.

"Breakfast?" I asked.

He nodded, studying the bloodstain on the wall again as I set the fish on the stove and watched them steam and curl, filling the inside of the cabin with their smell.

We ate in silence and half an hour later we were back in the boat chugging upstream, the outboard the only sound between us.

The river was heavy with silt and we hugged the western shore, darting across the thick current only when it was unavoidable. I searched the edges for some sign of a trail, the sight of which I hoped would put the events of the previous day be-hind me.

The awkward silence remained, soaring out along the riverbank. Every once in a while I caught glimpses of wasted chinook working their way upstream in the turbid current and instead of pointing them out to Burke I kept them to myself.

Several hours later a large cross-shaped shadow fell across the water, startling me out of the river trance. When I looked up a small bush plane dropped out of nowhere, its engine barely audible over the drone of the outboard. It banked, drifting twenty feet above the water before continuing upstream.

Spooked by the sudden intrusion I turned to look at Burke.

"It's nothing," he said. "Probably hunters or tourists."

"Let's hope," I said, wondering if they had seen something, scoped the two of us in the boat and passed judgment. Or worse, perhaps the pilot had noticed the body and was radioing the state police to come have a look.

But when we rounded the curve where the plane had disappeared I saw what it had been looking at.

The land on either side of the river was black and barren from a recent forest fire.

Burke held the engine steady, staring at the devastation. Twice we nearly ran aground, the propeller stalling in the shallow soot-colored mud. Everything smelled like creosote and ash and there were no birds or animals, just stripped timber and acres of bare hills. Early morning fog moved across the ruined landscape of skeletal trees and burnt stumps. An eerie calm descended on the whole valley and for great patches the river seemed to fall away as we floated like ghosts through the destruction, working our way closer to Nunn.

But there was the river slicing through the charred land like a blue-gray scar as we wound our way slowly through the heart of the ruin in Duke's battered aluminum boat.

"If the trail was here, it's gone now," Burke said as he ran the boat to shore.

"The camp too."

Burke squinted at the horizon and shook his head as the boat bottom struck rocks. He killed the motor.

We got out and wandered through the burn, the ash thick under our feet like fresh-fallen snow. Several times I reached out to touch a tree, half expecting it to be warm only to be disappointed by its scaly coldness.

I walked over a low rise, leaving Burke at the river's edge. The rise topped out over a large bowl-shaped depression. In the center of the bowl sat a massive haystack-shaped rock. Burnt tree trunks lay in concentric circles around the stone like straws dropped from above or toppled bodies.

I went to it, walking down the gentle slope, stepping over fallen trees. It felt as if I was walking into the center of some special place where the fire had paused, lingering, burning hotter until there was nothing left and then moving uphill, feeding on oxygen and fresh timber, frying all the little things in their warrens.

The surface of the stone was a polished dull black and I could just see my reflection on its uneven face. A long jagged crack split the stone into equal halves.

I put my face to the crack and stared into the slit hoping to see some flash of green or feel something in the rock. The stone was warm from the sun and seemed to vibrate slightly, but there was nothing inside except the striated swirl of stone and a fine layer of soot that stirred with my breath. I tried pushing the halves apart but nothing budged and I leaned against it, taking in the sky and clouds and letting the sun bake my face.

I heard something skitter across the ridge and turned to see a wolf loping along the edge, its fur catching the sunlight as it vanished into the clutter of timber and stumps. I waited for it to return and when it didn't I hiked back to the river without looking back at the stone, knowing Burke was probably waiting, anxious to get upstream.

He was at the water's edge, refueling and readying the boat. We said nothing to each other and got back on the water and rode through the burn for another hour. The mountains loomed closer, details of their snow- and rock-covered faces coming into view as we followed the river and a mile or two later the hills began to green again and then trees rose and it was as if the fire had never happened.

•

An hour later I spotted the tip of a canoe tucked under a swag of pine boughs and pointed at Burke, who steered the boat to shore, grinning slightly.

Brush had been piled around the other canoes and farther up the river at the head of a deep pool that stretched for nearly a quarter of a mile around a bend, there was a small spit of 2x4s extending out into the gray water, just as Duke had predicted.

We'd found our way in and I should have felt something besides the dread of beginning all over again, this time on land. So I looked at her picture again, the brown eyes, hair falling in what I'd determined was a deliberate cascade over her tanned shoulders.

"Put that away," he said. "You start jacking off to it, I'm gonna take it."

I flipped him off, even started to laugh until I remembered the shooting, and got out of the boat without saying a word to examine the canoes. There were four of them and a drift boat outfitted with a small outboard which had been tarped over. Rotten paddles were bungee-corded inside each canoe. Fetid rainwater and a scum of dead mosquitoes filled the bottoms of the boats. A heavy chain ran through an eyebolt on the prow of each. The chain was padlocked to a tree.

I walked up the swampy bank toward the makeshift dock, my boots slipping into the river. Several five-gallon buckets filled with concrete anchored the dock. Bits of rope dangled from a nearby tree and a tattered trash bag caught in the branches flapped in the slight breeze like a dying bird.

Burke came crashing through the underbrush. "We're in business," he shouted. "The trail's up there."

I followed him up a narrow wash to a gnarled fir tree which had an empty milk jug nailed to it. Inside it were slips of paper no larger than gum wrappers with writing on them, but the words were too smeared to make out anything except a few letters.

"What is it?" he asked.

"I don't know, paper—something," I said.

"Maybe it's a message box?"

"But why would they be in jugs?"

He stared at me impatiently, whipped out his knife and stabbed the bottom of the jug, spilling slips of paper out in a soupy mess of stagnant water and mosquito larvae.

"What good did that do?"

"Now you know," he said. "It's just some wet paper. Now let's pack it up and get the girl." He pointed at the trail with his knife, waiting for me to say something else.

But I didn't and instead followed him to the boat, where we loaded our backpacks in silence, taking pleasure in the fit and snap of gear into the pockets and hooks.

Then he did his usual G.I. Joe bullshit, securing a fillet knife and waterproof match case to his thigh with duct tape. He was proud of the knife because he'd honed it until it was thin and flexible and could bend without snapping.

"Hey, *Force Ten from Navarone*," I joked. "You ready to strike out into enemy territory?"

He smiled. "You never know, do you?" he said, holstering his gun. "And when you do, maybe it's too late."

"I'll take my chances."

"Like yesterday?" he jabbed, smile gone.

I ignored him and shouldered the rifle before taking one last look at our boat.

We were living on our wits now, no easy river to follow or sink bodies in. If Duke was right there would be a camp and as inconceivable as it seemed, looking at the tangled brush, people in the camp.

The trail was marked by can lids and dull red reflectors nailed to trees every fifty yards or so. The ground was damp, full of puddles

in the low spots and treacherous stumps and stubble in the places
where it rode up over the ridges. All the cut limbs littering the
edges of the trail told me it had been maintained recently.

We hiked. The sound of the river dropped away and I stopped
thinking about the abandoned boat, giving myself to the rhythm
of the hike, the blur of trail markers and trees, glad to have the
steady exertion, the burn in my quads and the tick of sweat burst-
ing from my pores. The dead weight of my pack kept me going
until my shoulders were numb.

Burke set the pace, swearing and swatting at cobwebs and stray
branches as the trail coiled endlessly and in some places almost
doubled back on itself. When the wind blew I could smell wood
ash from the massive burn downriver mixing with my own sweat
and the now pungent odor of ripe grayling guts. Not good for
bears, I thought. But gradually the fears dropped away until it was
just the hike and the sight of Burke working steadily up the trail in
front of me, locked, loaded and ready for anything.

Twice we stopped to drink from small creeks that appeared for
brief runs before sinking back into the muskeg. The water was
cold and tasted alive in my mouth. Burke stood, his stubbled jaw
dripping with creek water, shirt dark with sweat. Two days ago
one of us would have said something, a crack or an insult, but now
there was the body between us and it was easier to let the silence
take hold.

We kept walking.

Animals darted ahead of us in the distance, snapping branches,
spooking birds from their nests. In places the trail all but disappeared and I began to think that we were following a dead end
to some vanishing point in the forest. Or worse, a trap. But just
when the doubt became too much another of the markers would
appear and I would walk faster, trying to keep up with Burke,
who seemed bent on reaching the camp before the last of the
midnight sun set.

We walked for hours, everything both wild and unremarkable in
its sameness. My thoughts zoomed pitilessly until I latched on to
her—Duke's daughter, at the end of the trail, waiting for me to

stumble to her step by step, pack numb, bone tired and full of questions.

•

By early evening we'd made it over a large hill and were in a bright green meadow lined with blueberry bushes. We were nearing something. Burke could feel it too and began walking quickly, doubling his pace, racing the setting sun, while I jogged behind him, the rifle knocking against my shoulder as we swatted our way through swatches of delicate white and purple wildflowers.

We stopped at the edge of the meadow where several small game trails crisscrossed and then disappeared into the surrounding woods like jet trails.

"How you holding up?" he asked. It was the first word he'd spoken since the trail.

He unhitched his pack and began picking handfuls of blueberries, popping them into his mouth. He looked wild, sprung from some hole in the ground, his face covered with dead bugs and sweat.

"Right behind you," I said, grabbing berries and letting them explode both sour and sweet against my tongue.

"My guess is over that rise there oughtta be a lake," he said, glancing at the rocky incline and wincing. "It's got to be there. I mean we followed the trail and it's exactly like Duke said it was."

"What then?" I asked.

He shrugged. "It's on you how we go about it from here."

I thought a minute while Burke picked berries, shoving them into his mouth.

"Well, no guns would probably be a good idea," I said.

"No guns?"

"We can stash them and come back after we've checked out the ground situation."

He stopped. "No fucking way, Jack. After yesterday?"

"Especially after yesterday. It's the only way. Hell, what if she's not there—what then?"

"She'll be there," he said. "Don't look like she has a lot of other options."

"I'm dead serious—suppose she's not. I'm betting they're hippies who'd get pretty worked up about firearms."

"We have to tell them something, guns or no guns," he said. "Hell, we can't just charge out of the woods and invite ourselves in."

"I'll get to that," I said. "But you walk in there with that strapped to your leg and you're walking in without me."

He stared at me a moment, his jaw working as he thought. "You're gonna get us killed," he said finally.

"That's exactly what I'm trying to avoid."

"Well then, you'd better hope these are the peace-and-love types, Jack."

"What the hell else is there to do up here?"

Burke patted his gun. "My question precisely," he said.

I walked ahead for the first time, talking over my shoulder at him. "We're backpackers and we heard about the trail from an outfitter and thought it would be fun. We hiked the Cascade last year, right?"

He tossed a few blueberries that pinged off my pack, leaving small blue stains.

"It's not gonna work," he said. "No one hikes way the fuck up here, maybe if it was just off the river, but not this far inland."

"Okay, then we tell them the truth," I said. "Tell them her father's dying."

"And they could say tough luck, join the cult or die."

I scanned the dim wend of the trail, letting him think about the approach. "Which is it?"

"Fuck it, we'll stick with the story. I never got anywhere telling the truth."

"And the guns?"

He hesitated, shifting his pack around.

"We try this my way and maybe no one gets killed," I said.

"What the fuck's that supposed to mean?"

"Nothing—just that whatever happens'll be on me."

"You bet your ass it will," he said. "You bet your ass."

I nodded and walked on ahead into the dark tent of trees, glancing back at the meadow one more time as the trail began to climb gradually, winding around small rocky outcroppings and rising until there were no more markers. We doubled back, trying to pick up the trail again, but we'd lost it.

"Now what?" I asked.

He pointed straight up. "You hear that?"

I listened and heard the distant thrum of machinery coming from somewhere over the hill. Burke went into his confidence mode, retaking the lead from me, doubling my pace with an effort I could only guess at.

There was nothing resembling a trail, just random gaps in the stunted trees that clung to the talus and deltas of topsoil spilling down the incline. He went straight up, through, around and over, skittering loose rocks past my face as I struggled to keep up with him.

We emerged on a rock rim overlooking a narrow horseshoe-shaped valley. In the middle was a beautiful lake, its water reflecting the surrounding trees and mountains like one of those canned postcards of all the pretty perfect places. The sight of the camp pressed against the shores of the lake shattered any notion I'd had of what we'd find. I'd expected a weed-choked pond, a small campground with tents, maybe an old cabin. But what I saw seemed peaceful, set perfectly in the landscape as if it had always been there and needed to be there.

We dropped our packs and stretched.

"At least Duke was right about the lake," I said.

Burke tossed a rock over the edge. "Yeah, but how the hell do we get to it?"

"We must have missed something."

"Missed what?" he said. "We followed the trail until it ended."

"Maybe there's something else—another way in—some sort of secret path."

He walked along the ridge, surveying the lake as if the whole place was thumbing its nose at him. "Where?"

I shrugged, noticing the cluster of tin-roofed buildings on the lake's southern shore, each with small plumes of smoke spinning out of spindly chimneys. There were woodpiles and green-bodied canoes sitting on the shore and what looked like fish racks with the fat steel-gray bodies of trout on them.

But there were no people.

"What about down there?" I asked, pointing to the far side of the lake where the hills tapered into lowland swamp.

"That's two miles away if it's anything," he said. "Besides we've only got a couple hours of light left. We can climb down. It'll be slow going, but . . ."

"No way I'm climbing down," I said.

"Okay," he said. "We've been lucky with bears. You go into that swamp over there, provided there's even half a trail, and you're asking for it. Our best bet is straight down. I've got rope and I don't know about you, but I'm hungry and hope there's a little hospitality down there."

"What if they can see us?"

"The shadows will give us a little cover going down."

I thought about it a minute, scanning the heavily treed valley floor and the lake draining away into the stretch of the swamp. He was right, there was no other way that I could see and the thought of hiking even a hundred yards through the muskeg without a trail did not seem inviting.

"We can make it," he said. "Trust me."

I still wasn't sure and went to the ledge and pressed my chest against the cold stone, wanting to feel some sort of relief for having found the camp, but as I looked down dread settled in my belly.

He shifted impatiently behind me. "You meditating on me?"

"Thinking."

"No thinking involved," he said. "We rappel down. That's the easy part, going up's the bitch. Going out we're gonna need to know the secret trail out of there."

"If there is one."

He scowled. "Are you with me on this?"

"Okay," I said, knowing there was no turning back now.

That was all he needed to hear. He moved quickly, pulling rope from his pack, looping knots and peeking over the edge, trying to decide which angle would present the least problems.

I tossed a few rocks over and heard nothing, just the wind swirling out of the valley cool and damp and the thrum of machinery running somewhere below.

With the rope tied off against two trees and nestled in a groove, Burke tossed the coil over the edge and looked relieved when it stopped with slack. "Not that high."

He pulled me to the edge and pointed at the route he'd chosen. "You wanna keep to the right because there are trees if we need to take cover. Remember to punch it hard, you'll get beat up if you baby-step it down."

I suddenly felt less sure of going over the edge exposed and wondered what would happen if we were spotted. I'd rappelled with him only once and come away pretty banged up.

"You go first," I said.

"You sure?"

I nodded.

"I ain't climbing back to come get your ass. Just remember you're on your own with the bears."

"Get out of here," I said.

He grinned, ran a bit of rope through his belt and had me do the same. Then he wrapped several strips of cloth around his hands and grabbed the rope.

I watched him go over, keeping one eye on what I could see of the camp. There was still no activity, just the faint sound of a generator echoing up the cliff wall.

Burke gripped the rope tightly, his face clenched as he let a few feet of line slip between his palms.

"I was wrong—it's a long way down," he said, peering over his shoulder. Then he squatted against the stone face and pushed out, letting the rope fly between his fingers as he disappeared from sight. I pulled back. It would be easy to walk away, find the trail again and be drifting down the river by morning. *Lost* and *looking*. I'd been thinking about the words and the look on his face underwater, wondering if there had ever been a time when I wasn't lost or looking for some other way to live.

When the line went slack I looped the length of it through our packs and lowered them down. The rope went slack again and this time I pulled it through my belt, grabbed a T-shirt I'd set out from my pack, tore the shirt in two and wrapped it around my palms.

At the edge I picked up the rope, the wind blowing it against the rock like a stray hair as I straddled it, lowering myself over the edge, hands shaking. I pushed out hard.

And dropped into the nothing.

The first landing was clumsy and I smashed my shoulder against an outcropping, but I kept going, pushing off even harder, free-falling and then landing with a shock, sending debris skittering down. Gradually the bottom came into view and my heart slowed. I could feel the heat of the rope through the cloth as I dropped the rest of the way.

Even with both feet on the ground, things felt strange and out of balance. There was no wind and the trees looked like knives. Burke stepped out of the shadows and smacked me on the back and for a moment I flashed back to when he'd saved me from the trusses by pushing me off the edge of the building. He seemed different now, cut down to size.

"Thought you'd turned tail on me," he said. "That or a bear got you."

"Sorry to disappoint."

He laughed. "Let's get the bitch."

I turned and followed him into the forest. When I glanced back at the rope I realized that it would be immediately noticed by anyone in the area.

I stopped. "What about the rope?" I asked.

He looked troubled. "There's not a fucking thing we can do about it except find them before they find us."

We continued, keeping to the edge of woods, following the buzz of the generator until we came to another line of plastic milk jugs nailed to tree trunks. A path opened in the forest between them.

Burke pointed, but I was focused on the jugs and ignored him as I went to the first one and looked inside. There were the scraps of paper again, only this time they were relatively dry, having been sheltered by the thick canopy of pine boughs. I could make out a single word: TRAFFIC. I rattled the jug until another slip shifted into view that read: BAD HABITS. I shook it again until another slip with the words BABY KILLERS written on it in thick pencil came into view. Before I could say anything Burke was staring over my shoulder.

"You find the secret of the universe?" he asked.

I quickly decided to keep what I'd found to myself. "Just words," I said.

He turned down the trail and I scrambled down after him, toward the thrum of engines and the smell of exhaust. We skirted a hedge of stunted pine trees behind which sat a rough log shed with a tin roof. Burke immediately went for his gun.

"C'mon," I said. "Put it away. Remember the deal?"

He grumbled and took his hand away, creeping around the weed-choked side of the building. The front of the hut was littered with red plastic fuel jugs and there were more under a small awning tacked between two trees several feet away. A heavy insulated electrical cord snaked out of the doorway toward the clump of cabins surrounding the lake.

We stepped into the shack where the air swirled in hot gusts, exhaust coating the inside of my mouth with a sour film. Six generators sat in the middle on pallets, but only two of them were running. On wooden shelves sat dozens of car batteries and sets of neatly coiled jumper cables, wires, voltmeters and extra extension cords. There were a few tools just inside the door, some burlap sacks and a series of tick marks on the wall.

Afraid of being seen we ducked behind the shack and retreated to the cool of the woods.

"The guns," I said.

He shook his head. "Might seem foolish, us walking all this way without guns."

"It's better—"

"It's fucking unconstitutional is what it is."

I ignored him and pointed at the .45.

"Give it up," I said.

He stared at me for a minute before unbuckling the holster and handing me the gun. The Colt felt heavy and cold.

"I still got my knife," he said.

I ignored his taunts and stepped off the trail a bit, walking until the abundance of trees and brush reduced me to crawling.

I could hear him right behind me in the tunnel of brush, still trying to keep an eye on what I was doing with his gun. When I could go no farther I turned to him. "Right here, see?"

"The fucking squirrels are gonna get 'em."

"Just give me the shells."

He groaned, reached into his backpack and withdrew two boxes of cartridges and handed them to me. I placed everything in a trash bag and wrapped it against the trunk of the tree.

"They're here if we need them," I said, still hoping to placate him.

But he wasn't having any of it and backed out of the tunnel, snapping branches in his wake.

By the time we emerged mosquitoes and black flies were having a field day with us.

I stood back, inspecting the hiding place. From the trail the broken limbs were barely visible. Burke gathered stones and stacked them into a little cairn opposite of where we'd entered. Then he untied his hair from the short ponytail and flashed me the peace sign. "Time for peace, love, understanding and the girl."

"Just let me do the talking," I said. "The whole thing works if we get her to come willingly."

"How come I don't think that's going to happen?"

"Maybe you got it all wrong and we're in for some free love, granola and mind-altering drugs."

"Don't get your hopes up," he said, striking out along the electrical cord.

"We're backpackers, remember? We saw the trail and . . ."

". . . and unless these people are stoned out of their minds that ain't gonna float," he said. "We don't even look like backpackers. They're going to find the rope, so what's the use in trying? We should just grab her and go."

"Finesse," I said.

"Fuck finesse," he said.

"Okay then, go get your gun and start shooting."

He turned and glared at me. "Either you get past what happened yesterday or we're gonna have trouble," he growled.

"What's that mean?"

"It means, maybe you don't trust me anymore and think somehow you would have done something different if things had been the other way around," he said, pointing at me. "I saved your brains from being splattered all over those rocks and now you're tellin' me to relax and trust shit's going to work out?"

"I didn't say that."

He stuck a finger in my chest. "Then what are you saying?"

"Nothing," I said. "Let's just drop it."

We stared at each other a moment.

"Noted and dropped," he said finally. "Now let's do it."

I said okay and kept walking through the waist-high brush into a narrow field where the first of the buildings sat. Like the generator shack it had been built recently. Scraps of 2x4s lay scattered on the ground next to hunks of flesh-colored insulation rotting in wet piles. We squatted down beside a windowless wall. I could see the lake glinting blue not too far away and for a moment I thought this would be a pretty nice place to settle down, provided you could get out or weren't being thumped on the head with a Bible. Then I remembered the words *baby killers* written on the scraps of paper, wondering why the camp's inhabitants bothered dropping words into jugs.

There were other buildings closer to the lake and some heavy canvas wall tents with smoldering fire rings in front of them. But still no people.

I crept around to the edge of the building and that's when I saw them. It was a man and a woman and I knew even from this distance that there was something wrong. They were skinny and their clothes were tattered and unwashed. They didn't look like creatures bathed in paradise.

The woman wasn't Duke's daughter. She was older, her hair shot through with strands of gray. The man was younger, skinny, though with a thick black beard and stained hands which made him look like some old prospector plucked from a photograph. I watched them a moment, hoping they'd turn and spot me and make things easy. I could react and not have to think something up.

But when I turned around to motion Burke forward another man stepped around behind us holding a shotgun loosely in his hands. He was tall, his face a large blank white oval that seemed to float over the rest of his body. His skin was pale and there was a stillness to him, as if he'd been waiting for us for a very long time.

Burke spun around and started to move but the man raised the gun and pressed the barrel to Burke's cheek.

I tried looking the man in the eyes, but they were useless, the irises shrunken gray dots against enormous whites. We were just something at the other end of his gun.

He nudged the shotgun off Burke and pointed it at my face.

"You came a long way to get shot like this," he said. His voice seemed to rattle up from somewhere deep.

"We didn't . . ."

"Shut up," he said, calmly putting the shotgun back on Burke as if he knew in his gut that my buddy was the man of action and I was the talker.

I thought about our guns lying under the tree and what Burke must be thinking. I locked eyes with him, trying to feel out the right move—how to play the man or if I should leave it to him. But the steel double barrel was stuck to his cheek like a syringe.

Burke started to inch away from it slowly and I tried to say something, but it was too late.

Burke moved quickly, spinning his knees as he cleared the barrel from his face and raised a fist. But that was as far as he got. With a crisp snap the man twirled the shotgun around and crumpled Burke to the ground with the butt. He sank, legs collapsing beneath him like rags as a gash opened over his eyes, There was blood everywhere and the man advanced on me, gun out in front of him, pale face still blank. I kept waiting for Burke to spring back up and tackle the man, but he was slumped on the dirt, bleeding into his shirt quietly.

"Please," I said. "We were . . ."

He put the gun on my shoulder, sliding the barrel until it was cradled under my jawbone, the steel cool against my skin.

I reached up to grab the gun but he pulled the trigger, firing over my shoulder. The explosion shattered my eardrum and the barrel recoiled harshly against my jaw. I felt the vivid sting of powder and the whine of lead pellets sailing past me, plunging into the cabin wall, some bouncing back. Then he punched the smoking barrel into my temple and knocked me to the ground. My neck burned. Blood dripped. I got on all fours and looked up into his eyes, which seemed to suck in all of the light. His face was dim and simple, focused on the gun as if he'd just discovered something about it.

"Wait . . ." I slurred.

But he brought the gun down again, punching the words back into my mouth. The ground quivered and then everything went white. Then black.

THE CAMP

I woke into darkness. I couldn't move. Everything smelled like gunpowder, burnt hair and flesh. Mosquitoes buzzed. Somebody was breathing loudly next to me. Then I remembered the gun and the man with the dead eyes. I put a hand to my neck and it came away sticky. The skin was powder-burned all the way to my ear. I wasn't shot or dead, just alive with pain and for the moment it was enough. But then the darkness pressed in on me and I realized that we had made a terrible mistake in agreeing to get Duke's daughter.

I moved toward the sound of breathing. It was Burke dipping in and out of sleep, his body twisted, legs bent back under him, arms at bad angles.

I straightened him out and stood slowly, seeing if my aching head would let me have balance.

We were in a small cabin, the insides of which had been lined with tar paper. There were no windows. The floor was dirt. I felt around the perimeter for a door and there was only a narrow square seam in the wall, locked no doubt from the outside.

I sat down next to Burke and let the situation come back to me in degrees. Fairbanks seemed a million miles away. The guns were under a tree. I had no idea how bad he was injured and I knew by the viciousness of our capture that it would be useless to cry out or bang on the walls.

They would have to come to us and we would either be killed or we would not.

Burke came to several hours later. I heard him sit up and groan as if he'd merely been napping.

"You there?" he called out in the dark.

"Nowhere else to be," I said.

"How bad is it?"

"How bad is what?"

"The situation?"

I stared into the darkness, to where I thought the door was. "Nothing." A word for the jugs.

"What do you mean nothing?"

"I mean nobody's come yet," I whispered. "How about your head?"

He was quiet a moment. "Sore, but okay. You?"

"He barrel-bitched me," I said. "Knocked me upside the head with the gun and that's the last I remember."

He shifted around and then I heard the unmistakable sound of tape peeling off flesh.

"Guess what they didn't find?" he said.

"The knife?"

He flicked the blade. It made a stiff metallic ting, vibrating like a tuning fork.

"And matches," he said, striking one against the hilt of the knife. "Enough to kill and burn that motherfucker who chopped me in the face."

Remembering the letter and picture of Duke's daughter, I stabbed at my pockets only to find them empty.

"They got the letter and picture," I said.

"Fuck it. We're still gonna get her or die trying," he said. "What other choice do we have?"

I watched the match burn down to an orange tip.

"Let's just see what happens."

He snorted and struck another match. In the flickering sulfur light his face looked thick with dried blood and dirt. His hair was matted, eyes sunk deep, like he'd risen from some shallow grave.

"You look like shit too," he said, lighting another and circling the room. The ceiling was low and tar-papered as I'd guessed and there were iron eyebolts spaced unevenly in pairs on the ceiling with chains hanging from them. Shackles, I thought.

He found the door and stood by it, letting the match burn itself out.

"We'll wait," he said. "You figure it's late?"

"Dark at least."

"Good then," he said. "When they come for us in the morning I'm gonna put the knife on the first person through that door."

"What then?"

But he didn't answer and there were no more matches struck. He'd plotted his course and I was no longer in charge. My plan to talk our way in had failed miserably and Burke knew he didn't have to remind me of that fact. What was needed now was pure action.

I went back into a corner and sat, waiting for morning and Burke to make his move.

•

He was wrong. An hour later the door fell in with a heavy thud. He sprang into action, moving shadowlike across the blue-black light of the open door. I stood, hands out in front of me like a blind man. There were voices outside and then nothing as I waited for Burke to pounce, knife slashing in front of him.

When my eyes adjusted to the murky light entering from outside I could see the silhouettes of legs and beyond that stars up in the sky, bright and clear, taunting me.

Then I saw the barrel of a gun enter the door frame, splitting the square of night outside the shack. Burke moved slowly, doing something with his hands I couldn't make out.

"Slowly," a voice said. There was more banging around outside the door and then the beam of a flashlight probed the floor of the cabin until it fell on me, tracing the outline of my body.

"Now the other," the voice said.

The beam searched the darkness for Burke, who stepped out of the corner, very near the gun barrel. His hands were empty.

It was my play again.

I crawled out of the door and entered the night. The air was cool and hung with a fine mist. The man with the gun and dead face stepped up and looked right through me as Burke crawled from the shack, head bent, hands at his side.

There were a couple of other people standing in a loose semicircle, staring, their faces thin and drawn. I looked into each of them, hoping to see Duke's daughter, but she was not among them. A tall woman with ash-blond hair edging to gray watched me carefully. Her cheeks were etched with fine scars and hard wrinkles. Other figures retreated into the shadows, whispering, the white of their hands the only thing visible.

We were close to the lake. Moonlight glowed on its surface and the sound of lapping water seemed then oddly reassuring.

"We were just following the trail," I said to the crowd.

The woman stared at me and then smiled. Her teeth were a mess, the scars on her face filled with blood and then went white again as the smile dropped.

"What trail?" the man with the gun asked.

Burke pointed. "From the river."

The gun went on Burke again.

"There is no trail," the man said flatly.

"Okay," Burke said. "If that's it for the hospitality, well then we'll just be on our way."

The woman stepped closer and put her hand on the gun. "It's okay, Boothe, really . . ."

Boothe shook his head and pressed the gun into Burke's stomach. "He wants to see you now."

"Look," I said, "we just lost our way. Hiking, I mean . . ."

"Shut up," Boothe said. His face began to twitch. "You came for a reason. We found the rope."

"We've been waiting," somebody else said.

Boothe snapped around to see who it was—the faces were indistinguishable in the dark. The woman whispered something to him and he turned to us again.

"He wants to see you," Boothe repeated. "Now."

It was quiet for a long while.

Then Burke stepped forward. "Let's do it, then," he said brightly, clearing himself from the gun.

He looked at me and nodded.

Boothe stood back, somewhat surprised at our sudden cooperation, and pointed to a building behind him. The crowd drifted away toward campfires and tents, whispering amongst themselves. I could see others in the half-light, watching us follow Boothe.

Burke had his hands inside his shirt, gripping the knife no doubt, formulating some plan. I pretended to stumble into him before we reached the door.

"Don't," I whispered. "You'll get us killed."

Before I could say anything else I felt the cold steel of the gun in my ear and backed away, but not before Burke gave up on the knife and let his hand dangle out of his pocket.

The building had been built with stripped logs, plywood and 2x4s. There were windows cut in at irregular intervals and flat river stones stacked for steps.

Boothe opened the door and pushed Burke through with the gun. Then he stared at me until I swung in after him.

He latched the door behind us.

The interior was suffused with the dull red light of several oil lamps set with rose-tinted globes. Next to one of the lamps was a tattered print of a Blake illumination depicting a well-muscled man kneeling with the stars, the sun and the moon on his thighs and women gathered around him like angels plunging a knife into his chest. A dusty dream catcher made from fishing line hung just below the print. Farther down the wall were other illustrations tacked to beams. Some of them I recognized as Blake's. Others were just pictures torn from magazines that seemed to have no connection to one another—a photo of Stonehenge, several Far Side cartoons with talking bears and puzzled hunters, a black-and-white photo of a mother holding an infant in her arms, an old AIM bumper sticker, several sheets of paper with lists of names written on them in the same neat hand I'd seen in the jugs. But it

was the Blake print that my eyes kept coming back to. Somebody
had written the word YES across the man's chest and below it was
a poem that I couldn't make out in the poor light.

The air was thick with woodsmoke and other, more exotic
odors. Boothe parted a heavy curtain, revealing a long, low-
ceilinged chamber simply furnished with a bed, several makeshift
shelves full of books, a table set about by chairs made from willow
branches and a large bench against the back wall. Sitting on the
bench was a man. I could only see his profile but the whole room
seemed to tip toward him, even the light.

We stepped closer. I could make out just one side of his face.
The rest was hidden in shadow. He had a strong chin, weathered
skin and dark gray eyes flecked with gold. His hair was jet black
and long and fell around his shoulders like rotten straw.

Sensing our presence, he turned and the whole room seemed to
flicker.

Burke gasped. The man's face was split in two—one half normal, placid almost, the other furrowed with deep ruts and thick
red scabs. In places the red flesh erupted into yellow curds the
color of ham fat before tapering into what looked like new skin.
Even in the dull light of the room the skin seemed to hang from
the left side of his face in great scabbed sheets. His ear slid into his
neck and his nose melted into his cheeks, making it look as if
something had stirred his features with a hot wand.

There were other scars running down his throat and chest.
Some of it was scabbed over, other parts were still heavy with scar
tissue. But there were his eyes, perfect and untouched amid the
mess.

I knew that whatever had happened had nearly killed him and
that the healing had taken place without antibiotics or stitches.

Boothe nudged us closer until we were at the foot of the bench.
The man smiled. His teeth were perfectly white.

He nodded to Boothe and the gun slipped back.

"Welcome," the man said. "My name is Nunn."

He did not hold out his hand for us to shake or even so much as
nod in our direction. His voice made all that unnecessary.

My eyes kept tracing the ruin of his face and the scars that were now visible on his arm—deep gouges and missing chunks of flesh where there should have been muscle. I turned around. Boothe had vanished, but I had the feeling that there were others in the room, huddled in dark corners under blankets, watching.

Burke stepped closer and I looked to see if he had the knife out, but his hands were empty.

"What happened?" he asked.

Nunn stood, hair falling across the ruined half of his face, making him look normal again. He paced the room slowly, as if turning great thoughts over in his head. When he spoke it was slow and deep.

"The bear."

He stared at us again, then bent over and leaned in close to me until I could smell the slight rot of his face and feel his breath on my neck. "You can't have what you came for," he said, fixing his eyes on me until the face seemed to fall away. "The girl is one of us and will remain so until it is time."

I stared back at him.

"What—" I started.

"We leave things behind here," he said. "It is the whole reason for this place. There is the world and there is the camp. It is a special place and coming here like you did will undo some things I have expended a great deal of time and effort trying to keep out. Already Boothe has had to do the necessary."

"That's what you call this?" Burke asked, jabbing at his bruised face.

Nunn didn't react.

"We'll leave then," Burke said. "Walk away right now and not tell anyone."

"That's not possible," he said. "But you can help us set things right. Then maybe . . ." coming closer, his words trailing off.

Burke started to shake his head, but Nunn leaned in and said something that caused him to stare ahead blankly. For a moment the room was utterly silent. Burke's hands went slack and dropped to his sides.

"How . . ." he muttered.

Nunn shrugged and moved to the back of the room. He stopped at the door, turned and gave us a look with those eyes.

"Come," he said, "I have a test for you."

I glanced at Burke, who was still shocked at whatever Nunn had said to him.

"You all right?" I asked.

He nodded.

Nunn grinned. "Come," he said, motioning to a doorway covered with a dusty Navajo blanket. "I want to show you something."

We followed him outside and into darkness again and when I looked at Burke he was frowning, his eyes fixed on Nunn. I thought about running, taking my chances in the woods, but it was like being in a dream where my legs seemed leaden and wouldn't move except to keep pace with Nunn's silhouette.

Ten minutes later we were deep in the woods, pine branches sweeping my face, twigs crunching under my feet like tiny bones. My nose began to throb again and there was some blood seeping out of the burns on my neck.

Finally Burke turned and whispered, "Let's just go along," he said. "He's a *deeply crazy* motherfucker but I think we're going to be okay if we play his game."

"What did he say to you?"

He started to answer, but stopped and continued walking until we came to a small clearing. The moon hung low in the sky and stars trembled like bright moths humming through the trees.

Nunn stopped and spoke in that same even voice. "It does not have a name."

He paused for a long time, wind tossing his hair across his scarred face. "The beasts go into dens and remain in their places. Out of the south cometh the whirlwind and cold out of the north."

"What does that mean?"

"God speaking to Job from the whirlwind," he whispered.

Suddenly the words from the jug, *baby killers,* flashed across my mind and I worried that we'd stumbled into some bizarre fundamentalist cult. Burke glanced at me, raising an eyebrow.

Nunn smiled at my apparent unease. "When I was young I had to memorize the Bible," he said. "I was raised Methodist because my parents didn't know any better. They wanted me to believe, but I couldn't, not after I realized that the Bible was just another book with some interesting things in it. Nothing more and nothing less. I went looking when the pastor couldn't answer my questions."

"Looking for what?" I asked.

"Answers," he said. "But that's too simple, even now looking back there was a pattern. It wasn't visible to me then, but it was there. Do you understand?"

Neither of us nodded.

"The pattern is everywhere—even here," he said. "And this whole place is a reaction."

"Reaction to what?" I asked.

"Against whatever you desire—whatever you fear, whatever you came here for . . . but there is no religion, at least not in a conventional sense—just people and what they bring or what the world gives them. They come here and I help them quiet the yearning and striving. I help them see the pattern."

I looked at him confused. Burke stood nearby, staring absently into the dark.

"But then the bear came like a god in a whirlwind. It was trying to tell us something," Nunn continued. "Everybody wanted answers, but there weren't any."

"Answers to what?"

"Why the bear came," he said. "I have seen it only once and tried to face it, but I was struck down and chosen. When it was on me all I could remember was that verse from Job—my life didn't flash before me or anything else—just that stupid verse my father had me memorize when I was a child. I saw and felt nothing outside of what it was doing to my face. Nothing mattered. Not even the stars which were the only thing I could see or the fact that it had left me alive—none of it mattered. And when I got up I knew

I'd been transformed, rewritten by the wilderness. Transfigured by the bear."

"How?" I asked.

"Inside," he said, pointing at his chest. "It was a wonderful and horrible thing to be under its snout, my flesh being torn off, its weight crushing into me until I couldn't breathe. I fought it at first, but that was useless and when I could no longer raise my arms I gave myself to the bear. The pain dropped away and for a good long time it was just the two of us staring into each other's eyes—there was the blood of course. But the bear knew that I was not afraid, because it left me for dead. And I was dead for a long time until something in me told me to get up. I knew I was needed here. So I got up and walked. And the rest . . ."

I studied his face in the dark, unable to get past what the bear had done to it; the curls of half-healed flesh, the black crust of scabs edged with new pink skin.

He continued. "It has taken two others," he said. "It carries them into the woods and hides their bodies."

"Why don't you kill it?" Burke asked.

He laughed. "Because there is a reason for the bear—something more than territory. It has been sent into the valley to warn us and now it seems you too have been sent."

Burke stepped forward. "Sent for what?"

"To hunt the bear," Nunn said. "I can't kill it, not now, after I've been marked. There are lines being drawn. Choices that do not support the group and upset the balance that I have worked long and hard to create out of the nothing of this woods and the lake. The bear is a sign—a manifestation."

Burke said, "Manifestation of what?"

"The lurking god in nature," he said, smiling, moonlight chopping his features into shadowy lumps. "True wilderness, nothing more than true wilderness."

He pointed at his chest and then was quiet.

"What is this place?" I asked

Nunn turned to me. "The camp?"

I nodded.

"It's something different for everybody. It's whatever you want it to be." He swept his hair back. "Or whatever you fear."

"What the fuck is that supposed to mean?" Burke asked, sounding like his old self.

". . . what I mean is that for some it becomes nothing and they are asked to leave. But for now it is important you understand the bargain I have offered you."

"What bargain?" I asked.

He stared at me with those eyes. "If you choose not to I can give you over to Boothe. Things are sometimes more simple that way."

"You want us to kill the bear?" Burke asked. "Is that what you want or think we came up here to do?"

"It doesn't matter why you came, not anymore," he said. "Penny has chosen to stay and nothing you can say or do is going to change her mind. What's important is that you demonstrate your worth to the camp. Winter is coming and you were not invited . . . yet you came."

Burke faced him. "If you want the bear killed, why not have Boothe do it?"

Nunn blinked. "Because he has his place in the order, because you were sent, because—"

"—what fucking order?" Burke blurted.

Nunn stepped deeper into the shadows and sighed. "Do we have an understanding?"

"What if we walk away?" Burke asked.

He smiled. "Careful what you wish for, especially up here."

"What the hell does that mean?"

As if on cue I heard a rustling ahead of us in the dark—the sound of something large, moving through the trees, snapping branches.

I turned to look, but couldn't get a fix on the sound, it seemed to come from all around. Burke began backing away, his hand instinctively going for where his gun should have been.

"What the fuck?" he spat.

A low growl sounded through the trees, followed by a deep coughing sound.

Nunn turned on us.

"Of course you're free to go," he said. "But . . ."

"The bear?" Burke asked. "You want us to believe the bear is out there waiting on your command to come gobble us up?"

Nunn smiled and glanced over his shoulder at the murky wall of brush and small trees, his torn face glistening in the half-light. Whatever was coming through the trees was getting closer, coughing, growling and breaking branches.

I believed.

Burke grabbed my arm and tried to yank me into the woods, but I slipped from his grip and stood my ground and when I turned to say something he was gone.

Nunn made no move to stop him. I froze and stood there staring at the dark trees. The crashing in the woods stopped and for a moment all was dead quiet. Even the wind quit as blood pounded through my chest and my legs felt dull and heavy. I was afraid to move, fearing that whatever direction I chose would put me in the path of the bear's rush and I would go under its fur and claws just as Nunn had. Only I would die.

So I went down into a crouch and waited for the clouds to shift and spill more moonlight. Whatever had been in the bushes went quiet and when I looked up Nunn had vanished.

I shouted Burke's name. And when there was no answer I began to move, keeping low to the ground, expecting gunfire or somebody to step out of the woods and stop me, tell me the test or trap—whatever it was that Nunn had led us out here for—was over. I knew that Burke was looking for the guns and all hell would break loose if he found them.

I had to find him before that happened.

As I stood surveying the field something large began moving through the woods to my right. I turned toward the sound just in time to see a shadow break from the darkness. It was the bear and it thundered across the clearing recklessly, loping quickly, almost silently except for the thudding of its paws on the ground. In the poor light of the moon it looked long and thick, terrifyingly quick for its size, its hump rolling like another head, almost gray in the moonlight.

My breath caught in my throat as it jetted across the field, disappearing without a sound. I stood, frozen, waiting for the bear to lunge out of the dark and drag me off bleeding and screaming.

When the normal forest sounds returned I began to move around the perimeter, ducking into the wall of trees, hoping a trail would present itself, wanting to put as much distance as I could between myself and the bear. I knew it was all a matter of luck. I was a clumsy night-blind creature to the bear and if it wanted to find me it would sniff me out.

But I had to move. To stay and do nothing would be death. Nunn's story of his attack was there with me, working on the shadows, transforming a crippled tree into the outline of a bear or the snap of a twig into the beginnings of its final charge.

So I picked up a branch and groped through the trees swinging the stick in front of me at the darkness, knowing it would be useless against the bear or a gun.

After ten minutes I found a small crack in the forest. There were stumps on the ground and just enough moonlight to see that a path had been hacked. I listened hard, trying to pick out the sound of somebody moving, and with the stick out in front of me I moved toward a dull light hanging low in the trees. Branches swept at my arms like children and mosquitoes thrummed inches away, waiting for me to stop.

The light grew closer and closer until I was moving without listening anymore, thrashing blindly, falling into a rhythm, legs moving with certainty.

When I saw the source of the light I knew that the trail I'd followed out of the clearing had not been the one we'd come in through. The light emanated from a Coleman lantern hung in the narrow window of a small cabin. There were no other buildings in the immediate area and it seemed that the lantern had been placed in the window to guide me.

The cabin was little more than a shack built from logs and warped plywood sheeting, dotted with nail holes bleeding rust down the sun-bleached side. Firewood was stacked neatly outside in chest-high ricks and a small porch covered the front, its roof sagging. On the door hung two hammered steel charms: a crescent moon, the other a six-pointed star.

I moved closer, imagining Boothe or Nunn waiting for me inside. I no longer cared if they found me. I was cold. The thin shirt I'd woke up in was damp with sweat and blood that had seeped from my nose and neck. And I was tired. The running, the river and the hike into the camp as well as the crack with the gun had turned me into a simple animal wanting very much to find shelter and collect myself, even if it meant surrendering to Boothe and agreeing to hunt the bear.

It didn't matter what Burke wanted anymore. He was gone, running somewhere in the night. He would either kill somebody or get killed and for once I didn't care. After seeing Nunn and the cold look in Boothe's face I knew we'd bumped up against something too large and deep for Burke to change by sheer dint of his will. This was no longer some game hatched over a few beers and the romantic notion that we were rescuing a dying man's daughter from Nunn.

I approached the cabin cautiously. Suddenly the light blinked, just for a moment, but long enough to let me know that there was someone inside.

The shadows surrounding the door shifted to reveal a hasp and lock. I stepped up, put a hand on the padlock and pulled. It held tightly. Thin vibrations rattled the porch boards and to my left I could see the light shift again, plunging me momentarily into darkness.

I was being watched.

Shouts echoed through the woods in the distance as the night sky lifted at the edges to reveal the deep blue of dawn to the east.

I went around to the window, keeping low against the wall, before rising slowly to have a look. Moths bounced off my face, fluttering across my lips, chasing the ever-present mosquitoes away as the inside of the cabin came into view. The first thing I saw was several scarves nailed to the raw plank walls. A pair of dim oil lamps sat on the floor. The bed was made from 2x4s and plywood and stood near a small homemade-looking woodstove. I had shifted to the other side of the glass, and was brushing moths from my hair when I saw her. She was sitting in a rocking chair reading. Her hair hung across her face obscuring all but the point of her chin. It was her—Duke's daughter. She wore a loose white smock, pulled off her shoulders, and a dark red skirt that was faded and tattered at the hem. Her bare feet poked out, moving back and forth slowly against the dirty wood floor as she read.

She turned the page and pushed the hair from her face. Her hands were rough, the nails chewed to the quick, and there were small scabs on her forearms. Her shoulders were slim and straight, catching the graceful taper of her neck and the tumble of brown hair.

A large moth brushed against the burn on my neck before knocking loudly against the glass. She looked up, studying me carefully, her eyes even more interesting than they were in the photograph, serious and cautiously bright.

I heard more shouting echoing through the trees and the sound of the generators grinding to life like the roar of distant animals. After a while I imagined the sound would become part of the landscape, like the wind or the trees. But now it sounded ominous and out of place. Birds darted through the trees snaring insects as spiders dropped webs from the roof eaves and when I turned back to the window she was standing, the skirt sweeping the floor as she crossed the room to have a look at me. I put my hand to my face and tried to wipe away some of the grime and pine needles, but it was useless.

She came to the glass, pulled the lantern off its nail and set it on the floor behind her. I could see the outline of her legs through the thin fabric of the skirt now and the faint cup of her breasts soft and full under the backlit glow of the smock.

She cocked her head. I must have looked a wreck, because her expression darkened to one of concern, then possibly fear.

"Duke," I said into the glass. "Your father."

The words rattled back at me and for a moment I hesitated, not knowing what to say next or how I should explain what to her must have been a very puzzling situation.

She stared for what seemed a long time and then put a hand to the window.

"Go away," she said, her voice dulled by the glass. "You must go away."

"Your father asked us to come for you," I said.

She crossed her arms and regarded me, working on her bottom lip with her teeth. "Please," she said. "Before they come."

I didn't move.

"Go," she shouted, drawing closer to the window. Even through the glass she was beautiful. She had thick upturned lips and a soft round face. Around her neck was a braided leather necklace with a small twisted gold nugget hanging from it.

Her hands clenched into small fists. "I don't want you here."

I stepped back to the porch to have a look at the door and lock. A little chest and shoulder was all it would take to pop the screws.

I looked back at the trail. It was empty.

Sunlight was just beginning to pour over the horizon, lifting the fog that crouched along the dark edges of the forest.

I knocked on the door until I heard her rustling behind it. "Step back," I said.

I waited and then plowed into the door. The screws tore and the door popped open.

I stuck my head in. All the lamps and the Coleman lantern had been blacked out and what little light trickled in from the window cast dull shadows.

"Penny?" I said into the gloom.

The rocking chair creaked back and forth across the buckled floor. I stepped inside and walked toward the sound. "Penny," I said. "Is that your name?"

The rocking didn't stop. I moved closer, my eyes adjusting to the dark all over again. Her hair swayed gently across her face, hiding it for a moment and then parting to reveal those eyes I'd admired in the photo for days—the same eyes that had caused the man at the cabin to pause just long enough to allow Burke to line up his shot.

"Your father is dying," I said. "He asked us to come get you."

The rocking continued and I felt compelled to fill up the space with more words. "Why are you locked up?"

"Please go," she said in a tiny voice. "My father . . ."

I waited, but she just stared.

"I had a letter from him, but it was taken."

"You should not have come," she said, glancing out the door nervously. "They will come and find you here and it will only cause further problems."

"Who will come?"

"Nunn, or one of the others," she answered blankly.

"What will they do to you?"

A moment of silence followed as the first of the morning sun began to break through the window in blunt shafts, stirring small whorls of dust motes. For some reason this simple observation comforted me. I could have been anywhere—back in my apartment in Fairbanks staring at the cheap paneled walls and piles of unopened letters from my family or in some bar watching the sun rise through cigarette haze and hungover eyes. It was a minute of utter silence and calm, perhaps the last one I'd have for quite some time.

"I saw the bear," I said, hoping this would illicit some reaction from her.

"Nothing's been the same since the mauling," she said, her voice hollow again.

I knelt down beside her and tried to look into the shadowy pit of her face. "Come outside with me," I said.

She hesitated and then rose slowly and moved with me toward the door. We stood on the porch and watched the ground squirrels dash about the woodpile for a few minutes. She pulled her hair away from her face, tied it in a loose knot and smiled and it was as if some spell had broken.

"We came for you," I said.

She turned and then looked me straight in the eye. "You must have a lot of questions," she said.

"Some," I said.

"It's not what you think," she whispered. "But for now at least it's safer here than in the camp."

"The cabin?"

She nodded.

"And the camp?" I said.

She looked at me vacantly.

"I don't understand why everybody's here," I said.

"That's complicated," she said. "Maybe you'll see, once you've been accepted."

"Accepted?" I said. "Boothe nearly killed us. If that's—"

"—it could have been worse," she said. "They could have taken you out into the woods and tied you to a tree until you lost your mind. You've met Nunn, haven't you?"

I nodded, watching the morning sun hit her face. "Last night he took us out to this field and said we were free to go if we wanted," I said.

"And?"

"And then he gave us an option."

She brushed a cloud of gnats from her face. "He asked you to hunt the bear."

"How did you know that—were you there?"

"I was here all night, waiting," she said. "Did you give him an answer?"

"About the bear?"

She nodded.

I shook my head. "Not exactly. Burke ran off and I haven't seen him since."

"Burke?"

"My friend," I said. "It was his idea to come here."

She looked worried a moment.

"How did you find your way here?"

"I was lost and then I saw the light in the window and followed it through the trees."

She smiled again, started to say something and then stopped.

"What is it?"

"Just you ending up here—it's strange."

"What do you mean?"

"You'll learn that there is very little coincidence here." She looked at me with a slight prompt. "I forgot to ask your name."

"Jack," I said. "Are you telling me Nunn arranged for me to find you?"

"I don't know anything anymore," she said with a shrug. "Well, Jack, you seem to know all about me. Now what?"

"Your father arranged this," I said. "He told us you ran away with Nunn."

"I didn't run away," she snapped. "I came here for a reason."

"But he's dying."

"You don't really believe that, do you?"

"I saw him," I said. "He looked sick to me, I mean are you telling me he's not?"

"That's not what this is about."

"What is it then?"

"Did he tell you why I came to Alaska in the first place?"

I shook my head.

"Then you don't know the whole story or even why it makes sense I should end up here. My father knew exactly what he was doing and your friend bought it . . ." She stopped herself.

"What?"

She stared at me. "You really don't know, do you?"

"Know what?"

"Never mind," she said, putting her finger to my lips. "It's not important. What's important is what we do now before everything comes undone. Your friend didn't get far—not in the dark."

"Well then you don't know Burke," I said.

"There's only one way out and that's through the cave."

"Cave?"

"Isn't that how you got into the valley?"

"We climbed down," I said.

This seemed to catch her off guard. "Well then unless your friend can fly or climb cliffs in the dark he'll be found or let himself be found after he's considered his options."

"That's not good then," I said. "Because your father paid us to find you and Burke won't stop until he's done that."

"What about you? You seem to have found me. Now what—not what you expected?"

"What do you mean?"

"Before you go trying to save me, Jack, you might want to figure out what it is you're saving me from."

"I don't understand," I said.

She put her hand lightly on my arm. ". . . let it find you."

"Let what find me?" I demanded.

But she didn't answer because there was someone coming down the trail. She retreated to the door of the cabin and examined the hasp. "You'll see," she said. "Just don't fight it."

The voices grew louder and I went to her, grabbed her arm. "What the hell's going on here?—I don't wanna hear any shit about some *way* or philosophy. Your father's dying and he wants to see you. It's all we came for—don't you understand that?"

"You don't know my father," she said, pulling away. "It was foolish of you to come, especially now. They won't let you leave."

"Is that why you're locked up then, because you want to stay?"

She didn't answer, instead her eyes flicked toward the path.

I looked back to see Boothe standing, the sunlight at his back casting tall shadows across the field. There were two other men with him. They were young—no more than twenty-five. One had greasy blond hair and a long goatee. He was shirtless and shaking his head to keep the mosquitoes away. The other man had a dense curly black beard and was wearing a T-shirt, the front of which had a cartoon deer standing on two legs holding a shotgun. His nose was fight-crooked and he had broad linebacker shoulders.

The blond guy stepped forward, pulling at his goatee. As he got closer I could see his back and sides were heavily tattooed—drag-ons, chicks with big tits and swords. He flipped a butterfly knife out, his arms flashing in the sun, slick with bug dope as the other man stood watching, a rope coiled over his shoulder. It was the rope we'd left hanging off the cliff.

Boothe pointed the gun in my direction and remembering his thuggish negotiating tactics, I raised my hands above my head in surrender and looked to Penny. "What do you want me to do?"

She shook her head. "Help is coming."

"But . . ."

". . . learn or you will die. They'll show you a sign."

"Who?" I blurted.

She leaned over and quickly brushed her lips against the scab on my neck and kissed me. "The ones who know," she said.

They were on me then, grabbing my arms and separating us. I struggled until the tattooed one cuffed me on the neck. "Go easy, mate," he said, pressing the knife against my face. "I'll start punching holes, if you want."

I went limp and let them twist my arms behind my back.

"Penny?" Boothe said in his dead voice.

The dull, downcast expression quickly returned to her face. The girl in the photo was gone, but I'd seen her and knew I wasn't going to leave without her.

"I tried to stop him," she said flatly.

Boothe nodded and waited until she'd crept back into the cabin before turning to me. "Meet Tozer and Quinn," he said, pointing at the two men holding my arms vise tight.

Quinn, the shirtless one, smiled. His teeth were green and brown. He swung the knife shut, tucked it into his waist and gave me another cuff.

"Nothing personal," Tozer said. He was younger and his face, while weathered and obscured by beard, looked broad and friendly. Cleaned up, he could have been any college kid, backpack slung over his shoulder, dirty friendship bracelets corded around his ankles.

Quinn snorted and let out a high-pitched laugh as he swung on me, his fist stopping inches from my nose. On the back of his left hand FUCK 'EM ALL was inked in indigo.

"You like?" he said in a slight Australian accent.

When I didn't answer he swung again, catching me lightly on the chin.

Boothe started walking toward the trail and Tozer and Quinn muscled me for a while until I gave up and walked, waiting for one of them to peel off and lock Penny into the cabin, but they didn't and within minutes we were in the pines again.

•

In the daylight the whole camp looked different. I felt like a chain gang escapee who'd been tracked by hounds, captured and dragged back to face the music. Several campers stopped to watch, their faces giving nothing away.

On the lake there were two canoes. Nets flashed in and out of their green hulls with fish wriggling in them and every minute or so the thump of fish being clubbed echoed across the water.

Hawks and eagles canted across the gorge and I could see the brown outlines of moose feeding at the far end of the lake where the water turned into a tangled swamp that seemed to wend for miles into the distance. The sky was impossibly blue as was the lake. The high rock walls of the canyons were bleach white over the thrum of greenery and looking at them it seemed impossible that we had climbed down and lived.

As for the camp, it consisted of several small cabins set near the water's edge with the lodge-sized building in the center. The shack where we'd been locked up sat nestled in the woods next to three other similar structures. Hammocks had been strung in several places and what looked like car speakers were hung from the trees, their cords winding toward the lodge house.

There were people gathered around the lodge eating from bowls and sitting on crude picnic tables. Most of them were young and dressed in grimy clothes and heavy hiking boots. They reminded me of photos a friend of mine had taken during his hitch in the Peace Corps. He'd shown them to me trying to convince me that two years in some third-world country building bridges and toilets would be good for my soul. The people in the photos were young and dirty, but they had this strange indescribable glow, almost as if the trash-strewn village they were standing in was the greatest place on earth.

I recognized the woman with the scarred face from the night before. She was cleaning trout on a table. She was good with the knife, indifferent to its edge, trusting each slip and pull as she flicked offals into the bushes where ravens fought noisily over them. She looked up from her task and smiled, waving a bloody hand at me.

"Good morning," she said.

Quinn sneered and jostled me past, handing the coiled rope to Tozer.

Nunn was nowhere to be seen.

Instead of tossing me back into one of the detention shacks they muscled me through the camp and toward the lake. Quinn eventually let go and Tozer led me to a large bowl-shaped stone that sat at water's edge.

He motioned for me to sit. "It's okay," he said. "I'm not going to hurt you."

"Where's Burke?" I asked.

Quinn shot Tozer a look. "He'll be just fuckin' fine," Quinn said. "Now worry about yourself, mate."

"Take it easy," Tozer said.

Quinn scowled and watched as a woman appeared with a basin of hot water. She was slim and pretty in a beat-up sort of way. Her nose had been broken and her arms were covered with tattoos of flowers and chains. Around her neck hung a piece of gold.

She set the basin down on the stone and smiled at me.

"This is Lila," Tozer said.

She brushed a strand of hair from her face. "Thought you might want to clean up," she said, dropping a frayed washcloth into the water.

Quinn finally wandered off and exchanged words with Boothe

for a minute. Then Boothe turned and walked toward the house where we'd been taken to see Nunn.

I reached into the warm water for the washcloth, wrung it and rubbed it against my face and eyes until I could feel the fatigue of the last few days drain out of me.

"Are you hungry?" Lila asked.

I nodded.

"We can fix that too," she said, heading off toward the lodge.

I dabbed some water around the thick scab that had formed on my neck, remembering the flutter of Penny's brief kiss and her warning. I wondered if Tozer would be able to answer a few of my questions and waited for him to say something else.

I scrubbed until the scab loosened slowly and without looking in a mirror figured it would heal okay, but the split across the bridge of my nose would be with me for a while.

When I finished Tozer uncoiled the rope from his shoulder and dropped it at my feet. "You left this," he said. "Most people turn away when they miss the cave."

"We didn't know about the cave."

He grinned. "Fuckin'-A right, you didn't," he said. "So you climbed down, one of you knew what the hell you were doing."

"My buddy's the mountain climber."

"Really?" Tozer asked. "How many summits?"

"I don't know."

"I used to climb," he said. "Then I met Denali and it put me in my place. Humbled me big-time." He looked away, hands trembling.

Even during my brief time in Alaska I'd heard dozens of Denali stories. The mountain was impossible to avoid. On clear days it looked almost fake, the way it loomed in the sky like some white oxygenless planet.

"That was a while ago," he said. "Ancient history. Hell, nowadays anybody can climb it if they've got enough ching for guides. Ever since those assholes went and killed themselves on Everest, the tourists are lining up to call their friends from the summit on their cell phones. Me—I'm rootin' for the mountain to kill a few more dumb motherfuckers."

He laughed and eyed a line of people leaving the camp with tools slung over their shoulders.

"Where are they going?" I asked.

"Work."

"What sort of work?"

"Mostly mining. Some of them are on wood detail with Ogre or traplines."

"What about you?"

He smiled. "Today my job was to collect the newcomer before he hurt himself."

"What about Boothe?"

He checked over his shoulder before speaking. "In case you didn't notice, Boothe's not big on surprises," he said. "To be honest we thought you'd put up more of a fight than you did."

"Why's that?"

"It's a little late for tourists or stranded kayakers to be bumbling into camp so we thought maybe you were BLM, DNR—the jack-booted thugs, you know."

"You were expecting us?"

"Sanders spotted you on the cliff so Nunn sent Boothe."

"Sanders?"

"Don't worry about it," he said. "You'll get to know everybody if Nunn decides you can stay."

"But I thought there was no leaving this place."

He didn't answer. I hesitated, staring into the basin of dirty water. The washcloth had succeeded only in making me want to wash everything.

"Mind if I go for a swim?" I asked, pointing at the lake.

"It's colder than a polar bear's ass," he said.

"Do you swim in it?"

He nodded, grinning.

That was all I needed. I began stripping away my dirty clothes, placing them on the rock. "What if I kept swimming?"

"That would be up to you," he said. "The lake's bordered by swamp. Everybody calls it the Land of the Lost and unless you have a canoe and know where you're going it's easy to get lost and die in there. Me, I don't mess with it."

"No way out then?"

"If you're lucky you might make it to one of the Indian villages on the river and unless you've got whiskey I don't think they'd exactly throw you a warm Native American reception. But why would you want to do that?"

"Maybe I don't like having guns pointed at me."

"Hey, man, like I said, that's up to you," he said. "It would be stupid—but . . ."

I eyed him uneasily and walked to the water's edge. From the first touch I knew that there would be no wading in or easing myself under the surface. So I jumped. The cold forced the air out of my lungs and I let out a yell that made Tozer smile and wink. Plunging under again, I scrubbed furiously at the layer of grime and dead bugs. When I glanced at the shore I realized I was being watched by several people whose faces were white blurs against the green backdrop.

Finally the cold was too much and I splashed out of the water and sat panting on the rock, wishing the sun was hotter.

"You clean up pretty good," he said, grinning. "Next time you'll have to try the hot spring."

"What?" I said, shivering. "You mean?"

He laughed and nodded. "You didn't ask."

I liked Tozer and he didn't seem brainwashed or stirred in the head. In fact he seemed normal, like he was a traveler who'd discovered the lake and decided to stay. The more we spoke the harder it was to figure out my status in camp. I was no longer being held prisoner, but there was Penny's mention of help coming, the lock on her cabin, not to mention Boothe and Quinn.

"Can I ask some questions?"

He scanned the buildings nervously. "I know you've got questions and that's cool, but maybe you should see for yourself."

"See what?"

"Everything in time," he said. "It's Jack, right?"

"Yeah," I said.

We shook and he pulled me close and whispered. "You're being watched because not everybody's cool with you being allowed to roam. Understand?"

"So it's some sort of test to see how I behave?"

"If you wanna call it that, sure," he said, letting loose my hand. "The alternative is to go back to the detention shacks and have Boothe watch over you."

"I prefer this."

He smiled. "Solid, man, because I'm not in the mood to go chasing after you."

Lila returned with a wool blanket and a bowl of food. "Moose stew with chanterelles?" she said, setting the bowl on the rock and draping the blanket over me. The blanket smelled of campfire and fresh cedar as I huddled under it, still shivering from my plunge in the lake.

I ate the stew quickly, barely tasting it. "Good," I said, pointing at the bowl.

"You can thank Gant when you meet him," Lila said cheerfully. She'd moved next to Tozer and laced a thin arm around his waist.

"Gant?"

"He's the cook and lucky for us his personality doesn't affect his cooking."

I stood and eyed the pile of filthy clothes, not wanting to put them on. The sun had started to warm the stones under my feet and the stew sat like a punch in my stomach, making me feel sleepy.

Tozer and Lila whispered to each other and began walking slowly away from me.

"What now?" I called out to them.

He turned and Lila kept walking toward the lodge.

"Whatever you want," he said. "You might wanna find some clean clothes."

"I thought maybe you were going to lock me up or something."

"If you want I can lock you up," he said.

They left and I began rinsing out my dirty clothes on a

rock, beating them like I'd seen women in third-world countries do.

A string of fish guts washed ashore and lay glistening on the damp pebbles like some small dead alien. Voices echoed across the water, but when I looked I saw no one.

I wrung out the last of my clothes, set them to dry on a series of large flat stones and wandered the camp, blanket wrapped around my waist.

Behind the lodge I noticed the dogs, massive half-wolf-looking things. They were all over the camp: crouched under porches, sprawled next to woodpiles and glowering from muddy warrens in the heavy brush that skirted the entire clearing.

Between buildings one of the dogs broke away from the pack and followed. It was thin and had a thick collar of salt-colored fur that tapered to gray then black at its enormous paws. It looked hungry enough to kill and I tried not to tense up or show the dog that it was making me nervous.

I kept walking past the tents toward the small shack where we'd been held the night before, hoping I'd discover the whereabouts of Burke. The first shack was empty as were the others. The dog was still behind me as I headed toward the building where we'd met Nunn. The cabin looked smaller and more dilapidated than I remembered. The roof buckled in places and bright pink insulation had been stuffed around the door frame to keep the draft out. Even the porch stones were cracked.

I knocked and when there was no answer I tried the door but it was latched shut.

The dog stayed ten paces behind letting out faint whines. Twice I turned around and tried to shoo it away but it only flattened its ears and pawed at the ground as I made my way back to the lodge.

Attached to the side of the lodge was a crude greenhouse strung with Visqueen that snapped and popped in the wind coming off the lake. I pressed my face against the plastic and could make out two rows of raised planting beds and dozens of five-gallon buckets holding tomato plants. Most of the vines were brown and withered already and only a few of them had any fruit on them.

On the other side of the greenhouse was a large open door leading to the kitchen. The place reeked like some foul stew of rotten fish and wet fur. There was a bucket of freshly gutted trout on a table. The floor was filthy with wilted vegetables, dirty rice, flour, mouse shit and bloodstains. Several fly-choked garbage cans sat overflowing with animal bones and fish heads. Long stainless-steel-topped tables lined the walls. Pots and pans were scattered all over the place and dozens of well-cured cast-iron skillets hung from spikes set in the log walls above two large woodstoves. In front of one of them was a wiry man bent over a steaming pot. His arms were thin and pale and covered with small red grease burns. What little hair he had was plastered down the back of his neck in a long greasy blond curl.

He looked at me, nodded and then went back to the pot.

"If your name's Gant—thanks for the stew," I said, rattling the empty bowl and setting it on the counter.

"You the new guy?" he asked, his forehead shiny with sweat and grease. "Semper Fi" was tattooed in blurred ink on his right arm and he was missing a front tooth.

"Jack," I said.

"You'll be sick of moose in a week," he cackled. "Then fish too. Then the cold, the snow and whatever else you wanna piss and moan about—welcome to paradise lost, pilgrim." His head twitched a few times, and he scratched at a scab on his elbow with the back of a knife.

I smiled.

"That wasn't a joke," he said, stepping away from the stove. "Bowl goes over there and unless you wanna work stay out of the kitchen, stay outta my way and we'll get along like Fred and Ginger."

I shrugged and walked back outside. The dog was immediately at my side pushing its nose into my hand until I reflexively stroked it a few times.

"You hungry?" I asked.

The dog nudged my hand again and flicked its tongue between my fingers.

"Okay, okay," I said.

I ducked back inside the kitchen and making sure Gant's attention was focused on the stove, snatched several half-eaten portions of stew off one of the tables. I scraped them together and set it down in front of the dog, who gulped the bowl clean and then sat back on its haunches staring at me, wanting more. I stroked its strong neck, feeling the hard rope of muscles hidden under the fur.

"She's yours now," I heard a voice say.

I stopped petting the dog and looked up to see the woman I'd spotted earlier come around the corner. She was wiping her hands on a stained towel and smiling. Her hair was gray with just a shadow of straw blond beneath. She reminded me of one of those slightly crunchy older women who hung around health food stores posting drum circle flyers and ordering bulk millet. But it was her eyes that drew my attention. They were bright and full of something I couldn't quite place.

"This one's been trouble since it showed up," she said, pointing at the dog. "She won't take a sled harness and she likes to fight."

"Where'd she come from?"

"Oh," she said. "There's a couple of dog mushers in the area and every year they cut a few dogs loose. It's either that or shoot them. And if they don't go wild, sooner or later they find their way here or to one of the Indian villages upriver. Sanders keeps his own pack. It's all one big circle of life."

She smiled dreamily as if she'd been momentarily transported somewhere else.

I took my hand off the dog's head for a minute only to have it press its nose to my hand again.

"If you want her, she's yours," she said. "She can be your reason for coming. But when winter arrives you can feed her if she still don't want to take a harness."

I looked at her again.

"Grace," she said, holding out a hand for me to shake. "My name's Grace."

Her hand was small and dry like snake skin.

"Jack," I said.

"Do you want some clothes?" she asked, pointing at the blanket. "You look like some kind of holy man with that blanket."

"That would be good," I said.

"The clothes or you being a holy man?"

"Dry clothes," I said as she stared past me at some noise coming from the kitchen. "I was looking for my friend."

"They're out searching for him now."

"But . . ."

"Don't worry about him," she said. "He'll come out when he gets tired of hiding."

"Maybe I should help."

A worried look crossed her face. "It's being taken care of," she said. "You should work—help the camp at least until your friend is found."

"Is that what I'm supposed to do?"

"You can do whatever you want but sooner or later the others will grumble about you not pulling your weight. It's how we do things here."

I agreed before I realized how tired I was.

She smiled brightly. "Follow me," she said, leading me into a narrow cabin lined with cots. Bedrolls lay crumpled on the floor in a circle around a large wood-burning stove that dominated the space. She motioned me over to a pile of garbage bags stuffed with clothes and rummaged around, setting out a pair of stiff jeans, a work shirt and a pair of heavy wool socks.

"What happened to our packs?"

She ignored me. "These oughtta fit you," she said, tossing them at me.

She turned and I dropped the blanket, pulling the clothes on quickly, feeling human again.

"I liked the blanket better," she said, spinning around. "Now you look like an ordinary, average, everyday, earthbound man."

The dog was waiting outside the cabin and fell in step behind us, closing the distance every once in a while to bump my hand with its nose.

"What are you going to call her?" she asked as we left the circle of buildings and entered the woods. "She has to have a name if she's going to be yours."

I knelt before the dog, studying the narrow wolflike pinch of her muzzle, the gray eyes flecked with yellow and the powerful neck tapering into her chest.

"Lassie," I said to the dog. "How about that?"

Grace looked back, said something I couldn't hear and kept walking. I followed. She led me over a few low hills to a graveyard of large rocks and boulders that looked as if they'd fallen from the cliffs. Chain saws buzzed in the distance, axes thudded in an uneven cadence and I thought I saw a figure high on the canyon wall, but when I looked again it was gone.

Grace went over to the tumble of rocks and began pulling out wooden crates and spools of wire. The crates were full of leghold traps, basket snares and whiplike noose snares which she held up in a tangled ball.

"Put these on," she said, handing me a pair of stiff, grime-covered leather gloves. "We keep them out here so they don't get people smells on them," she explained.

I nodded and watched her unpack a dozen more crates from under the rock shelf each with larger and more vicious-looking traps in them.

"The snares are for rabbits. We start now for winter," she said, rattling a crate of small spring traps. "Number 1 jumps for marten, and these"—she held several large rusty traps by their chains—"are for fox, bobcat, coyote and wolf."

"What about the dogs?" I asked.

"Every once in a while, yes," she said. "It's my least favorite part of the job—a small unpleasant thing. But you get used to the killing. I know that sounds bad, but ten years ago if you would have told me I'd be setting snares and clubbing bobcat I would have told you you were crazy. But now I guess it seems normal because it's what the country calls for."

"Killing?"

"If you want to survive," she said, sounding oddly bright and cheerful. "It's tough country, even in the summer, but winter's when everything we didn't do in the summer comes back to haunt us—it's why we work and prepare."

"But I'm outta here before the first snow," I said.

She sighed and smiled at me without answering as if the very thought that I wasn't in the camp for the long haul was crazy. She busied herself with arranging the traps and wire coils on the rock and after several minutes she looked up from the empty crates. "Are you ready?" she asked.

I nodded.

She worked quickly, her hands moving sure and deliberate among the steel traps as she showed me how to hang them in pairs for weathering and how I should handle them with a Y-shaped stick of pine. On some of the larger traps she greased the springs, mended broken chains and rubbed them with this foul-smelling concoction she kept in sealed Mason jars.

After countless trips into the woods with traps at the end of the stick, Grace nodded with approval and rewarded my efforts with small talk about the camp.

When I finished, hands reeking of the rotten bait and scent masker, Grace tapped the bundled wire. "Snares," she said, deftly peeling back the plastic insulation. She twisted and knotted the wire, working quickly with a pair of snips until a long oval noose began to take shape.

"See," she said, putting her hand through the hoop and pulling on the tag end until the wire cinched quickly and smoothly around her wrist, gathering the flesh in a bright red ruffle. "The heavier the animal, the deeper the cut. The key is to make the hoop slide smoothly, that way they don't feel it and keep going until it's too late."

She loosened the wire and began again with a fresh length, slower this time, and after a dozen or so I got the hang of it, losing myself in the simple repetition of twists and knots, the slick wire forming crude, inelegant nooses.

When they were done she handed me a match and pointed at a small tepee of green cedar boughs.

"Light it," she said.

The minute the twigs and pine needles caught fire and began to smolder she held each snare over the blaze until the bright copper turned black. Then she handed them to me to hang from a nearby branch. I kept pace, falling into the ritual of trap preparation as she talked.

She was not exactly forthcoming, but by the time we'd plunged into the woods to set some of the snares and test my craftsmanship, I'd begun to get an idea of what sort of place Burke had led me to. According to Grace, almost every person had reason for having left their lives and coming to live in the camp.

I asked her if they were running away from something.

"Some," she said. "But not everybody. We're here because of what we can learn about ourselves and what he can show us, that is, if we are open and receptive."

"Are you talking about Nunn?"

She nodded. "He's the one that makes this place special," she said, smiling. "Come on, it's easier if I just show you. That way you don't go jumping to any unfair conclusions about our valley."

"You mean I get the guided tour?"

"Sure," she said, pointing left, down an overgrown trail. "We'll set snares while we're at it."

I followed her down trails, snares out in front of me on a stick as we crossed fields, boggy creek beds, low rocky outcroppings and sudden clearings in the forest. The other campers seemed to materialize out of nowhere, working or on their way to a job. Everybody was responsible for some detail in the camp. Some fished, others cut and hauled wood—an endless job and according to Grace the most dangerous. The loggers were led by a large chunk of muscle named Ogre who had some unpronounceable Polish name. He'd been dishonorably discharged from the army and was missing two fingers on his left hand.

Two Canadians whom everybody sarcastically called Lewis and Clark maintained trails and hunted. There was of course the kitchen, which meant you had to work with Gant, not the camp's most talkative or friendly inhabitant. Two hippie girls, Jenny and Veronica, helped Gant cook, manage the small greenhouse and watch the food stores for signs of mold or mice infestation. Jenny had dropped out of Reed College to follow a third-rate carnival around the Pacific Northwest, where she'd met Veronica. Veronica was strong and sinewy. She had a gap between her teeth, tons of soft brown hair and eyes rimmed with dark, sexy circles.

Ralph and Mary gathered berries, mushrooms and other edibles from the woods. Before coming to the camp, they'd spent time in a community near Brasília after Ralph had quit his job as an EMT in Chicago. He was tall and lean with a heavily creased forehead and a ring of gray curls around his bald head. He had a thick, gnarled fighter's nose and calm blue eyes. Mary looked sick, her skin stretched tight over her bones, lips chapped and cracked, eyes sludgy as if she'd just woken from a nap.

At the creek Grace introduced me to the miners.

The head prospector was a thin man named Shipley who looked like some sourdough version of Rasputin. He had a long black beard and walked with a monkeylike stoop, skittering over stones to check pans, unexpectedly dropping to the ground every so often to examine tailings. He rattled two stones in his mud-stained hands like dice as he gave me a tour of the operation, mumbling and pointing and then stopping every so often to watch my reaction.

He explained that there was a small creek that fed both the swamp and the lake. It had yielded a fair amount of gold already, but most of the group's efforts were focused on the cave where they'd discovered a vein of gold. The cave wasn't much more than a crack in the cliff wall. I took one look and decided it was a miracle that there hadn't been a cave-in yet. Water seeped from soft earthen walls, rock ledges hung cracked and propped up by stripped pine limbs.

"Inviting, isn't it?" Shipley said, rocks clacking in his palms.

"Is that the cave that leads out of the valley?"

Grace shook her head, gaze narrowing. "Maybe later when Nunn says it's okay somebody'll show it to you," she said.

I nodded.

"What about the jugs?"

She smiled. "So you saw those?"

"Yes."

"They were Nunn's idea. Used to be whenever we came back to the camp we would write down all that we were leaving behind on a scrap of paper and drop it into the jug. Nobody ever does it anymore."

Shipley, who'd been fiddling with a screening box nearby, looked over at us and said, "Wants out already, does he, Grace?"

I started to shake my head when I spotted a small jar sitting on a rock. It was the same kind of jar we'd pulled from the man on the river.

"Is that gold?" I asked, coming closer.

He snatched it off the rock and held it to the sun for me to see. "Lookin' at our gold, askin' about the cave. Hey, Grace, who's gonna vouch for this one?" He winked at me. "Lighten up, I'm just messin' with you."

I tried smiling, but it came out all wrong. "It's gold, right?"

"This here's a week's worth of work," he said.

"Funny, it doesn't look like much," I said.

"People kill over this," he said, grinning. "It's not the same as money. It's gold and the only way you find something like that is to work for it—go looking in the creeks, move tons of rocks, just to see that glitter, and when you do it's all over, man, 'cause it grabs hold of you and you're doomed. Hell, I can still remember my first nugget."

"You mean gold fever?" I said.

"It's deeper than that," he said, pausing to look at the jar. "But that's not why I do it. Not now at least. It's just work, plain and simple work that's good for the camp. You know what work is?"

It was the kind of question that I would have been a fool to answer so I looked off at a pile of rocks and waited for Grace to move toward the path.

He was setting the jar down when I realized that if they had our packs, they must have found the jar of gold Burke took from the man. More troubling was the fact that nobody had said a word about it.

Grace bent over Shipley and whispered something in his ear that caused him to smile and nod.

"What's the matter?" she said.

"Nothing," I said, looking away from the jar.

She eyed me and then began walking toward the trail.

I caught up to her. Every fifty yards or so we stopped to set snares where the heavy thicket of brush parted, forming a natural funnel, or at the edges of small breaks in the trees where tender grass had managed a spot of green.

My job was to search the surrounding area for a short stick to anchor the snare and then sprinkle the area with dry grass and pine needles. It was quiet work and as I staked the snares I tried to imagine a rabbit wandering through the small coil and hanging itself.

I asked her about Boothe again and she sighed, pausing to hang the remaining snares on a birch branch. After a long silence she said, "Ask me another question."

It was a game.

Right questions were rewarded with information, wrong ones with silence and uncomfortable stares.

"Okay," I said. "Does Tozer work with Boothe?"

"Balance," she said. "Everything we do here is for balance or at least it used to work that way. Until . . ."

"Until what?"

"Well, the bear and what happened to him."

"Nunn?"

"And the others," she said. "Things sort of tipped over, but now we're working to change all that. Make a fresh start and the most important thing I can tell you is that work is very important around here. Find a job and you'll find your place. Would you like that, Jack—would you like to help us?"

"Help with what?"

"The camp," she said, laughing lightly and pointing at the sky and trees, like some kind of game show host on lithium. "You get out what you put in. That's the beauty of this place. The rest of the world's not like that."

"I don't plan on staying that long," I said, trying not to sound too irritated.

Her eyes narrowed, the smile faded. She looked old and tired. "You'll stay."

"After the welcome we got?"

"You've got to understand that under normal circumstances that would have never happened. We thought . . ." She turned and squinted until the finely etched scars turned a deep ruby. ". . . I mean there's been trouble and winter's coming."

"So?"

"So when the two of you came down the cliff, carrying a picture of Penny and a letter from her father, naturally we panicked, but you must understand it was for the camp—to protect all the work we've done since the bear."

"But Boothe didn't give us a chance."

"He's not supposed to," she said. "When Sanders first alerted the camp that we had visitors we thought you were DNR or maybe the state police." She leaned in whispering, "Some of this is state land."

I looked at her. "Is there something to hide?"

She ignored the question and busied herself with setting a snare. Wind rattled the birch leaves, momentarily lifting the cloud of mosquitoes hovering between us.

"Okay, why are you here?" I asked.

"The simple answer, I suppose, is to get away from everything, escape the world, whatever that means," she said. "Others have different reasons and I suspect only Nunn knows them all. The thing about the camp is that in some way it *finds* you. Does that make sense?"

"No," I said.

"I don't expect you to believe anything, Jack," she said in a motherly tone. "You wanted to see the camp and I showed it to you. Other than the work I don't know what you want me to tell you. It changes, just like anything that's good. Some days I want to leave, pack my bags and live a normal life—move back to Ann Arbor, see my family. But then I catch the sun coming up over the cliffs and the air's so fresh it seems almost alive and I don't ever think I can leave here. Before Nunn found me I'd managed to mess up my life pretty good. I was good with the bad stuff, but normal, everyday life—forget it, I was horrible with people and selfish, caught up in my own little rackets. But then Nunn invited me to come with him and things started to change—deep inside." She pounded her chest with a fist. "There was only a few of us and the first winter was hard on me, but I did it, I mean, I made it through. Then summer rolled around and he brought others and I suppose it felt like a family, then after a while it was my family and maybe that's how things are supposed to be. Can you understand that?"

I nodded.

"What about Penny?" I asked. "Why is she locked in that cabin?"

She put a dry hand on my arm. "Because she's safer there."

"Safe from what?"

"All I can tell you is that Penny brought this on herself," she said. "Nobody forced her to stay, not here or anywhere else. Everybody's free here, Jack."

I looked at her.

"Everybody," she repeated.

She hoisted the snares and started to walk again. Question time was over; I'd been shown what I was supposed to be shown and still none of it made much sense. The people seemed happy. They weren't zonked or babbling about UFOs or some other shit—just Grace and her *everybody's free* line. It still all came down to Nunn, how he was pulling the strings and to what design.

Ten minutes later we were back at the camp. Tozer and Lila were gone and I didn't see Burke. Everybody else had gathered around the lodge house, sitting on log ends and eating. Scanning the unfamiliar faces I tried placing names with the stories Grace had told me, hoping some pattern would emerge.

I grabbed a bowl of food from Jenny and mingled. Grace kept

nearby, always listening, interrupting when I asked about the cave or Burke. I talked and ate, my head muzzy from lack of sleep, each face blending into the other.

Nunn appeared down by the lake and huddled with a few people. They scattered when I got close enough to recognize Quinn and Lewis and Clark. Nunn vanished into the woods and I went back to the lodge, Lassie two steps behind me like a shadow.

I stood there listening. The slightly blighted expression and numb empty tone of the campers reminded me of a group of Rainbow Children I'd run into in Colorado. I was on my way to a job in Seattle, driving cross-country, when I stopped at a rest stop. There was a camper van giving away free coffee and Peaceable Kingdom pamphlets. I got out, took a piss and stretched my legs. I hadn't shaved in days and my ears were still ringing with the Hüsker Dü and X tapes I kept on full blast to help me eat up the road. I started watching this old man walking his small dog in the field behind the parking lot. He was smoking a filter-tipped cigar and staring at a van full of dirty, slack-haired girls and shirtless guys. They had camping gear spread all over the warm pavement, drying. I started watching them too, a little road lonely from all the miles, when all of a sudden one of the girls strolled barefoot across the stained parking lot toward me, smiling. From a distance she looked sexy. The sun was in her hair and the wind kept blowing her skirt open. I thought maybe the faded bandanna I'd wrapped around my head to keep the sweat and hair out of my eyes had marked me as one of them or maybe she too was lonely. I could smell patchouli and hear the faint sound of the charm bells she wore on her ankles. But as she got close I saw that her face was pocked with large black sores, her neck was lined with dirt rings and under the sweet patchouli lay the sour odor of someone who hadn't bathed in a long while.

I let the smile go and folded my arms across my chest.

"Hey," she said, moving closer. "Are you going to the gathering?" Her teeth were yellow with black peppery spots on them.

"What gathering?" My voice sounded strange after three days of not talking to anybody.

She frowned, drifted a finger down my forearm and despite her grubby appearance I found myself getting aroused. One of the shirtless guys glared at me. He was talking to a dreadlocked dude dressed only in chinos and combat boots.

She leaned closer. "The Rainbow gathering," she said. "We heard it was in Winter Park. You hear that too?"

She removed her finger from my arm and scratched at a spot on her neck. I peered into her eyes and realized that she was tripping on something because I couldn't see much pupil and she kept smiling and rolling her eyes as she spoke.

"No," I said. "What is it?"

"I need a ride," she whispered. "Is that cool because these people I'm with are like no good—it's just too much tension for me—so *not* what I need now, so I'm like looking for some other way to the gathering. How about you?"

Just then one of the guys approached. He was young, his skin tanned and dirty and he was wearing a large red-and-white-striped Cat in the Hat top hat with a peace sign embroidered on the brim. He looked right through me and grabbed her by the arm. "Let's go, Cinda, he doesn't wanna buy any," he hissed. "Are you stupid or something?"

I put a hand on his shoulder and squeezed until Cat in the Hat let her go and turned on me. "Not cool," he said. "Not cool at all, you fuckin' Nazi!"

Dreadlocks came over and started snorting, laughing, snot running from his nose.

I wanted to swing at Cat in the Hat, but stopped when I saw that his fingers were wrapped around a knife that was laced to his belt in a homemade-looking buckskin sheath.

The girl started to shout frantically like a drowning person. "Peace! Peace!"

And the commotion caused the old man who'd been walking his dog to tottle over, the dog barking and strained at its leash.

She suddenly stopped shouting.

"See!" Cat in the Hat said, grabbing the girl. "Just stay out of this, right? Live and let live or . . ."

"Or what?" I said, raising both hands and giving the girl a look that said I was sorry.

"Or maybe I do something you're not going to like," he said, pulling the knife halfway from the sheath.

I backed off. A knife was as far as my Good Samaritan intervention would go. Cat in the Hat leaned over her and whispered something that made her smile and then giggle into her hand.

I knew I was probably being mocked.

"Thanks," she said, too stoned to realize that we'd almost come to blows over her. "I just thought you were one of us, one of the children. My mistake, peace, okay?"

She skipped away and crawled back into the van, taking a seat next to the other girls.

I watched them until the old man walked over, shaking his head in disapproval. There were cracks in his shoes and his shirt was missing a few buttons. He looked at me, hands trembling, and said, "Do you have a personal relationship with Jesus?"

I shook my head, still trying to make my mind up about the girl.

Across the lot Dreadlocks squealed, laughing with Cat in the Hat.

"Do you want to have a personal relationship with Jesus Christ our Lord and Savior?" the old man repeated, bolder now. "I can help you with the lack, the hunger deep down in your soul, because you look like a nice young man—a man ready for positive change."

I tried to walk away from him, toward the van, but he followed, dog snapping.

"I have materials you might like to read, written by learned men, biblical scholars." He was nearly yelling. "Men of vision who have insight into how things will be in the new Kingdom. You need to know the signs and prepare for the Rapture—"

I whirled around, snarling, still thinking about the girl and her laugh. "—I don't know what the fuck you're talking about."

The dog lunged at me and the old man seemed to shrink down

into his clothes. He put his old eyes on me, burning holes, accusing and judging until he was just this used-up thing between me and her and the road.

He began quoting Bible verse as I walked back to my truck. The van pulled out, tires screeching, tailpipe scraping the pavement like a fingernail on a chalkboard. I saw her for a brief moment in the window, waving at me.

I waited a few minutes before following them, keeping a good distance. The anger drained away and I was left wondering about the gathering and the way her finger had traced its way down my sunburned arm. The skin still tingled and I entertained little fantasies about cleaning her up, taking her to Seattle with me and then . . .

It was the first time I'd seen some pulse under America; a glimpse into a world below the daily grind and green grass suburban sprawl that I'd known all my life and for some reason I remembered the story my father had told me about the tiger in the jungle and how he'd let it slip away, unharmed.

Two hours later the van stopped for gas at a busy truck plaza. I followed, parking behind a line of idling tractor trailers and waiting until Cat in the Hat and two others had gone inside to pay for the gas.

A short-haired woman ran out of the van and skipped toward the rest room. Then I saw her. She emerged from the van, rubbed her eyes at the bright sun and went over to a large trash can with something cradled in her shirt.

I went to her. The cement between us was dotted with old gum and gasoline stains. Wind danced trash past us, stranding it in the thistle near the median.

"Remember me?" I asked.

She looked up, pupils shrunk to pinheads. She smelled like dope. "Huh?"

"You okay?"

"Come again . . . I hear you talking, but . . ." Her words trailed off.

"I want to know if you still need that ride. We could go right now, before they come back."

She went back to staring at the trash can where a clot of hornets were swarming over a glob of dried ketchup and a half-empty Coke bottle.

"Do you know where you are?" I asked.

She gazed at me with those eyes. Under the dirt and tangled hair I saw a college girl who'd had one bad trip too many, fell in with the wrong crowd and just started drifting. Or maybe she'd never been to college—a job dropping fries at McDonald's, little shoplifting here and there, some drugs, older men, one thing leading to another. And now this. She was lost and maybe somewhere deep down inside she knew it and wanted to do something about it.

"Yes," she said, rubbing her nose against the back of her fist until it came away wet with snot.

"But you're okay, right?" I paused. "I mean . . . my truck's right over there." I pointed, but she didn't follow my finger.

One of the other girls yelled out the window. "Cinda, stop feeding the animals and get back in here before Seth sees you!"

She smiled. "I'm okay," she said, coming close again. "I'm just nowhere, it's cool, really, peace, okay?" She flashed me the sign.

I turned to go but Cat in the Hat and his buddies had emerged from the store and were coming at me quickly. Before they reached me she tossed a crumpled photograph into the trash, disturbing the hornets. It was a Polaroid of her in a graduation cap and gown, standing with her parents. Then she skipped toward the van and got in. Cat in the Hat pulled his knife and watched as I walked back behind the line of tractor trailers, the heat from their engines and smell of diesel exhaust comforting me long after I was on the road driving toward the setting sun and a new job.

•

After I'd finished eating, Grace led me past the lodge to a small canvas tent. Only Ogre smiled and gave me a wave with his gnarled logger's hands as I left the group.

I smiled and waved back.

"You can sleep here," Grace said, pointing at the tent. "Nobody's using this one anymore."

Without another word I crawled inside. Several hornets buzzed against the canvas as I kicked my boots off and fell onto the crusty sleeping bag. The air coming in through the open flap was crisp and smelled of wet stones. Outside I could hear voices and the sound of the lake and for a moment I thought I heard music, but it faded as I drifted into a thick sludgy trance that promised sleep.

•

When I woke a couple of hours later the camp was glowing with long-shadowed midnight sun. There were people outside talking over the lap and ruffle of the lake. Two dead hornets lay on the floor inches from my nose. My first thoughts were to get the guns—find the cabin, take Penny and force her to show me the caves.

But Burke was still out there somewhere.

I rose stiffly, crawled out of the tent and sat on a log outside, pulling on shoes. The dog padded over and licked my hand until I stroked her, scratching behind her ears. There was a group of people huddled on the lodge house porch and Boothe sat by himself on a log, the shotgun cradled in his lap, zoned-out look on his face.

The sleep had done wonders for my legs and the stuffy feeling in my head. I felt strong and clearheaded and much better about my prospects of getting out of the camp as soon as I could find Burke.

Tozer peeled away from the group on the porch and approached me with a smile.

"Take a walk?" he asked.

I nodded and followed him as he reached down to give Lassie a pat on the shoulders.

"Looks like you've been adopted."

"Meet Lassie," I said.

"Lassie?" He laughed and we began walking toward the lake.

At the water's edge he grabbed a few rocks and sailed them into the blue before speaking. "Your friend hasn't turned up, Jack."

"Yeah?"

"Well, we took a vote and decided maybe you should help us

find him." He paused and side-armed a few more rocks into the water. "Between you and me the only thing stopping Boothe from finding him with extreme prejudice is Nunn."

"Where is Nunn?"

"He's around," he said, looking back at the group on the porch. "It's better this way if you go."

"You think he's gonna come out from wherever he's hiding just because I'm looking for him?"

He shook his head. "No, man, it's just that a few of the others are into testing your loyalty."

"Loyalty to what?"

"The camp," he said.

"Why?"

"Take it from someone who's been all over, this is one of the last unfucked-up places you're going to find. It's too remote for the timber and oil companies to get their grubby paws on it and no way the National Park Service is going to be bussing tourists in here to stare at grizzlies anytime soon."

"Why are you telling me this?"

"Because if you were looking, you found it."

"I wasn't looking for anything," I said, slightly confused by his sudden enthusiasm.

"Well this is it, Jack, off the grid. Paradise. Middle of fucking nowhere. Shangri-la. The Golden Bough or the end of the line," he shouted. "Now come on and let's go find this friend of yours."

He led me over to the group, introduced me around again. Lewis and Clark said they were coming too. They looked at Quinn, who glared at us for a moment from his perch on the railing and then stalked off toward Boothe, who was still sitting with his gun looking at the lake.

"You're going like that, eh?" Clark sniffed.

"Like what?"

Lewis tossed me a bottle of bug dope. "Ya might want to put a hat on and lace them shoes."

Tozer rolled his eyes and I bent down and reluctantly laced up my waterlogged boots while Clark produced two rifles, an old well-oiled Marlin .30-06 and a bolt-action Savage .30-30. He handed the Savage to Lewis, who chambered a round and checked the scope before slipping the strap over his shoulder.

"What are the guns for?" I asked.

"The woods," Clark said. "And maybe your friend if he gives us any trouble."

I tried to grab the gun from Clark but Tozer jumped between us.

"Just relax," Tozer said, pulling me aside. "Nobody's gonna shoot anything. They always carry guns—they hunt for the camp—kill things, right?"

Lewis winked at me, made a gun out of his finger and pointed. I ignored him, grabbed the bug dope and doused my bare skin.

We set out along the path. Tozer trailed behind, walking slowly, while Clark fell in beside me and began telling me his life story.

He was thirty years old and from Calgary, where he'd played semipro baseball. He was the local golden boy until he injured his shoulder, got hooked on painkillers and dropped out. He took a job as a seeder for a logging company and discovered he liked being in the woods so much that cities began to make him nervous.

"My two loves, eh," he said. "Baseball and drugs. And I had to give them both up. Know how it is?"

"What about hockey?" I said. "I thought all Canadians loved hockey. Gretzky . . ."

"Fuck hockey," he said.

"Even Gretzky?"

"Fuck Gretzky."

I nodded, remembering what Grace had told me about people having their reasons for being at the camp, but Clark seemed a little overzealous and Canadian, though normal.

I asked him about Lewis.

"Guided in the Cascades," Clark said. "Best woodsman I've ever known and probably the only one in the camp who could survive, all things being equal."

I tilted my head at him.

"No generators," he explained. "No gas, no gold, just the

woods and whatever ya can get out of it. Like the old days—Lewis would not only survive, he'd conquer, eh?"

Lewis looked back at us, frowned, made a fist and pointed it down. It was a signal to Clark, who nodded and readjusted his gun to the crook of his arm.

"How did he end up here?" I asked.

"Got sick of it all," Clark said. "I guess he got sick of taking rich American assholes fishing and hunting, cleaning their kills, making sure they got what they'd come for and seeing to it that they didn't have to touch the dead things except with a fork and knife over a bottle of wine."

Tozer slapped at a deerfly and muttered something under his breath.

Lewis doubled back, gun out in front of him.

"That's all he needs to know," Lewis growled at Clark.

Then he turned and started eyeballing me. "You know she'll turn on you," he said, pointing at the dog.

Lassie licked my hand as if she knew we were talking about her.

"Drop it, Lewis," Clark said.

But he continued. "The wolf takes over—ya never know when or why but it'll happen. Mark my words."

"I'll take my chances," I said as Tozer stepped between us.

"We get the point," Tozer said, pushing Lewis away. "No need to impress the new guy. Everybody knows you're the last of the fuckin' Mohicans—certified Canadian badass."

Lassie growled and pressed her shoulders against my leg.

"Everybody just take it easy," Clark said. "Come on, Lew, let's find this guy, eh?"

Lewis shook his head and pushed past us, taking the lead, branches snapping back in his wake.

After he'd disappeared around a bend in the trail I turned to Tozer. "What was that all about?" I asked

He looked over his shoulder before speaking. "Nothing, just let it go," he said. "They're the camp hard-asses and all the killing has gone to their heads. Watch them, though, those dudes are not to be trusted. I'll fill you in later."

I nodded, not sure what he meant, and followed the Canadians deeper into the valley where they stopped to examine broken branches and talk in quiet tones.

The sun hovered low in the sky, still bright when it poked through the dense canopy of cedar and willow and the towering cliffs overhead. Birds shifted through the trees in front of us and ground squirrels scampered in our wake like children.

The trail topped out on a small rise overlooking a clump of yellow aspens. I stared at the aspen leaves, glinting yellow and gold in the fading light, and knew fall was coming, knew that the sun was working against the land, setting nine minutes earlier each day, eating up the midnight sun until the whole valley would be plunged into cold and darkness. If anybody else noticed the yellow and gold leaves they didn't say a word. I knew that I didn't want to be in the valley when the snow started to fall.

Once Lewis and Clark were out of earshot Tozer resumed his talk about the camp and I began to suspect that the real reason he'd asked me to look for Burke was for the chance to peel away from the rest of the group and recount the sudden turn of events that had taken place since spring.

Until the bear Nunn acted as a sort of father figure—an old hippie with a trust fund who'd discovered the lake and bought it in parcels from a wilderness guide who'd gone belly-up.

"There was almost nothing here, man," Tozer said. "Couple a small shacks, a falling-down dock. It was raw, lots of fish and animals and not much else. But he had a plan to build the last good place before the tourists overran the state and killed it with their 4x4s and Polaroids, so he had supplies coptered in and began building cabins with a ragtag crew of volunteers."

He stopped walking and stared at me a good long while through the haze of bugs before continuing.

"Every year he'd talk another person into coming with him for the summer," he said. "All he promised was hard work and a chance to get away from it all. From what I heard this place was full of dropouts, fry brains, paranoid radicals and people in trouble. Not everybody stuck or worked out, but every year a few more stayed and it grew."

"That's it?" I asked.

He stopped to pluck a pale yellow leaf from a branch. He tore it to pieces and let the pieces fall from his hand.

"Depends what you mean," he said. "That's what I know and what I've been told and unless you haven't already noticed this ain't exactly the place to be askin' a lot of questions."

"What about Nunn?"

He squinted. "Before the bear, when I first came here, he was different. Hell, this whole place was different. He talks and you want to listen, does that sound weird?"

I told him no.

"Well," he said, stopping to swat mosquitoes, "we took walks and he explained certain things to me that made a lot of sense."

"Like?"

"Fuck it, I'm just not doing it any justice. He's got this whole rap on the way things should be and how people spend all this energy fucking things up, creating problems. Coming from him it sounds a helluva lot better."

"I still don't get it," I said. "You mean he counsels you."

Tozer nodded.

"About what?"

"All the stuff you waste your time on, I guess," he said. "Don't look so disappointed, Jack. What did you think was going on?"

"I don't know, something else, maybe."

He smiled. "Well then, expect nothing and see what finds you, man, see what finds you."

I froze, remembering what Penny had said about things *finding* me. I tried to laugh it off, but he'd caught me staring.

"There are stories about what he did before the camp and maybe all of them are true," he said, voice dropping. "The point is it doesn't matter. When I first got here all he asked me to do was work and get along. After what happened on Denali I was freaked and that was about all I was capable of."

"What happened on the mountain?"

"I thought Grace told you everything."

I shook my head.

"I was doin' a little guiding, nothing too heavy," he said. "Mostly I was livin' off my parents, getting into little adventures, havin' fun, you know . . ."

I nodded.

"Then I watched my best friend die," he said. "Froze to death right in front of me in the tent along with two other people."

"Sorry," I said. "I didn't mean . . ."

He looked away.

". . . fuck it, I don't have anything to hide. We made the summit, began the descent and then the storm hit. People started panicking. The guide lost control of the situation, broke his leg and from there things just went to shit. For a long time I thought I bailed on him—you know, let it happen."

"How did you get here then?"

"I was in Fairbanks after the accident, trying to figure out how I was going to tell Mitch's parents about how he froze to death. All kinds of crazy stuff was going through my head like how I should just get lost in the bush and go hermit or how I should cut my hair and go back to college. To tell you the truth I didn't know what I was gonna do."

He paused to stare up at the bank of cliffs hemming the valley. In places they almost looked climbable. "You met Shipley yet?" he asked.

I nodded, recalling the way he'd stared at me when I'd asked about the jar of gold.

"I ran into him at a pawnshop," he said. "I was selling off all my gear for a plane ticket back home and there he was dumping gold nuggets on the counter like they were goddamned pennies. We started talking and all I could see was that gold, man, and all those bills sliding across the Formica. He asked if I wanted to come and well . . . I wrote Mitch's parents a letter and followed Shipley here. I haven't been back since."

"And?"

"I liked it."

"So this isn't some kind of cult?"

"Who told you that?" he said, laughing nervously. "It's just what I told you—a place. Some people need to be here. They can't hack society or else had nowhere else to go so they came here. That's it, man, sorry to disappoint you but this ain't no Waco or Heaven's Gate."

We were wading through a damp section of woods. Lewis and Clark were just visible in the distance. Mosquitoes seemed to be multiplying in the air and we stopped to crush them against our skin.

"What about you?"

"I'm a carpenter."

He nodded. "Always in need of that sort of thing around here. You're gonna fit right in."

"That's not why we came."

He laughed and kept walking. The trail led to a small opening under the cliff walls. I could see Lewis and Clark bent over something on the ground.

"What is it?" Tozer yelled.

Clark looked up. "Bear scat," he said as Lewis raked the pile with a spruce branch searching for bones.

"But not our bear," Clark said finally.

Lewis gave a little nod and they disappeared into a thicket of stunted pines that skirted the base of the cliff.

"What happened with the bear?" I asked.

Tozer sighed and looked around again before speaking.

"You and your buddy came at a bad time," he said. "Everything fell apart after the bear. The nugget didn't help either."

"Nugget?"

"The Golden Heart, man," he said. "You'll see it soon enough. Shipley dug it out of the cave two months ago and things haven't been the same since."

"Nunn told us about the bear, but he didn't say anything about gold."

"I figured as much," he said. "The bear's the camp ghost story.

The Canucks shot a sow this spring. But if you ask me I don't think it's just one bear."

"Nunn said it's taken two people."

He shrugged. "Maybe, maybe not. They're dead, that's for sure. We didn't find any bodies, just a whole shitload of blood."

"Who were they?"

"Frye—Shipley's best friend—and PJ, a steelworker from Detroit. He and Penny used to talk books all night and hook up from time to time."

"If you didn't find the bodies then how do you know the bear got them?"

"That's the problem," he said. "Half the camp don't buy that Frye and PJ got taken by the bear. Hell, PJ slept with a pistol and was pretty good in the woods. No way he'd go without a fight."

"I saw the bear, right after Nunn told us about it."

Tozer's eyes brightened. "Yeah?"

"It came across the field like he'd called it."

"I betcha somebody hung a dead dog in the field to attract it," he said. "You sure it was a griz, it coulda been a black bear."

"It was a griz," I said.

"No shit? I was in Alaska for a year before I saw one and even then it was just this fat thing Dumpster diving at a Pizza Hut in Anchorage."

"We saw one on the river, too," I said.

"Yeah, the country's thick with them, but they're shy and you only see them when they want you to see them."

"What do you really think happened?"

He narrowed his eyes. "I think you saw a bear, the rest . . ."

Clark suddenly appeared out of a bank of willows and glared at Tozer. "If I was you I'd be careful Nunn doesn't hear ya or . . ."

"Or what?" he snapped.

Clark stepped back. "Suit yourself."

He waited until Clark went ahead before muttering, "Paranoid Canucks."

We kept moving along the canyon walls, past piles of talus and large boulders which had fallen from the cliff face, embedding themselves in the permafrost like stone angels. Lewis and Clark continued their search, Lewis stalking, gun in front, eyes on the ground.

I lingered behind with Tozer.

"What did he mean about Nunn?" I asked.

"He's right. He could be anywhere," he said, pinching a branch back and allowing me to pass through a narrow cradle of pine trees.

Lassie trotted up and bumped my hand.

"Scared the shit out of me!" he said, jumping back. "What did you do to get her so loyal?"

"Fed her," I said, remembering Grace's strange reaction to the dog. "Is there something wrong with that?"

He looked around. "Just doesn't happen much is all. Ogre runs whatever dogs he can get a harness on in the winter. But ever since Julia left, the dogs have pretty much gone wild and become a camp nuisance. They've got their own agenda."

"And what might that be?"

"Let's just say they kinda compete for food," he said, stopping to consider a three-way split in the path. "Except for the ones Sanders keeps with him."

"What did Clark mean about Nunn?"

"Nunn wanders," he said. "Sometimes for days. Nobody knows what the hell he does. It's like he's looking for something, meditating. After the nugget was found he began disappearing. That's when he got mauled and everybody thought he was going to die."

"Why didn't you take him out to a doctor?"

"He asked to be lashed to a cot and shot full of morphine. He screamed for days and most of us stayed away and then one day he walks out of his cabin, right down to the lake, and looks at his reflection. Didn't say a word or even scream. Let me tell you it looked a whole lot worse than it does now."

"I still don't understand why."

"If you ask me I think he liked it."

"That's pretty hard-core," I said.

He nodded. "It drew some even closer to him, especially the originals, like Grace and Mary. Ralph, I don't know about, he's a tough one to read. Ogre plays stupid half the time and the rest, go figure. I don't ask, especially after what happened to PJ and Frye. The mauling changed Nunn. He's not the same person I first met when I walked in here three years ago."

"What about Penny?"

He stopped and let a smile slip as he peered up the trail, looking for the Canadians. "No need to be coy, bro, the whole camp knows you came to rescue our resident damsel in distress."

"Her father's dying," I said.

"That's some tough luck, but I gotta be honest with you. That chick don't need no rescuing. She's right where she ought to be."

"You mean locked up?"

"No, here, man, I mean where else is she gonna go?"

"She could leave."

"She wouldn't make it," he said. "Not with Boothe and Quinn. They take turns watching the cave for people coming or going. The only reason you got in was because you climbed down. But Sanders had already spotted you."

"How come I haven't met Sanders?"

"He's the ghost in the trees."

"Huh?"

"The lookout, keeps to himself. Around here he's a necessity because every summer some stupid tourist canoeing down the river finds the trail and hikes in. Most of the time they turn back when they see the cliffs or get run off by bears. The trick is to get invited to the lake like everybody else."

At that moment Clark called out through the pines, "We found him."

We stepped up our pace, pushing through the tangled boughs as swarms of mosquitoes and black flies descended on us. But before I could break through Tozer grabbed me. "What I told you—keep it to yourself. There's more going on here than you think, comprende?"

I looked at him, momentarily confused.

"Now put on a happy face like me," he said, smiling. "Miles of smiles. Now all you have to do is get your buddy Burke to go along with us and we can all get out of this mess."

I nodded and plunged through the branches toward the sound of their voices where I expected to find Burke holding a gun to somebody's head.

When I emerged from the snarl of trees into a rock-strewn meadow I immediately recognized it as the field where Nunn had taken us to see the bear. In the daylight it appeared smaller, peppered with crooked saplings, several uprooted trees and a large circular fire pit in one corner. Several paths fingered off in all directions—one of them leading to Penny.

Tozer jogged up behind me and pointed to the far end of the meadow where the Canadians stood, gesturing over a dark heap on the ground.

I rushed over and saw that it was Burke lying facedown on the ground with a large teardrop-shaped pool of blood fanning out from under him.

For a minute I thought that perhaps they had beaten him while Tozer and I had been talking. But then I saw the drag marks leading into the bush and how the pool of blood had soaked deep into the dirt. I knew that whatever had happened to Burke had occurred a while ago and elsewhere.

I knelt to have a closer look.

Lassie began licking the blood and Lewis snorted, as if his point about the dog not being trusted had been proven.

I pushed the dog away and felt for a pulse on Burke. It was there strong, pounding through his veins.

Tozer helped me roll him over.

His face was a mess and in addition to the gash Boothe had given him, there were fresh cuts on his chin and another running the length of his forehead. His knuckles were bloody and swollen and several fingers hung at wrong angles.

"What do you think happened?" I asked, trying to recall the blurry sequence of events that night: Nunn's face in the moonlight, the bear, Burke's sudden flight and then Penny.

"Somebody sure did a number on him," Clark said. "Looks like they dragged him, eh?"

Lewis nodded and began his great white hunter routine again, poking at broken branches and the spatter of blood with his Spiderex knife.

Tozer helped me drag him under one of the trees where we propped him up. Remembering the knife I quickly patted Burke down.

It was gone.

"Looking for something?" Lewis asked.

I shook my head and dabbed Burke's eyes open with my thumbs. His pupils were rimmed with ruptured veins and did not react to the light.

"Fuck," Tozer said.

"Help me," I said, lifting Burke to his feet.

His breath whistled in and out weakly. He looked dead and then some. His arms were slack and mushy. Blood continued to drip out of his hair and I could feel myself beginning to panic— that Burke might die and leave me stranded in the camp.

I settled him against the bark, his torso lurching side to side like a ship taking on water. Tozer steadied Burke's listing body with his knees until he began breathing more evenly and the muscles around his swollen eyes twitched, but didn't open.

Clark returned, set the gun against a tree and hunkered down in front of Burke. "The drag craps out about fifty yards in. What I can't figure is why not use one of the trails, eh?"

He pointed to a slight part in the trees, hung with heavy brush.

"What's over there?" I asked, still confused which way the camp was.

"Not much," he said.

I eyed him, thinking maybe the cabin where Penny was being held was somewhere in that general direction.

"What do you mean not much?"

"Nothing," he said. "Trees."

"So somebody does this to him and then drags him through heavy brush and leaves him here to die?"

"I didn't say that, now did I?" Clark snapped. "Maybe he got lost and scared and started to run, hits a couple of trees and on the way down he catches a rock to the head."

"It didn't happen that way," I said.

"Let's just get him back," Tozer said, helping me to lift Burke between us and get my shoulders under him.

"Just get us back," I said. "I don't give a fuck what you think."

"Careful," Lewis said as Burke's head lolled back and forth, drool wetting the dried crust of blood and hanging yarnlike from his busted chin.

Clark whistled for Lewis. They had words and then Lewis pointed down a trail, spiderwebs glinting in the tree-filtered light, a slight breeze rattling the aspen leaves overhead.

We followed them, Tozer struggling under the dead weight of Burke. I kept waiting for his legs to stop dragging, for the battered eyes to open and tell me he didn't need any help—that he wanted payback for whoever had done this to him.

●

Our arrival in camp was met with very little fanfare. Boothe was still sitting on his stump. Lewis and Clark disappeared without a word and only Veronica and Jenny came out of the kitchen to help us get Burke into the lodge.

We set him on a cot. His breathing seemed even and strong and the bleeding had stopped.

Lila arrived, took one look and said, "I'll get Ralph."

She ran off toward the lake and while Veronica wiped Burke's wounds clean I excused myself, asking Tozer to point me toward the outhouse.

"I gotta go," I lied.

He held my gaze for a minute. "Straight up?"

"Straight up," I said.

"Behind the pines left of the second cabin," he said briskly.

I nodded and making sure Lassie didn't follow, walked quickly out the back, past the cabin and through the pines, the shit smell of the outhouse trailing behind in the cool air and into the woods where we'd first entered the camp.

I had to know if the guns were still where we'd left them or if Burke had managed to get to them before he'd been beaten.

I hustled past the generator shack, worrying that the mysterious Sanders would spot me and tell Boothe what I was up to. The generators were silent, the air still thick with their exhaust from the morning run. Several broken shovels lay on the ground outside the shack, next to the empty fuel cans and buckets full of stagnant rainwater.

Farther down the path I found the pile of rocks Burke had made and waited a few minutes, acclimating myself to the forest noise—birds moving from branch to branch, wind knocking anemic green and yellow leaves from their stems. But there were no human sounds, so I plunged into the tunnel of branches and crawled.

The guns were where we'd stashed them and I sat for a while, hands wrapped around the butt of Burke's .45, wondering how I could smuggle it back to the tent. Walking into the camp with a gun that big would be an announcement. People would know. But it felt good in my palms, the solid burl of its butt, the steel, cool like steak pulled from the refrigerator. I thought it through, recalling Boothe with his gun and empty face. I would have to kill, pull the trigger and run. But run to where and who to kill first and why? The camp was a maze of featureless trails. Only the lake and lodge house were familiar to me and I knew I had to find out more so that when Burke did heal—and he would, because whatever he'd run into had not killed him, could not kill him— we could get out.

Feeling only slightly better I wrapped the gun back in its plastic bag and crawled out, trying to reconstruct what had happened that night in the field after Nunn had told us about the bear. Burke had simply bolted off into the dark after the bear. Nunn had vanished and nothing seemed to make much sense anymore.

Mindful of how long I'd been away I hustled back to the lodge house, the weight of the gun in my hands now only a comforting memory. I turned a corner and ran into Grace, who was staring at something across the lake and didn't even acknowledge my presence. I faded back a few steps off the path and saw what she was staring at. On the far shore Nunn was sitting with Lewis and Clark. They were just visible through the crack in the trees. Nunn was gesturing with his hands and pointing at them. I looked at Grace again. She was transfixed, her face slack, hands at her side. She didn't move or turn in my direction even as I stepped back onto the path and walked past her.

•

In the lodge Ralph was hunched over Burke, gently lifting his eyelids, shining a small tape-encrusted flashlight into them. He shook his head, then snaked his fingers through Burke's blood-streaked hair, examining the lumps and gashes.

Tozer sat on a stool not far away chatting with Jenny, who kept nodding and twisting a strand of hair between her thumb and forefinger. She looked stoned.

"Find it?" Tozer asked, coming over.

I made a face. "Nasty."

We locked eyes and he knew that I hadn't been to the outhouse.

"Good then," he said, cutting me silent with a glance. "Did you meet Jenny yet?"

Jenny untucked her legs and drifted over. "Hey," she said in a soft voice.

"We met earlier."

Jenny nodded, put her teeth against her bottom lip and bit softly. She was thin. Her eyes were a light green and pretty, but she had a weak chin that made her look shy and a high strangled voice that set my teeth on edge.

"Your friend just needs to take it easy and stop fighting for a while," she said. "It's not good for you."

"Fighting?"

She blushed. "Especially up here with no doctor. Any crazy little thing can kill you."

Ralph stood, his weathered face deep in thought as he looked at Burke. He'd cleaned and bandaged the cuts with butterfly strips and swabbed iodine into a large scrape. Burke appeared to be sleeping peacefully, his arms at his sides.

"He needs to rest," Ralph said. "That's the first thing. The second . . ." His voice trailed off and he stood there staring at Burke as if he'd forgotten something.

"Is he in a coma?" I asked.

"Mmmm . . . he's got a broken rib and some pretty deep cuts. But until he comes to I guess there's not much else we can do except wait." He pushed at the skin under his chin. His fingers were stained with Burke's blood.

"What can we do?"

"The best-case scenario," he started. "I mean what should happen is that his body does what it has to do and he comes out of it."

"What about taking him downriver and getting to a doctor?" I said.

Ralph sighed.

"Not a good idea," Tozer said.

"Why's that?"

Jenny quietly excused herself and headed toward the kitchen, where Gant was rolling trout in a pie pan of flour and cornmeal and then setting them in a large cast-iron skillet where the fish sizzled and gave off a thick blue smoke. Several minutes of silence welled up between us, during which the even labor of Burke's breathing was the only sound in the room.

Finally Ralph said what we'd all been thinking. "Maybe somebody in the camp did this to him."

"I thought that much was obvious," I said. Then remembering the scab on my neck, "What about Boothe?"

Tozer shook his head. "He didn't do this to your friend. But he didn't run into a tree either."

"How do you know it wasn't Boothe?"

It was Ralph who spoke. "Because he would have killed him . . . that's why."

Without thinking I said, "Sanders?"

His face darkened a minute. "Who told you about him?"

"Grace."

Ralph scowled, no longer spacey and slow. "I doubt it and

unless you've got proof, I'd keep your suspicions to yourself. They won't make things any easier, I can tell you that."

I looked around the room. Except for Gant and Jenny in the kitchen we were alone. "What the fuck's going on here?" I asked.

He shook his head and began packing his medical supplies into a worn black leather satchel with an old Chicago EMS patch sewn into its side.

"If I was you," he said, stepping out the door, "I'd worry about your friend."

Tozer followed Ralph out before I could tell him about seeing Grace down by the lake.

I was left alone with Burke. His eyes were clenched tight, face swollen, there was only the rise and fall of his chest and looking at him, it was impossible to imagine him astride some roof peak swatting nails and swearing at the foremen. The cot seemed to swallow him, even his normally powerful hands looked soft and pink. But I was calm, determined now more than ever to get out and get out with Duke's daughter, maybe even Tozer.

Get out alive, I told myself, before the sun goes and the snow comes. With or without Burke.

Dinner was served late, after the rest of the people had filtered back to camp. Gant doled out fried trout and bowls of warm rice from the porch steps, fanning his hands over the food to keep the hornets from landing.

I ate quickly, pulling the crispy skin off the fish, slitting it and pulling the neat line of bones from the middle. Tozer continued to introduce me around, most of the time to blank stares or shallow nods. There was no sign of Nunn.

I even went inside to check on Burke and study his face for some indication that he was coming around. But he slept, his face yellow and blue where blood pooled under the skin, and after an hour of staring at the even movement of his chest I resolved to find Penny and start looking for a way out. When I knew that Burke recovered we would have to move quickly if we were to make it out at all.

We still had the guns though.

And even though I didn't believe it for a minute there was Nunn's offer of hunting the bear as a way out of the camp.

Lassie padded over, demanding to be petted.

"What's the way out of this place?" I asked her.

Her ears perked and she let out a yip before settling at my feet to watch the sun play down over the horizon, slow and haze-ridden. The mountains to the north turned a soft peach color and the lake water suddenly looked dark as Ogre built a large fire, tipping eight-foot lengths into a large tepee and then packing dry pine and leaves under it and lighting it with a single match. Several smudge pots blanketed the ground with a thick soupy smoke that for the most part kept the mosquitoes away. Shipley stood over one of the pots feeding green cedar boughs and moose bones into the coals.

Near the fire, Peter, a thin, serious-looking guy with Coke-bottle glasses and a large Adam's apple, was playing Dylan songs on a beat-up guitar. He sang with his eyes pinched shut, dirty fingers dancing up and down the guitar neck. Veronica sat cross-legged in front of him, occasionally singing along in a thin sweet voice to "Visions of Johanna" as dogs wandered through the small group of people, quietly sniffing for handouts and leftovers. It reminded me of a Dead show an old girlfriend had once dragged me to in college where we ate mushrooms and spent most of the show roving the parking lot, watching the freaks dance, shuffle and mumble bad poetry to each other.

Tozer staggered up to me and pressed a plastic canteen into my hand.

"Drink?" he asked.

I took it from him and held it to the firelight. "What is it?"

"Nasty homemade blueberry wine," he said. "But man, does it do the trick!"

I raised the canteen and drank. It was thick, strong-tasting stuff that warmed my stomach and made me forget about the various aches and pains I'd managed to gather over the last couple of days. After a few more swigs I heard a sharp electronic crackle

come from the trees and then Neil Young's "Cortez the
Killer" warble from the dozens of small car speakers hung in the
branches.

Tozer leaned in. "Like the tunes?" he said. "The whole system
runs off a car battery."

Over by the fire, Peter put away his guitar, yelling something
about not being able to compete with Neil, and Veronica leaned
back and stared up into the sky, letting the ash fall on her face.

"Besides," Tozer said, "in another week you'd be sick of guitar
boy there, the dude plays the same shit over and over."

"It wasn't bad," I said.

"Wait," he said, passing me the wine. "Just wait."

I laughed and drank the wine. Lassie was at my side. The surrounding woods were dark and I thought of Penny in her cabin,
wondering if I'd be able to find it again. Twice I thought I saw
Nunn in the distance, but when I looked again he was nowhere.

Later, after the wine was gone and the music and generators
shut off, couples started drifting back to their cabins. Boothe
stood as if he'd been called, shouldered his gun and disappeared
down one of the trails and I suddenly found myself all alone
watching the fire bank down and die. I kept waiting for Nunn to
amble out of the woods or for somebody to lock me up again.
But no one did and I was free for the moment and wanting to
test it. So I wandered to the edge of the clearing and stepped into
the woods, studying the sprawl of the camp behind me. The
remains of the fire glowed dull and smoky like a crack in the earth
and there were lights in several cabin windows that faded as I
walked farther into the comforting silence of the forest, head
buzzing with wine.

Lassie whimpered as we passed the shadowy humps of other
dogs going about their business in the gloom. I kept moving,
picking up what I thought was a small trail in the moonlight and
following it toward the cliffs. Remembering the snares I'd set
earlier with Grace I was careful not to let the dog wander into
the nearby brush and several times I stopped as something
crashed through the trees in the distance. After two hundred

yards or so in the dark woods I was shaking and had to stop to get my bearings. The trail narrowed where several large gray stones sat in the middle of the path. The clouds shifted and moonlight tilted in through the trees and in the brief illumination I saw the silhouette of a man step across the trail and disappear into the gloom. Several dog-shaped shadows trailed behind him, blending into the black until they were indistinguishable from the trees.

Lassie let out a low growl and stood at attention, fur on end. There was no way to tell if I'd been seen and what might happen next so I jumped off the path and waited, desperately trying to sort the shadows. The moon clouded over again, plunging me into utter darkness, and when it came back the path was still empty and except for the wind the woods was silent. The figure I'd seen move across the path had been short, compact and walked with a stealth that seemed impossible for someone of Nunn's size.

I waited drawing shallow breaths, careful not to shift my weight and give myself away with the snap of a branch or crunch of dead pine needles. My eyes played tricks on me. Trees turned into men, branches into guns, the white of moths flitting through the under-growth shimmered like knife blades catching moonlight. Grad-ually I began to block out the shifting shapes and see only the cleft in the trail where the figure had disappeared, sure that at any moment something would rush me from behind or drop down from above and that would be it. They would lay my body next to Burke and the women would wash my wounds or maybe do noth-ing as they waited for me to die alongside my partner.

But nothing came and I began moving again, withdrawing from under the tree, fighting the urge to slap noisily at the mosquitoes covering my neck and arms.

Within minutes I was back on the trail, putting distance between myself and the figure. At a three-way fork in the path I stood there a moment trying to decide which direction would lead me back to the camp and my tent. I was still drunk from the crude blueberry wine which did little to quell the tight bubble of paranoia swelling in my chest. If I chose the wrong path I could find myself lost in the valley with the possibility of meeting the bear or the shape I'd seen dash across the trail. Neither option seemed particularly appealing. What I wanted was to be back at the lake with the others, sleeping, waiting on Burke to rise and get us the hell out of here.

Again the moon faded behind clouds, making the choice somehow easier as I crept down the right-hand trail, the least dark of the three. I heard more crashing, the snap of branches, and saw other shadows rising and then fading into the dim black grid of trees.

I froze, convinced I'd chosen the bear. Lassie let out another low grumble and I crouched against a tree trunk as dead pine needles rained down around me.

After ten minutes the woods remained silent and I began to think that I'd imagined seeing the man, that it was the wine and all the stories I'd been told. I started walking again, stumbling over tree roots, branches slapping at my face as I checked the urge to turn back and run blindly to the intersection and choose again.

At last the path widened and I spotted a series of lights in the distance and moved toward them with renewed confidence. When the trail twisted away from the lights I pushed through the brush, arriving not at the lake but in a small clearing ringed with stunted pine trees. The light was still in the distance.

I walked the perimeter, keeping the lights in front of me, hoping for a seam in the wall of trees and brush that would lead me to them. I found a trail and turned to take one last look at the field before going after the lights when something caught my eye—a dark mound on the far side of the clearing that didn't appear to be a stone or fallen tree.

I went to investigate and halfway across the field tripped on a pile of dirt and fell face-first to the dewy ground. I waited, listening for sounds to emerge from the thrum of night noise. The dog paced, stopping to nose me several times as I rolled to a sitting position and saw two piles of fresh earth next to a pair of shallow holes. In the poor light they looked like graves of some sort. The largest one was no more than four feet long, too short for a man. Dog, I thought, or some other kind of animal. The chill of exposed permafrost traveled up my arm as I pressed my hand along the bottom of the hole and sniffed at the damp air, expecting to find the sweet coil of dead things mixing with the dirt. But the air was cool. I could see my breath against it and there were no dead smells, just pine and the rich loamy aroma of freshly dug soil.

Beside each mound of earth was a small cairn of rocks. I kicked one of the piles over only to find undisturbed ground beneath and a beetle, its back catching the moonlight as it scurried away.

I searched the rest of the field, head low to the ground looking for other signs of recent digging, but found nothing and returned to have a second look at the holes, recalling the people I'd seen heading into the woods with shovels and pickaxes over their shoulders.

I tried to explain away my discovery, remembering that two hours earlier the camp had seemed like one big friendly party; everybody gathered around the campfire, the liquor and music, catching Tozer and Lila kissing by the lake. But the memory slipped away as I stood staring at the black gash that had been cut into the field.

There were secrets here. Different versions of the same story.

The snap of tree limbs crunching under my clumsy gait brought me back to the purpose and I calmly walked out of the field, picking up a small trail that fed into a larger one, keeping the lights in front of me and the graves behind until I arrived back at the camp.

In the lodge Burke was still out of it, the sheets pulled up to his chin. Veronica appeared from nowhere and stood behind me in the dark holding a thick candle and looking a little high. She smelled of woodsmoke and the heavy grease of the kitchen.

"Exploring?" she asked, the candle fluttering.

I looked at her blankly.

"You can tell me," she said, coming closer.

"A little," I said.

She reached out and put a damp hand on the side of my neck, touching the scab. It felt good.

"See anything?" she asked.

I considered telling her about the holes I'd found, but when I tried to look into her eyes she dipped her chin and stared into the sputtering candle.

"Trees, darkness and mosquitoes," I said.

Her hand fell away from my neck. "I don't believe you," she said. "You're a liar."

"What do you mean by that?"

She smiled. Her lips looked swollen in the candlelight; a come-on wrapped in a smile and a threat.

I heard something else in the room—a zipper scratching open or shut and the sound of someone besides Burke breathing. She turned and blew out the candle.

"You'll see," she said, retreating into the shadows. "It'll *find* you."

I heard more rustling and she whispered something I couldn't hear and then there was silence. I knew it would be a mistake to go to her, so I turned and took one last look at Burke, reaching down to squeeze his hand until his grip tightened.

He was coming back.

I went outside and took a piss down by the lake and splashed water on my face to scrub away the film of dead mosquitoes and gnats. I searched the gloom for my tent, remembering the dead hornets and musty, dirty hair smell when I sat to take off my boots. I could hear the dog arranging herself outside as I crawled under the sleeping bag and fell asleep with the lap of the lake timing my breathing.

•

The next morning I woke early and checked on Burke. He looked better but didn't stir when I tried pinching his hand.

Veronica and Jenny came out of the kitchen and watched me for a minute and I turned, searching Veronica's face for any sign of our conversation the night before. But she seemed bright and cheerful, peering at me with her soft brown eyes as if it hadn't happened.

"Ralph was here already," she said.

"And?"

Jenny sat at the edge of the bed, smoothing the sheet. "He found blood in his urine," she said.

"Where is he?" I asked.

"He's gone," Veronica said, brushing small clouds of flour from her shirt.

"Then I'll go find him."

"It's okay, everything's going to be okay," Veronica said, "just relax, it's gonna be all right."

I started to say something but she frowned and pulled a joint from behind her ear. "Attitude adjustment?" she asked, offering the joint to me.

There were fish scales stuck to her arm and a thin layer of sweat or kitchen steam on her brow.

I hesitated.

She giggled and stuck the joint into my shirt pocket. "Save it for later," she said. "Shipley's been waiting to talk with you."

They left me standing there with a puzzled look on my face so I went outside and found Shipley filing shovels by a pile of old dog sleds which lay in a tangled heap of bent wood, rotten leather traces and rusty wire. His hands moved quickly, swiping the file harshly against the dull rusty edges of the shovels. The sun was burning off the early morning fog on the lake and a light breeze stirred ash from the extinguished smudge pots, exposing delicate half-burnt bones.

"You wanna work with us?" Shipley asked, waving me over. "Earn your keep until your buddy gets healed up and Nunn gives you a permanent job."

"I'm not staying," I said.

He cracked a smile and scratched under his beard with the end of a file.

"I heard you," he said, narrowing his eyes at me, his face darkening suddenly, smile dropping. "And I'll ask you again—do you want to work today or did you have other plans?"

"Will I get gold fever?"

"If you're lucky," he said, laughing and handing me a bundle of shovels. "Come on, the others have already started. It's cave and creek day and I warn you, it's work, none of that pansy-ass carpentry stuff."

"That's okay," I said, ignoring him.

With several shovels on his shoulder he set out quickly. "Stay close and don't let the bears get you."

He laughed again and led me to a trailhead at the edge of the lake. I dragged the bundle of shovels he'd given me and kept pace, trying to commit the various trails to memory so that even in the dark they would make sense. At the same time I was thinking about the snares I'd set with Grace, trying to picture her checking them for dead rabbits and fox as the trail wound away from the lake and the camp dissolved from sight. All that was visible was the blue water through the trees and the sun cracking off its surface.

We followed the trail for a mile or so until we came to a small creek lined with undercut banks and heavy brush. The water ran clear and fast around rocks and larger boulders and a school of minnows held steady along the edges, moving as one in jittery swarming darts. And in the deeper pools where the water piled over rocks into clear tumbles I saw larger fish, shadowing the pebbled creek bottom, their sleek outlines shimmering as the water moved.

Shipley stopped to point out a ptarmigan before it vanished into the thick brush in a blur of feathers and squawks. The disappearance of the bird was followed by the sound of something larger crashing away from us in the thicket.

Shipley froze, studying my face for a reaction.

"Moose, most likely," he said.

I nodded, trying to imagine a bull navigating the undergrowth with its rack, barreling over saplings, trampling bushes. They were massive animals and on the few times I'd run into them at close range I'd been awestruck at their sheer mass and the mange of moss and lichen creeping across their enormous shoulders. There were stories of them charging men, stamping bears to death and killing wolves with a single kick. But from a distance they looked cowlike, placid, hardly capable of anything but grazing and trudging the muskeg.

The bush remained quiet and Shipley continued upstream and then a minute later two rifle shots split the morning air, the boom echoing off the cliff walls harshly.

I started to say something.

"Nah," he said. "Too far away. Musta been the Canucks shootin' at their own shadows." He began moving again, scurrying over the stones until the white curve of the cliff walls became visible.

The creek meandered along the canyon, cutting into the rock, gliding under heavy brush, and in places it seemed to flow from someplace underground, the water welling up in large pools that fed into a series of shallow riffles. The riffles were dappled with sun and large dry-backed boulders that seemed to have been dropped in the creek for some purpose.

Two dark-skinned men I'd spotted in the camp but hadn't talked to were bent over a wooden sluice in the riffles. The gate hung between two rocks. Coffee-colored water spilled out of the sluice, staining the creek water. Each of the men wore bright yellow hip boots over heavy canvas pants. Their shirtsleeves were dark where the water had soaked through to their shoulders. Columns of gnats and mosquitoes hovered over them and as they glanced up from their work the insects momentarily shifted.

Each man nodded slightly as if I'd interrupted something.

"Jack, this is Sherman and Mooner," Shipley said.

They ignored us and kept working. Mooner was the larger of the two and wore his hair in a long black ponytail. Sherman was slim with a narrow hard-cheeked face. His eyes were pinched and dark and he stared into the sluice, his hands raking the larger chunks of gravel free. I noticed a long knife strapped to his thigh.

Shipley leaned in. "Tanana Indians and in case you're wondering, they're not being unfriendly, shy is all."

"How come I haven't met them?" I asked.

He considered the question a minute. "Well, they pretty much live here at the creek. It's been that way for a while."

"They're not part of the camp then?"

"Oh, no," he said. "They guard the claim during summer."

"Guard it from what?"

He sized me up again, his thick brow drooping. "You never know, do you? DNR might send its goon squad to check our claims if they hear we're mining. Poachers, claim grabbers—you name it. This far out it's still every man for himself. You don't exactly see any law, now do you?"

I shook my head.

"Back when I still had the paste I worked a claim for this old-timer in Bethel who shot at anybody who so much as set foot on his creek—no questions asked. He finally killed a man."

"And?"

"And nothing," he said. "We buried him where he fell and nobody missed him."

With that he walked farther upstream to where Lila sat hunched on a boulder panning, looking intently at the water, silt spilling over the lip of the plate. She saw me and waved, calling out for Tozer, who emerged from under a bank of willows, shirtless, a pick slung over his shoulder.

"Pulled some strings," Tozer shouted over the creek. He began hopping boulders across, slipping several times and soaking his tattered jeans.

"What's that?" I asked.

"Pulled some strings and got you with us."

"Lucky me," I said.

"Hey, man, if stranglin' bunnies with Grace is more your speed, go for it." He leaned in. "But just remember, she likes it and don't let her tell you any different."

Shipley shot Tozer a look before treading down a narrow rock-lined path that led away from the cliff. Tozer motioned for me to follow and within minutes we were standing in front of a small opening that had no doubt been worn into the cliff by the creek thousands of years ago.

He pulled on a T-shirt that was so thin his chest hair poked through. Over that he slipped a heavy wool shirt and pointed to the cave. I stepped closer, peering into the damp opening. A pool of groundwater sat just inside the entrance. It was peppered with muck-filled footprints and bits of crushed stone where the rock shelves had been chipped away to widen the entrance. Farther in I could see the bounce of Shipley's lantern as he crawled into the gloom.

Tozer grabbed a lantern from a storage box, pumped it, struck a match and crouched into the cave entrance.

"Come on," he said. "It's pretty cool."

I hesitated.

"I know it doesn't look it, but trust me it's as safe as anything else around here."

Avoiding the mud I inched into the cave behind Tozer, running my hands along the damp walls that seemed to get colder the deeper we went. In places I had to crawl on all fours through slender portals into even smaller chambers crusted with rippled sheets of ice and frozen mud. The sides were held up with gnarled spruce logs and rotten plywood sheeting. Dozens of small chutes, some no bigger round than a dinner plate, branched off from each room. Broken hammers, rust-frosted chisels and scads of white five-gallon buckets lay scattered everywhere like bones and as we made our way deeper my hands grew cold and then finally numb. Every time I thought we'd come to the end of the cave some dark twist would reveal another passage or hidden room piled high with earth and stones.

At a fork in the tunnel Tozer set the lantern down and ducked into what looked like a narrow indentation in the uneven surface of the cave wall.

On closer inspection I saw that the indentation opened into a tight chimneylike passage that emptied into a large room, the sides of which I couldn't see.

We went back down into the hallway.

"Ship wants us working here," he said, pointing.

"Looking for gold?" I asked.

"Maybe, maybe not, Ship says dig, I dig," he said. "The dude's got a nose for the stuff. Mud means there was water in here at some time or another and water washes gold out. Besides unless you wanna get wet and possibly lost, this is the best for now. And we can talk."

He slipped into the chimney and a minute after his legs had disappeared his torso suddenly popped down the opening and he grabbed the lantern off of its perch.

"You coming?"

I scrambled after him, my hands slipping against the cold stone floor, damp refrigerated air filling my lungs.

"We'll take turns chipping and filling," Tozer said, setting the lantern down in the center of the chamber. I stood carefully and looked around at the striated layers of earth that gave way to chalky mud on the far end and then finally stone.

"It's cold in here," I said, wishing I'd worn a sweater.

"What's not rock is permafrost," he said. "Some of the rooms further down are impossible to work in and if you warm them too much you risk cave-in."

"Has that ever happened?"

"Cave-in?"

I nodded.

"I wasn't here, but yeah, when they first started work on the cave two guys died in one of the back chambers," he said. "Only Shipley knows about it. Their bodies are still in here some-where."

"I thought you said it was safe."

"It is."

"Then . . ."

"Hey, man, voices carry." Then whispering. "It's safe now. All I'm sayin' is something else happened—I don't know what because it was before my time, but it wasn't good."

He took the lantern and walked to a dull white stripe at the far end of the room.

"Check it out," he said, swinging the lantern in front of him.

The light hit the object—a massive column of ice that hung from the ceiling, fanning out along the floor like liquid glass. He stepped behind it with the lantern and the ice seemed to glow, magnifying and refracting the light in dull green and red waves.

I pulled out the joint and tossed it to him.

"See you've wasted no time getting friendly with Jenny and Veronica," he said, taking the joint and carefully lighting it off the lantern and inhaling.

He passed it to me.

The smoke burned my lungs and I ended up coughing half the hit. But after ten minutes the dope made the cave seem warm, as if I was in the belly of some large stone animal.

Tozer toked up and then went behind the ice wall again, shattering the light into small prisms that shifted and tilted around the room like a giant kaleidoscope.

"It's awesome," I said.

He laughed and came out from behind the ice to grab the last of the joint from me.

"Shipley showed it to me on my first day in." He paused to look around. "They found a pile of bones just over there."

"Human?"

He nodded. "Ship thought they were Indian, but they could have been some old prospector's who wandered in looking for gold during the rush and died. Plenty of that around here."

"Plenty of what?"

"Old bodies," he said, grabbing a trowel and mud-spattered bucket. He paused. "You met Ogre, right?"

"Yeah."

"Well, he used to work for the park service and one of the jobs they had every spring was to hike into the remote campsites and look for unlucky pilgrims who'd either frozen, starved to death or met up with bears."

"Not a lot of leeway up here, is there?"

He lifted a pick and checked its tip. "Not anymore."

"What do you mean by that?"

He was silent a moment and then handed me one of the plastic buckets and began striking the wall, stopping only to whisper. "We should be quiet. There's always somebody listening."

"Look," I said. "I'm getting pretty sick of all the fucking mystery. What are you trying to tell me?"

He put a finger to his lips and smiled. "Nothing and everything. Right now it's important you get along. I vouched for you yesterday with the others. So it's cool for a while at least. And as long as you don't do anything stupid and help out you'll be accepted."

"Stupid meaning?"

"Leave or try leaving."

"What?"

He hunkered down and dimmed the lantern, speaking into his hand to dull the echo. "Just what I said—you can't leave."

"But yesterday you were the camp cheerleader."

"It was part of the act for the Canucks," he said. "They don't call me Tozer the poseur for nothin'. That's all this place is anymore, a lot of pretending. Even Grace with her Earth Mother act—what a load of crap. Next time you go out executin' bunnies with her, ask her how she got those scars all over her face."

"How?"

"Her first husband put her head through a glass coffee table," he said. "That was after she stabbed him with a steak knife."

"Grace?"

He nodded and then started to say something else when a series of clacks and thuds echoed from one of the tunnels.

Tozer stiffened, quickly handing me a trowel and pick and pointing at a pile of loose rocks. "Fill the buckets then haul them out and let the Tontos run 'em through the sluice."

The sound grew louder until Shipley crawled out of one of the tunnels dragging two buckets behind him. The opening was one I hadn't noticed before and he emerged covered in mud, shivering like a newborn calf.

"You assholes working or talking?" he asked, dropping the buckets with a heavy sigh.

"Hi-ho, hi-ho, it's off to work we go," Tozer sang out, attacking the wall with a pickax so hard that sparks flew. I grabbed a bucket and jerked gravel into it until Shipley slithered out of the chamber dragging the load behind him.

It was cold, damp work and when the dope wore off I began to doubt that the mining detail was one of the better jobs in the camp and I figured it was merely an excuse for Tozer to spill the camp politics to me. I still wasn't sure I could trust him, not with all he was throwing at me because he hadn't really come out and said he wanted to leave. I'd met plenty of guys like him on jobs, ready to pitch a bitch at the drop of a nail, but the minute the bossman showed his face they bent right over and became company whores who would make you look bad in a heartbeat if they thought it would hold off the pink slip or bump them to a better crew. Or maybe Tozer was just scared and confused at what had become of his Shangri-la. So I worked, tossing things around, trying to get a fix on whom to trust and how I could escape.

It was too dark to tell if what I was loading into the buckets contained gold, but I kept chipping away as Tozer hammered at the rock ledge, stopping every once in a while to catch his breath or spit rock grit from his mouth.

We filled two dozen of the buckets without talking. My resistance to the work finally gave way to long stretches where I thought of nothing except the shovel and the jerk of muscle as I hauled each bucket to the exit, lowering it down the chimney.

He paused from his work and listened for the steady rhythmic blows coming from a nearby chamber. It wasn't until the sound stopped that he began to talk, swinging his pick at the rock every once in a while and urging me to shovel in order to keep up the appearance of work.

I asked him about the nugget—the Golden Heart.

"I'd show you where they found it but I haven't been that deep," he said. "Only Shipley knows the cave well enough."

"You've seen it though?"

"Everybody has, that's the problem. Frye thought we should sell it and do something with the money."

"Like what?"

"I don't know," he said. "It's worth a lot of money though. I figure Ship and Nunn are the only two who know exactly how much. Frye started yammering about selling it and two days later he meets Mr. Bear."

"And PJ?"

"Penny convinced him to leave and get help."

"Help?"

"Who knows what she wants," he said. "Could be she wants the Golden Heart. I haven't been able to talk to her since Nunn banished her to the cabin. Funny you should show up so soon after."

"What do you mean?"

"I don't know, just seems like perfect timing to me. You and your buddy appear out of nowhere looking for Penny."

"Her father hired us to come get her after he heard rumors about the troopers picking up a couple of backpackers who'd nearly died getting out."

"From here?"

I nodded.

Tozer paused to look at me over the lantern. His face was covered with a fine rock powder, his lips and eyes now pink holes in the gray mask. "That's impossible."

"Impossible how?"

"There weren't any backpackers," he said. "Either he was lying or they were talking about some other camp."

"Why would he do that?"

Tozer shrugged. "I dunno, there's a bunch of dopers living in tepees above Delta Junction. Maybe that's where they came from, because nobody's made it out of here since last fall."

"What about PJ, did he get out?"

He nodded. "Yeah, and two days later Nunn shows the camp a pool of blood and some bear tracks. But . . ."

"But what?"

"No body," he said, brushing the rock dust from his face. "We searched the valley and didn't find a fucking thing except the blood. Penny thought somebody killed a dog, spread the blood around to attract bears to make it look like PJ got eaten."

"I don't get it."

"After what happened to Nunn, people were pretty freaked out about bears. Maybe he did it to keep everybody quiet."

"Quiet about what?"

"The gold," he said. "And not just the Golden Heart, there's a lot more gold than that around here someplace, only problem is that nobody seems to know where it all goes."

"Did Penny?"

"She was talking about it, getting everybody all hopped up."

"Where do you think it is?"

He looked around. "Some of it is spent on supplies, but look around, these ain't exactly luxury accommodations, know what I mean? I'd do some pretty evil things for a chocolate bar or a supply of razors. Ever since this bear thing Nunn has refused to send someone out for supplies. Now we're looking at winter with no rice and half the usual lot of flour and sugar—almost no Tampax and not enough diesel to make it through till spring. It doesn't matter how much fish we have, people are going to starve."

"What about leaving?" I asked. "Why can't you just leave?"

"It's not that easy. Some of the people here aren't ever going to leave," he said. "They've been all over the world and as far as they're concerned they've found paradise. You can talk to them until you're blue in the face and it won't do any good."

I studied him in the soft lantern light.

"I left everything behind when I came here," he said. "I didn't know anybody, it was a fresh start. And I needed it because I was fucked after the mountain and my friend dying. All I know is that if I could make things different—show you how this place used to be before the Golden Heart and the bear—I'm not so sure you wouldn't want to stay."

"Plenty of good country around."

"That's not what I'm talkin' about," he said. "Nunn made this place special—I mean it worked because he made it work."

"How?"

Tozer paused to pump the lantern. "He's a perceptual athlete," he said.

I shot him a look.

"No, that sounds wrong," he said. "What I mean is he does

things, they may sound crazy, but they work, like he'll take you into the woods at night, no food, no water or shelter. He calls it a vision quest. You walk until dark, sit down, let night fall and listen to the animals."

"Sounds like a lot of New Age crap," I said.

"You're wrong," he said. "It's not like that, I know what that stuff is like—trust me, I've seen way too much of it."

"He takes you out in the woods?"

He nodded. "I was scared to death the first time, especially when he disappeared and I started hearing things, imagining bears moving in the trees. But then I broke through all that and drifted, just like he said I would. Even the bugs didn't bother me. And before you ask, I wasn't stoned. I was straighter than I'd ever been—it was like being plugged into the woods. I couldn't even sleep. The next morning Nunn appeared and started telling me everything he'd observed since I'd arrived in the camp and I know this sounds flaky, but it worked. I got my center back and I guess that sort of made me loyal to the camp. Others got help too and are grateful to him, even now after all that's happened."

"I didn't come to have my life sorted out," I said. "I only came for Penny."

"I've heard that line before."

"What do you mean?"

"I mean this place ain't exactly easy to find," he said. "Hell, you guys came down the cliff, not too many do that. Did you ask your buddy why he wanted to get here so bad?"

I dropped the shovel. "Look, I already told you why—we got paid. Burke met Penny's father in a bar, they started talking and that was it, nothing else to it."

He smiled. "Whatever you say, man." He started banging with the pick.

We worked and a little while later I told him about my midnight stroll.

"I know," he said. "You shouldn't have done that. You were in danger."

I looked at him, paranoia welling up through my chest.

"Was that you on the trail?"

He shook his head. "It was Sanders with the dogs, and that, my friend, was a warning."

We stared at each other.

"And the field?"

"What field?" he asked, light coming back into his eyes as he shifted the lantern closer and dropped the pickax.

"Someone had been digging. I mean they looked like . . ."

He waited, staring at the dark, his breath fogging the damp air. "Graves," he said. "Or mistakes waiting to happen, according to Grace."

"Mistakes?"

"Dead babies."

"What the fuck are you talking about?"

He scowled and then bent to cut the pressure on the lantern until it faded out and we were in the dark again.

"You see any children around?"

"No," I said quickly, not really getting what he was trying to say.

"Took me a year to notice," he said. "And when I finally asked, everybody said they were careful. There were more women in the camp and I'd just hooked up with Lila when she told me about the graves. The ones you saw were empty, but there are others."

"I still don't understand," I said.

"Camp rules," he said. "No children."

"This comes from Nunn?"

"Yes, but then again, this ain't exactly the best place to be pregnant. But shit happens and the women go see Grace. She feeds them some mixture of herbs that causes them to abort. Most of the time it gets caught early, Grace goes to work and nobody knows about it except Nunn and the guilty parties."

He struck a match, lit the lantern and when my eyes adjusted he was back at the wall with the pick.

"What about Penny, did she . . ."

He turned and nodded.

"With who?" I asked.

"PJ—they tried to hide it from Nunn."

"And?"

"She didn't want Grace to go near her, so they made plans to get out. But somehow Grace managed to slip her the poison and take care of the problem."

"What happened then?"

"All the other crap started, the bear got Frye. And then some of the gold went missing and they locked Penny up."

"What about PJ, did they kill him?"

"I didn't say that, now did I?" he said.

"But you suspect?"

He shrugged. "Doesn't matter what I think, man—Nunn showed us some of his clothes and a bloodstain and told us a bear got him. Don't ask me if I believe it—it's what everybody else believes that matters."

I knew then that it had been PJ who'd fired on us at the cabin and PJ who I'd watched sink into the river. Then I recalled the look on Penny's face that morning when she'd mentioned that help was on its way. It was full of hope and we'd killed him and now nobody was coming to save Penny or anybody else. But I had a secret—one that might help get me out of the camp.

I went over to Tozer until he stopped swinging the pickax, trying to decide whether I should tell him what I knew about PJ.

Instead I lowered my voice and said, "Then leave with us when Burke gets better. Show me the cave and where they keep Penny and we'll get the fuck outta here."

"First of all she's not exactly being kept and second I wish it was all that easy."

"She was locked in."

"That's what you saw, right?"

"What the hell's that supposed to mean?"

"Nothing is what it seems here," he said. "Besides, I've got Lila."

"She can come too."

After a long silence he said, "She won't."

I thought a minute. "You've asked?"

He stood, studying a handful of rocks under the lantern's dull glow. "She's afraid."

"Afraid of what?"

"Her old life," he said. "Nunn brought her here and she changed and she doesn't wanna go back to all that. I can understand, I mean I didn't know her before so who am I to tell her she should leave this place?"

"Even now?"

He stood. "Even now." He went back to work, chipping away at the wall, and I knew the conversation was over.

The rest of the morning sped by as we hauled the buckets out for Mooner and Sherman to sluice. The dog was waiting for me patiently outside the cave in a small patch of sun that reflected down off the canyon wall.

At lunch Lila returned with food. Shipley took his sack and disappeared into the cave while Mooner and Sherman sat down on a bank of tailings and began throwing rocks at a ptarmigan pecking its way along the creek bank as it searched for seeds and insects.

Lila and Tozer walked down the creek and sat on a large rock jutting over the water. I wondered if he was telling her, trying to convince her that they should leave with me before the first snow. I found a sunny patch of ground and stretched out, my hands still frozen from handling the cold tools and my back and arms aching from hunching in the low passageways. I fed half of my fish to Lassie, who swallowed it in one gulp along with the stale slab of bread.

Mooner came over and stood, his shadow blotting out the sun. I squinted until his chubby face came into focus.

"Don't get too comfortable," he said in a soft high voice. He wanted to say something else, his face curling into a broad friendly smile, but just then Sherman emerged from a bank of alders and glared at Mooner until the big man peeled off and followed him back to the pile of tailings.

After an hour Shipley crawled from the cave dragging another bucket.

"Time to hit it," he shouted, dropping the rocks loudly into the sluice.

On cue everybody slowly dragged themselves back to work. Lila grabbed a pan and squatted at the creek's edge, her face pinched and worried looking.

Tozer drifted over, looked back at Lila and bit his lip.

"Ready?" he asked. "Ship thinks we're doing too much talking, so let's put one together and make up for the morning."

I flexed my arms.

"Okay, tough guy," he said.

I followed him back into the cave where we worked the wall for a couple hours, speaking only sporadically because Shipley was digging in the adjacent chamber, the sound of his spade rising and falling like the clack of a time clock.

After several hours of backbreaking labor we quit and watched the last of the dig put through the sluice. It felt good to be in the sun. Sweat cooled against my skin. My hands were raw with work and I had that bone-deep weariness of an honest day.

When the last of the dirt and stone had been washed through, Mooner clicked off the small sluice pump and dragged it from the creek, wrapping it in a blue plastic tarp while Shipley examined the catch screens.

"Piss poor," he said, shaking his head. "And then some."

Sherman displayed two pea-sized nuggets in his damp palm for Shipley to inspect.

"And the others?" Shipley asked, flapping his hand at Mooner.

"That's it," Sherman said.

He kept after them. "Give it up, Moondog, or I'll have the new guy beat it out of you," he said, pointing at me.

Mooner broke into a wide, toothless grin and slipped a fat hand into his shirt pocket and produced a small jar with a thin layer of moist sludge on the bottom.

Shipley snatched it from him, held it to the sun and then set off walking back to the camp.

"In case you were wondering," Tozer said, "that happens every day. It's a game between them."

•

At the lodge I checked on Burke. His eyes opened when he heard me approaching. A grin cracked across his swollen face and his hands scooped air, motioning me closer. For the first time I noticed the gray in his thick dark hair. His eyes looked old too.

"How long?" he whispered.

I leaned in. "What?"

He put a gnarled hand to his throat and massaged until his voice came. "How long was I out?"

"Two days," I said.

He grimaced and lay back down on the bunk with a groan.

"What happened?" he said, struggling to swallow. "I was going after the guns . . ."

"They're still there," I said.

He tried to grin, but then seemed to drift off again and within minutes he was snoring loudly, eyeballs whirring under clenched lids. I pulled the blanket up to his chin.

In the kitchen I found Veronica sorting blueberries into a plastic tub, her fingers stained with the crushed fruit.

She looked up from her work. "Come here," she said, dipping a hand into the tub of floating berries and fishing out a handful.

"Taste," she said, pushing a few of them against my lips as berry-stained water purled down her arm, dampening her shirt.

I resisted at first and then opened my mouth, taking in the berries and the dirty water from her water-pruned fingertips, all of it exploding sweet across my tongue.

She took her hand away. "Pretty amazing, aren't they?"

I nodded.

"Bears like 'em too," she said, popping a few into her mouth and drying her arms on a towel.

I was trying to come up with something witty to say when Jenny stomped over and frowned at Veronica.

"Ralph's coming to have a look at your friend," she said. "Now go on, we've got work to do."

I hesitated and Jenny started shooing me, "Out, out, out."

Veronica bit her lip and returned to the berry sorting and I went out and sat down next to Burke, thinking the whole time of the way the water had tasted on her fingertips and the sudden sweet and sour of the berries.

•

Ralph arrived an hour later with his black medical bag. "Sleeping Beauty awake?" he asked, setting the bag down on the bed.

"Yeah," I said.

And as if on cue Burke's bloodshot eyes flashed open, hands reaching out trembling.

Ralph lowered Burke's arms to his side and went to work, checking him over. Burke blinked and struggled as Ralph pulled open his shirt and pressed at a series of banana-shaped bruises that were black in the center and a jaundiced yellow at the edges.

"It's okay," he said. "Got to see what's going on here." He shined a light into Burke's eyes, nodding when the pupils promptly shrank to small black points.

"How's the head feel?" he asked.

Burke looked around the room. "I got a monster fucking headache," he rasped.

Ralph stood back, put his hand on his chin, thought a minute. "Okay, let's start with the basics. Can you stand?"

Burke set his jaw, swung his legs off the bed and stood into a quaking hunch, slowly straightened his back. He looked thinner, his face soft and swollen. A shadow Burke.

After a minute he sat back down with a groan and held his head in shaking hands.

"Somebody did a number on me," he said.

Ralph busied himself with his bag, dipping cotton swabs into iodine and pressing them against the still infected gash that ran the length of Burke's nose. It looked as if somebody had tried to chop him in half. Yellow ooze trickled from the cut and Ralph kept pressing until he saw fresh blood.

Jenny brought a bowl of broth and a chunk of corn bread and Burke ate slowly, wincing with each chew and swallow.

"Easy," Ralph said. "You've got a long way to go."

Burke ignored him and drained the broth, nodding as Ralph asked him a few more questions before leaving.

When he was gone I helped Burke to the outhouse and waited outside until he emerged several minutes later, his eyes tired looking, hands shaking as he reached out to steady himself against a small birch.

We took in the camp as the sun set over the western edge of the lake and smoke drifted across the grass. There was music in the trees again and people gathered around the large stone down by the water's edge, their voices a dull murmur under the music. From a distance it looked like a party and for some reason I wanted to be down there with them, talking with Tozer or staring at Veronica and not standing with Burke waiting for him to snap back from the beating.

He took one look at the people gathered around eating in groups and shook his head. "You find a way out yet?" he whispered.

"Not yet," I said. "I tried last night."

"And?"

"I saw somebody."

"You mean they tried to stop you?" he asked.

"Not exactly, more like a warning," I said. "There was somebody following me, letting me know I was being watched."

"You find anything else?"

I looked at him.

"Like what?"

"Gold," he muttered, "the girl?"

I paused, wondering why he'd asked about the gold so quickly.

"I saw her."

"Duke's daughter?"

I checked over my shoulder to see if anybody was nearby listening or watching. "They had her locked up."

"But you talked to her?"

"Yeah and she didn't make a whole lot of sense."

"Make whole lotta sense about what?"

"This place," I said. "What everybody's doing here. She tried to warn me about something, but then Boothe tracked me down and brought me here."

"What did she warn you about?"

"Getting out, I think," I said. "And taking her."

He thought a moment. "What about the others?"

"Tozer's cool, you'll meet him," I said. "Jenny and Veronica seem normal and maybe Ralph's okay. The rest I'm not sure about."

He nodded, hands trembling less. "There was somebody in the room."

I looked at him.

"Last night," he said. "They were sitting on the floor, staring at a candle."

"Was it Veronica?"

"Which one is she?"

I described her, thinking of how I'd seen her in the lodge carrying a candle and how I'd heard another person in the room.

"They coulda fucked on my bed and I wouldn't have known." He laughed lightly and then held his chest, pointing at his ribs to signal they were too sore. "What about Nunn?"

I shrugged, not wanting to tell him my suspicions.

"He's around," I said carefully.

"Yeah?"

"Yeah what?"

"You figure it out yet?"

"Figure what out?"

"The angle," he said, lamping me with his swollen stare.

I shrugged. "He's some kind of guru," I said, knowing the word didn't exactly fit what I'd seen.

He was quiet a minute. Then he said, "Promise me you won't leave without me."

I gave him a long hard look.

He grinned and I saw that he was missing a chunk of tooth. "You thought about it, didn't you?"

"No, I . . ."

"Fuck it," he said. "I would have, matter of fact it woulda been my first thought—get out, save my own ass."

"Really, I didn't."

"Now you're lyin', Jack. It's okay—I got us into this mess and I'll get us out."

I studied his face, trying to decide whether or not I should tell him that he'd killed Penny's boyfriend. But he seemed strange and just as full of secrets as everybody else in the camp. So I didn't.

"What did he say to you?"

He stared at me, confused.

"Nunn," I said. "When we were in his room. He said something to you."

"It was nothing."

"That's bullshit," I said. "You were scared."

His face closed in on itself while he kicked something around his thoughts.

"He told me I'd killed," he said, his eyes clear again. "I mean he didn't say anything to you."

"That's because I didn't kill anybody," I said.

Leaning back he said, "Not yet, at least." I waited for him to crack a smile but he remained stone-faced, staring me down.

"How did he know?"

He shrugged. "Guess he took one look at us and figured I was the outlaw—the one to watch—and decided to shake my tree, see what came out. Until that crap about the bear, he had me going."

"What happened after you ditched me?"

"Now I ditched you, huh?"

"What was it then?" I said.

"I thought you were gonna follow me," he said. "But when I looked back you were gone, so I kept running . . . and then fuck, I don't know. Somebody clocked me from behind. Maybe I ran into a tree first, but I went down and that's all I remember. At first I thought I'd been shot. There was so much blood."

"Did you see who?"

"No, but when I find out I'm gonna give it right back." He tried to make a fist, but gave up when one of the scabs cracked

open and began bleeding. He frowned and began rubbing a kid-
ney-shaped bruise on his forehead when his knees buckled and he
sank to the ground with a loud thud.

"I better get back to bed," he sighed. "The Burkster ain't feeling too good."

I helped him back to the lodge where he collapsed on the cot
without saying another word. Ten minutes later he was sound
asleep.

•

The next morning Burke was running a slight fever and couldn't
get out of bed. The camp was empty except for Jenny and Veronica, who were arguing with Gant about the greenhouse. Jenny was
shrieking at him and waving a knife around while Veronica sat
perched on the prep table staring at her hair.

I went outside and found Grace waiting for me at the trailhead.

"See if the woods left us anything?" she asked.

"Huh?"

"Check the snares."

I hesitated, still hoping to talk with Veronica or maybe explore
the paths and find Penny's cabin.

"It's better to get out," she said. "Help the camp."

I took one last look toward the kitchen, nodded and followed.

She walked at a good clip, a mesh bag slung over her shoulders.
Several times I managed to anticipate which trail she chose when
we were confronted with a fork in the path. I made it a game,
pointing right or left, behind her back.

Lassie padded behind me, never quite letting me out of her
sight. Sometimes she'd stiffen and stare at some noise only she
could hear. I scanned every small field and opening for signs of
the graves or the cabin where Penny was being kept, but each
clearing blurred into the next and I imagined that Grace was
intentionally steering clear of any such field. Although we did cut
across the place where we'd found Burke bleeding and uncon-
scious and saw that some sort of animals had been digging at the
bloodstains.

Grace, however, pretended not to notice and ducked down a trail, motioning me to follow.

The first rabbit surprised me. It had been caught in a snare next to one of the open fields. I'd seen plenty of dead things but this was different. The thin wire hoop had cinched tight around its neck, making it look like a balloon that had been twisted and pinched to resemble an animal. A small pink tongue glistened from its tiny jaw and on its nose there was a bright red clot of blood. Hornets hovered over the body, landing on the fur for brief moments and then darting off as if they expected the rabbit to jump awake. Grace bent over, pulled a short knife from her pocket and worked the blade under the fur where the wire had pulled tight. The hoop loosened and she slid it gently over the animal's head as if she might harm it in some way. Even with the wire off, the deep crease remained, frozen like a smile, as she put the body in the sack, reset the snare and continued walking.

By noon I was carrying five rabbits and my shirt was damp with sweat where their bodies lay curled against my back. We topped a low rocky hill which rose out of the valley floor, affording a good view of the valley. The lake flashed before us. There were no canoes, just tight waves chopping the glare into thousands of small bright blue reflections. Beyond I could see the swamp wending through the tangled trees and undergrowth until it melded with the horizon in a gray haze.

The woods was full of trees that had begun to yellow and drop leaves when the wind blew. The ferns blanketing the ground were beginning to brown and turn inward as if in retreat from what was coming. I tried to picture the valley smothered in snow, the lake with five feet of ice on it and the wind curling off the canyon walls under a cold black sky hung with noontime stars. Then I imagined the members of the camp huddled around stoves, waiting for the sun to rise and set in the span of three hours.

I'd always liked winter, especially the sight of trees bare against the sky and the way the cold burned your nose and lips. I felt more alive, always measuring myself against the cold unforgiving bar of winter. Maybe it spoke to that little part of me that wanted to die or fight, I don't know, I just saw the world better when there was black ice on the roads and snow falling over everything. But winter in the camp would be different: the snow and cold always at the door waiting for the fires to blink out or the lack of food and planning to hit. But as I stood looking over the valley the idea that this green and vibrant place with its busy people would soon be compressed into small stuffy cabins as winter approached scared me and made me want out.

Grace stood blinking at the bright canyon walls.

"Will you show me the cave?" I asked. "I just thought that if something were to happen . . ."

Her face went still like cement. "What could happen?"

"What about a fire?" I said, remembering the massive burn downriver.

"Already happened," she said. "It skipped over us. It was never meant for the valley."

"Okay, then," I said. "I just thought . . ."

". . . you thought what?" she said, face coming back to life a little. "We're checking the snares we set, Jack, because it's my job— your job too. Everybody must work for the good of the camp before winter comes."

"But I didn't ask for a job," I said.

"But you came." She thought about this a moment. "Do you want to tell me about it?"

"About what?"

"Why you came. Why you really came, maybe about your job if you want. Sometimes it helps to tell the story of your former life."

"Helps with what?" I said, slightly irritated. "I don't have a former life."

She arched her eyebrows at me. "You said you came to get Penny," she said. "Do you really think it's that simple? You don't even know her or why she's here. You came for a stranger. What do you think, now that you're here? What do you see when you look around, do you see anybody who needs rescuing?"

I paused, staring at the scars on her face. "I'm not sure."

"You're not sure because you don't know," she said. "You're here now—in Alaska, in this valley—because you were meant to be."

I turned on her. "Look—I'm not playing this game. Whatever it is you do here, that's your business. I don't give a fuck."

Without flinching she stared directly at me and spoke in a smooth even tone. "When I first arrived I didn't want to be here. I wanted to run out screaming, but I stayed because nobody just comes to Alaska without a reason. This was true for me and some of the others. I really believe we were meant to find this valley and learn from it."

Just then I saw an eagle drifting over the valley. A black cross against the blue sky. Grace noticed it too and paused to watch as the bird circled back lazily before disappearing over the horizon.

There was nothing else to say. I didn't trust her, not with what Tozer had told me, so I shrugged and with that she took off briskly down the hill. I followed, the dog behind me, her nails clacking on stones.

I waited until we were deep in the woods and Grace was well ahead of me before I ducked down a narrow side trail that splintered off the main. Lassie came quickly to my side, the trail dipped to the right and within minutes I could no longer hear Grace.

I proceeded down the path, part of it vaguely familiar, as the generators roared to life in the distance and then faded into the background noise. I thought of Sanders—watching, waiting, wondering if he'd been the one to do the number on Burke.

I rounded a tight bend in the trail and came to another fork.

"Which one?" I asked, glancing down at Lassie.

She didn't move, so I chose left. There were footprints where the rain had gathered in shallow mud puddles and the tree limbs on either side had been sawed recently to widen the track. I kept moving, the rabbits bouncing against my spine, like little fists, their bodies hunched into stiff poses.

The trail descended into a narrow ravine which I hadn't seen before and judging by the sound of the generator I couldn't have been more than a couple of hundred yards from the camp. But the thick impregnable snarl of bush and trees made the camp seem miles away and the valley infinitely larger. Several times I thought about turning back, but the newness of the trail urged me on, so I kept moving.

At a large willow the path veered to the right and the canyon walls loomed closer. As I turned the corner the path opened onto a clearing littered with animal bones and rotting hides. A heavy curtain of sweet rot wafted over me and made my knees weak. I'd found the camp dump.

Waves of flies lifted off the partially decayed pieces of caribou. Hornets swarmed a web of fish bones. Ptarmigan feathers hung in the bushes like bouquets springing from the rich jumbled mounds of rabbit parts, stiff hides, half-bare skulls and yellowed teeth. There was a moose head just sitting there at the edge, half of it gone to rot, the other half locked into some sort of smile as things moved under its skin.

There were birds everywhere perched on the moldering remains, picking at bits of flesh that hung from some of the dump's more recent arrivals. I caught a flash of movement along the back of the clearing. Lassie growled and stepped back into the shade of the trail. I saw the dog then or what I thought was a dog. But as it stepped out from behind a heap of moose skeletons I realized it was a wolf because it was taller than the camp dogs and its eyes seemed different, hungry and wild in some indefinable way. There were others behind it, slinking in the tall grass and stunted cedars. The lead wolf stood its ground, baring its teeth as the rest of the pack gathered behind, whining, yipping and growling.

I backed up slowly, keeping my eyes on the ground in front of me, and that's when I saw the tattoo of bear tracks in the mud leading to the dump. They entered through an impassable stand of cedar and larch and they were fresh, no more than a day or two old. My senses snapped alive, amplifying every chirp and shift in the surrounding forest. The fear plugged me in, connecting me to the land, and for a moment I felt as if I knew every twisted trail in the valley, where the caves and bears were, how the water sank into the swamp and all the dark places where gold lay hidden.

When I looked up, the lead wolf had retreated under the shade of a drooping aspen. Two other animals tussled nearby fighting over the rotten hindquarters of a moose, the flesh coming off in ripe chunks, maggots and small beetles flying in the air as they shook the meat, swallowing it without chewing.

The sudden acuity I'd felt soon faded and I began to creep away from the dump. I felt stupid and small. My legs filled with dread, imagining the rush of the bear or the swirl of wolves tearing at my clothing, sinking their teeth into my back.

I forced myself to move, avoiding twigs and branches, stepping only on hard earth until I arrived at the fork in the path again where I heard somebody moving up it, heedless of the noise they were making.

I stepped to the side, pulling Lassie with me, and hid behind a bank of bushes as a swarm of mosquitoes descended on me, crawling up my nose, fluttering against my eyes. From my hiding place I could see down both paths. Sunlight pushed soft and green through the canopy and in the distance I heard the generators again as Grace appeared on the trail, her face flush with a fine layer of sweat.

"Jack!" she shouted. "Jack!"

I stifled a laugh, suddenly not sure why I'd chosen to hide from her, other than I felt in control of something for the first time since the river. The hiss of Grace's voice brought me out of my thoughts.

"Jack," she called, straining now, momentarily freezing the other forest sounds as I inched farther into the cool, dark woods. Tiny black and gray spiders dropped and hung from webs, waiting for me to walk into them and carry them off, and a ground squirrel rattled through the undergrowth to my left as I tried to make myself invisible.

She raced past my hiding spot, calling out my name. Only the birds answered back, masking my nervous breath and the now constant swiping motion I employed to keep the mosquitoes from settling on bare skin.

I waited until she was out of sight before stepping back on the path and moving quickly to where I'd originally strayed.

The trail began to level out, certain trees and stones set along-side the path took on familiar patterns, but when I broke into the clearing Grace blurred out of the woods calling my name.

"Where were you?" she shouted, twisting the bag of dead rabbits into a tight knot.

"Got turned around," I said in my best fogged-out voice. "I couldn't find you and I thought you'd gone on without me."

She shook her head, strands of gray hair whirling about her face. "You should be more careful," she said. "If something were to happen it would be my fault. I'd be blamed and . . ."

I put on more of the fog—mouth open, eyes blank. "What could happen?"

She clicked her tongue at me and looked down at the dog, who sat leaning against my shins, panting.

I shrugged. "Where do you want these?" I asked, hoisting the rabbits at her.

She pointed to a large crooked tree.

I walked over and dropped them against the trunk. There was dried blood on the ground and bits of fur tangled in the nearby brush.

She gave up with the questions and went to work as Sherman and Mooner sauntered over. They were dirty and tired looking. Mooner must have fallen into the creek because the entire left side of his body was wet and muddy. He smiled at me, his face smooth and childlike.

Sherman turned and stared blankly at Grace, who was hanging the rabbits by their necks from thin nooses on the tree. When she ran out of nooses she nailed the remaining carcasses to the trunk with a rusty hammer, the small bodies jerking, making soft splut sounds when the hammer hit them.

Then she picked up the knife again and with a quick pull gutted each rabbit, tossing the strands of offal into a large white bucket in an easy practiced motion. Next she ripped the hides off with a pair of pliers, exposing the soft gray flesh, stripping the small bodies until they twisted, glistening and obscene like aborted Christmas ornaments.

The smell of blood stirred the dogs from their resting places in the nearby bush. Several of the larger males circled closer and closer to the tree until Grace raised a knife at them. Lassie, who had been watching impatiently, let out a low moan and then hunkered down, her fur standing on end.

Sherman and Mooner watched Grace work a moment and then began walking toward the lake. Mooner took a few open-handed swipes at the smaller Sherman, who countered with a handful of dust and several well-placed kidney punches that seemed to have no effect on the larger man, who kept coming, arms outstretched like Frankenstein's monster. Grace looked up and shook her head at them.

Gant emerged from the kitchen to inspect the take, poking at the soft rabbit flesh with a charred skewer. "We'll can 'em," he said to Grace. "The girls'll take care of it from here."

After Gant had slipped back into the kitchen Grace rinsed her knife in a bucket of water, wiped it on a stiff grime-laden towel and left without telling me what I should do with the rest of the day.

So I checked on Burke and found a half-eaten bowl of stew on the floor beside him. He was still sleeping and must have moved since I last saw him because the blanket lay tangled around his legs like a second skin he was trying to shuck. He stirred, mumbling something in his sleep, and then was still. His face was bright red and I reached over and put my hand against his forehead. It was hot and damp and for a minute I thought that perhaps somebody had tried to poison him, so I sniffed the stew, even tasted a bit, but it was only cold and greasy.

I went to find Ralph, hoping he was around somewhere and could determine if the fever was anything to worry about. Instead I found Mary sitting on a collapsible canvas stool in front of their tent. There was a smoke stain on the tent the shape of Tennessee and some words I couldn't read written on the flap in black marker. Mushrooms lay drying on chicken wire racks beside baskets of freshly dug roots.

She was repairing a torn wool shirt with a heavy needle and thread and didn't even glance up when I arrived. Her hair curled lightly, framing her broad, almost plain face which pinched into crow's-feet around her narrow blue eyes. Her hands were rough and callused, the nails chipped and ringed with dirt. A Tibetan prayer bracelet hung loosely around her left wrist.

She looked up and nodded.

"Ralph around?" I asked.

"He's away," she said curtly.

"Away as in . . ."

She stopped sewing and stared at me. "What is it?"

"My friend needs Ralph," I said. "He's sick."

"He'll be back," she said, slipping the needle into the shirt. "I just don't know when."

"It's just that my friend . . ." I sputtered.

". . . he's out," she repeated firmly. "He'll be back and when he's back he'll find you."

I waited for her to say something else, but I could tell from the blank tone in her voice and those faraway eyes that she was done talking. So I left to explore the woods around the camp, trying to familiarize myself with the trailheads and who lived in what cabin or tent.

I had several awkward conversations with people who were returning from the creek or logging detail with tools in hand. They all had tired faces, gaunt eyes and flat voices.

Lewis and Clark cornered me near the lake. Lewis had a wad of chew in and was spitting every few seconds. Clark was dragging a dead porcupine on a rope that had a jagged bloody stump where its head should have been.

"How's your buddy holding up?" Lewis asked. He had several dead ptarmigan lashed across his back and smelled of gunpowder.

"Better," I said.

"Good," said Clark, jerking the porcupine carcass. "The sooner he gets up the sooner you can hunt the bear. Just do yourself a favor and make it look good, eh?"

"What do you mean?"

"There ain't nothing in this valley except black bear, ya know."

"No griz?" I asked.

"Not unless it came in from the swamp," Lewis said. "In that case, we'll get him, and you and your buddy came here for nothing."

"We came for Penny," I said, not caring who knew anymore.

Clark laughed. "It doesn't matter what ya think you came for, you'll get what Nunn gives. Do what he wants and you'll be okay."

"Is that a warning?" I asked.

"Take it anyway ya want," said Lewis, fingering the stock of his rifle and spitting chaw between us.

Clark started walking away, the headless porcupine tumbling behind him like a child's toy. Watching them go I thought I saw one of the ptarmigan flap its wings against Lewis's back, but when I looked again the birds appeared dead and dull, their wings bent into crashed angles.

•

I returned to the lodge and sat watching Burke for a long time, trying to match the limp broken figure before me with the guy who'd walked into the valley just a few days ago. I tried to picture him up on some roof, hammer singing through the air, exploding into nails, shouting at the whitehats as I struggled to keep up with him.

Ralph arrived before supper and carefully examined Burke again, laying hands all over him, taking his temperature even though the fever had recently broken and the sheets were still damp.

"Well, uh, I think he has an infection of some sort," he said. "Could be anything, but my guess is it's nothing serious, but then again you can't be too careful up here." He eyeballed the room before pulling a small bottle of pills from his shirt pocket and slipping it into my hands.

I stared at the pills. They were expired and the address of the Fairbanks pharmacy in smudged type made me think of my apartment and the few things I'd left there.

I turned to thank him but he silenced me with a sharp glance. "Those are between you and me."

"But . . ."

"Like I said—they're between you and me," he said. "Not a lot of medicine around here, especially with Nunn canceling the supply runs."

I looked at him.

"It's been kinda harsh with nothing in or out," he said. "Not since the bear got PJ. And if you ask me it's dangerous to think we can go the whole winter without supplies from outside. But who am I to question?"

"I thought there were snow machines in the winter."

"Maybe, maybe not," he said, gathering up his things with a tired familiarity. "Nothing's for sure anymore . . . not up here at least."

At the door he put a hand on my shoulder. "Just get the pills in him as soon as you can."

I nodded and he stepped outside, shrinking when the cold wind hit him.

•

When Burke woke he was clear-eyed but groggy. I shook two pills from the bottle and gave them to him. He swallowed them without protest and then motioned me closer. "I want you to try again, tonight," he whispered.

"Try what?"

He glanced over at the kitchen where Gant and Jenny were finishing the jars of canned rabbit meat, wiping the tops with a hot rag before screwing the rings down tight over the lids and dropping them into large pots of boiling water.

"Try finding a way out tonight," he said. "There's weird shit going down here."

I studied his face, worried the fever had fried his brain. "What?"

"Nunn. He sat right there," he gasped, pointing at the rickety stool I was perched on. "He talked to me . . . whispered in my ear."

"You have a fever," I said. "You must have imagined it."

He shook his head and reached out for me. "Just get us the fuck out of here before . . ."

"I will," I said, prying his fingers off my wrist.

He nodded and sank back into the bed, eyes closing, his face dream-locked again.

Before joining the others outside for dinner I pulled the blanket over him and left.

Food was some kind of stew or hash. Gant hovered around the pot scowling, his eyes pink where they should have been white. His hands were shaking and sweat was running down his neck, soaking his thin T-shirt.

For dessert Jenny and Veronica circulated with bowls of berries, rationing out tiny spoonfuls of sugar. Veronica approached, smiling, a wooden spoonful of sugar stained blue from the berries.

"I liked them better the other way," I said.

She smacked my hand with the wooden spoon. "We're too far north for that kind of crap," she said with a stoned smile. "Try again."

"Thank you?"

"Better," she said, dumping a small amount of sugar in my bowl and moving to the next person.

Shipley raised an eyebrow at me and grinned.

"Careful with that one," he said after she was out of earshot.

I nodded, still thinking about her—what she'd look like naked or how her mouth would taste.

We made more small talk, about the mine and a little about the gold, and after dinner I checked on Burke again. His forehead was cool and he was sleeping, despite the banging of pots and pans emanating from the kitchen. Instead of sitting and waiting for him to pop awake and tell me to go exploring I went back outside and walked down to the lake.

The fire was going again, sparks whorling over the water under a rain-gray sky as Peter strummed and howled "Idiot Wind" over the snarl of the fire and the pop of lake stones splitting in the heat.

Grace was talking to Ogre and when I strolled past she stopped. Ogre faked a laugh that withered into a series of wheezes and Grace smiled tightly. Everywhere I went long creepy pauses and dead silence followed as if they were waiting for something to happen.

Ralph glanced up, his eyes knifing me. Mary sat beside him, her hands flopped loosely in his lap like an afterthought.

Tozer saw me through the crowd and waved me over but before I could make it to him, Nunn appeared, walking out of the trees, the setting sun at his back. He was dressed in a long black shirt, dirty blue jeans and mud-encrusted hiking boots. He walked like a king, each step full of purpose and familiarity, as if he had nothing to hide or fear. Grace ran to him and installed herself under his arm, looking up occasionally, a smile tacked across her wrinkled face.

A murmur rippled through the crowd as people rose expectantly to greet him. Jenny and Veronica came skipping out from behind the lodge, their arms glistening with water. Music cracked out of the speakers, drowning out Peter, who upon seeing Nunn, stopped strumming and set the guitar down. Ogre jumped up and stiffened as if he was at attention.

Lewis and Clark, who had been cleaning their rifles on an old army blanket, began assembling the guns without looking, snapping bolts into place, locking stocks and scopes with military precision.

I searched for Tozer and Lila, but they were not among those gathering around Nunn as he led the group closer to the fire, the heat lifting his long black hair, revealing the knotted scar tissue dividing his face. He gazed directly at me, his gold-colored eyes flashing red in the firelight.

I nodded slightly, but before I could raise my hand to offer a small wave, he bent his massive head to Grace. She whispered something to him.

My cheeks reddened as I imagined her ratting me out, telling him of my little disappearing trick or maybe how I'd been on the trails at night. Just then Boothe walked out of the smoke and shadows, dragging the butt of the shotgun in the dirt. I studied Nunn, trying to see if he was somehow directing Boothe's slow steady movement, wanting to see some order in the camp—a design or some communal pattern to emerge and reveal the ragtag assembly of cabins and people hiding from the rest of the world to be something more. But Nunn's attention remained on Grace and Boothe lingered a moment before continuing past the fire and blending into the dark without a word to anybody.

An immense gray vault of storm clouds shifted in from the northeast, covering the darkening sky like a shroud. A chill wind blew off the lake and for a brief moment I saw in a flash the cruel winter that would descend on the valley in a matter of weeks.

The commotion around Nunn made me feel awkward and out of place so I decided to look for Tozer, hoping he'd show me the hot springs.

The farther I got from the fire, the better I felt, but the wall tent Tozer shared with Lila was empty. I checked the lodge and found only Burke, sweating, dreaming, perhaps waiting for Nunn to return and whisper to him.

I went out and stood on the porch and watched lightning ripple in the distance. The people gathered around the fire looked small and moonfaced like children, all of them wanting his attention. I knew that if I wanted to understand what I was up against and why I'd been allowed to roam the camp then I had to get closer, see who was truly with him and who was against.

So I went to them, striding through the spray of bugs and smoke toward the bonfire where I found Veronica sitting by herself, smiling and holding an unlit joint between her legs. Her shirt hung open, exposing the soft curve of her breasts, and the firelight did wonders with her skin.

"Hey, it's Wolfman Jack," she said, patting the ground. "Looking for something?"

"Tozer was supposed to meet me," I said, lowering myself down beside her.

"Must not have been too important because he checked out with Lila." She made a face. "Those two . . ." Her voice trailed off and I was left listening to Nunn as he talked about trees and watching a moose feed in the swamp. Grace and the others gathered in a semicircle around him were hanging on every word. I listened hard, trying to understand what they found so important.

He continued. "There are moments, when the sun is just right, warming the rocks, and the birds are in the trees, when everything seems perfect and in its place—everything, that is, except me." He made a broad gesture with the flat of his hand, then pointed at his face. "If I'm cold I can lie on the stones and receive their heat. I can burn wood. And for hunger there are berries and animals everywhere ready to take and fish in the lake, dumb and willing to give themselves. But there are barriers to taking from the land, not to mention the sheer work of it all and the knowledge that you are still alone but never safe, because that's all wilderness is—the absence of any absolute safety. Wilderness is the opposite of safety and comfort. You can't simply do *nothing* and expect to go on living, not here at least. That way of life works only in the cities and after generations all the old reflexes, the deep dark stuff, goes flabby and becomes forgotten so much that the mere sight of a pathless woods or deer in the headlights is cause for fear."

He stopped and took a minute soaking in the faces, doing slow acid waves with his hand to his face like he was drawing them in somehow, speaking in code. I looked about uncomfortably, wanting to trade smiles with somebody, but all eyes were on him as he continued. "So when I rise to forage in the blueberry bushes I see bear tracks. Rabbits run and hide from me. Birds fly away. Fish catch my reflection and dart into the shadows because I am the *other* to the wilderness—the thing that can never belong because it knows fear, realizes the violence—the necessary *murder* of nature. But to the valley we are merely voices in the trees—things that kill and take and rarely give back. That is our fragile dominion and every year, in the dead of winter, that dominion crumbles a little because it has to, because there are only two things you can count on if you choose to live in the middle of nowhere outside the comfort of cities."

He paused to hold up two fingers, his gaze sweeping the faces before him. "One is that wilderness, true wilderness, is never that far away and once you've seen it—really been in it—you will always know it when it comes for you, quickening the blood, letting you know your place in the order because to take is to give and all that work, all that careful planning, can be undone by a hole in the ice or the swipe of a paw or a spark from a bad stovepipe. The second thing is fear. True fear and trembling before all the indifference surrounding us. It's a fear that most people will never know because all they do is take without knowing what's behind the taking: the slip of knife that starts the steak, the lost fingers in houses, the stillborn calves in every glass of milk, the miles of dead water and stripped land in every newspaper and book—all of it taken, ripped out and packaged only to be consumed without thought or toil. One chooses wilderness only when you know that it takes indiscriminately and asks only that you fear it as you fear the *other*."

He went on like some scar-faced Thoreau and I remembered what Burke had said to me that first night, after Nunn had whispered something in his ear. *Deeply crazy,* he'd said.

But here he was: a true believer who knew that the others had come searching for some meaning to attach to their lives because they had nothing left or because they were natural followers. Everything that I'd seen told me that however crazy Nunn seemed, he knew things—knew how to reach into the campers and pluck strings.

Nunn's voice brought me back to Veronica and the others baking in the heat from the fire.

Across the way Grace sat gawking at me. She looked old. The Alaskan bush had gone to work on her skin, the midnight sun tanning it, wind and cold winters leaving wrinkles. Her hands were thick and rough, the nails blunt and half-mooned with dirt and rabbit blood. There were, however, the scars on her face to remind me that whatever it was she'd run from in her past life had most certainly been worse than making a go of it in the bush.

I leaned into Veronica, pointed at the joint and whispered, "What are you waiting for?"

She giggled. "Company? The right mood?"

"Well," I said, thumping my chest, "aren't I some kinda company?"

"Later," she said, clenching her shirt tight but not before I saw a flash of silver hanging from her nipple.

"Caught you," she said.

I raised both hands in mock surrender and she held my gaze until I had to look away uncomfortably.

Ogre rose from the shadows and heaved a large Y-shaped log onto the fire. Sparks splashed into the air like burning sparrows fluttering gold and orange and for a minute the place looked like some exotic tribal gathering. I half expected to hear drums, women wailing and all that voodoo crap, but then Veronica jumped up, slapping at a few sparks that had landed in her hair. She managed to put them out, but not before the air filled with the acrid odor of burnt hair.

Nunn stopped talking and was now staring at me, his eyes bright with reflected fire.

"Come closer," he said. He pointed at a large copper-colored lump of what looked like gold sitting on a square of tanned moose hide at his feet.

Veronica nudged me. "It's okay, he won't bite."

I hesitated until she grabbed my hand impatiently and led me over to the circle of people gathered around him. Lewis moved aside, making room as Veronica curled into my lap, her tailbone pressing insistently against my crotch until I felt myself getting hard.

Nunn reached down and cupped his hands around the object on the moose hide, raising it until it caught the orange glare of the fire, becoming almost incandescent for a moment.

"The Golden Heart," he said. The good half of his face curled into a self-satisfied smirk while the rest collapsed into a trauma of scars and scabbed ridges.

My chest tightened as I stifled the urge to reach out and touch the gold. It resembled a real heart and not one of the fake Valentine's Day hearts kids cut from construction paper or carve in trees. It was twisted into two nearly identical lobes the size of a baby's fist that met in the center. Several thick spines radiated from the top and bottom like calcified veins, giving it a fragile, other-worldly appearance.

He set the gold down gently on the hide. Remembering Tozer's story about how Shipley had found the heart in one of the cave's back chambers I looked around for him, wanting to see if his face was blank like the others. But he'd moved away from Ralph and Mary, and his attention wasn't on the gold. Instead he was staring at the outline of someone in the trees not too far from the shacks. It was Boothe and there was another figure beside him, nearly indistinguishable from the trees.

Veronica pressed herself against me. Her skin was aglow with bug dope and sweat and I wanted to touch it almost as bad as I wanted to hold the chunk of gold.

"It's amazing," I said, pointing at the gold.

Nunn nodded slowly. "What to do with it is the problem," he said, folding the gold gently in the hide and slipping it inside an ordinary-looking canvas sack. "Nothing has been the same since."

"It's just gold," I said.

He settled a hand on the bag. "Worth is context," he said. "A simple wristwatch in ancient Rome would fetch the wealth of nations. During the gold rush men would have killed for something like the Golden Heart. And now it seems that it's my task to assign it some worth both inside the camp and outside." He scanned the audience again before continuing. "Perhaps it would have been better if we hadn't found it, left it in the ground to be broken and bent into smaller nuggets."

Several people nodded vigorously as his hands stroked the bag like a magician and I stared at him blankly.

"Things are never what they seem, Jack. You ought to know that." There was a small hint of menace in his voice that caused Veronica to stiffen against me. "Your friend is getting better, do you still remember our bargain?"

I said nothing and tried to hold his gaze without staring at the scars.

"I'd still like to know what happened to him," I said.

He considered this a moment. "Perhaps he attempted to go back on our deal and suffered the consequences or perhaps . . ."

I could feel the others staring at me, waiting for me to say something.

"What if we can't find the bear?"

"I can help with that," he said, leaning forward. "Just like I've helped the others to find things. The secret is you get out of this place what you put into it and after coming all that way it would be a pity for you to leave empty-handed with nothing to show for your efforts."

He smiled enigmatically and wrapped his arm around Grace again.

I said nothing for a long while and finally had to look away from his face and focus on the fire. Peter was silently fingering his guitar, nodding to himself. Ogre winked and Jenny seemed to be staring daggers at Veronica, who sat curled against me as the heat of the fire blanketed us in great rippling waves.

Then Nunn went back to telling his story of his time in the woods—staring at animals, noticing the sun and clouds. Veronica nodded along with the others, lulled by the steady drone of his voice and the slow series of hand motions. The more I tried to follow his voice the more I thought about the gold. I'd heard stories of whole families sitting on claims, working the river for years and coming away with a mere handful of gold dust, only to have their fortunes suddenly turn with the discovery of a new vein or nugget. Or worse, stories of men shooting each other when the gold played out and the liquor and women were all gone. Everybody on the job knew somebody who'd vanished into the bush looking to get rich; guys who'd quit it all and did the Fred Dobbs bit—going after gold, getting greedy and sometimes falling off the face of the earth. The story always ended with them on some tax-free island, knee-deep in little brown girls, enjoying the good life. The truth was that just as many men returned broke and dissipated and others died on their played-out claims, swallowed by Alaska, frozen to death, leaving behind only sleeping bags full of bones in remote trappers' cabins. It was what the woods would do to you if you didn't enter it on the right terms.

There were ways to die everywhere. And now after three days in the camp I could see how it happened—how the woods could pull a person in with its endless possibilities and vast green spaces, forcing you to knit patterns, make order of it or die. Alaska was, after all, the last wilderness, a fact that I'd been reminded of several times in smoky bars as old-timers slurred and rambled the story of their lives, somehow wanting the coincidence and lost things to all make sense. Perhaps I wasn't any better off. I was a carpenter, a guy running away from his mediocre past. Nothing more and nothing less. Any romantic, Jack London notions I'd had of making a go of it in the wild, simplifying my life, stripping it down to preparation and survival, had been erased. Nunn was right: life out here in the bush, this far away from the nearest city, pared things down to the essentials—survive or surrender—and there wasn't room for anything else. But I knew there was more gold here than the Golden Heart. It had to be hidden somewhere and maybe all that crap about the wilderness was just an excuse to look for gold.

So I listened to the steady drone of his voice, sneaking glances at the others looking for signs as he talked on and on. More logs were tossed on the fire. The music in the trees quit. Somebody passed a bottle of the blueberry wine and Nunn concluded his speech with a loud clap.

Everything returned to normal. Veronica smiled and people began to drift in and out of the circle, dividing into small groups, talking mostly about work and what still needed to be done if the camp was to prepare for winter.

"We'll need gas for the saws soon," Ogre complained. "Maybe not 'til December, but we're gonna need it." He swatted at a few mosquitoes and stood squinting at Nunn, who seemed not to react to the news other than to smile slightly.

Ogre moved off and Sherman and Mooner told Nunn they were going to the fish camp for the last of the salmon and would need help bringing the salmon back.

Again Nunn nodded and said nothing.

Peter reported that the lake fishing was still good and the nets were holding up. Lewis and Clark assured Nunn that there were plenty of moose in the area and that they were waiting for the weather to turn before harvesting them.

And then Ralph, who had been sitting quietly meditating with Mary, uncurled himself and told Nunn what sort of mushrooms they had gathered and were in the process of drying.

"We need to borrow Quinn and maybe a few others for the berries," Ralph said. "Frost could hit anytime now and it'd be a shame with the amount of berries this year not to get everything we can."

Nunn nodded. "You'll watch out for bears?"

"Uh . . . naturally," said Ralph. He turned to Mary, who was twirling a strand of hair between her dirty fingers, and shot her some kind of private couple look.

"Good then," he said.

Ralph relaxed and pulled Mary closer to the fire until I could see steam coming off them.

Then Nunn looked at me and for a minute I thought he'd simply volunteer my services to the berry pickers. Instead he started talking again. This time it was about winter and the hard dark times coming.

I tried to listen, see the pattern under the ramble. And there were moments when everything seemed to make sense in a crazy scattershot way and I found myself nodding like the others as he spoke of the importance of place and of the shadows all of us had and how it was our job to confront that part of our personalities.

I coughed into my hand and looked about skeptically, trying to break the spell, but those around him continued staring even as he stopped speaking and looked at me as if he knew what I was thinking.

"Coyote energy, like Peter," he said, pointing at Peter.

Silence followed. Peter went pale, his mouth hung open, lips quivering as he sat there, staring blankly at his guitar.

Nunn then recounted how he'd found Peter and his girlfriend

penniless in a no-name bar outside Seward, ready to fight a gang of local Indians who didn't like his white face.

He stopped and nodded at Peter, who began talking.

"I hit her," he said, his voice cracking. "But only sometimes and . . . afterwards I could barely remember it. But there were the bruises and I couldn't look at her, not in the eye because I loved her full-time, like it was my job to love her, and then I dunno, I'm not proud of it. I'm not proud of anything I've done, except maybe up here."

He looked at Nunn, who seemed to be staring right through him.

Peter continued. "We came to Alaska hoping to kick. I figured there wasn't any smack up here and I'd heard about all the summer work entertaining tourists, how if you could sing or play guitar there was always work." He faltered, strumming the guitar absently as color crept back to his face.

"Go on," Nunn said.

Peter set down the guitar and looked at his boots, fingers nervously pecking at the mud-encrusted laces.

"At first the plan seemed to be working but then I stopped gigging and got on the smack again," he said. "I mean it just sort of found me. Some old junkie from Portland tipped me out with a bag, told me where I could get more and that was all it took. She was right there with me and things were like normal again. We loved each other and she helped me sell the guitars when we couldn't pay the hotel bill and after that we just sort of wandered like it was the high old times all over again. We dined and dashed, broke into trailers and took TVs, guns, stereos—anything we could pawn. We had to leave a few places pretty quick and then I don't know, but somehow we just sort of ended up in Seward, hanging around this bar, trying to stay drunk so we wouldn't get sick. That's when I got my face kicked in by the Indians, I mean I had it coming or at least I think I did. But when it was all over and I was just sitting there on the floor . . . I mean it was the first time in a long while that I actually felt I knew something . . . like it was the end and I couldn't go back to the real world because it didn't work anymore, at least not for me it didn't. It was just a matter of time before I got one of us killed, I mean she knew it too and without having to say it I left her and came here and found what I was really looking for."

Nunn sat studying my reaction to Peter's story. I kept waiting for Peter to say something else, praise Nunn or admit to bad things, but all he did was spit into the fire and look away from the others. Ash drifted down from above, landing in his dirty hair, and after a moment, he picked up the guitar and began strumming again, humming along to some half-song, his eyes closed, maybe thinking of the woman he'd left behind. He looked older, teeth pitted, skin stretched tight over his skull. I studied his arms, hoping to see pockmarks or needle tracks, but there were none. His arms were tan and well muscled, work ready, and the only thing to suggest his former life outside of the guitar was the three holes in his right earlobe.

As if on cue a cold drizzle started and all the connections I felt seemed to melt. Even Nunn's voice didn't seem too important to me anymore.

Ralph and Mary said something I couldn't hear, unfolded from lotus, waved, said good night and walked like they were arguing, shoulders hunched at one another, faces bent to the ground.

Nunn stood abruptly, grabbed the sack with the Golden Heart in it and walked toward the cabins.

Grace followed suit. The rest of the group staggered away, work bleary and tired. Jenny came over and tried to pull Veronica out of my lap. "Time for sleep," she said.

"I'm going to stay a little longer," Veronica whispered.

Jenny gave her the eye. "It's just . . ." She stopped herself and Veronica peeled her hand away, saying, "Don't worry, I'm completely in control. See?"

Jenny frowned and crossed her arms, the rain soaking her shirt as she turned her disapproving glare on me.

"I'm okay, really," Veronica said. "Everybody needs to relax around here."

Much to my surprise she shrugged and walked away into the dark.

Veronica turned, face tense. "Mother hen's not happy," she said, making a pecking motion with her hands.

"We're both adults," I said.

She laughed. "That's the problem."

The hot updraft from the fire exploded the rain into a heavy mist that settled over us like warm oil and when the last of the logs finally fell into the bed of coals she took my hand and led me along the lake shore. The drizzle had flattened her hair into stringy clumps that hung in dark coils against the white of her neck like curled wrought iron. Even in the dark with rain on her cheeks she was beautiful in an unusual way. Her nose had been broken, her mouth was too large and full of teeth.

"You still want to leave, don't you?" she asked.

"Is that a problem?" I asked.

"Only if you make it a problem," she teased.

I laughed uncomfortably, remembering the flash of silver on her nipple and the way she'd pressed herself into me while Nunn spoke. As we walked, the rain soaking through our clothes, I watched her hips shift under the thin skirt fabric, pink where the rain made it cling to her skin. I didn't care where she was from or what any of it meant because I wanted her because I could, because here in the camp the rules had shifted under my feet. I didn't know the way out. I'd watched a man die. And the more I looked the more it seemed that this valley was full of lies.

As if to seal what was about to happen she lit the joint, took a hit and passed it wordlessly. The fire gave into the storm and huddled into a heap of coals hissing where the rain hit it, blinking black and bright red.

"I still don't understand what happened tonight."

She gave me a funny look.

"With Peter," I said. "I mean it was strange."

"It's because he's full of shit," she said, exhaling. "There was no girl, I mean maybe somewhere, but not like he tells it. What I think is true is that Nunn found him two seasons ago and he can play guitar. Other than that he fishes and keeps to himself. He's got nowhere else to go. You pass a guy like that on the street and you look right through him. But up here he fits right in because there's nothing else for him to do."

"Why did Nunn have him tell the story?"

"Why?" The smile dropped from her face again and we stood there just looking at each other, the joint burning between us as I palmed it against the rain.

After what seemed a long time she said, "Because he wanted you to hear it."

I didn't know what to say, so I took another hit, trying to play it off. She shivered. The fire sputtered, losing to the rain, and I stared at the moon, a dull cloud-fuzzed disk slouching just over the trees, knowing that if I questioned her the moment would break and I would go back to my tent, alone, stoned and wet.

"Well," she said, standing. "Are you coming? I want to show you something."

"The hot spring?" I asked.

"What hot spring?" she said.

"Tozer told me there were hot springs."

She laughed. "It's just a story," she said.

"What do you mean it's just a story?"

"Does it look like there could be a hot spring here?"

"So he was fucking with me?"

She laughed some more. "Come on," she said, tugging me to my feet. "He was fucking with you."

I stood and followed her back to the cabin. It was small and the walls were unpainted. Eighteen penny nails that had missed the studs pierced the inside at odd intervals. Insulation hung in pink globs, held here and there with bits of duct tape. Two beds sat against each wall under tiny double-paned windows and Jenny was asleep on one of them, buried in her mummy bag. A paperback, *Masters of Atlantis,* lay facedown next to her on the floor, its spine white with cracks. She didn't stir, even as the drizzle switched to rain and began banging against the tin roof.

The only light was an old coffee tin filled with wax and a shoelace for a wick. Black smoke rose in curled gouts and hung in the rain-heavy room like funeral ribbon. Bras, skirts, underwear and jeans spilled from lumpy garbage bags and old tattered duffels.

Veronica shut the flimsy cabin door, sending the tattering of photos and postcards tacked to the back of it fluttering. She led me over to her side of the cabin where above the bed a half-burnt sage stick hung from a piece of twine. She brushed past me just as the dope began to hit. My senses pinwheeling together, images popping and then sinking back down until the only thing that seemed to make any sense was that I wanted her.

I grabbed her and pulled her close, my movements dope slow and clumsy. "Wow," I said, still tingling from where she'd touched me. "That stuff went right to my head."

"Alaskan skunk weed," she said. "It'll put you in another place—make you do things . . ." She stopped, bit her lip and said, "Wanna burn another one?"

I nodded, let her go and watched as she extracted another thin joint from a battered wooden box. Grinning, she stuck it in my mouth, struck a match and watched as I made the tip glow, the smoke coming into my lungs sweet and sticky, easier now. I passed it to her, still holding the smoke in, riding a series of heavy waves, watching as she pulled a thin blanket across a piece of rope, dividing the room in two.

She moved in a sexy loose-limbed shuffle, her dark brown hair falling off her shoulders, wet shirt flapping open to reveal a V of pink skin. There was a faded tattoo near her collarbone that looked as if she'd tried to scrape it away. I thought to ask her about it, but that too slipped away. With a deep sigh she sat on the floor and leaned her head against my chest. Cold damp air crept across the floor as the rain continued to pound the roof.

I wanted to kiss her, but it felt like Jenny was watching somehow, faking sleep, even though the blanket across the room made her invisible to me.

"Tell me what you thought," she whispered.

"About what?"

"Tonight," she said.

"What was he talking about?" I asked.

"Us, them, everything, I guess. That's how it is with him."

"How's that?"

"The way he makes everything sort of make sense. For a while I thought that maybe you weren't listening."

"I was listening, for what it's worth."

"Good," she said.

"Good why?"

"Because he holds the camp together," she said. "Most of us here managed to muck up whatever lives we had before. But up here it's okay—everything's okay. It doesn't matter who you are or what you did."

I looked down into all that hair, feeling her voice vibrate into my chest. "But . . ." I said, trying hard not to let the thought skate away on some dope tangent.

"Yes?"

"There's something wrong," I said. "With him, I mean . . ."

"I know what you're thinking," she said. "You were going to ask me if this is some sort of cult."

"I was . . ." I sputtered.

"It's okay," she said. "To tell you the truth it probably looks like a cult, but the way I prefer to look at it is that we let him tell us things in exchange for living here. The camp's a lot of different things to a lot of different people, but until you've wintered over, you're in no position to judge."

"Judge what?"

"Why we're here, why we stay. I can see it in your face, Jack, you're not as subtle as you like to think."

"And the gold?" I asked.

"You mean what he showed you tonight?" She crinkled her nose. "We don't know what to do with that thing except talk about it."

"I meant the other gold," I said. "The stuff you're taking out of the creek and cave."

She thought a minute. "The rest is ours."

"What do you mean?"

"Each of us gets a share when we leave."

I stiffened. "How come Tozer didn't tell me this?"

"Because he's not supposed to, not after what Penny did."

"You mean sending PJ out?"

"Sort of," she said, her voice barely audible over the ping of rain on the roof. "I'm really not supposed to be telling you any of this, but you would have found out sooner or later. It's not like this is any big deal or even why anybody is chosen by Nunn to come here, but it helps. I mean I didn't know about it when I came here, but then I saw the gold and I guess it kinda makes things easier."

"Where is it?"

She giggled. "You didn't come all this way to steal it, did you?"

"No . . . I mean it's just . . ."

"I was joking," she said. "You can have all the gold you want, you just have to get out of here with it."

I looked down at her. She was still smiling, holding it a little too long until I thought maybe it was the dope.

"How much is there?" I asked.

"A lot," she said, curling her lips at me.

"And everybody's seen it?"

"Except for you. Although you did get to see the Golden Heart, which means he trusts you."

"But he doesn't even know me."

"You'd be surprised what he knows, what you've already told him without knowing it—how he finds you before you even know what's happening."

"That's right," I said, hoping to steer the conversation back to gold. "I forgot, he's some kind of mind reader."

"I didn't say that," she said.

I paused. The dope had warped the dimensions of the room so much that only the drone of rain seemed normal, like we were inside some steel animal, hearing its blood pump.

"And you?"

"And me what?" She did that thing with her mouth again and then sighed.

"You worked in a carnival?"

She killed the joint and tossed the roach behind her.

"Grace told you, right?"

I nodded.

"It was a sideshow," she said. "We opened for rock concerts and freaked people out."

I looked at her.

"Fun stuff," she said. "Live body piercing, chain saw jugglers, razor eaters, fire walkers, contortionists, tattooed man and a chicken geek. We had it all."

"What did you do?"

She smiled. "Don't ask unless you really wanna know."

"As long as you're not Harry the Hermaphrodite," I said. "Tell me, I'm a big boy, I can take it."

"You're stoned, you don't really want me to—"

"—no, go on," I said. "It'll be good."

She smiled tightly and went to a wooden box at the foot of the bed and took from it a long satin bag and a bottle of rubbing alcohol. She dampened a rag with the alcohol and began scrubbing her arm.

I started to say something, but she silenced me with a finger to my mouth, the alcohol burning my lips, cool, bitter and dry.

"You can't chicken out now," she said, removing a half dozen brass needles from the bag. She held one for me to inspect, tapped it against the bed frame to prove that it was solid and then with a quick jab, pushed it clean though her arm. Blood began to drip and land on the dirty wood floor, matching the splat of rain outside.

She repeated the trick with three other needles and seesawed them back and forth, her skin making small tents where they'd entered. Blood ran down her arm, staining her fingertips.

"Tah-da," she whispered, taking a mock bow. "I'd have the geek come out and catch the blood with his mouth. The crowd would go crazy, throw their nose rings at me and scream for more."

"Sounds glamorous."

"Hey," she said, flipping me off and grabbing another needle. She punched it through her upper arm, with a small wince.

She was still beautiful, even with the needles.

She did more of the in and out, taking pleasure in my squeamishness.

"Does it hurt?"

"If I hit a nerve wrong, yeah, but mostly it's all up here," she said. "Many different kinds of pain and not all of it's good if you know what I mean."

"Okay," I said. "I think I've got the picture."

She began pulling the needles out as quickly as she'd inserted them, wiping each with the alcohol and tapping them briskly against the bed frame, still part of the act.

With each rap of the needles Jenny stirred in her sleep, but Veronica was either too stoned or too into the act to notice.

After she'd put the last of her gear away she sat down next to me, rubbing her arm where the needles had entered. "Haven't done that in a while."

"I feel honored."

"You should," she said. "Old habits die hard. Even up here."

"Why did you quit?"

She wrapped her arms around her knees and rocked.

"I didn't come here right away. At first I liked the idea of drifting from city to city with the show. We crawled bars and after-hours clubs, collecting other freaks. It was like being a member of some tribe and only we were in on the joke and everybody else was full of shit—suckers with money for us to take. Do you know what I mean?"

I nodded.

"But it got old," she said. "Especially after you've been through Sioux City five or six times and the same drunk punk rocker hits on you every time at the very same bar and asks for your number. You start doing things you regret, deep dark things to break up the monotony and maybe kill a little of yourself so that nothing ever seems that bad when it happens." She pressed her face against her knees. The holes in her arm seeped, sticking skin to skin. "But then I . . . I mean . . . I mean I kinda split with the whole program."

She was quiet for a long time. I couldn't help remembering the way Nunn had made Peter confess in front of the others, wondering if this was more of the same.

"I met this guy after a show in Detroit," she continued. "I'd seen him hanging around before, talking to some of the others. Sometimes he bought us all dinner when we came through town. He was kinda creepy, but then so was everybody else who hung around and he had money. Jenks vouched for him, said he owned some kind of auto detailing business. I was stoned all the time so what did I care? The only thing worse than being bored was dead. So after the show one night he asked me if I wanted to go get a drink with him. I said yes and before I knew it he had me in his car. We split some acid, smoked a little dope and then it got bad. I started seeing things—his face falling apart, blood dripping from the car upholstery. The car engine sounded like some screaming medical test animal. But I maintained and kept my cool and just when I thought I'd peaked he took me to this club. It was a real freak scene—anything you can imagine. And I got scared. He kept laughing, wanting me to do something with needles for him, said he liked seeing my blood. I knew then that I'd made a big mistake and tried to leave. That's when his friends showed up and took me to a hotel room."

She looked up, wanting me to ask.

"What happened?"

"I gave in," she said. "I let them do what they wanted to me. He would have killed me, so I just curled up and let them have their fun, putting cigarettes out on my back and . . ."

I stared at her until she nodded.

"Yes, that too," she said. "I don't remember it much, though. When they passed out I called Jenny and she rescued me. It took me three days to get my head straight. The show left without us and went to Chicago. Some other stuff happened and then she asked me to come along with her to Alaska and visit her brother who was stationed at one of the bases. One thing led to another and pretty soon I'm here."

"How long ago?"

She unwrapped her arms and moved closer.

"I don't remember."

"Before or after Tozer?"

She pressed her teeth against her bottom lip until the blood drained away. "Before."

"He told me he came here because something bad happened to him. It seems like everybody has a reason for being here."

She laughed. "Everybody except you."

"And Burke," I added.

"I wouldn't be so sure about that one. Not after what I heard him talking about in his sleep."

I studied her face to see if she was feeding me a line.

"What sort of stuff?"

"He kept talking about guns, pieces of skull," she said. "I don't know, it didn't make a lot of sense."

For a minute I was back on the riverbank, gun pressed to my spine.

"Do you know what he was talking about?" she asked.

"I don't know," I lied. But she saw it in my eyes. "He's just a guy I met on a job."

There was a long uncomfortable pause. I let the dope and guttering candlelight fill the gap. I put my hand on her shoulder, pushing her shirt away until it was bare. She made no move to stop me.

"Tell me about Penny," I said.

She sighed. "She wanted out and tried to get others to leave."

"Why?"

"The gold, I guess. She knew about it before she came and when Nunn told her she had to leave empty-handed without even a canoe, she and PJ took some and tried to get out."

"Gold?" I said. "I thought she was pregnant."

She nodded. "Probably—but it was the gold that started everything, and now she has to decide."

"Decide what?"

"About the camp," she said. "Just like Nunn's going to ask you."

"There's nothing to decide."

"You're wrong about that."

"Am I supposed to take that as a threat?"

"No, what you should do is wait—let him talk to you and figure it out for yourself."

"Figure what out?"

"Why you came."

I immediately recalled what Nunn had said to us that first night. "We didn't come here to kill the bear."

"That doesn't matter now, does it?"

"Listen to me," I said, shaking her. "If we can get out of here will you come with us?"

She covered my hand with hers. "You shouldn't ask that question, not now—you're stoned and . . ."

"What?" I demanded.

She bit her lip, gave me a blast of those eyes. "There are things you don't know about me, about the camp . . ."

"What?"

"Plenty of things," she said. "Secrets and . . ." She leaned in to kiss me, her tongue slowly working its way into my mouth.

I gave in and pulled her to me, the dope making everything soft and blurry as I reached inside her shirt and cupped a breast. I felt the cold silver hoop on her nipple and waited until I felt the metal warm. She put her hand over mine, her fingers searching for and finding the hoop. She tugged on it lightly until her nipple hardened between my fingers.

She let out a moan and pushed against me, her hand going to my neck and finding the scab from Boothe's gun trick.

Outside the rain beat harder on the roof as she pushed me back and straddled me, her skirt coming up around her hips. I struggled to free my pants from around my knees, careful not to make too much noise and wake Jenny.

"Secrets, secrets, secrets," she hummed. Her eyes were red with the dope and there was a faint blush on her cheeks. She took my face and pushed it to her breasts. I licked around them until she pushed her nipple into my mouth and I sucked.

"Harder," she said, reaching back and guiding me inside her quickly and then shuddering as I slid in all the way.

It was all I wanted.

She didn't move for a long while and every time I tried to thrust my hips into her, she pushed back until I stopped, letting the moment linger like the hum of a tuning fork.

Then she reached down, spread herself on me, grinding slowly, her stomach quivering from inside as the candle popped and strung black ribbons of smoke which seemed to fall over us like a net. The rain continued to beat against the roof and I watched her move in the half-light, head back, eyes closed, hair damp with rain. I grabbed at her, pressing my hands into her hips and breasts, wanting to feel it all.

She seemed detached, floating above me, her body rocking slow and steady against mine. And then something began to clutch inside her and she moved faster, both of us breathing now in muffled gasps. The room opened up and I imagined I could see the sky, feel the rain on us again. I let go and came, feeling her right there with me.

When it was over she collapsed beside me on the floor. Exhausted I watched a large moth with two black eyes on its wings sail into the candle. It struggled to free itself but then a tip of its wing caught fire and it was all over. The room filled with the unpleasant smell of burning flesh.

Veronica moved her arm across my bare chest, raking the skin with the scrape of new scars where she'd put the needles. I happened to glance back under the crude frame of the bed and saw the knife. My senses crawled back. It was the thin boning knife Burke kept taped to his leg; the very same knife he'd had on him before he was beaten and now there it was sticking out from under a clump of dirty clothes, begging to be noticed.

I stiffened and stopped her hand on my chest.

She lifted her head to look at me.

"What's the matter?" she asked. "Did you hear something?"

I stared at the knife.

She sat up and pulled her shirt on, smoothing her skirt down and rubbing her face sleepily. I dressed quickly.

"What's wrong?"

I pointed under the bed and watched the color drain from her face as her gaze fixed on the knife.

Then I leaned under the bed and reached for it.

"What are you doing?"

I held the blade out in front of her. "Yours?"

She looked at it carefully. "I don't know . . . I mean it's just a knife, so what?"

"It's my friend Burke's knife," I said, watching her reaction. "He had it on him before he was nearly beaten to death. Did you know that?"

She stood stiffly and pointed at the door. Her eyes went cold. "Leave then, if you want, and take it with you."

"I just wanna know how it got here," I said. "It's important."

"I don't know—Quinn, maybe?" she said. "I don't understand how it matters."

"How does it matter?" I shouted.

Jenny sat up, saw me holding the knife. "Jack? . . . Veronica?"

I turned on Veronica, shouting. "Just tell me how this got here."

She sank to the floor and began crying, mumbling that she didn't know, over and over. Her sides shook and her face was draped with hair, tears smearing it into sticky curls.

Jenny stood and went to Veronica and comforted her with a few whispered words while I tried to hide the knife behind my back.

"You don't know what you're talking about," Jenny said, scowling at me. "You should never have . . ."

I cut her off, sober now, things clicking into place. "All I want to know is what's going on here."

She stepped away from her friend and approached. "You're going to find out now," she said, her voice calm and even.

"What's that mean?" I shouted.

But she turned her back on me and returned to comfort Veronica, who was now curled in a tight fetal tuck.

I left, stepping out into the dark bug-drenched rain with the knife in my hand. My head cleared quickly as I ran down the list of possibilities about how the knife had arrived under her bed.

As the rain began to soak through my already damp shirt I figured it would only be a matter of minutes before Boothe or Quinn rushed out of the trees, pointing guns and forcing me into one of the shacks.

But nothing happened, no guns or shouting, just the rain and me in the heart of nowhere waiting.

Several tents were aglow with lamp light. I called out for Lassie a few times, but she didn't come. So I trudged toward the tent, changed my mind and headed for one of the shacks, figuring that sooner or later they'd come looking for me.

I darted into the first shack. The floor was damp and cold so I sat in the highest corner soaked to the bone and shivering as voices echoed outside and I could hear people moving about in the mud. But nobody came for me and I shut my eyes, forcing sleep to come, knowing I would need it.

•

I woke after having slept very little. I was stiff, my clothes still damp. I poked my head out of the shack. Sunlight splintered off the lake, making the banks of fog glow in the dark spots under the trees. The place looked deserted so I went to check on Burke, stepping across the muddy field.

Burke was gone.

I checked the kitchen and found Gant feeding kindling into one of the stoves.

He turned and shook his head at me. "If you're looking for your buddy, Nunn came by and took him for one of his walks."

"But he's sick," I said.

"Not anymore he's not," he sneered. "Got himself the cure." He tossed more wood into the fire, laughing now. "The all-purpose true north cure."

I ran out of the kitchen and headed directly to where we'd stashed the guns, thinking that if Burke was well enough to go on a hike with Nunn, perhaps he'd managed to get to the guns sometime during the night.

The camp was still empty except for a single canoe drifting on the far side of the lake. Chain saws whined and droned in the distance. I half expected Veronica or Jenny to emerge from some path and begin shouting and make a scene.

Within ten minutes I'd arrived at the generator shack and crawled quickly through the thick canopy to where we'd hidden the guns. When I reached around the trunk for them my hands came back with nothing but rotten pine needles and broken twigs.

Trying not to panic I set out on one of the paths, calling Burke's name, fearing he was going to threaten Nunn, shoot Boothe or force some other unsuspecting camper to show him both Penny and the cave and I would be stranded behind, left to answer for him, maybe even pay his tab.

I still had his knife though. I could stab, cut and kill, but only up close, face-to-face, and I didn't have that in my gut, not now at least. What I wanted was the heft of gun iron—the power to point and crumple living things from a safe distance.

It all swirled together, my head still fuzzy from lack of sleep and the dope. I could smell Veronica on me: rain-wet hair, patchouli and tears. Then I remembered the look on Jenny's face when she saw me holding the knife. And Burke, coming out of his fever, his face full of lavender bruises, black scabs, telling me I should find a way out.

•

An hour later I was still thrashing through the undergrowth, afraid of who or what might find me on one of the paths. I was following a mess of unrecognizable animal tracks through the mud into a dense green nowhere. The mosquitoes seemed to multiply the deeper I ventured into the muskeg, buzzing for my blood as leaves dropped from the trees and settled on the ground in a bright autumn quilt.

At the edge of a narrow clearing I saw something brown in the bush and bent to investigate, half thinking I'd find Burke dead this time, beaten beyond recognition. But it was only a rabbit, caught in one of the nooses I'd helped Grace set. It had been dead for a few days and the smell of it hung thick and sweet in the air. Hornets crawled from its mouth and anus and its eyes had been pecked out by ravens or maybe something else.

Just then I heard a rustling in the bushes. My hand went for the knife and then stopped as Quinn emerged from a trail, dressed in dirty coveralls, his beard rubber-banded into a long goatee, tattered baseball hat shoved down over his head. He seemed to be leaning, reeling back and forth, walking to right himself, like he was drunk or crazy.

"It's a dead rabbit, mate," he said. "Real dead, judging by the smell."

He skittered toward me, snatching at stray branches, stopping every few feet to lift his cap and scratch his head. Blood rushed to my face and without thinking my hands curled into fists.

"I found the knife," I said.

"What knife might that be?" he said. "Plenty of knives around."

"The one my buddy Burke had on him when he was jumped," I said, pointing now. "The one that somehow ended up under Veronica's bed."

He played it cool, chuckled. "Lots of people been in that bed. Some quicker than most."

"What's that mean?"

"The slag's not exactly a pillar of virtue," he said. "Let me guess, she got you stoned, ran her stupid trap about the camp and then fucked the shit out of you?"

My face must have registered shock because he smiled crookedly. "I'll take that as a yes," he said. "Well for your sake I hope you brought some of those New World rubbers with you, or you my friend are going to be visiting the field. That one's fertile as the Nile, mate, and you might have a little problem on the way for Gracie to take care of."

"The knife," I demanded.

He got in my face, swaying back and forth.

"You want me to do what?" he asked, blasting me with his rotten breath. "Apologize for fucking her before you or apologize for the knife?"

I shook my head. "I wanna know why you did that to my buddy," I said.

His shoulders tensed. "Maybe you oughtta ask him why he dragged you up here. It ain't about Penny, I can tell you that."

I stepped back.

"Come again?"

Quinn laughed and rearranged the rubber bands in his beard. "Got your attention now, do I?"

I didn't say anything.

"He came for the gold and you're the wanker who followed him."

"Back the fuck up," I spat.

"We can do that too," he said, hands snapping into broad fists as he rushed me, snarling.

I met his charge, grabbing him by the coveralls. Everything went bright around me as my hands slipped instinctively to his throat and I struggled to find solid footing in the spongy underbed. He was light, his neck thin and soft, and I kept squeezing until his hat fell to the ground.

He kicked and swung punch after punch. But I outweighed him by a good fifty pounds and my grip was strong from all the hammer work.

It felt good and pure.

I drove him through the trees as his fist mashed at my face but I held tight and let him swing until I could taste the gunpowder of cracked teeth mixed with blood vapor. He landed one solid jab and I saw orange for a second, felt that ticking in my neck, like I was going down. I kept squeezing even as he tried screaming, his throat working, coming alive under my hands. I pushed harder until pine branches slapped by like needled turnstiles.

I slammed him against a dead tree and he went limp for a moment, his sallow body folding under me. I fell to the ground with him, both hands still wrapped around his throat, tight like snares as he gasped, his eyes bulging. For a second I saw how easy it would be to kill him, the realization blooming in my chest, black and needy.

He kicked and thrashed against me, his throat straining to form words as I gazed directly into his eyes, imagining the light going out of them like color bleeding from a dying salmon.

And then suddenly the spell broke and I looked away, my hands relaxing until his breath came back in shuddering heaves.

I could feel blood oozing from my nose and my lips swelling.

"Enough?" I screamed. My lip burst, filling my mouth with hot salty blood.

He nodded and I rolled off and let him catch his breath.

"He put up a fight," Quinn gasped. "Your friend, it was either put him down or let him get shot so I put him down."

A line of blood ran quickly from his nose, dotting his coveralls in grape-sized drops.

I stood over him and put a hand on his throat again, felt things crunch. "What are you talking about?"

"Nunn told us that you came for the gold and that Penny was just some excuse," he said, his voice breaking. "He's talking to your friend about that now."

"Where?"

He smiled and arranged the rubber bands in his beard again. "Around," he said finally. "The woods. He'll come for you and talk plain sense, mate, talk and talk until it's all you hear, all you ever wanna hear. Then you'll see how it's to your advantage to help out the camp and help yourself at the same time."

"Do what?"

His eyes widened. "Kill the bear," he said.

"Why don't you just hunt it yourself?"

"We already tried that and it's bad karma, mate. The bear hides. We kill innocent ones and the meat goes bad because nobody wants to eat it." He rubbed his throat again. "Besides it makes sense that strangers should be the ones to kill the bloody thing."

"Is that why you nearly killed my friend?"

He sighed. My handprints were still visible on his neck. "All I did was save him from himself and if you had any sense you'd do the same," he said.

His face grew dark as blood continued to drip from his nose and without warning he scrambled to his feet, grabbed a heavily knotted branch and swung it, catching me on the shoulders and knocking me into the willow scrub. I managed to roll away from the next blow, slithering through an opening in the thicket and then breaking out into the harsh glare of sunlight.

"Wait," I screamed.

But he was on me with the club, this time thudding it into my rib cage, knocking the breath out of me, his eyes blank slits, beard flying about.

I reached around and found Burke's knife and brought the blade up.

He smiled and then froze as his eyes fixed on something over my shoulder. I turned to look and at first I thought it was Lassie trying to find me, but when I saw the animal I knew it was one of the sled dogs—a large one, half wolf, its fur matted, ears ripped and scabbed from fighting. Another dog moved into the space behind it like some vapor, smooth and silent. Others followed.

Quinn shook his head and drew a long serrated Gerber knife, staring at the wall of greenery as more dogs shot through the woods and into the clearing like bullets, assembling themselves around him.

A dog brushed up against my leg and moved past Quinn, who was still frozen, knife in one hand, club in the other.

He began backpedaling out of the light and into the cool shade, stopping against the wall of pines.

I'm still not sure what happened next, but he tripped or was pitched forward and the club flew from his hand. He shrieked loudly and several of the dogs matched it with deep howls that made the hair on the back of my neck stand on end.

I inched closer and saw that somebody had ahold of Quinn's ankles, dragging him into the heavy brush. It was a man with thick strong arms, a full beard and a wild tangle of hair obscuring his face. He was dressed head to toe in dirty camouflage and he moved vinelike up Quinn's body, punching, grabbing and subduing as the dogs swirled, yipping and baring their teeth.

It was Sanders, the man whose silhouette I'd seen on the trail.

Quinn struggled, stabbing blindly behind him and missing, the blade sinking into his own thigh. He dropped the knife and the dogs closed in, licking at the blood, lunging and nipping at his clothes.

Sanders grabbed his wrist and twisted it quickly and something cracked. Quinn howled in pain. His arm stopped working and seemed to just hang there, twitching like some half-dead animal.

"For Chrissake help me," he hissed.

Sanders was on top of him now, both arms cinched around his chest in a bear hug. I noticed a small gold nugget on a braided strip of leather hanging from his neck. It caught the sunlight and glinted, a bright spot in the camo and dirt.

Sanders looked up at me. "Go," he said. "Get out."

Then he said something in a language I didn't know and the dogs halted, sitting back on their haunches silently.

"Help me," Quinn hissed again.

"Go," Sanders repeated. "Go now and there'll be no word of this to the others. You are in danger and must get out of this place, before . . ."

Quinn elbowed him in the jaw and Sanders answered with a short punch to Quinn's Adam's apple that left him gasping and clawing at his throat with his one good arm.

"What?" I asked, coming closer, blood rushing to the bruises.

Sanders motioned me away over Quinn's pleas for help. We locked eyes. He took one hand away and pointed at the gold around his neck, smiled and then winked at me as if he'd given me some sort of sign.

"Go," he repeated. "Leave everything."

I nodded, pushing carefully past the dogs as they growled and stamped at the ground with their paws. I knew that with a word they would be at my throat.

Sanders didn't call out or try to stop me as Quinn made one last pain-racked attempt to get my attention.

Then there was silence.

I kept walking into the sun and when I turned they were gone. Only the dogs remained, regarding me like statues, their mouths half-open.

Sanders had given me some sort of sign by pointing at the gold. The only problem was I didn't know what it meant other than he'd saved my ass from Quinn. I knew there was no going back, that some change had taken place in the camp and now maybe everything was coming undone, so I kept wandering, keeping to the cliff edge, looking for the cave opening, still hurting from my throw-down with Quinn and puzzling over what he'd said about Burke.

Water oozed down the rock face and in other places small waterfalls formed, spilling dirty streams into dank pools rimmed with lichen and moss. Hawks soared overhead through columns of shifting white clouds. I was hungry, tired and confused—floating through the landscape, scrambling across the litter of stones and deadfall. I stopped to call for the dog a few times, but she didn't come. Twice I heard gunshots and moved toward them, but after a half an hour I gave up and drifted back to the cliff wall.

I killed most of the morning, just wandering, staring up at the cliffs wishing I could transport myself up them, hike out to the boat and be done with this place. So I searched for the cave and had covered more than half of the valley wall when I heard someone approaching. Moving on instinct I scampered behind a large boulder and hid, pressing my cheeks flat against the cold stone.

The crashing grew louder and for a minute I thought it might be a moose or, worse, the bear, but then I heard voices. It was Tozer and Lila and they were calling my name. I kept hidden and watched them—saw the way Lila reached out for his hand, face knit with worry as they called for me. Again I was struck by how young they looked, under all the filth and tangle.

I waited until they'd vanished down a path before I followed, walking quietly, keeping the sound of them just in range until I recognized the path as the one that led to the dump. Remembering the wolves and bear tracks I retraced my steps, found the fork and chose left instead of right and ended up back at the lake.

The camp was empty, the generators silent and a slight breeze hissed off the lake. Birds darted over, casting shadows on the water as I hid in the bushes, watching things, hoping some plan would come to me. My hands were still trembling from the fight with Quinn and the sound of his voice as he pleaded for me to help him. Sanders had saved me from being beaten to death, but why?

•

After an hour of watching and waiting I began to move along the apron of trees. I darted out to check Nunn's cabin for any sign of Burke. The door was locked. I pounded on it and when nobody answered I checked the rest of the buildings. They were all empty.

Somebody had cut the ropes on my tent and tossed my bag into a mud puddle. Lassie trotted out of the bush to greet me and despite all the aches and pains I felt good and alive as I made for the cliffs again, determined to find the cave.

A hundred yards into the woods I ran into Tozer.

"Hey, man," he said, "we been looking all over for you."

I shrugged.

Lila stood off to the side looking at something through the trees. Her face frozen, seconds from tears and a scream.

He came closer, braced me. "Where the fuck've you been?"

"At the camp," I said, not sure whether I should tell him about the fight with Quinn. "There was nobody around."

"What happened?" he asked, pointing at my face. "You're bleeding."

I touched my swollen lip. "I fell."

He shook his head. Lila turned and began to lose it, lips quivering, eyes rolling seizure white. "It's back," she said.

"What's back?" I said.

"The bear," Tozer said. "It took Quinn this morning."

The news hit me deep as I remembered the look on Quinn's face as he pleaded with me to help him.

"But that's impossible," I said.

"They found blood and his hat," he said. "Lewis and Clark are out looking for him now with some of the others."

"How do you know the bear took him?" I asked.

"Because we saw the blood," Lila said.

There was a deep silence. My plan for getting out began to crumble.

"He's the one who beat Burke," I said. "I found his knife under Veronica's bed and then . . ." I stopped.

"Never mind that," he said. "Tell me what you saw."

"First show me where Penny is," I said.

He nodded. "Deal."

"And the cave," I said. "I wanna see the cave too."

We stood there a moment. Lila was clutching at her neck, fingering something on a string. It was a nugget and without thinking I pointed at it.

"Where did you get that?" I asked.

"Nowhere," she said, tucking it into her shirt.

I glanced at Tozer to see if he was wearing one. He wasn't and I knew it meant something, especially after Sanders had pointed to it. I remembered that Penny had one too.

"I know about the gold," I said. "Veronica told me."

They stepped back under the shade of a pitiful-looking willow. Leaves fluttered down around them as Lila shot him a look and grabbed his arm. "Don't," she said.

"He's not stupid," Tozer said, giving me the eye.

"No," she said, shaking her head.

He ignored her. "I mean why else would we be up here?" he asked.

Before I could say anything she spoke. "For him," she said quietly. "For him and what I was when I came here. I don't care about the gold."

"Tell me," I said.

Lila began crying and dabbing at her eyes with dirty fingers.

"I haven't seen all of the gold," Tozer said. "Just a few canvas sacks and coffee tins full of dust and pea nuggets. But we know it's here somewhere."

"Is it why you stay?"

He thought a moment, put an arm around Lila and shook her gently. "Part of it, I guess. Hell, I don't know anymore—it's all different, everything's changed."

"But you've been looking for it?" I asked.

He nodded but wouldn't look me in the eye. Lila just stood there fingering the nugget nervously, twisting the rope tight and then letting it spin.

"What about the others?"

"Some of 'em know," he said. "Penny was telling people that Nunn was sneaking the gold out and that we were working for nothing."

"Do you believe that?"

He shook his head. "I don't know what to believe anymore except that he's not going to let anything go easy. Before all this shit started happening he could just talk to you and that was enough. Now . . ." He tossed his hands in the air. "Now everything's fucked up and coming apart fast."

"What's going to happen?"

He shrugged. "He's gonna put us through some kind of test to see who's with him and who's not before winter hits and as long as he has the Golden Heart people will listen to him." He pulled close, examining the work Quinn had done on my face. "Now fess up and tell me what happened with Quinn."

"You'll show me the cave?" I demanded.

"Right on," he said.

So I told him about Quinn coming at me and the dogs and then Sanders.

"What do you mean he tried to kill you?"

"He came out of the woods and we argued about Veronica," I said.

Lila rolled her eyes. "The whole camp knows about you and Veronica."

Tozer nodded. "What were you thinkin'—that chick's out to lunch."

"Take a guess," I said.

He ignored me. "So then Sanders shows up with the dogs?"

I nodded.

He paced, stripping pine needles from an overhanging branch. In the distance I could hear people shouting and the dull concussion of gunshots.

"Quinn had to have come back to the camp," he said. "Or . . ."

"What?" I said.

"Tell me you didn't kill him."

"I wanted to," I said. "I mean, I could have, but I didn't and neither did Sanders."

"Then how does Nunn end up with his bloody hat?"

"I'm telling you it wasn't like that . . . I mean Sanders could have killed him right there or had the dogs do it, but he didn't. He was holding him down so I could get out, then he gave me some sort of sign."

This seemed to catch him off guard.

"What kind of sign?"

"He pointed at that," I said, gesturing to Lila's necklace.

"That doesn't mean a goddamn thing," he said. "Not now, at least."

"What did it mean?"

"It doesn't matter," he said, waving me off.

Lila stepped up. "It meant we knew."

"Knew what?" I asked.

"Nothing," Tozer said, clearly annoyed.

I looked at them. There was a strange otherworldly smile on her face and Tozer was staring hard at his boots.

"The truth," she said. "Nunn gave them to us after we'd wintered over, but not everybody wore them."

"I lost mine in the lake," Tozer said.

"I still don't understand."

"That was before," Lila said.

"Everybody knew there was gold here, but nobody really talked about it until Penny showed up. But then Ship found the Golden Heart and not too long after Nunn got mauled by the bear. Penny nursed him through the worst of it. She kept asking him about the gold, wanting to know where it was all hidden."

"Why?"

"Because she wanted to take it," Lila said. "So she started talking to people. Touching the nugget was the signal that you were with her. But it sort of blew up because nobody trusted anybody and now this . . ."

"And now everybody's just pretending it's the way it was," Tozer said. "I'm not sure Nunn knows the fucking difference. Or Penny for that matter because after PJ had his accident Nunn took her into the woods for a week. Who knows what went on, but she came back changed or at least broken, that was until you showed up—"

"—PJ got out," I blurted.

"What?"

"Burke shot him," I said.

"What are you talking about?" Lila said.

I told them what had happened and how we put the body into the river and when I'd finished, Tozer stood there, shaking his head. "Penny was sure he'd gotten out," he said. "How do you know it was PJ?"

"Because he had gold on him."

Tozer nodded. "Nunn's been using the bear to brainwash and scare half the campers back to the way they were. The rest of us just wanna get out alive with a little something."

"You mean the gold?"

He nodded coldly and Lila stood, shaking her head in disapproval.

"What was Sanders trying to tell me?" I asked.

"Who knows," he said. "He let you go—you're lucky for that."

"He said I was in danger."

"You are," Lila said. "And so is everybody else who wants to leave."

"If Sanders didn't kill Quinn then who did?" I asked.

"It doesn't matter," Tozer said. "All that matters is that Nunn has everybody believing a bear got him. He's even called a gathering tonight."

"What's a gathering?"

"You'll see," Lila said.

"If you want to get out of here just talk to Burke and keep quiet about Quinn," he said. "We'll talk to the others and see who wants to go."

I nodded. "Now show me," I demanded.

He took the lead, skirting the edge of the field. Lila followed close behind and I brought up the rear, snapping branches every thirty yards, committing the route to memory. We were on trails only half the time and after hearing voices through the trees I figured the path was not the most direct one, but meant to provide minimal risk of running into anybody else.

At a narrow clearing Tozer halted before motioning us through the weeds and dead branches. Lila turned and put a finger to her lips and I steadied the dog with a few errant pats until she sat, wagging her tail.

I advanced, crawling, trying not to make a sound, and when I reached him he parted the branches, revealing the lower half of the cliff walls still white with late afternoon sun. I could make out a pile of talus and larger chunks of fallen cliff stone peppered among the stunted pines and alder.

"I don't see it," I said.

"You're not going to," Tozer said. "Just watch over there by the tree." He picked up a stone and heaved it toward the cliff wall where it smacked loudly against the outcropping. A figure rose from the shadows immediately. It was Boothe and he had his gun out, scanning the brush. We ducked, waiting as he walked a small semicircle before returning and then fading from sight again.

"You can't see it until you're right on it," Lila said as we made our way back. "There used to be a marker, but I'm not sure anymore."

"It's going to be guarded, twenty-four seven," Tozer said. Glancing back I could see my trail of broken and bent branches. If

Tozer and Lila noticed them, they didn't mention it. Besides I hadn't really seen the cave and had to trust that it was there and would be there when the time came.

"Why is Boothe guarding it now?" I asked.

They looked at each other a moment.

"Because of what's about to happen," Tozer said.

"What's that?" I asked. But he didn't answer. Instead he grabbed Lila by the hand and dragged her through the woods expecting me to follow them back to the lake.

•

At the end of the trail they stopped and told me to stay out of the way and say nothing.

"Find Burke," Tozer said. "We'll talk to Ralph and some of the others about getting out."

"Tonight?" I asked.

He nodded grimly and walked on ahead.

The dog sat at my feet. A cold wind whipped off the lake, stinging my cheeks as I watched people moving about the camp, hauling wood, cooking and preparing for the gathering.

When I walked into the center of it all, looking for Burke, nobody stopped me.

I found him down by the water, washing himself. He stood slowly, his face looking better, water dripping from his great head.

"I'm back, Jack," he said.

There was too much to tell him—the gold, Veronica, Sanders and Quinn, so I said nothing except, "I saw the cave."

He smiled. "Good," he said, rubbing lake water on his neck.

"That's all you're going to say?"

He stood. "I talked to him."

"Nunn?"

He nodded. "We can have the girl if we do what he wants. And . . ."

". . . the guns are gone."

"I know," he said, something in his voice causing me to back away. "They were part of the bargain."

"What bargain?"

Just then Grace came down to the water's edge and stood listening, the wind tossing her hair. She had that too-far-gone look in her eyes and her face slack like she was watching some private horror show shit.

Burke stopped and pointed at her and I tried my best to talk low, hoping she wouldn't hear what we were saying.

"What bargain?" I repeated.

He shook his head as Grace crept closer.

"We've gotta get out of here," I said.

He smiled again, slicked back his hair and wrung out the lake water. His eyes were calm and sober.

"We will," he said.

"Tonight."

Glancing at Grace, he came close, slopping an arm around me and whispering, "Just make it look good."

And with that he strode off toward the others that had assembled around the front of the lodge, leaving me to puzzle over his remark. I watched him move among them talking as if he'd always been a part of the camp. Ogre slapped him gingerly on the back. There he was, back to full strength, transformed somehow by the beating. All sorts of paranoid thoughts ran through my head. I wondered what he and Nunn had talked about in the woods and worried that perhaps Quinn was right and Burke had known about the gold all along and Penny was just some story to get me to come along. Or that Tozer had lied to me from the start, filling my head with hope, commiserating, letting me in on false secrets to gain my trust. And now there was no time left to sort anything out.

Grace came over, stared and pointed at me and then inexplicably walked away toward the lodge.

Instead of joining the others for dinner, I walked along the lake shore, idly skipping stones, going over all I'd been told, trying to sort out some truth I could latch on to. The signs and secrets were all there drifting down around me like fallen leaves: the needles in Veronica's arm, her curled and naked and me with the knife,

Burke's awkward hug. Grace's scars and her tiny graves in the woods. Penny's confused warning and her kiss before Boothe had taken me away. Even PJ's dead face came floating back, mouth open through a halo of bloody river water. And there was the clink of skull falling on the cabin floor, the dead beetles under the bloodstain and Burke's secret. But most of all there was the Golden Heart, the sight of it cradled in Nunn's hands reminding me of what Veronica had said about the promise of gold to those who stayed.

I had to find out about the gold for myself, especially if half the camp was out there looking for it and all that was left now was some elaborate charade.

I wanted out.

I wanted the gold and I wanted the girl.

Nobody rushed to stop me when I faded into the woods with Lassie close behind. As I snaked through the woods around the camp making my way toward Nunn's cabin the sun failed behind a bank of soft white clouds, and smoke from the rekindled smudge pots began drifting through the trees like ghosts. I crossed several trails, keeping the tin roofs of the camp well within sight.

Ten minutes later I'd made Nunn's cabin and was hiding behind a large woodpile. I could hear the others, not too far off, eating and talking as I waited, swatting at mosquitoes, watching the cabin for any sign of movement. I sat there for two hours and then the speakers crackled to life, music lifting the pregnant hum that had fallen over the place. I saw Lewis and Clark jog by, guns out in front of them, and Peter paddle out to the middle of the lake, drop something in the water and then paddle back.

I was hungry and my arms were sore from where Quinn had clipped me with the club, but I had a plan and I was going to stick to it or die trying, because Burke could no longer be counted on, not after what Quinn had said. And the more I waited, the more I knew I wanted not just gold, but the Golden Heart.

So with the shadows growing longer I told Lassie to stay and looked around a moment before slipping from the woodpile and heading for the back door. A large rug hung across the opening and I hesitated, sure that at any moment Grace would appear and stand pointing, calling me a traitor.

I ducked inside the short foyer, my hands groping for the rough wooden door in the dark. I found it and pushed gently, expecting it to be locked, but much to my surprise it swung open silently. The large hook and eye made a low snick as I looked inside the dim rectangular space. Red oil lamps glowed, their wicks low, smoke blackening the glass as my eyes adjusted to the gloom. The room was thick with incense. I glimpsed somebody in the far corner and squatted to see under all that smoke. It was Nunn and Veronica lay beneath him naked on the mattress, legs spread wide. He was naked too, his scarred back glowing in the lamp light as he moved between her legs.

My stomach knotted up and I wanted to run, but I didn't. He was talking to her as he moved in and out of her almost mechanically, his hands wrapped around her thighs gripping them hard.

She was either crying or moaning—it was impossible to tell because of his voice droning, "Tell me, tell me, tell me." Over and over, chantlike, and for a minute I thought about stopping him. I even reached for Burke's knife. But then he rose from the mattress and stretched his thin arms to the ceiling while Veronica folded her legs and rolled onto her side, grabbing at a blanket to cover her nakedness.

He turned and appeared to be looking at me for what felt like a long time. I practiced stillness and becoming one with the dark as I stared through the cracked door waiting for something to happen. Maybe even ready this time to kill.

Veronica stood, her legs trembling, and came to him. They were no more than fifteen feet from me, but they seemed distant, lost in the red glow of the oil lamps as I retreated into the darkness, wondering what it was I'd expected to find or do. The Blake prints pinned to the wall above them fluttered as she fanned the blanket around her shoulders and stretched to kiss him, pressing her damp face against his ruined one. The blanket slipped from her shoulders and fell around her and I saw the glint of her nipple ring.

He stood there like a statue as she moved her lips across the fold of scars and scabs, arms pinned to her sides as if she was afraid to touch him. She kissed him one last time and then turned to dress, leaving him to stare at a table covered with various stones. Some of the stones were marked, words scratched into their surface; others were just ordinary-looking lake stones with white lines in them. But nestled in among them was the canvas sack containing the Golden Heart and a dirty baseball hat I instantly recognized as Quinn's, the brim of it crumpled and bloodstained.

Veronica came up behind him. "Sorry," she whispered. "I'm so sorry. I don't want to go back, not in front of the others."

If he heard her, he gave no indication.

She stopped and he pulled a small brown thing from a basket and held it in front of her mouth until she opened it.

"Take it," he said, setting it on her tongue like a communion wafer. He waited until she'd swallowed it.

"Good girl," he said. "You'll see things more clearly tonight."

She nodded and he began dressing, pulling on his clothes slowly. When he was finished he grabbed Quinn's hat and tucked the Golden Heart behind a stack of books in the corner. He pulled back his long black hair and bent to a small piece of polished steel, staring at his reflection for a long time.

He turned to Veronica. "Bring her," he said. "Bring her and we will let them make up their own minds. Either it will be all over or we can start again."

She nodded and without looking back exited through the front door.

He returned to the polished steel, bending his face to it, and poked at a bright red ridge of scar tissue then held his finger to the light, examining it. He muttered something to himself I couldn't make out and then quickly turned and followed Veronica out of the cabin.

The minute I heard the door bang shut I moved swiftly, my heart beating in my throat, sweat pricking out of my pores as I knocked the books away reaching for the sack. I half expected Nunn to step through the door and kill me with his bare hands.

It wasn't as heavy as I'd expected so I opened it until I could see the Golden Heart reflected in the red lamp light.

Everything changed around me when I slipped the sack into my shirt. I moved with a clear purpose, gold knocking against my ribs.

Outside the air was heavy with smoke. The dog rose stiffly to greet me from behind the woodpile.

"Good girl," I said, before dropping into the bordering woods, the sack pressing against my stomach.

There were others moving along the trails, checking tents with flashlights and scanning the water's edge with lanterns as dusk fell. Somebody had built another large bonfire and I could see people gathered around it staring into the flames as if deciding whether or not to walk into them.

Anything was possible now that I had the Golden Heart. I even considered making for the cave with the gold and leaving everybody else behind, but something stopped me and I started looking for a place to hide it before joining the others. If and when Nunn discovered it was missing the slow unraveling that Tozer had hinted at would spin out of control and there was no telling what might happen. Perhaps the confusion would allow some of us to slip away.

Each time I set the sack down behind a pile of stones or old brush I came back to it, knowing that if all hell broke loose I'd never find it again. So I decided to hide it in plain sight, in the rabbit-skinning tree behind the lodge.

I found the tree with no trouble. The nooses hung empty, and coiled against the trunk were the snares I'd made with Grace. I placed the sack with the Golden Heart in a wide crook and stood back to make sure it wasn't visible from the ground.

Already I wanted it back, but I forced myself to go down to the water, walking past my collapsed tent and into the thick white smoke of the smudge pots.

They saw me coming and I wanted to yell, wake people up, cut through the smoke and stories and get out before winter frosted down from the mountains. That was the loose plan. But then I saw a few of the faces and knew I was in trouble. People sat next to each other, not speaking, staring at the blaze which seemed to burn brighter with each branch Ogre fed into it.

Tozer gave me a nervous glance and then looked away quickly.

Burke sidled over. "Thought the bear got you," he said. "That or you ran off."

I couldn't look him in the eyes. All my thoughts swirled back to the Golden Heart up in the tree waiting for me.

"I'm here," was all I said.

The music suddenly became very loud, the tape hissing and popping.

"You know something," Burke said, his voice flat.

I answered him with more silence and took in the scene. Nunn sat cross-legged on the ground next to the fire. Ash fell from the fire plume like fresh snow. Peter was nearby with his guitar on his lap, face pinched tight against the heat. Grace kneeled, coiling noose wire into small bracelets. Ralph and Mary stood next to the pile of wood, watching the fire, and Mooner looked up at me, his face smudged with dirt and ash, eyes bulging slightly. He was sitting on his hands, rocking back and forth slowly and talking to himself while Shipley paced by rattling stones in his thick palms.

Jenny and Gant were sharpening knives and she glanced up from her work to stare right through me.

As if on cue Nunn stood, holding up Quinn's bloodstained hat for everybody to see.

"It has come," he boomed. "And now we must do something about it before it takes another. We need to come together and remember all that we've left behind, all that we will leave behind. We must prepare for winter and allow the newcomers to prove their worth before the snow comes."

His voice came at me in surreal chops and overly dramatic pauses. Nobody else seemed to notice.

Grace began crying.

"Here comes the Kool-Aid," Burke whispered, smiling slightly.

"Looks like they've already had a few party favors," I said.

He nodded. "Some kind of mushroom and seeds."

Nunn circulated through the crowd, inspecting faces, and when he came to us he smiled. Something passed between him and Burke, but when I looked again he'd moved on.

Lila brushed past me. "You were right," she said. "Ralph saw Quinn, said his arm was broken or something before Nunn took him into the woods."

"He was killed after?"

She nodded and left when Grace suddenly appeared out of the smoke.

Burke gave me a look and I started to ask him about the gold just to see how he'd react but there was a clattering sound behind us and I turned to see Lewis and Clark coming out of the shadows from the lodge, dragging something large, their breath chugging white in the chill night air. At first I thought they were dragging Quinn but as they came closer I saw that it was a moose carcass. It was no larger than a pony and its legs pointed stiffly at the sky. The rack had been sawed off and the chest cavity scooped clean. Whole sections of its hindquarters were missing.

Jenny stood and with the knives in her hand like Chinese fans began stripping away the hide, carving off large chunks of flesh while Gant grabbed several sharpened sticks and impaled the meat on them.

Ralph and Mary rose, took a skewer from Gant and held the meat to the fire. Others did the same as I tried to process what Lila had told me about Quinn.

"Play along," Burke said, thrusting a stick into my hand. I nodded and followed the others to the fire, holding the meat close until my face burned with the heat and the flesh sizzled, spitting fat into the fire.

"What did you talk about?" I whispered.

He looked at me blankly, his face still swollen and yellow at the edges.

"With Nunn," I said.

He shook his head. "Not now," he said. "We've got to do something first."

"What do you mean?"

"The bear."

I looked around, people had begun eating, tearing at the half-raw meat with their fingers. "There is no bear. They've killed them all."

He pulled his stick from the fire and tore into the meat, juice running into his half-beard. "How do you know?"

"I was there with Quinn," I said. "He came after me because I found your knife."

His eyes glowed. "Yeah?"

"Under Veronica's bed."

"Go on, I'm listening."

"Quinn had been there the night before."

"You've been a busy man, Jack. What else?"

"The bear didn't get him."

"What about the hat?" he asked. "I was with Nunn when he found it. There was blood everywhere."

"They tried the same thing with PJ."

He eyed me blankly.

"The man you shot at the cabin, the one who was trying to escape."

"We'll talk about this later," he said.

"There's not going to be a later."

He grabbed my arm. "We'll see about that," he said.

Tozer walked by and pointed as two figures emerged from the darkness and into the ring of firelight. The first was Veronica and behind her walked Penny. Nobody else seemed to notice, not even Burke, and I quickly pulled the stick out of the fire and dropped the moose meat on the ground, where Lassie fell on it hungrily.

Penny stopped at the edge, looking pale and fragile—the girl in the picture was gone.

After a minute Nunn came to her, bent his massive head and began whispering into her ear. Her hands began to shake, her knees wobbled. He held her up and tried to press her close, but she straightened and pulled away, her face breaking into sobs.

He left her and went around speaking to the others. Some

peeled away and left after he'd finished with them while others just sat back down and resumed eating the moose meat. He spent a long time with Tozer.

Lanterns bobbed around the perimeter and flashlight beams tilted through the trees as the fire spat sparks red against the night sky. The music cut off and Nunn came to us as the others gathered around in a loose circle.

And then all the plans went to hell.

Burke stepped up to meet Nunn.

For a minute I wanted to push them into the fire and run, but then I looked at Penny, her face wet with tears, the fire burning higher and higher behind her, and I couldn't move, couldn't possibly think what came next. Nothing seemed to make much sense anymore even if it was all about the gold.

Clark appeared cradling a pair of rifles in his arms and stopped in front of Nunn, who in turn nodded silently at Burke.

He reached out and took a rifle and turning to me he said, "You with me, partner?"

I stumbled away from them.

Penny came toward me, crying, pointing her finger, and Grace stopped her.

"I told her about PJ," Nunn whispered. "She knows everything."

"Told her what?" I asked, trying to keep my cool.

Nunn smiled. "How you shot him. How you gave his body to the river."

"It was Burke," I said.

But Nunn kept smiling and I looked at Burke, who turned away from me and went to the others with the gun in his hand. There were people emerging from the woods dragging skinned dogs and disemboweled rabbits on ropes.

Everything was coming apart.

"Come with me," Nunn said.

Penny slumped to the ground in a heap at Grace's feet, glaring at me.

I started toward her, wanting to explain, get back the girl in the picture, the one with the dying father. Just then she lifted her head and out of the tears I saw her wink and her hand go to the nugget around her neck.

It was a sign—enough to keep me going.

But then Nunn stepped between us. "Come," he said, the smooth half of his face blinking in the firelight.

I got lost tracing the scars and before I knew it I was following him away from the fire and into the dark. The last thing I saw was Burke with the rifle, stuffing shells into his pocket.

We went deep into the woods, Nunn navigating around the dim outline of trees, avoiding branches and swampy depressions, spooking thick clouds of mosquitoes into the air. I could hear Lassie trailing behind, keeping to the shadows. The fire was a distant orange glow through the lattice of trees and even though there was nothing there for me I wanted to be back sitting around its heat with the other zombies.

"She came for the gold," Nunn said.

I stopped. The heat from the fire was gone and I felt very cold standing next to him.

"Who?"

"Penny," he said. "At first I was fooled. She fit in and helped the camp. But when we told her about the gold she began to talk with the others. Some of it went missing and she tried to pass a note to the supply pilot. And then everything began to crumble— everything I'd built here, all the work, it meant nothing because of the gold."

I looked at him, trying to read his ruined face in the gloom.

"Her father told her about the gold," he said. "And sent her here to take it."

"Duke?" I gasped, replaying that night in his cabin and how Burke had convinced me to go along.

"He wasn't always called that, not when I knew him," he said. "He told you stories, how he was dying and wanted to see his daughter. Am I right?"

I nodded.

"And you believed him, didn't you?" He took the letter Duke

had given me out of his pocket. "Perhaps you should have read this before coming all this way."

I looked at him.

"What Duke didn't tell you is that she wants to stay," he said. "That she wants to be with us, even now, after all that has happened and will happen, with winter coming, she is part of us, just like you could be part of us."

I reached to take the letter from him, but he crumpled it and threw it into the brush. "Her mother's alive," he said.

"What?"

"It was all a lie," he said. "Everything you came here for was a lie, Jack."

"Why would he tell us that?"

He laughed, stepped back into the shadows. "Because you are a coward," he said. "Because he needed you to believe something and because she will never leave here, not now after what has happened."

I could no longer distinguish his body from the trees all around us. I knew I had to do something—think of some way out, just a chance to get back to the others and the Golden Heart.

His voice dropped into a croak. "I know about Veronica, too," he said. "Just like I know other things, pieces of everybody here because they trust and believe in me and because I've led them to this place in their life—this valley. Just like you were led here, deluding yourself that it was because she needed rescuing. You're no better off than they are."

"You're lying," I said.

"How can you be so sure? Or your friend Burke . . ."

"Burke what?"

He laughed. "Way deep down even you needed to find this place."

"I don't believe it," I said.

He shrugged. "Well then, I have a test for you, a choice just like your friend Burke gave you, only I'll tell you what you can expect because I have nothing to hide." He turned and came out of the shadows again and I stumbled away, wanting however crazy it was to be back at the fire with Burke and the guns.

He struck a match and held out his hand to reveal several small dark seeds.

"It's important you understand your place here, so in the spirit of free will I offer you a choice," he said. "You can hunt for the bear with Burke or take one of these and join the others."

He rattled the seeds in his palm. They resembled shriveled insects.

"What are they?" I asked.

"Some of them are harmless. Two of them are jimson seeds. Are you familiar with it?"

"They're poisonous."

"Only to some," he said. "Only to some."

"Is that what you gave the others?"

"Some," he said. "Others required something else."

He lifted the seeds until they were right under my nose. "If you don't die you'll see things you haven't seen before. Perhaps even the cave or maybe you'll discover why you decided to come here. Or maybe when this night is over you'll find yourself down by the river, delivered from this place, delivered from everything you came looking for."

I stared at him.

"Once you know, you can never not know," he said. "You could go back to your life or whatever that is and you would know, Jack, you would know things others don't or maybe it will all be over tonight for you . . . Would you like that?"

"Know what?"

The match went out and he reached over and tapped me on the chest. "What's inside here when nobody else is looking."

"What about Burke?"

"He's elected to stay, for the bear, because there's always a bear, Jack," he said. "A lurking god. The whirlwind. Fear."

I felt blood rise in my cheeks as I tried to remember what Burke had said to me.

"There's no bear," I shouted. "I know what happened to Quinn."

He made a fist around the seeds and thought a moment.

"Yes, the same thing that happened to PJ," he said. "The same thing that happened to Frye—the wilderness took them. Or maybe you killed him because you wanted the gold. Either way it can be anything I tell them."

He was quiet again as I collected my thoughts trying to turn something around on him.

He put his face next to mine. "You're a coward, Jack, and now two men are dead because of you."

"I didn't kill anybody," I shouted.

He clamped a hand around my throat and brought the seeds to my clenched mouth.

"For them I am the wilderness, Jack—I am the dark woods, the one who brings the bears."

I struggled to push his hand away and he abruptly let go, grinned and swallowed all of the seeds as I watched in horror.

"They were nothing," he said. "And you did exactly as I'd expected. Now where does that leave us?"

"I know what you're doing up here," I said. "The gold—is that it?"

There was a long silence and then, "You don't even know what you're doing up here, do you?"

I didn't answer and instead darted past him and ran toward the light of the fire, branches smacking my face and arms. The dog fell in step beside me as I pushed and fought to find some sort of path back to the others.

Nunn suddenly appeared in front of me, blocking the way.

"Made up your mind?" he asked.

I moved close and ripped a wild roundhouse at him, connecting with the scarred half of his face, my fist making a wet sucking sound. He didn't move and I swung again but he caught it this time and smashed his elbow into my throat and I went down.

Pain rocketed through my whole body and I forced myself to stand, knowing everything from here on in was for keeps.

When I rose to meet him he was holding his face, his breath ragged and uneven from pain. Lassie lunged at him, but I managed to pull her back and run, letting it all out, trying to keep the glow of the fire in front of me. I hit trees and nearly fell several times as my throat began to swell, making it hard to run.

I broke into the clearing and ran along the lake edge and saw that there were only a few campers left around the fire.

Burke was gone and there were others in the trees with torches and lanterns. Wolves howled in the distance and I took off for the tree where I'd stashed the Golden Heart, pulse thrumming in my ears. I'd never felt so alive, so sure of my actions. I was running on pure instinct, reveling in each free moment.

When I got to the tree it was still there in the crook. I opened the bag and touched the gold before heading down the trail.

I heard my name being called again, and turned away from it, cradling the Golden Heart in my shaking hands when Burke grabbed me from behind, put a flashlight into my face and raised the gun at me. I slipped the sack inside my shirt. Lassie went after him, snapping at his gun arm, and he swatted her away and then knocked me to the ground.

The dog yelped and I slithered forward to grab her, digging my fingers into her scruff, feeling every muscle come alive somewhere deep in her.

He clicked off the light as the sound of others grew near.

"Where is he?" he demanded, searching the dark.

"Who?"

"Nunn!" he hissed. "I thought he was doing a little mind fuck on you."

"You could have stopped him, said something, I mean he could have killed me."

He lowered the gun, the old Burke coming back. "That's not his style, Jack."

"Tell me what his style is then. Because you knew," I said to the dark in front of me.

"Knew what?" he spat.

"About the gold," I said. "It was all bullshit—everything you told me. You never intended to get her."

He stood fingering the gun stock, hands white against the wood.

"Not now."

"No, now," I said. "I wanna hear about the gold."

"You don't know what you're talking about."

"Fuck you, I don't. He told me why you dragged me up here. It was just some game to you, wasn't it?"

Even in the dark I could feel him put the gun on me again.

"This ain't no game, partner," he said. "We're way past that. We can get out of this before the shit hits the fan. Get out and get out good, with a little something."

"I wanna hear it."

"Hear what?"

"The whole thing—why we came."

"I thought Duke was just some dying old man trying to sweeten the deal, telling me about all the gold and how we could just walk out of here with it because they'd be too far gone to notice."

"You could have told me."

"That wasn't it. I didn't believe it myself, not until we found gold on that guy at the cabin. Things changed then."

"Duke lied about Penny's mother," I said.

He nodded. "So I've been told."

Branches snapped behind us and he jerked me farther into the trees.

"It's not only the gold," I said.

He squinted. "It is about the gold, Jack. Why else would they come here?"

"That doesn't matter anymore," I said. "You've talked to him—you tell me."

"He knew things," he said. "He knew why we'd come. He knew what we wanted."

"So you told him?"

"Fuck yes, I told him," he said, coming closer. "I slapped all the cards on the table, because that's what he wanted to hear. Look, Jack, anything goes here except leaving."

"He knows because he found the letter," I said. "That's all, the rest you told him."

He hooked his shoulders. "It was more than that. He asked

about shooting that guy by the cabin, just like the first night. That wasn't in any fuckin' letter."

"They found the gold when they took our packs, that's how he knew."

"Did he tell you what happened before?"

I looked at him.

"That blood and bone we found in the cabin."

"Yeah?"

"It was Boothe," he said.

"What do you mean?"

"He and a couple of buddies were using the cabin for moose hunting. They got into trouble with a bear. One of them got mauled and Boothe snapped his leg trying to climb a tree. Three days later Nunn found them and asked Boothe to shoot his friend who'd gotten mauled. He reasoned with him, said they could watch him die or give him a little nudge into the sweet hereafter."

"What happened?"

"Boothe did him, shot him point-blank," Burke said.

I backed away from him, remembering the bartender's story about the moose hunters.

"What is it?" Burke asked.

"Nothing," I said. "Do you believe him?"

"Doesn't much matter now, does it?" he grunted. "Boothe does what Nunn tells him and right now he thinks the bear's back."

"But there is no goddamned bear," I shouted.

"And that first night in the field—what the fuck was that?"

"A bear," I said. "But not the bear that did the number on Nunn's face. Tozer thinks he baited the bear in with a dead dog, hell I don't know."

"They've been killing dogs all afternoon."

"Who?"

"The Canucks," he said.

"The whole camp thinks PJ and Quinn got eaten," I said.

"That doesn't mean there's not a bear," Burke said.

"It'll be a bullet in our backs or something and then the bear— he's put us out here to have an accident."

"What about this?" he said, lifting the gun.

"None of that matters if we can get out," I said. "Tozer and Lila want to come, maybe even Ralph and some of the others—"

"One thing first," he said, taking off down the trail, expecting me to follow.

And I did because even though I no longer trusted him I still held out some dim hope that he'd come through or that I could use the Golden Heart to bargain my way out of the valley.

•

We came on the first of the dead dogs in the clearing where I'd discovered the small graves. They were hanging in the trees, their bodies stripped of fur, throats slashed. Some of them had been shot. The air smelled of blood and other rich things and I imagined bears and wolves lifting their noses, following the scent, as I tried to block out the rustle of leaves and branches.

Lassie refused to come any closer. Burke bent to examine the blood trails crisscrossing the field. There were no bear tracks or lights in the distance and for a moment everything was quiet.

Burke circled nervously doing something with the gun, clicking the flashlight on and off, swearing as he jacked shells out of the magazine and stood staring at them.

"What is it?"

"No fucking good," he said, dropping the shells into the mud where they landed like punched-out teeth. "The rims have been messed with."

Then he ran the bolt home and pulled the trigger with his ear to the chamber. It sounded bad and a quick check revealed that the firing pin had been snapped off. He heaved the gun into the brush.

"Hope you're right about the bear," he said, loping off into the dark, leading me down a narrow brush-clogged chute. There were trails on either side and every so often someone would run by shouting. Twice I heard gunshots.

I asked him where we were going, but he ignored me and kept slithering through the dark.

Several times I thought about ducking away, finding Tozer and going to the cave with him. But I stayed, shadowing Burke through the dark until we emerged on a familiar trail. Ahead I could see the cabin where I'd first seen Penny.

I looked at him. He was grinning, moving now with a sureness I didn't think possible as he urged me forward and kicked down the cabin door. Before I could ask what he was doing he began searching the floor with his flashlight, knocking over the small woodstove and tossing the cabin.

"What are you doing?" I asked.

But he didn't answer. Instead he pushed away the rickety bed and I saw that some of the plywood flooring hadn't been nailed tight.

"Come on," he said, looking for something to pry it up with. "Gimme a hand."

I handed him a coal shovel and watched as he pried up a section of floor to reveal a large crawl space. In the hole was gold, lots of it, dozens of Mason jars filled with irregular-shaped nuggets, coffee tins full of gold dust, and he bent to it, laughing, pushing his fingers into the jars and scattering the dust in the air like pollen.

"See?" he screamed. "Cult, my ass, it's about the gold!"

I just stood there frozen by the sight of all that gold, wondering how much work had gone into it.

"How did you know?"

"I had Nunn show me where he was keeping Penny."

I studied his expression.

"Don't just stand there playing with yourself, get me something!"

"But how . . ."

"Duke said it would be hidden in plain sight. So when I saw the cabin, I knew, I just knew," he said. "Now find something to put it in."

"Bullshit," I said, sensing he was lying about something. "You did something for Nunn."

He got in my face. "Help me get the gold," he growled. "Help me get the gold and we'll get the hell out of here."

"Or?"

"Or, nothing. You can leave right now if you want—you know where the cave is."

I thought about it a minute, knowing I still needed him if we were going to get out alive. So I took another look at the gold and tossed the room for a sack to carry it in. The only thing I could find was a couple pairs of dirty Levi's and some mud-spattered blouses. He snatched the jeans from me, tied knots in the legs and began dumping gold into them, stopping every so often to feel how heavy they were. When he could barely pick them off the ground he jumped out of the hole and stood there staring at the remaining gold, wondering no doubt how he could take all of it.

"Now show me that fucking cave," he said.

"We've got to get the others."

"Fuck that, Jack," he said. "Look at all this and tell me you wanna go play hero. For what?"

"Because they'll die if we leave without them."

He thought a minute. "Fine," he said. "Show me the cave and I'll go my own way before things start getting really weird around here."

"I'm not going to do that," I said firmly. "We won't make it like this. They're going to find us."

"I don't wanna hear that, Jack. We're in the heart of it now. Piss down your leg and both of us are dead."

With that he shouldered both sacks of gold and was out the door.

Not wanting to be caught in the cabin I exited quickly and headed for the nearest trail.

Burke was waiting for me under a tree. He stepped out of the gloom and put a hand out to motion me still. The dog growled as we crouched, listening for the sound of breaking branches.

They were coming for us.

I saw the gun first. It was Clark, his face catching the moonlight, glowing like a mushroom. His eyes were black slashes and his gaze was locked on the ground beneath him as he stepped lightly down the trail. Burke slowly lowered the gold from his shoulder. But Clark had spotted us and he snapped the gun in our direction, yelling something I couldn't make out. But it was too late. He fired, splitting the night with a blue and white funnel of light.

Burke charged into it, low and centered.

And then nothing as the barrel flash faded and the woods went dark again. I was momentarily deafened by the gunshot and went to where they were wrestling on the ground. Others were coming now through the trees, shouting, shining their lights.

Burke was on top of Clark whirling away with his fists. He was trying to protect himself but Burke kept battering away until his arms fell limp at his sides. He went on pummeling Clark's face and neck with tremendous blows, each of them shaking the ground. Clark seemed to give in to them, his mouth hanging slack, taking each blow with a wet mushing sound. The rifle lay on the ground next to them and I went to it, but before I could reach it, Burke stood and pushed me away, grabbing the gun for himself.

I looked down at Clark. His face was a stew of blood and mashed skin and his nose had been pushed across his cheek. There was blood coming from his left eye and his chin was split to the bone like a vertical smile.

I turned to say something when I noticed that Burke was walking funny and that there was something dark pooling around his boots.

We locked eyes and I knew what it was.

"Are you shot?" I asked, pointing at the blood.

"Shot good," he said, his hands digging frantically at his side, just above the hip. "In and out, I think. That's good, huh?"

I bent to have a look as he put the flashlight on it. There was a hole and a lot of fluid coming out just below his ribs and white curds of fat mixing with the red torn stuff.

"How bad?" he asked.

"Not bad," I said. "But we've got to find Ralph now."

He shook his head. "Just take me to the cave and get us the fuck out of here."

"We'll never make it down the river. You'll die if we don't do something."

He put his hand back over the hole, fingers disappearing in the wet mess.

I looked around for something to bind him up and slow the blood. There was nothing except the jeans stuffed with gold. With Burke watching I dumped the gold out and shook them until they were free of the stuff. He started to say something, but then he looked down at his side and began pulling his shirt up for me to bind him. I did the best I could, wrapping the stiff denim around his waist, tying it tightly, not wanting to tell him the truth about how bad it looked. When I finished there were flakes of gold everywhere, mixing with the blood. He bent to stuff his pockets full with some of the larger nuggets.

I checked on Clark, marveling that Burke had managed to pulp the man's face while shot and bleeding. He still hadn't moved so I tried to see if he was still breathing. His eyes seemed to shine in the dark. This was not like the movies. He was still and bleeding. There were no last words or gasps, just the utter calm of a man dead or close to it.

The others were coming, drawn by the gunshot.

In the dark I saw two figures slip into the cabin and I turned to see Burke standing over the gold, still trying to stuff it in his pockets.

"Hurry," he gasped, grabbing the remaining sack of gold.

"Leave it," I said. "I'll find Tozer and Lila and come back for it."

He shook his head. "I'm not walking out of here empty-handed."

"What about him?" I whispered, pointing at Clark.

"He's all done," he said, heaving the sack over his shoulder, the gun steady in his free hand.

I had no choice but to follow him off the trail, hoping the

others would pass us by as he propelled himself forward with a massive effort deeper and deeper into the woods. The moon flashed on, revealing a bloodstain covering half his body. The wound was worse than he wanted to admit and in a tight stand of pines his grip finally failed and the gold fell around his feet like a dead man.

"Pick it up," he said, pointing.

I shook him off and told him no.

He shot me a look and tried again to pick it up, but it was no use, the jeans I'd wrapped around him had soaked through. He looked pale and moved now in jerks and shifts as if at any moment his body might quit and fall to the ground beside the gold.

We stood there, staring at each other a moment. I knew he wasn't leaving without it so I shouldered the gold and we pushed on, quickly crossing trails, sticking to the dark tangled places, toward what I didn't know. Animals I couldn't see moved all around us, ravens shifted awake, ground squirrels scattered and even the scrim of mosquitoes seemed to lift. As I struggled through the thick brush, stumbling into dead dogs and smelling Burke's blood, the old fear of bears roused itself inside me.

And the fear was good. It needed to be there urging me on as the Golden Heart knocked against my ribs and the gold cramped my shoulders, sucking every last bit of strength out of me. I knew then that if we were ever going to get out of here alive I had to burn everything. Lay it down and use it up.

At a dip in the trail he stopped and fell to the ground. I dropped the gold and went to him. Cupping the flashlight deep in my palms to hide the light, I played the pink glow over his shaking body to find that the bleeding had worsened. His boots were full of blood and he was shivering.

I asked him if he could go on and he nodded weakly, one hand pawing at the hole in his side, the other reaching out for the gold as I helped him to his feet silently.

"We'll get help," I said.

His head rolled to me. "Good, now get the gun," he gasped and gripped my neck tight.

I took the rifle and helped him down the trail, the moon giving us some dull light and a little hope even though I knew we would be found and that he was probably dying. So I followed a wide trail, past more dead dogs, staring at us gagged and gutted from bloody ropes until we stumbled out behind Nunn's cabin and made for the fire. Burke kept falling to his knees and each time I lifted him he felt heavier.

Down by the lake somebody was feeding green branches into the blaze and through the thick white smoke I could just make out a few figures sitting cross-legged next to the fire.

I pushed forward, Burke and the gold leaning on me. I kept waiting for one of them to rise and come for us, but they just sat there, arms and legs folded still as stones.

Fifteen feet from the fire I heard someone coming up fast behind us and before I could turn they blasted into me, sending the gun sprawling. Burke collapsed with a loud groan and I hit the ground hard and began crawling toward the rifle, not sure who or what was behind us. I rolled just in time to see Lewis pounce on me.

I kicked and struggled, but he put his weight into me, his fingers slipping into my eye sockets and pulling until I was blind and howling. We went at each other, fighting close like animals, biting and punching until I managed to separate him with two short jabs to the throat. Good things crunched under my knuckles. I saw blood.

As he sat there gasping I went for him, but before I could reach him a loud shot cracked and a bright silver hole opened just above his eye. The hole smoked and then flushed red, his head flopping lazily to one side, mouth coming open in a stupid grin. There were bits of meat everywhere and white chips of bone and the air was thick with gunpowder and the smell of blood.

I looked up to see Burke swaying over us, rifle in hand, his face empty and pale as if he'd lost something.

Lewis's body gave one last shudder and then slumped over to

reveal a large fleshy starburst in the back of his skull. Then he was still.

I grabbed the gun from Burke, who staggered and then fell beside Lewis and began crawling toward the fire.

"The gold," he gasped. "Get the gold."

I stood there stunned by it all, unable to move even though I had the gun and part of me wanted to just shoot Burke, show him a little mercy. Or maybe it wasn't even that.

Tozer was the first to arrive.

"Where have you been?" he shouted.

Stunned I looked back at the fire and the smoke billowing out from it, orange around the edges.

"Snap out of it, man," he shouted.

But I was too busy watching Grace, who had appeared out of the haze, serene smile plastered across her face. She moved past us to where Burke lay, half slithering toward me, pointing and trying to say something. The jeans I'd wrapped around his midsection had come undone and there was a trail of red dirt next to the ever-widening pool seeping out of the hole in Lewis's head.

Tozer kept pulling me away, shouting something about Nunn. But I was watching Grace, wondering what she wanted with Burke.

I went to her.

"He needs help," I shouted. "Can you find Ralph for me?"

"Where is the Golden Heart?" she asked, her voice a shallow croak.

I looked at her and knew she'd checked out.

"He wants it," she said as she bent and began going through Burke's pockets, roughly. He put up a small fight, pushing her away like a patient refusing treatment, wet with his own blood, eyes peeled deep and scared. She knocked his hands away and patted him down, leaning close and whispering in his ear, "Where is it?"

I remembered the Golden Heart and pressed the sack close to my skin, feeling its jagged edges, wondering if I should pull it out and begin bargaining for my life.

Burke kicked her and gurgled at me to help him when I saw Grace flip out a knife and lean over him. With a quick pull she opened a large grin-shaped slash just below his chin. The light went out of his eyes and he fell back, his face pointing at the starry sky.

I tackled her, the blade slicing up my palm, and for a minute I was lost in the tangle of her hair. Her small body crumpled under me and I expected to feel the cold push of the knife entering my stomach but then Tozer pulled me off. Lassie lunged at her and Grace swung the knife at the dog, narrowly missing her snout.

"You," she said, pointing the knife at me.

I picked up the gun and pointed it at her, imagining how her tiny body would fly with the impact and fall next to the others, but before I could pull the trigger Tozer wrapped his hands around the gun and pulled the barrel skyward.

"Leave it," he shouted. "This place is going fucking crazy."

So too was I.

Grace spun and jabbed her finger at me, shouting, "You should never have come here."

And then she was gone, running toward the dark scrim of cabins set against the woods, her body black and quick like a scrap of burnt cloth caught in the wind.

When I turned to look at where I'd dropped the gold I saw Mooner leaning over it, the gold sparkling as it spilled from the torn denim. Shipley and Gant rushed him and he fell to the ground cradling it like a fumble as they began kicking him until a gash opened across his forehead and there was something wrong with his mouth.

I forced myself to look down at Burke, wanting to feel something. I couldn't seem to get anything going and I knew that others would die and that the selfish trick was to not be among them, to claw my way out of the valley any way I could.

DOWNSTREAM

Tozer yanked me away toward the lake through a carpet of heavy greenwood smoke. Faces appeared only to be swallowed by the haze. The moon beamed down bright over the water.

"Where did you get the gold?" he asked.

I told him how Burke had led me to Penny's cabin and of the gold under the floor.

"There's a lot more where that came from," I said.

He just shook his head and stood there staring at me in disbelief.

"But . . ." He stopped, taken by the swirl of the camp: people running and shouting, the sudden dull pop of rifles.

"What's happening?" I asked.

"It's all coming undone," he said. "Somebody stole the Golden Heart and half the camp ate jimson, the other some kind of mushroom."

I turned just in time to see Nunn lope out of the woods and gather up several burning sticks and then run off again, the sticks bright streaks in the night.

"What the hell . . ." Tozer said.

"He's going to burn the place down."

Tozer nodded and ran toward the fire where I saw Penny sitting, legs crossed, staring at the flames. Her skin and hair were covered with soot and ash. Veronica stood nearby, eyes closed, body swaying as if to some music only she could hear, and next to the half-carved moose carcass lay Peter, naked from the waist up, a pool of vomit steaming next to him.

Lila rose and came to us. "I just saw Nunn," she shouted.

Tozer nodded. "He's going to torch the gas in the generator shack."

I started after him, but Tozer stopped me.

"It's too late, help me get them," he said, gathering Lila and pointing at the others.

I nodded numbly. There was nothing left to say or do now that Burke was dead. And as the fire baked my chest and legs I felt myself coming up against my limits. I was tired and sore, my hand still bleeding from Grace's knife. There were swellings and invisible sore spots across my chest and shoulders. The days of little or no sleep and the beatings had taken their toll. I was, it seemed, too tired to care about anything except saving somebody from the valley.

So I went to Penny and lifted her to her feet. She rose, staring at the ground. Veronica was next. I couldn't see her eyes and she was quivering. There was nothing I could say or do except lead them like children away from the fire, wondering if there were others hidden under the thick hover of smoke.

"Now, man," Tozer shouted. "The time is now."

Just then a loud explosion rocked the camp and I turned to see a bright red plume of flame and vapor rising from the direction of the generator shack. The smell of burning gasoline rippled through the air as fuel cans arced into the sky like comets. Some landed with a hiss into the lake while others thudded brightly in the woods, igniting other smaller fires.

"Let's go," Tozer shouted.

I ran to them, grabbing Veronica's and Penny's limp hands, tugging them away from the fire.

Penny let go and stood staring at the pillar of flames as it climbed, collapsing and fanning out black and orange over the entire valley. As soon as I let go of Veronica she sat on the ground again, her legs folding under her. I shouted at her to get up as gas cans continued to catch fire and roar in the distance and Penny mumbled something about the others.

I grabbed her by the shoulders. "They'll get out," I said. "Everybody who wants to get out will get out—they have to."

"No," she said, fighting to stay lucid. "He won't let them."

Out of desperation I unwrapped the Golden Heart from its sack and for a long time nothing happened but the whoosh of gas cans catching fire and exploding. Then some flash of recognition flickered across Penny's face as I turned the gold over and over, letting it catch the light. Veronica came closer, her eyes rising from half-mast to take in the Golden Heart. I imagined how Nunn must have felt showing it off to the camp, watching their faces fill with the base and primal wonder of it.

Penny reached out to touch it just as Tozer jogged out of the gloom to grab me by the shoulder. The gold slipped from my grip and I watched it hang for a moment, suspended as it gathered firelight on its curved surface and then fell, landing with a dull thud on a large rock. It broke into several chunks.

I immediately dropped to my knees and groped around the rock for the pieces, knowing there was something wrong by the sound it had made on impact. Penny knelt beside me and froze when she saw that the gold was only a thin layer that had been cast over stone and bits of gray metal.

"It's fake," I said.

Penny screamed and tried to run but Tozer stopped her and stood holding her in a tight clench. Veronica just kept nodding, blissed-out look tacked across her face.

"Did you know?" I asked Tozer.

He started laughing.

Lila took a piece of the Golden Heart and turned it over and over, struck mute by the sight of the rock and rusted metal under the bright surface. It was hollow—the whole thing was some hollow elaborately twisted hoax.

Tozer shook his head. "Besides Nunn only Shipley ever touched it," he said. "It doesn't change a thing, we've still got to get out of here."

But staring at the pieces I knew something had changed and I thought about slipping back to the cabin and grabbing enough gold to make it all worthwhile. What stopped me was that I knew I'd never make it, not with Penny and Veronica in the state they

were in or with the fires that had sprung up around the still burning generator shack. There would be a tipping point where if the
fire took it would level the valley in a matter of hours as it followed
the suck of air up the cliff wall.

Tozer took off down the path. Before following them I gathered up the pieces of the broken Golden Heart and stuffed them
into the sack along with a few nuggets I'd taken from the cabin.

We made our way in the dark as the fire spread around us. I
could smell tar paper burning and knew that the cabins were going
up and I kept expecting Nunn to grab me from behind and take
me with him to watch it all end.

For the moment I still had the gold, clinking and rattling like
dice in the bag, and Penny, moving surefooted, her face locked on
the path ahead, no longer tripping on whatever Nunn had given
her.

At a fork in the path we found Sherman dead with his head
bashed in. Tozer briefly played a flashlight over the body, revealing
the sparkle of gold dust on his clothing.

"Look," Tozer said, pointing out a single nugget clenched tight
in Sherman's palm.

Penny shook her head and kept moving. "Hurry," she said. I
dragged Veronica away from Sherman and followed the others,
wondering if we were all funneling to the cave in the dark only to
meet Nunn or worse—Boothe.

We came to a small opening in the trees. Tozer stopped and
pointed ahead at the cliff wall where I could just make out the
faint gray outline of rocks and trees.

"Is this it?" I asked.

He nodded. "I'm going to make sure it's clear," he said. "Then
I'm going back for some of the gold."

Lila began smacking him, whispering, "No, no, no."

He shook his head and started to say something just as Veronica
began running toward the rocks. I tried to grab her, but she got
past me. We went to the edge of the woods, watching as she
rounded the familiar pile of rubble and faded into the shadows
surrounding the cave.

We listened for a long while and there was no sound except for that of the fire crackling away behind us, filling the sky with light. Tozer stepped out into the clearing, hunkering low to the ground like some sort of animal, and then froze.

I crept forward, Penny pressed close to my side, her hair brushing against my arm as I squinted at the jigsaw of shadows until I saw what had caused Tozer to stop dead in his tracks.

Where the rocks spilled into the clearing there was a large griz rooting at something on the ground. It looked like a man. It was too dark to see who it was or for that matter if he was even alive, but from the way the bear stood on his chest, peeling away the clothing with his paws, I figured he was dead or close to it.

The bear was large, hump-shouldered and oblivious to our presence. Its fur seemed to catch the silver moonlight and watching it made all those old fears come back. The woods seemed suddenly more dangerous. The animal moved with a deliberate grace, glowing like a demon in the night as it tore at the man in some pure and indescribable way—as if it was merely fulfilling its duty—feeding on the stupid and unlucky. The pilgrims. And there we were, waiting for our turn with it if we were ever going to make the cave.

Tozer turned and pointed to something perched on one of the large rocks near the cave entrance.

I stepped farther into the clearing until the vague figure of Veronica took shape, no more than fifteen feet from the bear.

Clouds slipped over the moon, plunging the whole scene into terminal darkness, and when the clouds shifted back I saw that she was standing. Tozer leveled the gun at the creature as it lifted its thick head, aware of our presence.

And without thinking I started toward her, knife out, wanting stupidly to save her.

Everything happened quick. My legs began to fail me and I knew I wouldn't reach her in time. Even with the rifle the bear was in control of the situation. It moved off the body, hopping and barking at Veronica, who didn't veer or fall to the ground under its charge. When it crashed into her she flew into the air like a tossed doll and came down in a soft crush of hair and bent limbs, ten feet from where I'd frozen, puny knife out, fear in my belly like sand.

"It's Boothe," Tozer whispered, pointing at the fallen man.

With that the bear turned to me, swung its head from side to side and stomped at the ground.

And then it launched at me, full speed. Its ears flat against its head, claws slapping the ground. In those final moments before the bear plowed into me I swear I saw Veronica rise and stagger to the mouth of the cave.

Time stretched as the bear closed the distance and I thought, *this is how it ends,* not Nunn or Boothe shooting me in the back, but the bear with the wilderness behind it, stomping me dead a hundred yards from the cave.

I froze, eyes clenched shut, and when it plowed into me the moon seemed to tilt. Pieces of the broken Golden Heart rattled in their bag and the fire flickered as if the force of the blow was enough to extinguish it.

I heard voices and then the ground rose up and I crashed hard.

It was on me in an instant. The pain flooded in, everything on fire and aching at once. I knew things were broken and could feel its breath on my face as it gently nuzzled me, its fur smelling of fresh earth and rotting leaves.

I tried not to move. My thoughts spun until I remembered the gun and waited eagerly for Tozer to shoot the bear and save me. It was getting harder and harder to play dead.

But the shot never came. Only the dog barked and rushed and the bear swatted her away. She let out a long yelp and then was silent.

It returned to me, my skull pounding as I tried to take in all the sensations, the rake of its claws, its tongue and teeth pulling at my shirt, buttons popping. It was as if it was trying to teach me something by showing this brutal restraint and not killing me instantly. I had no choice but to take the lesson or die even though every fiber in my body was telling me to rise and fight.

But I played dead and let it pin me under its weight as I listened and steeled myself to look it in the eye. I wanted it to be my one last great thing, better than fighting or running. So I pried my eyes open and turned my head slowly, feeling things crunch deep in my spine.

It was snuffling my hand where Grace had cut me. It looked up and we locked eyes in the gloom. They were deep and large and I could see the fire reflected in them. Our breathing fell into synch and I kept waiting for something to show in those eyes—God or some other deep thing—but there was nothing except my own fear and the flicker of reflected fire.

I wanted to turn away but couldn't, holding out hope that Tozer was taking aim this very moment for its heart and I would get to see the very same nothingness it saw in my eyes as the bullet ripped through to its heart.

Instead everything began to fade, like those peaceful moments before a long deep sleep.

It broke our stare to bite into my hand, but I was too far gone to do anything except give in to the heavy dull feeling that was making it easier and easier to play dead.

•

I woke to see Penny leaning over me, her hair brushing my face. My hand felt as if it had been stapled to the ground. My head was stiff and heavy. Lassie stood next to her, bleeding, holding one leg up, her fur singed from the fire. There was smoke everywhere.

"Can you move?" she asked. Her voice sounded far away.

I tried to nod, not sure what was moving and what wasn't. My head felt like it was stuffed with broken glass and cotton.

"Bear?" I said, going in and out of it. "What happened to the bear?"

"It's gone," she said.

"Where?"

She shook her head and tugged at me. "Hurry," she said. "The fire's right on us."

I sat with great effort and there was a warm crackling in my chest. Broken ribs, I thought. My legs were okay though, nothing broken although my right knee felt as if it had been nearly twisted off. I looked down at my left hand. It was bleeding. Skin hung from the fingers like too ripe bananas and I could see bone and the white cording of tendon.

Penny covered the hand with a strip of cloth, wrapping it gently. When she finished I pushed myself up, expecting to see the bear dead in a brown heap nearby, its skull blown out, but there was only Boothe's trampled body. His beard had been torn off and his face hung in torn slabs. The bear had shattered the sinus bones and soft nose cartilage. There were deep ruts in the exposed skull and a pile of gore next to his shoulder.

"Where are the others?"

"Gone," she said.

"Tozer and Lila?"

She nodded and pointed behind her at a wall of burning brush. "The cave," she said. "They made the cave."

"Veronica?"

She shook her head. "I don't know," she said. "She's gone. It left her to charge you. Everything happened so fast and I thought you were dead. When it came after us we separated and the wind picked up and swung the fire around."

"What?"

"It's blocked," she screamed. "The cave's blocked. We can't get through."

"Huh?"

"I need to know if you can make it, I need to know—"

"—I can make it," I said, feeling my body struggling to rise. The air around was bright with the fire. Burning pine needles drifted past like fireflies. Leaves fell flaming orange and skeletal and then turning black as they crumbled into the earth. Sap popped and crackled and bushes seemed to vaporize under the wall of encroaching fire. I wanted to lie back and wait, but something was urging me up.

My knife lay in the dirt and I picked it up, gaining a little strength from the feel of its handle in my palm as I slowly crawled to my feet, taking in what was left of Boothe, noticing a bullet hole just above his ear. I looked around but the bear had disappeared like a tiger in the jungle.

Penny ran toward the cliff walls and the dog followed us as we picked our way over the rubble. I looked back at where the cave had been. There was only fire now and I tried to think of Tozer and Lila breaking through to the other side, seeing the valley from above and the blaze blooming in it.

The fire was all around us, thinning the air and making it hard to get any real breath. But I kept going, stumbling blindly after Penny, gaining strength just watching her scramble over the talus, her face locked onto the swirling dark even though I knew that chances were we'd be hemmed in by the fire and die from smoke or lack of oxygen.

But somehow we managed to flank the worst of the fire as it ate its way around the lake, jumping from tree to tree, snaking through the underbrush.

I didn't look at my mangled hand and kept a good grip on the knife with the other as I floated through the landscape high on some new kind of fuel, thinking about that goddamned bear and the way it had looked at me in judgment. I was this small, scared thing that wouldn't rise and struggle to live like the moose calf or sick elk it took down from time to time, always leaping brokenlegged to their feet only to be pinned back down to the earth to await the deathblow.

We arrived at the narrow creek and I could see the black gash of the mining entrance. Penny didn't pause or stop to see if there was anybody huddled inside waiting out the fire.

"Come on," she said, dashing down a path.

Twice I thought I saw bodies at the edge of the woods, a leg or pale hand glowing under the moonlight. But we kept moving, Penny leading the way while I trotted behind like a battered zombie.

We reached the lake and followed the shore, wading into the water when the brush became too thick until we found a trail that hugged the perimeter.

As the trees tangled into swamp, blotting out even the moonlight, I saw him coalesce out of the shadows, arms outstretched, hair blown back by some small wind. It was Nunn and he was laughing at the sight of us, his ruined face cooked into a half-smile. There was nobody behind him, no gun or knife in his hand, just that voice booming out to us, "I've been waiting."

Penny stiffened and reached out for me.

"Go," I said to her, thinking that maybe it was some sort of trap, that Sanders would call out his dogs on us or we would be shot. But he kept walking, closing down the distance, arms still outstretched as if he was calling us to him.

Penny tried to run into the forest and finally stopped under a pine like a child afraid to go any farther.

The bear must have jarred something loose in me because I no longer cared if I lived or died. I held my ground, the pain in my chewed hand mellowing into a warm tingle. In my good hand I had the knife and I tested it. All the muscles seemed to work. The knife jerked up, strong and quick, and it felt good and I knew that nothing mattered except getting past him.

He let me get close, arms still out as if to hug me, stopping only when he saw the knife. The grin melted off his face and his eyes looked old and tired as he studied what I had in my hand.

I brought it home—into his belly and then up, feeling his whole life vibrate through the thin steel of Burke's blade as it did its terrible job, slipping and bending around bone, cutting cords and other things.

I remember thinking how easy it was; a reflex like swatting at flies or recoiling from a snake.

He gasped and we locked eyes for what seemed a long time even though I wasn't seeing him—just looking through him at some black spot in the forest. And then he folded over me like a flag cut from a pole, his head resting on my shoulders as I tried to pull the knife out.

"The test," he whispered over and over. "The test." Until it began to sound like some sort of accusation. I wanted him to stop, but he kept on muttering. "You know . . . you know . . ." he said.

I let him fall. The knife went with him and I looked down at the blood on my hands, wanting his words to mean something, strike deep and double me over with guilt. Instead I felt nothing, just tired, sore and sick of it all. I had no curiosity about what happened after. He went on talking to the sky, his voice calm and level as blood poured out of him and he tried to scoop it back in with his hands.

I closed my eyes and was lost, hearing only his voice, extolling those last words, and when I opened them the news of where we were and what I'd just done rushed in for a moment and then was gone, replaced with that heavy, undigested blackness I'd felt strangling Quinn.

"Hey, pilgrim . . ." he said to the dark. He laughed and started to speak as his body shook one last time, chopping his final words into a series of low moans.

And then he was dead. His voice stopped and all that was left was his long body staring up at the night, blood around him. And me, somehow delivered to this point way up in the middle of nowhere, blood on my hands, his goddamned voice echoing deep down in me, vibrating for what seemed forever.

I felt a presence behind me in the dark and turned expecting to find the bear coming for me again but there was just the tangle of trees and the coming fire. A vast nothing.

Penny took my hand in her tiny one and broke the spell, leading me away, and neither of us gave him a second look. There were no words for what had happened.

We walked and fell back into the groove, the pain in my hand coming and going, my head full of nothing except the trail as the rock gave way to a cold swamp and I could see the lake on the right, fire reflected on its calm surface. And then we were in the swamp, sloshing through freezing muskeg, batting away at branches. I was happy to have the obstacles even though we were not alone. Bullmoose and panicked elk rushed past us, spooked by the fire, seeking shelter in the cool water.

By dawn I'd begun to falter, succumbing to what the bear had done to my insides. My breath rattled in my chest. Blood pooled in my arms and Penny kept picking me off the ground, pulling on my wrecked hand until I rose with the pain to chase after her.

And by the time the sun poked through the haze of smoke and clouds, my arm felt hot and infected. I was reeling, dumb with pain, hallucinating as DNR planes drifted over the fire, looking like silver-skinned hawks, and trees morphed into campers. Every shadow became the bear, stalking me, and I thought I saw Grace beckoning me closer with her knife. Penny turned into Burke and I followed, trying to keep pace with him, prove something. Still there was the swamp, wending on and on forever.

I wanted to quit, but it was easier to just keep putting one foot in front of the other, following her narrow back through the murk.

When we finally reached the river the smoke had blotted out the sun. The air was hot and dry. I collapsed on a mound of gravel and driftwood, happy to have the warm solid feel of earth under me. I thought I saw Sanders and his dogs or maybe it was Lassie I heard, circling, barking at me to get up.

I don't know how long I lay there pinned to the bank, like something rotting, returning to the soil. Dozens of planes buzzed overhead, the sound of their engines comforting me even as the strength I'd felt holding that knife in Nunn's belly left me, dribbling out into the landscape. I'd made it out to the river and was ready to quit, let the wilderness take me slowly and rake me back under because I'd topped Burke by getting this far and that was enough.

I remember floating. Hours? Days?—I lost count of everything except the hazy sun on water and the sound of a paddle dipping in and out. I slept and woke with my cheek pressed against the hull of the canoe, listening to the river beating beneath it like some great heart.

She gave me water and talked to me. The dog was there whining, shaking with what the bear had done to her. I don't recall much of it, only the sound of Penny's voice and the lap of the water and then a heavy bump that seemed to go right down into my bones.

And then there was land again and she leaned and put her face to mine.

"They'll find you," she said. "Let them take you back."
She kissed me lightly and then was gone.

•

I don't know how long I was on that bank, but when I got up the dog was still there and the gold was gone from my pockets. I managed to stagger out to a path and then a road where a logging truck picked me up and dropped me at the Fairbanks hospital.

The bear had done a number on my insides: two snapped ribs, some ruptured organs. The doctors asked a lot of questions and I lied, told them I'd fallen down a cliff, had a little misadventure in the bush. Thankfully there was a drunk German who'd been shot in the stomach and a lady who'd lit her housecoat on fire—plenty for the doctors to do. So they discharged me and I wandered Fairbanks sozzled on pills, trying to get it all straight in my head.

The paper ran a small article on the fire but there was no mention of the camp. It was a small fire by Alaskan standards and it had stalled at the river, eating up only the valley and some of the swamp. The smoke did, however, make for some interesting sunsets and at dusk I saw people sitting in the back of their pickup trucks watching the sun fizzle down over the horizon as they drank beer and snuggled.

I walked around town with this enormous secret sitting on my chest. I was sure there were still some of them out there—campers who'd made it out—and I figured I'd run into them sooner or later because Fairbanks was, after all, a small town especially in winter when the tourists began to leave, pulling out in their shiny RVs and heading east down the Alcan.

And Duke? I went by his cabin wanting to ask him about Nunn and Penny, but he was gone. The cabin had been cleaned out except the bear pelt, hanging on the wall. I thought about taking it, but didn't. I even spent some time checking the hospitals to see if he'd died but there was nothing and that was just as well because I imagined him hearing about the fire, thinking of the two of us, me and Burke, burning the camp down for his daughter.

Only I knew it didn't happen like that. I'd killed and watched others die like rabbits, I'd made it out and not a minute went by that I couldn't feel that bear pressing its paw to my chest, or the way it had looked me in the eye. Later I thought I saw Grace in the Safeway. Her hair was shorter and she was pushing a cart through the slush and there was a small boy in the front of the cart pulling at his jacket, but when she turned I saw it wasn't her. And that was good.

In a bar north of town I ran into Shipley. He was wearing nice clothes and buying the house rounds. We pretended not to notice each other and that was okay with me. Still I imagined the others drifting down into the lower forty-eight in late-night Greyhounds or borrowed cars. Other times I imagined they'd simply waited and died in the fire. I didn't know which was worse.

The only person I told was Day-Glo Bob, who smiled and asked me if Burke had died righteously.

I lied and told him he had.

"Epic," he said. "How about you? You've got that faraway look."

"What look?" I asked.

But he just laughed and then started crying as he sparked a joint in Burke's honor. Later we found the rest of Duke's money stashed under a pile of maps and half-written letters. We went down to the Club Alaska to get drunk and when I walked through the door the bartender stopped and stared at me, pointing as if he knew. But when I turned around I saw that he was only pointing at a sudden small whirlwind of dead leaves and trash that was dancing across the dusty parking lot.

•

I never found the canoe or saw Penny again and I don't know if she came back for her father or if she'd continued on down the river, looking for some better place to disappear, or even if any of what I thought was true. Perhaps they were somewhere warm together. It didn't matter because she'd rescued me and somehow I was going to have to live with the mystery.

I bought a plane ticket with what was left of Duke's money and

I even called home to arrange a ride. But I never got on the plane and when the first big storm hit I sat watching the snow pile up outside the window in thick wind-driven drifts. My hand still hurt. The medicine was gone and I was almost out of money, but for a moment the world seemed bright and clear. And even though winter was coming and the land would be dark and cold for months I knew that I wasn't going anywhere because there were secrets and bears out there waiting for spring under the fresh October snow and that was enough to make me want to stay.